Broken Voices

Broken Voices

Wilhelmina Fitzpatrick

St. John's, Newfoundland and Labrador
2005

We acknowledge the support of The Canada Council for the Arts for our publishing program.

We acknowledge the financial support of the Government of Canada through the Book Publishing Industry Development Program (BPIDP) for our publishing program.

Cover Design by Maurice Fitzgerald

Published by KILLICK PRESS
an imprint of CREATIVE BOOK PUBLISHING
a Transcontinental Inc. associated company
P.O. Box 8660, St. John's, Newfoundland A1B 3T7

Typeset in 12 point Garamond

Printed in Canada by: Transcontinental Inc.

Library and Archives Canada Cataloguing in Publication

Fitzpatrick, Wilhelmina, 1958-

Broken voices / by Wilhelmina Fitzpatrick

ISBN 1-894294-83-1

I. Title.

PS8611.I895B76 2005 C813'.6 C2005-900683-8

To Anne and Bill Fitzpatrick. We miss you.

In my little bed I lie
Heavenly Father hear my cry
Oh Lord protect me through this night
And keep me safe till morning's light.

(from a prayer my father said each night when he tucked me in)

PROLOGUE

When I was five, I saw a man in the woods. He had a white bum, the colour of the clouds in the heavy Newfoundland sky. His pasty flesh stood stark against the lush backdrop of dense evergreens and abundant berry bushes. My eyes blinked with disbelief. Still it was there, the sagging weight, the puckered cellulose of his bum. And then it was moving, each second a minute as his body turned towards me. My eyes shot upward, away from "down there", up to his hairless chest, his balding head, his bland pudgy face. He was older, my father's age, I thought.

"Hey, Lilly and Suzie, over here," my sister, Noreen, called out to us. "Me and Janie found a real ripe patch."

Suzie and I ran over with our nearly empty buckets. "Oh, look at them all. And they're so ripe," I said as we squatted right down next to Noreen and Janie and started pulling the bakeapples from their stems.

"This is better than yesterday, right, Lilly?" said Suzie.

"Yeah, that was creepy."

Suzie and I had been up there by ourselves the day before, but we hadn't stayed long because it was raining. The marsh was so boggy that our feet were constantly being sucked into the cushioned earth. It made the whole place feel strange, and we'd left with only a thin layer of pickings in the bottom of our buckets.

It felt better being in the marsh with our older sisters along. It was the perfect time of year to pick bakeapples, and our pails were brimming over with the pale pink berries in less than an hour.

"Let's play hide and seek," yelled Suzie.

Noreen looked at her watch and nodded. "Sure, it's only early yet."

We all took turns being "it". When it was Janie's turn to count, Noreen bustled me and Suzie in through a thick cluster of trees, where we scurried and scrambled into a mossy crevice under some fallen branches and a rotting tree trunk.

"Ready or not, here I come." Janie's voice was far away, muffled, yet we knew what she was saying.

It was right then that the man appeared.

"Who's that?" Suzie whispered.

Noreen held her finger to her lips to quiet Suzie. Noreen's eyes were wide, scared. I glanced behind me towards the boggy marsh. Nothing moved save the wings of a bird silhouetted against the overcast horizon. When I turned back around the man was closer.

Janie shuffled breathlessly into the clearing, her short, round body coming to a stunned halt when she saw him. They each stood staring, one at the other, Janie's chest rising and falling rapidly, his slower at first, then picking up speed as the seconds ticked by.

"Have you seen my doggie, little girl?" he asked finally. His voice was raspy, yet sickly sweet.

A deep gurgling noise broke from Janie as her plump hand moved across her open mouth. She started to back up.

Reaching his hand down below his flabby belly, the man began to move forward.

Bounding to her feet, Noreen dragged us from our hiding place. "Hah, stupid girl, you couldn't find us," she shouted at Janie.

The man stopped. I saw his eyes then. They were blue, small and lashless. Like marbles, but hazy. Eyes that seemed much too small for his large pale face.

"I've lost my dog," he said, his voice less certain than before.

I must have seen his entire body then because he was right there in front of us, naked. But if so, it was a sight my eyes refused to acknowledge. I knew instinctively that it would be wrong to look, that God, and my parents, would be very disappointed in me.

"We never seen your dog, mister," Noreen declared, her voice loud and rough. She moved steadily towards Janie and took her

hand. "Okay everyone, Mom'll kill us if we're late again. Let's go now," she yelled, pulling Janie for all she was worth.

They started to run but my feet would not budge. I felt stuck in place, stupefied, as they began to move farther away, my sister in the lead. Then Janie glanced back. Immediately she spun around and bolted toward me. I had never seen her move with such speed and determination. Hurling her berry pail at the naked man, she grabbed my hand and jolted me from my spot. Suddenly I could move, and we were all running like fire, pink bakeapples bouncing from our plastic buckets. I turned around once but there was no sign of the man. Just Janie, brown and round as a ripe summer berry, trying to keep up. Still grateful, I paused to wait for her but Noreen grabbed my arm and yanked me along. "No stopping till the end of the woods, Lilly," she warned, her breath ragged. "Janie, hurry up!"

And so we all kept on running, jumping over the rocks and grassy clumps, scooting around the trees. Finally, we made it out into the open, all of us wheezing and gasping for breath. Our low white-washed house was just ahead, the Corcoran's narrow two-storey farther on out the road. Mom was hanging clothes on the line and talking to Mrs. Murray, who lived on the other side of our short wood fence. Seeing them standing there, mumbling through the clothespins in their mouths as they attached another item to the line, the thin wet shirts and clean faded underwear waving in the light summer breeze, it felt like a plug was pulled from my heart. I burst into tears.

"Lilly, it's okay now, we're safe," Noreen consoled me. "Let's go tell Mom."

"No!" shouted Janie, her eyes wild.

"Why not?" Noreen demanded. Even though she was only ten and a few years younger than Janie, Noreen had long been the unspoken leader in our foursome. The role came naturally to her, and we never questioned it.

"Because we can't," Janie cried. "We'll get in so much trouble. We're not supposed to see that, you know, he had nothing on his arse,

and we were there and if Dad finds out—"

"Janie, it's not our fault. We didn't do nothing wrong," Noreen insisted.

"No, we can't tell. Please, none of us can ever tell. Promise me," she begged, her words tumbling over each other in their haste to be out. "Cross your heart and hope to die. Dad'll kill me if he finds out. Please, Noreen?"

"But Janie, that's stupid. We—"

"Please, Noreen!" she shrieked. Her panicked face was streaked with sweat and dirt. "I'd do it for you, you knows I would. Just don't say nothing, I'm begging you. Please?"

Suzie had moved to her sister and taken her hand. "Please, Noreen. Do what Janie said, okay?"

Noreen agreed to keep it quiet then, but I could tell she didn't like it. Spitting out the side of her mouth, she grabbed my arm. "Come on, Lilly, let's get on home."

When Mom asked us how the berry picking went, we handed over our nearly empty buckets of bakeapples without a word, our lips sealed with the promise we'd made to Janie.

Two days later, I was in the living room curled up with an afghan and a new book on baby animals. The phone rang on the table across from me and Mom hurried in from the kitchen to get it.

"Hi Ida," she answered. Her tone was warm and friendly. She'd always had a soft spot for Suzie's mother, although she never said a nice word about Suzie's father. "How are—?"

I could hear the voice on the other end, slicing the air as it made its way through the phone and across the living room. My mother said little in return, just stood there staring out the window, listening and nodding. And although I couldn't see her face, I noticed the shape of her free hand, balled into a fist inside her apron pocket.

"I'll call you back, Ida." She hung up the phone and turned to me, her mouth set in a tough line. "Where's that sister of yours?

Noreen!" she yelled at the top of her lungs. "Get in here this minute."

Noreen came running down the hall.

"That was Ida Corcoran on the phone just now. What do you suppose she was calling about?"

Noreen's face reddened beneath her baseball cap. "Mrs. Corcoran? What did she want?"

"You tell *me* what she wanted, Missy."

"I don't know…" Noreen hesitated, glancing uneasily at me.

"The hell you don't. Out with it, right now. What happened up in them woods the other day?"

When I saw Noreen's eyes fill up and spill over, I really got worried. She never cried, and denounced anyone who did as a big sissy. I started to cry then too.

"Don't be bawling at me," yelled Mom, shutting the both of us right up. "Just tell me what happened."

"There…there was a man. He was up there, and he had no drawers on," Noreen stuttered and stammered. "And he lost his dog he said, and we were behind the tree, and he was looking at Janie right funny, and we took off home."

"And did you leave Janie there then?" she demanded, pushing her flat brown hair off her forehead.

"Leave Janie? No, I grabbed her and—"

"Her mother said you were all hiding on her."

"Well, yeah, but—"

"And that he almost got her, and you were watching and stayed in the woods."

"That's not true! We were hiding because it was her turn to count, is all."

"And you didn't run off and leave her?"

"No way! We jumped right out and got hold of her and we all ran out the woods."

Noreen didn't mention Janie going back for me. Neither did I. I knew there was something odd about it, and was still surprised that it was Janie who had run back for me and not Noreen.

Mom stared at us both for a long moment. "Why didn't you say something before now?"

"Because Janie made us promise not to tell anyone," said Noreen. "She said her father would kill her if he found out what she did."

"What? For God's sakes sure, it wasn't her fault."

"That's what I said to her," Noreen insisted, throwing her hands up in frustration. "But she said she'd get in real trouble if we told. Right, Lilly?"

I nodded vigorously, anxious to support my sister and keep her out of trouble, even if it meant telling on Janie. "Yeah, she begged us not to say, cross our hearts and hope to die, she said."

"Good God almighty! Well, she's telling her mother a different story now, then. Blaming you for keeping it secret."

"Me?" yelled Noreen, her cheeks hot with anger. "That's not true, is it, Lilly?"

"Noreen wanted to tell you right away, Mommy. But Janie made us promise. Honest." Frightened and confused, as much by the man in the woods as by the scene playing out in front of me, I started to cry again.

Mom came over and put her arm around my shoulders, squeezing Noreen's arm with her other hand. Her greenish brown eyes looked hard at me, then moved to my sister. "It's okay. But the two of you listen to me now. If anything like this ever happens again, you're to tell me right off. If any man ever lays a hand on you, or shows you his privates, or anything like that, no matter who he is, I don't care if he's the frigging pope, you come straight to me. Okay? Promise?"

I nodded again, my heart hammering. My mother rarely spoke of such things. This was important.

"Yes Mom, straight off," vowed Noreen. "Just wait till I gets my hands on that Janie Corcoran. She's some liar, that one."

"And you're going to leave it be with Janie too," Mom ordered. "Just let it go, Noreen. Poor girl was too scared to know any better, so let her be. Her and Ida got enough to deal with having that Matt Corcoran around."

Noreen started to say something, but Mom gave her a particular warning look, one that even I knew meant that was enough, that no more should be said on the matter. Just then my grandmother, who was sick and lived with us and was always in want of something, called out from her bedroom. Sighing loudly, Mom went to check on her. Noreen sat down next to me but she said nothing for ages. Moving closer to her, I reached over and spread some of my afghan over her legs. She didn't seem to notice.

I tried to concentrate on my book but my thoughts kept flitting back to the marsh, and to the man we'd seen there. I still saw only his upper body, and when my mind began to drift below, I pulled it back to his face. That suddenly evil face. I remembered the day that Suzie and I had been up there alone. Had he been there then? Had we just missed him because of the rain? What would we have done, two little children alone in the dense swampy bog, with nothing but our buckets to save us? I shivered under the warm heavy afghan, and looked down at the pictures of the baby animals. They didn't seem so cuddly anymore.

Noreen got a royal tongue-lashing from Dad later that evening, about how she was never to keep something like that from them ever again. He was angrier than I'd ever seen him. Yet even as he railed at Noreen, he kept hugging her ever so hard, and looking at me over her shoulder, his worried eyes fast on my face. Then he hugged me too, so close and tight I could feel his heart beating against my cheek. As scared as I was, I'd never felt safer.

Nothing more was ever heard of the man in the woods.

PART I

1

The wooden birds craned their necks upward as if straining to break free and soar out into the night, their brightly coloured tail feathers iridescent in the clouded Newfoundland sky. Lill's father had carved them years before, their rustic charm belying their innate dignity. Much like the man himself, Lill had always thought, straightforward, salt of the earth. It saddened her to see them stuck on the wall behind her sister's back door, virtually out of sight, but she was hardly surprised. Marlene had never cared a fig for their father's carvings; she and Ted preferred more modern mass-produced trinkets that could be made anywhere, by anyone. But the birds were treasures to Lill, each unique piece carefully sculpted by Hank Penney's hands. The birds, the jewellery boxes, the bookends, to Lill they were creations straight from her father's soul. She had to resist the urge to snatch them right off their hooks and make a run for it.

A grease-blackened hand touched her shoulder, sending a residual whiff of motor oil drifting up her nose. "How's it feel to be forty there, Lill?" Jack Pitts asked innocently.

There it was again, that stupid question. Why did everyone keep asking it, as if no one else had ever strung the words together in a sentence before? How does it feel to be forty? How's it feel to be stupid, she wanted to ask them back.

Forty was thirty-nine plus one. It was finding wiry grey traitors in her thick brown hair, and, around her hazel eyes, tiny yet persistent wrinkles that no longer ironed themselves out as the morning progressed. Forty was a tightening of her belt although she hadn't gained an ounce, the settling of that extra inch of flab into its permanent nesting place on her waist. Forty was the acknowledgement that she would need every millimetre of her five foot three frame to support her one hundred and thirty-five pounds, and, according to the fitness gurus, extra calcium to keep that frame upright. But then again, that had been thirty-nine too, maybe even thirty-eight.

Marlene had been adamant about throwing her a birthday party, even though Lill had insisted she didn't want one. She had no desire to be the centre of attention, even for one night. Being a teacher in a town as small as theirs, it was not particularly fun to be in the spotlight, the focus of idle parents with nothing better to talk about when all had gone home. Not that all parents were like that, but the few that were made most teachers watch their behaviour out in public, a fact that Lill was still getting used to in her second year on the job.

Feeling strangely alone in the crowded room, Lill thought of Steve. It had been more than two years since the car accident, and at times like this she actually did miss him, almost as if she'd been as deeply in love with him as everybody liked to think now that he was dead. In truth, the marriage hadn't been so bad. In fact, if he hadn't depended on her so much, if he'd just taken the initiative some of the time, she might have been happy enough. He'd been better than lots of husbands, really. Lill recognised that. She just wished it had made more of a difference, waking up to him day after day, making love week after week, or, later, month after month.

Turning around, she answered finally, "Forty's much the same as yesterday, Jack b'y." She popped another chip into her mouth.

"I suppose you'll be heading to fifty soon enough yourself, won't you, Jacko?" wheezed Barb Reilly, squeezing in between them with a plateful of goodies, her equally round husband right behind her.

"Passed that train a long time ago, Babs," Jack answered. "About the same time you did, I'd say."

"Go on with you. I'm nowhere near it, sure," she guffawed, her body bouncing with the effort. "Still heading for thirty-nine, that's me."

They all laughed, even Lill, though she didn't find it very funny. Twisting the cork from a bottle of homemade wine, she poured a small glassful. The others were still chuckling. She smiled politely. God, how long did she have to stay here, she wondered? Raising the glass to her lips, she pictured herself leaving, just walking out the door alone. Would anyone try to stop her?

Lill glanced around the large pristine kitchen. Everything was new, from the bottom to the top, and she had to admit, it was nicely done. Her own kitchen was almost twenty years old, with barely a touch-up since the day it was born, except for a few coats of paint to hide the nicks and scratches. She couldn't see it getting anything else for a long while to come either, not with two teenagers to feed and put through university. Sometimes the enormity of that hit her hard, that there were two human beings who depended solely on her. To feed them, to clothe and educate them, to raise them into responsible adulthood. Could she do it? Could she face the years ahead of her, alone and, yes, lonely? She shivered. Best not to think about that on her birthday. She might end up bawling into her brother-in-law's awful wine.

Eyeing the stainless steel six-burner stove and the double ovens, she wondered what her sister planned to do with it. Lill was the only one of the three Penney girls who enjoyed cooking. She loved to try new foods, often with names she couldn't pronounce, and to experiment with new and different recipes. Of course, that had changed since she'd gone back to work full time. Marlene, who stayed home all day even though her kids were in school, boasted a repertoire of six basic meals that she rotated on a regular basis. On the seventh night, they ate out.

Just as Lill was starting to get a bad case of kitchen-envy, she noticed the dark-haired woman next to the stove. Janie Corcoran, make-up thick as pancake batter, dressed in a short skirt and skin-tight T-shirt. Although she was no longer fat, there was a flaccid look about her, a looseness to her skin, that did not seem healthy. Lill didn't see much of Janie anymore, and hadn't even known she'd been invited until she and Noreen dropped by Marlene's earlier in the week.

The house had been immaculate as usual, buffed and shining, everything in its assigned place. Marlene, on the other hand, was looking a little flustered. Lill had asked if everything was okay. "Of course, don't be silly," Marlene had said, hanging up the phone. "That was just Jack calling, Jack Pitts. He's not sure if he and Jane can come to the party." "Didn't know they were invited," Lill said, taking an apple from the fruit bowl on the sideboard. "Oh that, well, Jack's been talking to Ted about some sort of business deal, so he's been over here a bit and I thought it would be the neighbourly thing to do and all, to invite him. And Jane, of course," Marlene added almost as an afterthought as she rearranged the fruit in the bowl. "But apparently herself might have to stay in town and Jack don't want to leave her all alone. That's just like Jack, that is, so thoughtful. That Jane, she's some frigging lucky to have him. You'd never know it from the way she acts, though, always on the make when she's out for the weekend, sitting on other fellows' laps at the bar, dancing right close with them to the slow songs, sometimes you can't get a flea between them." Her voice went a tad breathless. "Swaying back and forth, first they're slow, then all fast and pushing, squeezing right into each other right out there on the dance floor." Lill glanced at Noreen, and they both raised their eyebrows. Noreen, ever the saucy spinster, winked at Lill and asked, "Cigarette, Marlene?"

Janie Corcoran was Jane Pitts now, and she and Jack had two grown sons. Jane had had another son, Rod, when she was fifteen, but Ida had raised him as her own. Lill remembered how she'd envied Janie going to St. John's by herself at sixteen, how Lill thought she'd do the same thing when she got older. Janie had lived in the city ever since; Lill had stayed put.

Just recently, Ida and Suzie had moved to St. John's as well, to be closer to Janie and to Ida's doctors. Lill had bumped into them at Hynes' grocery store the week before the move, Ida limping along, Suzie holding fast to Belle's leash, her ever present German shepherd. "I'll be missing you, Lill, girl," Ida said, patting Lill's hand. Lill remembered how much her mother had liked Ida, and on impulse, she reached out and hugged her. "I'll miss you too, Ida. And you, Suzie," she added quickly. Ida smiled sadly. "Me and Suzie be back lots of weekends. And our

Roddy'll be here during the week, now that he's teaching at the school and all," she added proudly. Suzie just licked her ice-cream, saying nothing, of course. Nothing had been heard from Suzie Corcoran in over three decades.

Lill hadn't realised that Rod Corcoran was Janie's son until she'd overheard her mother and Mrs. Murray talking about it years before. "Imagine young Janie having her own father's baby, and poor Ida having to raise it," Mrs. Murray had said, her tone filled with disgust. "Everybody knows it was his, the whole town says so." "That's pure baloney!" Lill's mother had retorted hotly. "Sure that young Rod was always fine in the head, smart in school from day one from what I hears," she proclaimed, "and you knows darn well he'd be dumb as a post if that Matt Corcoran had his hands on his own daughter. Well, at least to make that boy, though God only knows what he did to her before it. Anyway, Ida did her best, God knows she did, and it weren't easy." "Easier without him than with him," Mrs. Murray whispered. "Truer words were never spoke, my dear. Ida Corcoran's been a changed woman since she got shed of that good-for-nothing." Both women nodded their heads sagely at that. Mrs. Murray's hair was in curlers, covered as always by a pair of girl's underwear so that the rollers stuck out of two holes on either side. The Murrays had even less money than the Penneys, and Lill's mother often praised Mrs. Murray on how well she managed to make do with so little. "You can bet your drawers on it," Lill's father once said, slapping his knee in self-delight. Lill had started to giggle, but one look from her mother put a stop to that.

Some years later, when Mrs. Murray lay dead in her casket at the age of forty-four, Lill had particularly noticed how nicely styled her hair was, no torn underwear, not a curler in sight. Her father had winked at her as they knelt together by the coffin, and she'd had to cover her mouth to hide the grin on her face.

Lill smiled at the memory. Hank Penney had always loved a good joke, and would often mutter irreverent asides at Lill under his breath, careful that his wife didn't hear. It was many years before Lill realised that her mother was just as bad, that what Lill so loved about her father was what had attracted Marg and Hank to each other in the first place. God, how she missed them both. Never mind that he was still alive. Lill doubted if her father would ever have called what he was doing now living.

Lill felt the smile slip from her face. Good Lord, some party this was turning out to be! Surrounded by everyone talking and laughing, all she could think of were dead people. If only Noreen could have been there, it might have been better. Her older sister was alive and well, thank God, but had proclaimed she was stuck home all week, there was no way she was giving up a weekend near the start of the golf season just so Marlene could flaunt her perfect new kitchen, all under the guise of throwing a birthday party. Lill fully agreed with her.

Nevertheless, Lill knew she should be more appreciative of her younger sister's efforts. Heaping trays of food lined the table, sliced cheese and sausage, breads and patés, colourful dips and spreads surrounded by neat rows of crackers. Every so often, a fragrant platter of freshly baked, formerly frozen appetisers passed by—mini egg rolls, chicken wings, exotic things in puff and phyllo pastry. Lill had spent the better part of the evening sampling them all, and they'd formed a tight ball in her stomach.

She was still annoyed that she'd let herself be talked into the party in the first place. Why couldn't they have just had their housewarming and left Lill's friends out of it? Probably wouldn't have got enough people, Lill decided, then chided herself for being so catty. Just great, she railed at herself. Here she was, stuck at a party she didn't want to be at, but couldn't leave because it was supposedly in her honour. And now she felt guilty because of her suspicions about her sister's motives, and she was stuck talking to the Reillys and Jack Pitts on her fortieth birthday—fine people, all of them, but hardly her closest friends. On top of it all, she was having a PMS day and felt fat as a pig. It didn't help that she'd been eating non-stop since she'd arrived.

A movement by the stove caught her eye. Janie had seemed to lose her balance, and was leaning into a man who worked for Ted. They remained standing very close to each other, closer than was necessary despite the crowded room. He whispered something in her ear as his hand came up to her arm. Across the crowded room, Lill could see the glazed expression on Janie's face as she stared drunkenly up at him. Meeting no resistance, he placed his hand on the seat of her black leather skirt and led her outside.

Lill looked away, down into her glass. Barb and her husband were still talking about turning forty, or perhaps it was fifty. At one point, they both laughed loudly. Lill laughed too, as did Jack, briefly, half-heartedly. Excusing himself, he headed for the front door.

Several minutes later, Lill noticed that the man who'd been talking to Janie was back. He seemed to be having a hushed but heated discussion with Ted. Janie had disappeared, presumably with Jack. Lill wished she could leave as easily.

Eyeing the spicy wings, she was about to hit the food table again when Rod Corcoran came through the door. Strange, Janie's son was now her colleague. By the time he'd moved away to go to university, Lill had been a married woman with children. She didn't remember ever talking to him back then, although she probably had at one time or another, in passing at least.

As Rod was hanging up his coat, her brother-in-law called out to him. "Hey, Corcoran, you used to play hockey. You see that game last night?"

"Yeah, that was something, eh?" Rod answered, joining Ted and his friends where they stood by the sink.

"Stupid refs," Ted yelled, "if it wasn't for them—"

Ted was immediately interrupted by several other men, each of whom had something to say on the matter. Lill noticed how Rod paid attention to them all, unobtrusive, not barging in and forcing them to listen to his opinion. When he did talk, they paid attention, as if he had something worthwhile to contribute. He had a reputation for being smart, "despite that family he's from", as the old fogies would have put it. After completing two degrees at Dalhousie, he'd moved to Toronto to teach and had eventually gotten married up there. Last summer he'd come home alone, divorced. He'd been hired on at the high school after Nancy Nolan retired.

Watching him, Lill thought her mother might have been right—perhaps he wasn't his grandfather's son. He was a little too good-looking to be a total Corcoran, especially with that curly brown hair. That crowd all had locks straight as whips. Rod was tall too, not short and stubby like his mother's family. No, she decided, no way he was a double Corcoran.

He glanced up and looked right at her, then lifted his hand in a little wave. Her mouth full of chicken, she gave a half wave back and turned self-consciously back to Barb and her husband, trying to pick up the thread of their conversation. It wasn't hard.

Several minutes later, a low voice came over her shoulder. "Happy Birthday, Lill." A delicate shiver tickled her neck, and she blushed from her own silliness.

"Oh… hi Rod, how're you doing?" She turned to talk to him, leaving the Reillys on their own.

"Pretty good. Nice crowd you got here," he said, gesturing with his beer bottle at the people all around them.

"Yeah. Not like there's a lot else to do, though, is there? Besides, half of them are Marlene's friends."

Moving out of earshot of the others, he leaned in towards her. "So, anyway, how's it—"

"Oh, God, not you too! If one more person asks me that question, I'm going to scream."

He pulled back slightly. "Huh? What do you mean?"

"About turning forty. You want to know how it feels?" she ranted. "Frustrating, that's what, because everyone's always harping on with the same old line, like they're the first person to ask." His face had instantly reddened, and his shoulders seemed to rise up, making him appear even taller. Lill had the feeling he was about to turn and flee, and she realised that she must have sounded like an old shrew. "Lord, Rod, I'm sorry."

"No, it's okay… it's nothing, don't worry." He moved closer again, and she noticed his scent—clean, fresh, the faintest hint of after-shave. "I wasn't even asking about that, you know. What I was going to say was, how's it going with Jenny?"

"Oh, Jenny!" She lowered her voice. "Now I feel totally stupid for lacing into you." God, she really was a shrew!

"That's all right girl, forget it," he said, lightly brushing her arm with his free hand. "Anyway, how is Jenny?"

"I'm glad you brought her to me, Rod."

"I'm glad I did too. And thanks again for helping me out. Sometimes I wonder about being the only guidance counsellor in the school. It's not like the girls are going to tell me their troubles."

"They might. You're closer in age to them, and sometimes that's enough." She leaned in and whispered, "Jenny's doing okay, I think. She's not pregnant."

"Oh." It was several moments before he continued, and his voice was tight. "She's not, eh? It's for the best, I suppose. What would a seventeen-year-old want with a baby, right?"

"Especially her." Lill sipped her wine, the acidic aftertaste making her mouth pucker. She took another sip anyway. "That girl is so bright, she could really make something of herself. She's one of the smartest in the school. If she had a baby, that'd be the end of it, and she'd be stuck here like the rest of us." Looking at the red liquid sloshing around in her glass, she remembered Jenny's earnest face, the desperate eyes begging her to help. It was not a face she could ignore.

The noise bubbled around them as people leaned against the countertops and the stove, sat at the table or hung around the perimeter. Marlene and Ted had moved back into the renovated house just the month before, and everything had that brand spanking new look. Chrome and glass sparkled and shone, and mould and mildew had not yet found a home in all the hidden crannies. The whole place smelled just-opened, new and fresh. Unlike Lill. Compared to the gleaming kitchen, she felt old and used up. She'd worn her favourite dress-up clothes, the black velvet pants and grey silk shirt she'd placed under the tree for herself at Christmas, but she felt more like an old shack than a modern kitchen.

She looked at her watch. It was only nine o'clock. She knew she had to stay at least another hour. Maybe if she drank enough she'd get more in the mood. Unfortunately, her sister's good taste did not stretch to wine, and the nice bottle Lill had brought to the party had been finished off by someone else. She could hardly blame them.

Suddenly she realised that Rod was talking to her. "I'm sorry, what did you say?" she asked.

"I said, are you stuck? Do you really feel that way about living here?" He didn't smile or make light of it.

"You're really asking?"

"Yeah. I mean, is it so bad?"

"Good God, you should know. You've spent half your life away from here, enjoying the big city. Oh I know there's downfalls there too, but at least there are people who don't know every living thing about you every minute of the day and night."

"Well, yeah, but it's the same here sometimes, you know that." Pausing, he shook his head at her. "There's lots people don't know, though it doesn't stop them from guessing, does it?"

She eyed him curiously, wondering if he was referring to his own questionable history. They didn't know each other well, yet for some reason the conversation did not seem inappropriate. To hell with it, she thought, taking another gulp of wine. He was the one who'd opened up the subject, she'd see where it took them. "That's the point, though," she persisted. "Even if they don't know the answers, they know all the questions."

"True," he agreed. "Then again, anonymity's not all it's cracked up to be either, Lill. It can get pretty lonely in a crowd of strangers, let me tell you."

"Or a crowd of friends," she countered with a swift glance around.

He studied the mouth of his beer bottle. "Must be hard on you, Steve dying so young."

His comment took her by surprise, but she didn't mind. "Worse for the boys, losing their father."

"Yeah, I suppose it would have been." He picked at the label, studying it hard. Lill had the impression that he wanted to say more.

"Good story there?" she asked, gesturing towards the still-full bottle in his hand.

"Oh…sorry. It was just…" He stopped, his face pink with embarrassment.

"What? What is it?"

"Well, I was wondering, you know… do you go out much?" he blurted, seeming relieved to have the words out of his mouth.

"Out?"

"You know. Like with friends…or out with someone." His eyes touched hers for a second before lighting on his bottle once again.

"Let's see." She pretended to think. "I went to a play with Noreen a few weeks ago in St. John's. And a couple of months ago, Barb and I tried that new Mexican restaurant just outside town."

"Okay, fine," he laughed, then looked her straight on. "What I meant was, do you ever go out with a man?"

Good God, was he flirting with her? It had been so long, she wasn't sure. "A man? But what would people think, Mr. Corcoran?" she asked, giving it a go herself.

His evergreen eyes crinkled at the corners. "I don't know, Mrs. Dunn. Perhaps you should try it and find out?"

"First I'll have to find me a man."

He was just about to say something, his full smiling mouth closing in on the first syllable, when Ted slapped him on the back. It seemed to Lill as if the words back-fired straight down his throat.

"Time to toast the birthday girl. Marlene!" Ted yelled, then realised she was standing right next to him. "There's the Mrs.," he slurred, slapping her on the backside.

Marlene gave Ted a tight little smile that never quite made it past her lips. Everyone then did the obligatory glass-raising and singing. Someone suggested the birthday bumps but was pre-empted in favour of birthday kisses, and a half dozen or more men took turns giving her pecks on the cheek and, occasionally, a little more, none of which did much to satisfy two years of drought. Rod had disappeared, and she felt inexplicably let down. Giving up on the wine, Lill switched to tea.

By ten-thirty she was home in bed, utterly deflated, exhausted with the effort of trying to smile for three hours in her sister's perfect kitchen. She wasn't sure if she wanted to yawn or cry. It wasn't turning forty that had her in such a state. It was feeling like she'd been waiting for such a long time, in this town, waiting for her life to begin. Would she spend every weekend wishing for something different, hoping for some glimmer of excitement? Family dinners with her sisters, visits to her father rotting away in the Home, raising David and Max until they both moved away, like David would in the fall.

Lill had never lived on her own, never lived away except for short stints in her thirties when she'd gone back to finish her degree. And although she had felt the call of the city then, the lure of the new and unexpected, the pull to explore a different type of life, she'd kept it to herself. In the end she was glad she did. When Steve died and she was left on her own, she was grateful to be home; it was where she belonged. This town lived in her as much as she lived in it. It had been that way for as long as she could remember. There was comfort in that, she told herself, comfort and security. Yes, there were worse things.

A light snow had started to fall outside her bedroom window. Closing her eyes she rolled to her side of the queen-sized bed, the only sound her solitary breathing.

Another Friday night in Port Grace.

2

Rod Corcoran looked out his bedroom window into the stark stillness of daybreak. A typical spring snowstorm had blown through overnight and at least a foot of powder had fallen since he'd walked home from Lill's party. The world seemed suspended in a sea of white. A quick breeze slipped under the slightly open window; he breathed deeply, the crisp Newfoundland air sharp and clean in his lungs. He'd never been a late sleeper, always waking with or before the dawn. As a boy he'd hated early mornings like these. Stuck inside, no one to go sledding or skating with, nothing to do but watch cartoons with his mute teenage sister until the rest of the town woke up and ventured out into the snowdrifts.

By the time he'd turned fifteen, however, he'd come to look forward to the surreal anonymity of wintry Saturday mornings. He'd head out at first light to shovel the latest downfall, relishing the feel of his muscles straining under the heavy wetness. When their own house was done, he always cut a path for the neighbours on either side. After a change of mitts he'd deliver the weekend paper, each week counting how many souls he met on the streets, always hoping he'd be the only one. He loved living in Port Grace on those days, loved the freedom, the clean frozen-in-time innocence that pervaded the raw icy air. He was not so fond of the place most other times.

Except for warm and sunny spring mornings. Forced to hibernate for months on end, when the thaw set in and the sun came out, so did the people. Neighbours opened their doors early, shaking out their mats, getting the first load of laundry ready for the clothesline, and for the lucky few with a decent blade of grass, gassing up their lawn mowers. The ocean, visible from almost any vantage point unless you were lying down and staring up at the sky, glittered like firecrackers of gold and silver out to the horizon. The earth and the sea sang of green and blue, of trees and grass and aquamarine. Port Grace smelled of new dirt and sparkling water, fresh and clean, better than it did any other time of year. It seemed to Rod that spring brought out the best in people, too. It opened their hearts, allowed them to smile at someone they'd frowned on the week before.

Unfortunately, snowed-in Saturdays and sunny spring mornings left a lot of days unaccounted for.

To be back in the midst of it all at thirty-two still surprised him. There were times when he could barely believe he was once again living in a town with only nineteen hundred and ninety-eight people. The high-rise apartment complex where he'd lived in Toronto probably had more occupants than that. Still, with all those people living so close together, one on top of the other really, he'd never felt claustrophobic in the city. Yet that was precisely how he'd felt his last few years of high school in Port Grace. Like one tiny sardine, an insignificant little fish that never quite measured up to the other fish in the ocean.

Port Grace was Rod's home. Yet as much as he wished it otherwise, he had never truly fit in. He knew that was because he was a Corcoran. Lill, on the other hand, was a part of Port Grace. She was born a Penney, and the Penneys definitely belonged. They had always had an integral place in the town, like the sea air and the white-capped waves. Not so the Corcorans. In a community filled mainly with hard working Catholic families - neither rich nor poor, devil nor saint - Rod recognised that somehow his family stood on the lowest rung of the community ladder. And while he understood that it was a position they'd inherited, it seemed to him one they did their best to maintain.

Nevertheless, as a child he'd felt relatively normal, despite the fact that he had no father. His first warning that the Corcorans were different came one day in kindergarten when Jimmy Linehan and Luke Dunphy cornered him on the playground and started making fun of Suzie. Until then, he hadn't known that it was a strange thing for someone not to speak. Suzie was simply his sister, a lot older and very quiet, but a constant fixture in his life.

"How come Suzie won't talk?" he asked his mother that evening.

Ida was in the middle of making molasses bread, and she glanced briefly in his direction, then shifted her gaze to the open kitchen window. "I don't think our Suzie got much she wants to say."

"But could she, if she wanted to?"

Ida stopped kneading the bowl of bread dough and turned to face him. "Not anymore, Roddy. Not anymore."

"Did she used to talk?" he persisted.

Ida looked at him for a moment, then frowned. "Why you asking?"

"Cause Jimmy Linehan said she was so stupid God figured she didn't need her tongue for talking."

Ida's cheeks puffed out. "Jimmy Linehan should keep his mouth shut, talking about stuff he don't know nothing about."

"But he does. His father told him."

"Oh he did, did he?"

"Yeah, and he's a teacher, so he knows stuff."

"What else did little Jimmy have to say?"

"Oh…nothing," Rod answered, turning away.

"No? Come on, Roddy, what else did he say?"

"Just that…that…he said that all the Corcorans were stupid, and that we weren't there when God was handing out the brains."

Ida snorted. "Hah! You tell Jimmy Linehan he better look in the mirror if he wants to see a boy with no brain."

"What? How…?" He quickly realised what she meant and started to laugh, but after a moment he turned serious again. "Suzie got a brain, though, right?"

"Oh, Roddy, of course Suzie got a brain, and she got a tongue, too. Don't you be minding the Jimmy Linehans of this world. People like that are always looking down on somebody."

Rod had nodded, satisfied, for the time being at least.

Still, as he grew he started to pay closer attention, to listen to the words and the voices behind the words to try to discover why his family didn't measure up to the other families in Port Grace. What made the Corcorans less than the Linehans and the O'Sheas, the Penneys and the Foleys? Why did his teachers look down on him but spoil the likes of Luke Dunphy? Was it just because Mr. Dunphy was the mayor? Or did the fact that Rod's family rarely went to Mass have something to do with it? Although they were all baptised Catholics, they only went to church when Rod suggested it. "I went every day for forty years," Ida claimed when he pestered her. "Sometimes twice. As far as I'm concerned, that's enough for a lifetime." But was it enough for Port Grace, Rod wondered?

He began to think it was some defect buried deep inside of him, and inside his mother and his sisters, too, perhaps even inside his father before he died. He suspected it might have something to do with his father's death, that with the lack of a man to head the house, the women and children remaining were left to stand alone at the bottom of the chain. Then he thought about his mother, her cleaning job at the school, and it occurred to him that maybe having to clean up after other people made her less than them. One day he got up the nerve to say something about it.

He'd just come home from school. Ida was stirring a pot at the stove, the loose flesh on her arm wobbling with each rotation. He dropped his books on the wood table, and they landed with a resounding plop. Liking the sound, he picked them up and did it again, even though he knew it would irritate his mother. The second time, however, they slid across the table, knocking the salt shaker to the floor. The top, which had never fit well, came off, spilling salt across the clean cracked linoleum.

"Bad luck that is, to be spilling salt," Ida remarked. "You best be picking up them grains if you wants to be getting into heaven."

Rod was in a bad mood. At recess, Luke Dunphy had been picking on him again, calling Ida "the town mop", and making exaggerated humming and gagging noises that everyone knew were meant to mimic Suzie. "No Corcorans in heaven," Rod shot back at Ida, the words leaping out of his eight year-old mouth before he even knew he'd thought them.

Ida turned around and glared at him. "Indeed there is."

"Yeah?" he pushed, despite the growing pain in his stomach. "Probably cleaning toilets."

"You got a bee in your bonnet there, Roddy?" she asked sharply.

He hated when she said things like that. A bee in his bonnet! He was a boy, for God's sake. Boys didn't even wear bonnets. No wonder everybody thought they were weird. "Well, wouldn't we be? That's all we're any good for, everybody knows that," he yelled at her.

Ida rounded on him, wagging her callused finger in his face. "Don't you be letting me hear that kind of talk, Rodney Corcoran." Opening her rough hands wide, she thrust them up in the air between them. "'Tis an honest days work I does with these mitts, and it's a harder one than most around these parts. I haven't once gone on the dole in all the years since he been dead, though the devil knows we had to before it. So anybody says anything about me cleaning, you be proud to know we're making our own way in this world, and we always will if I got anything to do with it."

He could feel his bottom lip quivering, but then Ida reached out and hugged him to her, squashing his head into her chest. He didn't mind though. He liked to be hugged when no one else was around, except Suzie of course. Suzie didn't really count. And even though he knew he'd upset Ida, he was still glad he'd done it because what she had said in return made him feel much better about his family. If his mother believed they were equal, it must be true. Even so, he kept his eyes open.

It was a year or two later when he detected something else that was different. It seemed whenever Janie came home from St. John's, his mother changed toward him. If he cut his knee or fell off his bike when Janie was there, Ida would send him to her. And she would insist on getting Janie's advice about any little problems he was having, and tell her all the details of what he'd done since she'd last been out to visit. In the beginning he was okay with this. He liked when Janie came to visit because it always seemed to shake them up a bit. With more people and more noise, their family felt more normal. And he enjoyed the extra attention and his mother's obvious pride in him. But soon he noticed Janie's reactions to Ida's praise. It was as if she could barely tolerate him, at most giving him a nod. Usually she acted coldly indifferent, hardly glancing his way. Rarely did she look him dead in the eye.

By grade six, Rod had begun to excel in his schoolwork. Several times the previous year when he'd gotten high marks in a test, he felt as if his teacher actually treated him nicer. In fact, he could have sworn that the better he did, the more people seemed to like him, teachers and students alike. With that in mind, he decided to truly apply himself. His grades shot straight up. As expected, Ida was thrilled, but she kept harping on about Janie. "I can't wait for our Janie to see them tests of yours," she'd exclaim, or, "Janie got lots to be proud of there, my boy." When he got a good mark in a project, she'd place it on top of the fridge, "out of harm's way, for when Janie gets here. She be some pleased with you there, Roddy." Not wanting to spoil the moment, Rod always let it go.

Then Janie would come home, and his mother would prattle on, and it seemed to him that both he and Janie would put up with it until Ida finished and left it alone. The only time Janie did seem impressed, he thought she acted more proud of herself than anyone else, as if it was more his lucky fortune to be her brother than his hard work that got him such good grades.

"Well done, Rodney," she said stiffly when he came first in the class on his report card. "Good to see you got a decent brain in that head."

"Of course he does," Ida beamed, her voice filled with pride.

Sneering at her, Janie pronounced angrily, "Don't go patting yourself on the back there. It's me he got to thank for that, not your lot."

Rod wasn't sure what she meant by that. Then again, he often didn't with Janie.

Shaking her head, Ida tutted and sighed, then went back to her pots on the stove. Janie glared at the back of Ida's head for such a long time that Rod feared she might hit her, but in the end she just lit a cigarette and stormed out, her trim muscular legs marching out on three-inch heels. Confused and disappointed, he decided to ignore his moody sister. Besides, Ida and Suzie were proud enough for all of them.

His new confidence spurred him on and he studied even harder. From grade seven onwards, he finished each year at the top of his class, earning himself a lasting respect in the eyes of his teachers. By grade nine, between his mother's outright pride and the occasional approving grunt from his sister, along with the prizes he won for top marks and his more-than-decent showing on the ball diamond, he was starting to believe there were worse things than being a Corcoran.

Then everything changed. At fourteen he heard it for the first time. In fact, it was spat at him as he crouched on the ground, shivering from the cold and the wet and the fear of the bullies surrounding him.

"...dumb fucking Corcoran...mother's your slut sister...stupid retard...daddy's your granddaddy...granddaddydaddy..."

The noise swirled around him, the voices angry, sneering, mocking. The words, seemingly random at first, gradually merged within his head, so that finally he understood what it really meant to be a Corcoran.

He couldn't believe he was the last to know. Couldn't believe the women in his life, his mother and his sisters, had never let on, had never had the decency to warn him. Everybody seemed to know but him. Yet nobody but him had more of a right to know. He knew life wasn't always fair. His mother preached it often enough, and Janie must have said exactly that a thousand times. But this was more than unfair. This was unforgivable, when the only people you trusted, the women who took care of you and made you feel like you belonged even when nobody else did, when they lied to you that was the biggest wrong of all.

So as he crouched on the ground and the taunts rained down on him, he blocked out everything but the fury growing inside him. But he wasn't angry at the fools who eventually left him shuddering in the dirt. No, he was furious at those women. One of them in particular.

Rod tore through the woods in the afternoon cloud, his bleeding scratches drying up even as he created new ones from the branches and trees that tried to stop him. He didn't care. He barely noticed. Racing onwards, stumbling never falling, his heart smacked inside his chest. His head and face and eyes felt ready to explode with the effort and the rage that boiled within his heart.

Their house backed onto the trees, and he came around the long way, past the beach and up behind it. It stood there, grey and shabby, suddenly unwelcoming. A thin trail of smoke snaked out of the chimney, and a dull light filtered through the kitchen window. A shadow passed in front of it.

It might have been one of his sisters, or his mother. Or both. It might have been Janie. She'd come home the night before with her two boys. They were in there now, all of them, probably getting supper ready. His mother would be worried; he was never late.

He barged through the porch and into the kitchen. Ida immediately hurried over to him. "Roddy, what happened to you?" she asked, reaching up to touch one of his scrapes; he'd been taller than her for over a year now.

He pulled back and pushed her hand away. "Never mind it."

"It looks pretty sore there. Let me—"

"I said leave it be," he barked. He'd never in his life spoken to her in such a voice.

Janie was sitting at the table, eyeing them strangely. She stood up and walked over, fists tight against her bony hips. "Rod, who did this to you?" she demanded, glancing past him out the window. "Who's the cause of this?"

He looked at her then, this woman who was his mother. Although they were similar in height, she was thinner than he, with a dry pinched look about her face. Dark hair hung limp to her shoulders, the bangs not quite covering the purplish scar in the middle of her forehead. She had no make-up on yet. That would come later if she decided to go out on the prowl. "You are," he told her.

The room fell silent, the only noise the rhythmic cadence from a children's TV show in the living room.

Lighting a fresh cigarette, Janie asked contemptuously, "What in God's name are you going on about?"

"I said you are. If it wasn't for you, I wouldn't be all beat up."

She spit out a shred of tobacco. "Fuck's sake, Rod, don't be such—"

"Did somebody say something to you, Roddy?" Ida cut in.

"What do you think?" he yelled. Then he moved to Janie, and asked with all the hatred he could muster, "If you're the slut they say is my mother, then who's my fucking father?"

Finally, she looked straight at him. Then her free hand shot out and belted him hard. His head spun in a flurry of light and colour. For the second time that day, for the second time in his life, someone had deliberately hit him. Just as the thought occurred to him, she struck again. It was more a fist than a palm, punching him in the mouth, then across the head, her eyes raging. She looked insane, ready to pound him forever.

Ida jumped between them, pushing Janie back. "Don't you dare raise your hand to that child!" Ida warned. "I won't have it, I tell you."

"Oh, won't you, now?" Janie bellowed back at her.

"Janie, you knows how I feels about that. There'll be nobody getting beat in my house, not any more."

"Hah! What a fucking laugh! Butter wouldn't melt in your gob, it wouldn't. Christ!"

Ida hung her head for just an instant, then raised it to glare at Janie. "I've told you over and over that we're not going to be that way no more. Not in this house. Not since he died. No sir, never again."

"Too goddamn bad you didn't feel like that when I was his age, eh? You knew how to lay it on then, didn't you?"

"Maybe so, Janie," Ida said with a forced calm. "And I said I'm sorry a thousand times, and I still am. But them days are gone. That was then. This is now."

Rod watched as the two of them stared at each other, Janie's nostrils flaring, Ida's eyes hard and determined. As long as he could remember, no one was ever hit in Ida's house. Normally she didn't allow swearing either, but today she said nothing about that. She just stood there, chest heaving. The only sound came from Suzie. She had started to drone, a dull buzzing monotone that filled up the kitchen as surely as her short podgy body filled the width of the living room doorway.

Janie shoved Ida's hands away. "Shut up, Suzie," she yelled.

"Go in and keep the youngsters company, Suzie," Ida told her.

Suzie trembled in front of them, her eyes wide and frightened as she looked at Janie.

"Right, sorry," Janie said, her voice softening just a little. "Keep them busy for me, okay?"

"Is it true?" Rod demanded angrily as Suzie shuffled off.

Ida looked from him to Janie. "It's time the boy knew some things, Janie."

"Yeah, I suppose it is." Janie dragged deeply on her cigarette. As her lips scrunched around it, tough, tight crevices formed all around her mouth. These used to disappear after she blew out all the smoke, but they didn't anymore. Barely thirty, the lines around her eyes and mouth made her appear much older. In fact, since the car crash the year before, she seemed to have aged noticeably every time he saw her.

"Well?" he asked.

She sighed then, as if it was all too much bother. Rod had the urge to use his own fist to hit her back. It was definitely a day of firsts.

Janie flicked the cigarette into the sink. "Fuck it. I'm your mother. So what?"

He waited. There had to be more. Surely she'd have something else to say on such an important revelation. He gave her time to continue, but she stood silently defiant in the middle of the kitchen, nibbling the inside of her lip.

"And?" he asked.

Janie shrugged her shoulders.

"Mom?" he said to Ida.

Ida looked to Janie, who shook her head slowly from side to side, her face set and hard. "Janie, I think—"

"No! That's all he got to know."

"All I got to know!" he cried. "How can you say that? You weren't there. You don't know what they said, what they called you, and…and the other stuff."

Janie glared at him. "I can just imagine. My advice to you, Rod, is don't believe everything you hears."

"But what were they talking about? A granddaddy for a daddy, what did they mean by that?"

Ida rushed in. "Oh, Roddy, no. They didn't, did they? Them little bastards. They don't—"

"Mom! That's enough."

"But Janie…" Rod stopped. Suddenly struck by the truth, he wondered whether he was supposed to call her or Ida, "Mom".

Janie's hand ran through her hair, pulling at the faded roots for just a second. "I'm going to say this once, Rod. I am your mother, but I was young and foolish when you were born so she raised you. It's no big secret, the whole fucking town knows it. We're not going to talk about who your father was, and there's no sense asking around because nobody can help you with it." She looked pointedly at Ida. "No one. And for the last time, don't be believing rumours. They don't know nothing else, this crowd. Just remember that." Grabbing her cigarettes and lighter, she barged out of the house.

"Mom? Do you know?" he asked Ida.

She shook her head sadly. "I'm sorry, Roddy, but it's Janie's decision. I'm afraid I got to go along with whatever she wants."

As confused as he was, Rod still couldn't help but notice how worn out Ida looked. She was always tired now, ever since the cancer the year before. He'd been so frightened that she would die, scared senseless at times worrying about her, and what would become of him and Suzie if anything happened to her. He'd prayed and prayed and made a vow to be really helpful and not to upset her, if only God would let her live. And he'd kept his promise, until today. Today he couldn't do it. "But Mom—"

"No! I means it now. That's enough about it." She marched out and up the stairs to the bedroom she shared with Suzie.

He stood in the middle of the kitchen, his heart banging so loud he could feel its pulse in his throat. His chest hurt with the pressure of not screaming, the pain rising up his neck and into the back of his head. He needed to know. They had no right to keep it from him.

But neither of the women would budge from her position. The next day, he cornered Suzie, badgering her about what she knew. But she started in with that high-pitched humming of hers. Eyes frantic, mouth smeared with jam, she backed away from him, her sloppy sweat pants and baggy sweater hiding the layers of fat she'd spent years accumulating. The mouth that never spoke never stopped eating.

When Janie came in the room and caught him, she kicked him out of the house. "You won't be going on at her about it, Rod," she yelled. Suzie was her one soft spot; Janie was gentler with Suzie than she was with her own children. "She got nothing to tell you, nothing to add to what I been telling you myself. So leave her alone, you hear? Picking on the poor helpless thing, my God, what's the matter with you? Get out of here, and be gone for the day!"

She was right. He knew that. It all just made him feel even worse, and he already felt bad enough, about Suzie and Ida and everything else in his life, hopeless and frustrated for hurting them and for feeling so hurt himself. He didn't think that way about Janie though. He was more angry with her than he'd ever thought possible, but he knew it was useless to push her. He'd never seen her so determined, and she was no wilting flower on a normal day.

With no one to turn to, he took off for the beach and spent the rest of the evening in the place that Suzie had once shown him. She'd made such a big deal of sharing it with him, leading him secretly in the back way and spreading her hands so grandly when they got there. He hadn't had the heart to tell her he'd been there before, often in fact, and had up until that moment considered it his own little hideaway. It was the one place where he felt truly himself.

Around nine o'clock he walked home, past the homes of neighbours he'd known all his life. He'd never thought too much about them, the people inside, or the hard rock of land on which they lived. They had always been there, they always would be. He had never considered the brightly painted clapboard houses, garish yet strangely beautiful, how they stood out amidst the more conservative whites, the fading greys. Yet all were plopped down, as if stuck haphazardly on plots of land, some front, some back. Did the owners even know where one property began and another ended? Did they care?

He reached his house, one of the weathered grey ones, with patches of old white paint still stuck to the wood. Knowing Janie's boys would have just gone to bed, he crept along the side so as not to disturb them. He was passing underneath the kitchen window when he heard them, Ida and Janie, their voices rising in anger, then descending in secrecy.

"Why not tell him?" asked Ida.

"Tell him? Good Christ, Mom, you knows we can't do that," Janie answered.

"I don't mean everything. You could give him something though, all the same."

"No way. We don't want him finding out more than he needs to. He's just a youngster. God knows who or what he'll be telling."

"But he's got a right to know. It's his life we're talking on here."

"Yeah, well it's my life too, and yours. Besides it won't make no difference. It'll just bring on more questions and you knows I can't answer them."

"Oh, Janie, it don't seem fair to the boy."

"Mom, it's as fair as I'm getting. Just imagine if he ever knew the real truth, imagine how that would feel to him."

"I suppose," said Ida. "What about if it weren't the truth?"

"Christ Almighty! Isn't there enough frigging lies and secrets in this house already? Besides, what would be the point?"

"Make him feel better, it would."

"Maybe so, but I'm not doing it."

"Aw, Janie. Sure I suppose you might be right. We'll just leave it be."

"You promise not to tell him?"

"I promise. If he ever finds out, it'll be from you."

Their voices drifted off then, away from the window, towards the sink perhaps or out of the room. He didn't know or care. He let his body slump down into the cool grass. Was it true then, he wondered? Was the man he'd thought was his father his grandfather too? It had to be. If not, why wouldn't they tell him who his father was? Or was it somehow, in some twilight dimension he couldn't fathom, even worse? Could it even be possible to be worse than that? A shiver shot down his arms, and a dull ache lodged in his stomach. He rolled over and lay still, his head buried in the cold empty space between the grass and the dirt.

Throughout the remainder of high school, he tried to concentrate on what little he could control, focusing his life around school and sports, hockey and ball, and homework and chores. There was nothing he could do about his family. It was not within his power to change the course of history; he alone did not have the ability or desire to make good the Corcoran name. For the time being, he was stuck in Port Grace, and it was stuck with him. But not forever. He developed a plan, the GET he called it—get straight A's, get a scholarship, and get the hell out. And he did.

Over the years he thought often about who his father might be, but his attempts to daydream were always unsuccessful, and more often than not, hampered by the ghostly appearance of a hazy unshaven figure, a crazy old man. Even in his wildest daydreams he couldn't conjure up the mythical stranger who would appear to claim him as his own. Consequently, he rarely broached the subject. On the few occasions that he did, both Ida and Janie gave him that cold dead look they reserved for the most distasteful of subjects. It was the same look they got when people talked about old Matt, the man he'd grown up assuming was his father, the one he'd grown older fearing was the same. All Ida would ever say was that he should not believe the stupid stories people told or the idle rumours of old biddies. But she would never tell him anything else about who his father might be. He wanted to believe her, but always he remembered the words beneath the kitchen window. Always he wondered.

3

When Janie Corcoran was young, she shared a bedroom with her little sister Suzie. They had one twin bed that seemed to be the perfect size, especially on those nights when they wanted to hide from the world, or from their father.

It was around St. Patrick's Day that it happened for the last time, although they didn't know then that it would be the last time. Janie pulled the blankets over their heads as soon as the yelling started. "Let's play camping," she said to Suzie, who lay quivering beside her.

Under the covers everything was muffled. The air was thick with their hot breath and the double duty of darkness.

"It's warm in here," whispered Suzie's tiny voice.

Janie didn't answer. She was listening to the ominous quiet outside the blankets.

"Janie?" Suzie's frightened cry broke the silence. "Are you there, Janie?"

"Right here," Janie answered quickly. A shout, their father's voice, reverberated. "You want to hear a story?" she added, trying to hide her own fear.

"Okay. The one about Hanna and Greta."

Janie's version of the fairytale told of two sisters who ran away from home, leaving a trail of crumbs for their mother to follow. A bird ate the crumbs and the sisters got lost and wandered further and further up into the mountains. But a beautiful rich woman found them and took care of them and they all lived happily ever after. It was Suzie's favourite story. Janie liked it too.

She was almost finished the telling when there was a thump against the wall that separated their bedroom from their parents' room. Janie stopped abruptly.

"What was that?" gasped Suzie.

Janie said nothing. She waited, breathless with dread, for what she knew would follow. Finally, she whispered, "just…an animal jumped out of a tree," and pretended to make it part of the story.

There was a moan then, and shouting, loud even within their tiny haven. Janie felt Suzie curling up beside her, growing smaller. She hurried to finish, ending with "…happily ever after." Then, to fill the void left by her voice, she began to hum a lullaby, which usually worked to distract Suzie. "Hhmmm, hhmmm, hhmmm…" she droned, anything to drown out the moans and grunts and shouts that seemed to batter the dark empty spaces around their heads, ricocheting off her eardrums.

Janie hummed and hummed until the house became silent.

A long while later, she pushed the covers from over their heads. Suzie lay nestled beside her, asleep, her tiny thumb imbedded in her mouth. Beads of sweat trickled down her cheek. Janie reached over and wiped them away, careful not to wake her.

The next morning Janie waited as long as she dared. Just as she was about to give up and get out of bed, she heard the door slam. She woke Suzie, and they quickly dressed and hurried down the stairs.

Ida stood at the stove. Janie could hear the faint murmurs, the intermittent whispered phrases, the intoned pleas, as her mother recited the rosary while she worked her spoon round and round in a large charred-bottomed pot. Her frayed and faded blue cotton nightgown hung loosely over her slumped shoulders and short round body. "Eat up some of that now before it goes cold," she said flatly without looking at them.

Two bowls of porridge lay congealing on the table. Janie's stomach heaved at the thought of trying to get the glutinous mess past her lips. "Where's Dad?" she asked, pushing Suzie's chair in closer to the table.

"Down at the plant." Her mother's voice seemed to lift and brighten then, but Janie knew from experience it was a false cheer. "Gone to ask on that job. Thinks he'll get it this time."

The air in the kitchen felt mouldy. The day was socked in and only a pale light drifted in through the window. Nestled as it was between two hills, and open to the sea, Port Grace was often a very dreary place to live. A couple of miles over in Grenville the sun was probably shining, having burned off the fog early on in the morning. But not here. It could be hours before that happened, if at all.

Ida shuffled sideways to the counter; all the while the whisperings continued. When she reached up to get a mixing bowl, her sleeve fell back for a moment, just long enough for Janie to spot the large greenish purple bruise above her elbow. "I'll make some tea bikkies for lunch." Her mother's voice was low and distracted, as if she was talking to herself. "He likes them, he does."

"Yeah, great," muttered Janie. Keeping one eye on her mother's rigid back, with the other she watched Suzie making shapes in the porridge.

"I needs for you to stop on over the way and see to your granny for me, okay Janie?" Ida had stopped moving, although she didn't turn around. One hand rested on the side of her head, the other was somewhere near her face.

"Okay."

There was a low moan from the counter. "And take our Suzie with you. She's a right good help, and your Nana likes to see her." Again, she didn't look at them.

Suzie smiled at Janie. They both liked going to their grandmother's, where there was a bigger TV that always worked, and store-bought cookies and cakes and chocolate milk.

Janie got up and went over to her mother. "You need any help here?"

Ida stepped quickly away, keeping her face averted. Still, Janie saw her wince as she bent to look in the fridge.

"No," Ida said crossly. "Set yourself at the table there and finish up. Don't need to be wasting." Still with her back to them she straightened slowly, cautiously it seemed to Janie, then shifted to the stove to add some wood. As the cast iron cover settled back into place, Janie could just barely hear her mother mutter, "...Son, and the Holy Ghost...." Ida's fingers rose to her forehead, then swept quickly down towards her chin, and in a continuous motion, swished across her face. "Amen." She gingerly rubbed her nose, then recoiled from her own touch.

Janie wondered if old Matt had been rougher than usual. He was generally careful not to leave anything too noticeable, especially on the face. Just as she was thinking about how she could get in front of her mother to have a closer look, hard heavy footsteps could be heard from the back. The door banged open and bumped against the porch wall amid a muttering of "fucking idjits" and "Christly bastards."

Grabbing Suzie's hand, Janie raced toward the front. "Hurry," she whispered. "Get your stuff and come on."

Suzie needed no encouragement. Shoes in hand, she ran barefoot from the house.

As long as Janie could remember, it had been that way. For several days before each episode, the air in the house seemed to thicken. Sometimes she felt it was all she could do to just get a full breath of air. She would notice him watching her mother's movements, his dark eyes half hidden under thick lids. Then one day, he would go out with his friends. Drunk and belligerent, he'd return hours later with a bottle of Screech under his arm. Janie knew her father to be a mean, horrible man with a gut load of beer in his belly, but when he laid in a skinful of rum on top of it, Matt Corcoran was evil incarnate.

Then it would really begin. No matter how carefully they spoke, or how softly they tiptoed through the house, no matter how much they tried to fulfill his every need before he was even aware that he wanted anything, he would find something wrong, some word, some deed, some action left undone. If supper was not to his liking, he would fling it into the garbage, or worse still, throw it out the back door, plate and all, ranting that it was "nothing but pig slop, not fit for a dog." Or he'd go into a rage if they ran low on hot water, even though Ida would have used it to wash his clothes and his dishes and to clean up after he'd tracked mud throughout the house. Whatever it was, big or small, it would send him into a fury, his body and his voice thundering from room to room.

Janie had learned to go to bed early on those nights, to stay far out of his way. Although she worried after her mother, she was far more frightened for herself and Suzie. Huddled together in their little bed, the two of them would try their best to get through another night of fear. From start to finish it would last several hours, the shouts and threats, the pushing and shoving, their mother's voice begging him to stop, "no, Matt...don't...please don't." And throughout it all, Ida's muffled whimpers of pain. Then it would slow down, always ending with a series of grunts and groans from her father, different in timbre than her mother's, less painful sounding. Janie was eleven before she figured out what they were about.

It would only last the one night, thank God. It seemed to quench some need in him, some brutal force that had to be met, some desire he could not control. He wasn't exactly nice after that, but he was tolerable, and they all looked forward to a period of relative peace following each episode.

Ida never spoke to her children about what her husband did to her, and as far as Janie could tell, she never mentioned it outside the house either. Still, Janie knew that people knew. Their neighbours were not stupid, nor were they deaf. She could tell by the way they looked at her and her sister and her mother, sizing them up, making judgements in their minds. Janie knew that to most of them, the Corcorans were lesser beings, a verdict that was hard to dispute. The evidence was all around them, in the way her mother spoke, low and subservient, rarely making eye contact, and in the way she walked, trudging forward, head bent, hung in humiliation. As a child, it was hard for Janie not to emulate the posture of disgrace that Ida modelled for her. But even then, Janie failed to understand exactly why her mother felt such shame, why Ida seemed to be continually begging for God's mercy and forgiveness, day in and day out, in the church and out of it. Nor could Janie understand why she herself felt such humiliation. It made no sense when the one person who should have been ashamed appeared not to know the meaning of the word.

One Saturday around noon, Janie was looking through the cracked upstairs windowpane. She'd just finished her chores for the day—making the beds and scrubbing the floors. As she nursed a small splinter on her water-soaked finger, a big shiny black car with tinted windows pulled up and parked on the edge of their patchy front lawn. When the wide door swung open, Father O'Malley, their parish priest, wrestled his ample frame from behind the wheel. A large frown creased his forehead as he stood staring at the house. He reached behind his robe and pulled out a stark white handkerchief to mop the sweat from his face. It was not a warm day. A cold spring rain had let up just minutes before. But he was six feet tall, with a great thick neck that strained against his white collar, and a stomach that bulged forward, as if announcing his very presence. Janie ran to get Ida, but her mother was already at the door, beckoning "Dear Father" in from the damp cold. Janie watched wordlessly as his mud-spattered shoes smeared footprints across the freshly washed living room floor. As he hurried Ida into the kitchen, his booming voice ordered Janie and Suzie to their room with orders to kneel down and say their prayers, and not to come out till he called them.

They scurried up the stairs. As soon as the door was shut, Suzie knelt by the bed. "Our Father who art in heaven—"

"Shhh. To yourself, Suzie, okay?" Janie whispered.

Nodding, Suzie squeezed her eyes together and started to pray, her lips shivering as tiny whispers slid past them.

Janie lay down on the floor and wriggled silently to the wall. With her hands cupping either side of her head, she pressed her face to the cold metal register and stared down into the kitchen. She concentrated as hard as she could because it was hard to catch all the words. Father O'Malley was pointing his finger at her mother. Rosary beads clutched in her hands, Ida sat mutely across from him staring at the scarred wooden table.

"…God…watching you. Duty to…wife to him…promised …honour and obey."

Ida mumbled something then, which seemed to make him angry.

"They have to learn …sacrifices…eyes of God…girls should do…their father says. You have to…If you…God will take care of…"

Nodding meekly, Ida bowed her head.

"Now I don't want to…rumours anymore…windows closed…duty to be a good wife to him…keep this quiet…a word with Matt too."

With that he stood, gathered his black robes about him and raised his cross above Ida's bent shoulders. "…God bless …the Father…of the Son and …Ghost, Amen."

As Father O'Malley passed underneath the register on his way to the door, Janie could barely stop herself from gathering every last drop of saliva in her mouth and spitting it down on him. For even at ten, she had come to detest the hold that the church had over her mother. She'd learned that Ida's trust in the saving grace of God was a blinding force in her life, a window into a fantasy world where only good things awaited those who believed. Ida's pat answer when life looked hopeless was that God would look out for them, that they should leave it, whatever "it" might be on any given day, in God's good and merciful hands. "The meek shall inherit the earth," she would tell her daughters, then meekly bless herself and them, her eyes heavenward.

As Janie lay on the floor waiting for her mother to return from seeing the priest on his way, her stomach knotted with fear. And when she saw Ida slump into the chair and lean her greying head into her worn chapped hands, Janie finally did what the priest had told her to do. "Dear God and Holy Baby Jesus, please help us."

Later that year when she was no longer ten, and when she no longer slept on the other side of her mother's wall, she would wonder if either one of them had been listening, or if God had pulled rank on his infant son. In her innocence she had hoped that Baby Jesus might have been looking out for her more. But in the end she concluded that His Father must have had other loyalties. She also concluded that she could not count on God's good hands.

After the priest's visit on that cold wet spring day, Matt Corcoran did finally leave his wife alone. Even when he was drinking. Even when he was so drunk he could barely see the bottle in front of his face. Had the priest lectured him too, Janie wondered? Had Father O'Malley done some good after all?

As the weeks turned into months, Ida appeared to become calmer, less visibly tense. Several times Janie even caught her in a light-hearted moment. Whereas before she'd always seemed to be on nervous alert for the moment her husband would walk into the room, she began to speak of him with respect, even affection. It was as if she had completely forgotten all that had passed before. Janie wished she could so readily erase it from her mind.

It was around then that she noticed how much time her mother was spending at church. Every morning without fail, Ida went to Mass, twice on Saturdays and Sundays if Matt was not at home to notice. Sometimes she dragged Janie and Suzie with her, sometimes she went alone. She would arrive early and leave late, spending the extra minutes performing the Stations of the Cross, or in the front pew on her knees, head bent towards the altar. She was just as pious at home. During the day as she cleaned and cooked, she would sometimes fall to the floor and prostrate herself before one of the crucifixes she'd hung in every room, her voice a mumble of whispery intonations.

Janie knew it all should have made her feel better but it didn't. It frightened the daylights out of her. She had not forgotten, nor was she anywhere near as optimistic as her mother seemed to be. She sensed a tension about her father, a restless quality that made her eerily uncomfortable, especially when she caught him looking at her. Those dark brooding eyes would follow her around the kitchen, trailing behind her, searing into her back. It was as if an evil presence had invaded the room, clouding the very air they breathed. Her skin felt prickly, like something was crawling on it, and she kept thinking that she should tuck her clothes in, that something was sticking out and catching his attention. In an effort to stay clear of him, she spent more time in her and Suzie's tiny bedroom.

"We be shifting you to the downstairs, Janie," her mother told her one morning at the end of August. Ida was bent over the sink washing the breakfast dishes.

"Downstairs? What do you mean?"

"For sleeping. There's that room there in back of the furnace."

"I don't want to sleep down there."

"Now, now. Your father says you needs your privacy." There was a hint of pride in her mother's voice, no doubt regarding his thoughtfulness. "You been spending so much time in your bedroom, it be only right you has a room of your own."

Janie's skin shivered. "Mom, I don't need no privacy."

Ida turned to her, wiping one wet hand on her ragged apron and shoving her still uncombed hair back with the other. "Now why you being that hard to please? He's just on for doing something nice for you. We'll do it up good."

"But it's freezing and pitch dark down there."

"No, now he says he got a bit of rug from his mother. Make it all nice and cosy, it will."

"But Mom," she begged, dangerously close to tears but afraid to let them fall, afraid to lose control of what was happening to her, but knowing she had no control anyway, "I wants to stay up here. With Suzie. And you. Don't make me go down there."

"What in God's name is going on in that head? He's trying to do something nice for you and this is what thanks he gets. I don't want to be hearing another word out of you."

"Please, Mom—"

"Don't be so Godforsaken ungrateful," Ida shouted, just as familiar footsteps trudged up the back steps. They both spun around to stare towards the porch. "Now shut up about it," she hissed.

He trudged in, a rolled up piece of carpet under his arm, the frayed fibres hanging all about. "Your mother tell you?" he barked.

Janie glanced quickly at his unshaven face. A cigarette stuck straight out of his mouth, securely lodged in the missing bottom front tooth. The smoke curled upwards to where his permanently bloodshot eyes squinted at her.

"Well?" he shouted.

Janie nodded.

"Good then. Be done by tomorrow."

Next he lugged in an old rollaway cot, its hinges red with rust. Janie prayed it wouldn't fit as he pushed and pulled, forcing it down the narrow basement stairwell, his face puffed and raw with the effort, his mouth coated with spit. Grunting loudly, he shoved it the last few feet into the room and up against the far wall. The metal legs scratched the grey concrete; her grandmother's discarded carpet covered only part of the floor. A half-rotted chest of drawers salvaged from the dump and the termites completed the interior design. All of this was lit by a forty-watt bulb sticking out of the ceiling. Her mother promised to buy a shade as soon as she could. Meanwhile, she said Janie might as well move in and make herself at home.

It was cold in the basement, colder than anywhere else in their drafty house. That first night, Janie shivered in her bed, hugging her blankets to her chest and wishing she could be upstairs lying next to Suzie. An odd sour-sweet smell rose from her mattress. It took a long time to fall asleep. Even still, in the middle of the night, she woke up. She couldn't figure out where she was at first, and though she opened her eyes as wide as she could, there was nothing to see. Her heart raced as she stared into the black void. Then she remembered, the room, the dirty mattress, the rusted hinges. She turned into the wall and closed her eyes.

For Janie's eleventh birthday at the beginning of September, Ida presented her with a thin glass shade to cover the bare light bulb. It was not exactly what Janie had in mind for a present, but at least it was something. After her father finished putting it up, she went down to see how it looked. He'd been in the basement a long time, and she'd waited for him to come upstairs before going down herself. Ida and Suzie had gone to their grandmother's to tuck the old woman in for the night. Janie had wanted to go too, but her father had said no, that it was time to fix her light. She'd sat in the living room for ages, waiting for him to finish. He'd even called out to her once to come see it, but she'd pretended not to hear.

Just as he came up, panting at the top of the stairs, Ida and Suzie walked in the back door.

Two nights later, Janie was lying on her bed reading a comic book that Noreen had loaned her. Suzie was sleeping in her and Janie's old room on the top floor and Ida had gone to make sure their Nana was settled in, just as she did every night. It had started to rain outside, really pelting it down against her tiny window. Her basement bedroom was chilly and damp, and the weak light bulb was further dimmed by her new shade. She shifted to lift the blanket over her legs.

That was when she heard the knock on the door.

Her body froze. Her lips clamped shut. She could not move or speak. It was as if her mouth was broken, her limbs paralysed. Still, the door opened. Still, he came towards her, step, by step.

She tried to cry, but her father's big hand clamped over her mouth and his cold yet feverish eyes locked into hers. "Shut up," he rasped. "Do as I tells you and say nothing."

She heard her own muffled sobs beneath his hand, felt the snot trickling past her nose. And still he stared at her, the eyes dark and piercing as the rain battered the thin glass. The wind howled, its brute force whipping the dirt up off the ground to slam against the fragile window.

That was when she knew, in the darkest vilest recesses of her screaming heart, that Baby Jesus had been overruled.

She stopped crying then. She knew it didn't matter. This was going to happen. Besides, there was no one to know. Since the priest's visit, Ida had kept the windows shut, rarely letting a breath of air inside the house. With the curtains pulled tight, there was no one to see, no one to hear, and no one to help.

Finally, Janie understood her mother's shame.

By the time she and Suzie and Lill and Noreen saw the man in the woods, Janie knew full well what she was looking at. Her father had been visiting her bedroom for close to two years by then. Janie also knew that somehow, in some distorted perversion of events, the half-naked man in the woods would be her fault, in her father's eyes, perhaps in her mother's too. So she made the others promise not to tell.

But several days later, Suzie must have let it slip. Ida confronted Janie the second she walked through the door. "What's this our Suzie's on about?"

"What do you mean?" Janie asked, glancing sideways at Suzie.

"You knows full well. About some man with no clothes up in the marsh? What went on up there with them Penney girls?"

Janie sighed. "Suzie!"

"I'm sorry, Janie. I forgot not to tell." Suzie was sitting on the kitchen floor playing with her two dolls. The clothes that Janie had made for them out of scraps were spread out over the peeling linoleum.

"Why wasn't she supposed to tell?" Ida demanded.

Janie glanced from one to the other hopelessly. "Because...because Noreen hid away and then took off on me and Lill..." She didn't know what she was saying, only that the truth was unthinkable. She knew Noreen would be fine.

"Yeah? So?" demanded Ida.

"And I knew they'd be in trouble, and...and because Dad would be so mad at me."

"What? Why would he be mad at you?" Ida paused abruptly. Janie thought she saw a moment of alarm cross her mother's face, but then Ida shook her head, grabbed another potato and began to peel furiously, the short sharp knife hacking at the thick brown skin. "It don't matter no how. I don't want to be bothering your father with this stuff. He got enough on his mind, poor thing. We'll go to church and tell it to Father. First I got to phone Marg Penney though. That Noreen needs a talking to, she does."

"It wasn't her fault," Janie insisted, sorry she'd ever blamed it on Noreen. "It was me. I begged—"

"Of course it was her fault. Leaving you with the likes of that."

"It's not the first one I seen." Janie was horrified. She had not meant to say it, had never intended to utter those awful words. But there they were, out in the open.

"What are you talking about there, girl?" Her mother's mouth was hard. She did not look at Janie.

"I seen his too." She could hear the fear in her voice, the terror of speaking the unspeakable. Still, she went on. She couldn't seem to stop herself. "I seen Dad's."

Ida's eyes blazed at her. She dropped the knife onto the counter. "Suzie, get to the yard. Right now!"

Scrambling all her little bits and pieces together, Suzie piled the dolls and the clothes in her arms and hurried out. As soon as the door shut behind her, Ida whirled around and slapped Janie square across the mouth. "Don't you ever let me hear you talk like that again. God don't want little girls saying that stuff."

Her skin stinging from pain and humiliation, Janie persisted. "But Mom, I did. He takes it out and makes me—"

Ida backed away from Janie. "Shut up!" she screamed, her hands, dark and dusty from the potato peels, slapping her ears. "You're nothing but a sick fat whore with that talk, a horrible sinner blaspheming her own father." She threw herself to the floor and scrambled onto her hard fat knees. "Jesus God, forgive her. Oh holy—"

"It's true," Janie cried. "Honest to God, I'm not lying!"

Moving faster than Janie had ever seen her, Ida bounded to her feet. Her hands shook with rage. Grabbing both sides of Janie's head, she battered it back and forth. "Shut that dirty goddamn mouth of yours, you hear me? Shut it good before I shuts it for you."

"But Mommy, help me—" Oh God Almighty, Janie prayed, make her listen. She'd waited so long to tell, please dear God.

"You take that filthy mouth of yours and get out," Ida screeched. "Get down to that church and talk to Father O'Malley and beg forgiveness on your rotten soul."

"No, Mom, not that. Please don't make me."

"Goddamn right I'll make you. Now get out of here and don't ever speak of it again."

Janie felt the tears running hopelessly into her mouth and down her chin. "Please!" she begged. "Please, Mommy, why won't you believe me? He—"

Her mother picked up the knife again, her eyes wild and manic. Janie was suddenly scared witless.

"That's enough!" Ida screamed. Throwing the knife across the room, she grabbed Janie by the head close to the scalp and hauled her to the open back door. "Never again, I said," she hissed in Janie's ear. "Now you go pray on your big ugly knees that your dirty soul don't rot in hell."

Janie moaned as her mother gave her head and hair one last yank, sending a final bolt of pain down through her gaping eyes as the cruel words pounded her eardrums. Then she felt her entire body being shoved out the door. It slammed shut behind her.

The first thing she saw when her vision cleared was Suzie sitting on the sodden ground in a downpour, her small head rocking back and forth on her thin shoulders. She was humming and rocking, rocking and humming. Even through the driving rain, Janie could hear her, the dull lifeless monotonous refrain.

When she got her breath back, Janie went over and sat down next to her.

"It's okay, Janie," said Suzie's trembling voice. She lay one of her dolls in Janie's arms. "We'll take care of you. Okay?"

With the tears and the rain streaming down her cheeks, Janie shivered as her sister's tiny hand wrapped around her cold wet fingers.

PART II

4

When I was six, I had a dream I would never forget. It was extra scary because I'd been so happy and content when my father tucked me in.

"You'll sleep better with a breath of air," he said, opening the window a crack. The night was warm even though it was the end of summer. "Marlene can bunk in with your mother and me for tonight so she don't wake you." His strong warm hand brushed the hair back off my forehead as he smiled down at me. "Good night, my little Lilly," he whispered. Then he kissed the tip of my nose like he did every night, and turned off the light and left the room.

The door clicked gently shut behind him. It was a beautiful feeling, the breeze drifting through the open window, the late-day smell of my father, odours of clean sweat and faded after-shave floating on the air, the faraway chatter of the television in the living room. There was no better place to be in the whole world, no safer place to fall asleep.

I didn't usually go to bed with the window open. I had a secret fear that a bird would fly in during the night and steal my soul while I slept. But that evening I was too tired to worry about that. I'd had a sleepover at my friend Gina's house the night before. Suzie Corcoran was there too. Their mothers were sisters, so Gina's mother always insisted that she invite Suzie. Although Gina constantly complained about how unfair this was, it was fine with me. I liked Suzie. In fact, I felt sort of protective of her. She was the type of child who others teased and tormented, from a poor family, somewhat slow in school, and with a perpetually runny nose. From an early age, my father had instilled in us a sense of duty towards those less fortunate. He said it was wrong to make fun of others, and I generally listened to him. And Mom refused to hear anything bad about Suzie's mother. They had grown up together, and although their lives had taken different turns, she still counted Ida as one of her oldest friends. As for me, picking up for Suzie made me feel good. It put me in mind of the saints and martyrs the nuns preached about during religion.

The night after the sleepover my mother told me I was "too frigging crooked" to stay up and sent me to bed at seven-thirty, but I honestly didn't mind. When I couldn't find my new pyjama bottoms, I crawled underneath the covers with only the pink flowery top and my underwear on. The flannel sheet felt soft against my bare legs, and I moved them up and down several times, enjoying the cosy warmth and the anticipation of a long restful slumber.

But then I had the dream. I dreamed of a man. Under crusty eyebrows and mangled hair, his eyes stared at me, almost touching me they felt so close. His face seemed very old, and was covered with bristles and dirt. Deep wrinkles cut across his forehead. When he opened his mouth, I could feel the heat of his stinking breath, and the film of filth that covered his teeth and tongue. There was a wildness about him. He reminded me of an injured moose, crazed and frenzied, that I had seen on the highway one time. I had the eeriest feeling that I should know him, but I didn't recognise him because he wouldn't show his whole face at one time, and I couldn't put the parts of it together in my mind. Evil surrounded him. I wanted to scream but I was struck dumb with the overwhelming fear that if I did, he would know that I saw him and then he would have to hurt me. Somehow I knew that was what he wanted, it was what he had always wanted, to hurt me. I wondered if he was the man I'd heard the adults whispering about, the one that nobody ever seemed to see but everybody knew about. Or maybe he was the one my mother was always warning us to watch out for, the bad man who liked to do terrible things to little girls. I knew he had to be one or the other, maybe both. I don't know how I knew that but I did. Dreams are like that. So I kept my lips pressed tight together even though I desperately wanted to scream out to my father to come and save me.

The face disappeared when the rock came through the window. It crashed right in and landed on the floor next to my bed. Bits of glass lay all around it. I remember sitting up and screaming in the dark bedroom, my mouth so relieved to be open that it just kept yelling and crying for fear that the man would come back and clamp his large filthy hand over it and shut it up. But there wasn't any man. I turned to the moonlit window and there was no one there either. Just the curtains, half inside the room and half out of it.

Then my father was there. Turning on the lights and holding me in his big safe arms. My mother rushing in, running to the window. Looking at me, then the floor and the window again. My father's soothing voice, his steady hands patting my back and smoothing my hair, Mom asking me what happened, Dad saying, "Later, Marg. Give the child a minute." Then my mother muttering something about not resting until they found "that goddamn maniac what's on the loose". Dad shushing her, but looking just as worried.

I told them about the dream, about the horrible man and the rock and glass flying everywhere. I looked at the window again. It was broken. But there was no man. Suddenly I was scared senseless and started to cry. What if I hadn't woken up? Would the man have done something awful to me? And how did the rock become real, and the window, was it open in my dream? Was it broken in my dream? I held tight to my father, and let him rock me back and forth while Mom cleaned up the glass on the floor.

They said I could sleep with Noreen that night, so at least something good came of it. And I decided I would never sleep with the window open ever again.

~

Lill eased up on the accelerator. There was no hurry; her father wasn't going anywhere. The dread of seeing him in that place, the Home, his 'home', had made her foot as heavy as her heart. The long lonely drive over the highway always took the good out of her. Until recently, she and her sisters had shared the car ride. Then, about three months ago, it was decided that they didn't all need to go every week, that they'd take turns. He didn't know they were there anyway, what did it matter if there were one or three of them, Marlene had argued. Lill had reluctantly agreed, but part of her had died a guilty little death.

It was late afternoon by the time she arrived, and though she'd been there countless times, the rancid clash of human waste and disinfectant slammed her senses. Waving as she passed the nurses' station, the flat green walls of the endless hallway stretched before her, pulling her into a vortex of despair: old Nellie Power, her withered face smiling expectantly, waiting for the day the visitor would be hers, that day long past as her two sons had gone before her; the maintenance cart, laden with new and soiled rags, and cups and straws and toilet paper; Bertha Smith yelling "Bingo!", waving her empty hand in the air; the quiet twisted body of Paula Sampson, mother of two teenage girls, both of whom undoubtedly lived in terror of facing the same slow death from Huntington's, head lolling sideways, hands curled on her sunken chest, hardly the future this ex-cheerleader had expected.

Lill saw him then, at the end of that long lonesome corridor. He was sitting in his special chair, the type with a table attached - a table to eat from, a table firmly secured at the back. It prevented the patient from falling forward onto the floor, or, looked at another way, from escaping its confines. His invalid chair, Marlene called it. The word had stuck in Lill's mind, invalid, in valid, not valid. Lill hated those damn chairs.

His eyes seemed to stare right at her, even from so far away. Familiar yet unknown, they drew her onward, locking her in for that eternal walk to stand in front of him. It was a summons she knew intimately. These were the eyes that would haunt her sleep, phlegmy clouds surrounding misty pupils.

"Are you cold, Dad?" she asked. She didn't yell anymore. She'd learned not to be one of those visitors the nurses talked about, the type who "thinks she can shout the sense back into the poor old bastard." She spoke clearly but gently, and, she hoped, with a smile in her voice.

He didn't answer, but she imagined he had to be. His skin seemed thinner, an ashen canvas to blue-grey veins. Laying her hand on his bony arm, once so muscled and strong, she rubbed gently, soothingly, like one might a pet.

"Do you know who I am?" she asked again, the third time in as many minutes. There wasn't much to say to someone who never answered.

The film lifted just a fraction. The eyes focused, briefly alert. He peered hard, his eyes unyielding. Lill hung onto them, refusing even to blink. They stared into each other, pulling, pleading. His hand wandered upward, unsteadily, to his forehead. Cold flat fingers pressed the skin, shoving inwards. Was it physical pain, she wondered, or the strain of trying to remember? His face, a face that once so loved to laugh, seemed to be begging her. For what? Relief from the pain that possessed his frail pathetic limbs? Or a soundless scream for release from the nonlife that imprisoned him? He pushed harder on the pallid skin.

Lill couldn't let go of the eyes. "What is it Dad, tell me, please?"

Do you remember? You were my special one. Save me.

Always with her father, she'd believed she was special. She supposed Marlene and Noreen might have felt the same way, but she'd never asked them. Never needed to know. "Oh God, Dad," she cried softly, "I'm so helpless. What can I do?"

Please? Then, from nowhere, the fog began it's hazy descent. *Where is this? Who are you?*

"Lilly. It's me, Lilly," she rushed to answer her own real and his imagined question. She dropped her eyes, releasing his and hers. "Okay, Dad?" she asked, praying for the mist to descend fully once more. Reaching up with both her hands, she caressed his head, massaging backwards, slowly, tenderly. She watched his weak blue eyes. His face relaxed, and soon a trace of a lost smile appeared. In sluggish animation, the eyes closed as the fog slid slowly into place, lids coasting towards sunken cheeks. His head inert in her palms.

She imagined briefly that he had died. How heartbroken she would be. How relieved. Long moments slipped by. Soundless. Still. Ticking onwards.

He sucked back a shallow breath, exhaled, then another.

She kissed his forehead, held her warm lips against his clammy skin before she gratefully dragged herself away.

As she pulled out of the parking lot she started to cry. She usually did after seeing him, but always stopped herself after a few minutes. This time she didn't bother. The tears ran down her face. Yet even as she bawled her eyes out for her father, her heart yearned for her own self, wherever it was. There were times when she felt as out of touch with life as her father seemed to be.

The sun was setting when she stopped at Irving's gas station. Putting on her sunglasses, she bought a coffee and sat in her car for a good while to let the swelling subside. By the time she got home, it was dark, and Max and David were parked in front of the TV, gearing down for the week ahead.

"There's spaghetti in the fridge," said David.

"Thanks, honey," she answered, her stomach recoiling at the thought. She hadn't eaten spaghetti since she was a child. "I'm not really hungry right now. Maybe later."

"Sure. It tastes better the next day anyway."

After Steve's death, her older son had seemed to grow up overnight, especially once Lill started working. In fact, he did more around the house than his father ever had. Max, on the other hand, had been less sure of himself, and although he usually did what David or Lill asked of him, he appeared far less ready to take on more responsibility. Still, he was a good kid, and Lill knew she was lucky to have two sons as helpful as they were.

They were both extra nice to her on these nights, and she was grateful for their overt gentleness, realising that it was hardly typical in two strapping teenage boys. She knew that she projected her own sadness onto them, but she couldn't seem to help it. She had quit trying to cheer up just for them. Kids needed to know the down side of life as well, she figured. Besides, she didn't have the energy to fake it. She hated these days, when everything that was wrong in her life hit her like a ton of bricks. It was a funk that was hard to get out of, and as she'd gotten older she tried less hard to do that. She'd just learned to go with it, to take it and wait it out.

"Homework all done?" she asked the backs of their heads.

There was a burst of laughter at the television. She repeated the question.

"Oh… yeah, didn't have much anyway. So close to the end of the year."

She didn't stop to consider whether or not that was true. She was a teacher, at their high school, although thankfully not for either of them. Undoubtedly there was plenty they could be doing to prepare for finals, especially David, but she decided to let it go for the night.

Pouring herself a full glass of wine, she plunked down on the couch next to Max and settled in. They were watching a Monty Python special, and although she didn't usually like that type of humour, the pure sound of her sons' laughter was infectious, and she caught herself giggling as much at them as at the antics of John Cleese.

An hour later she shut and locked the doors and all the windows and went to bed. Shouting a good night to the boys, she smiled, at peace with herself for the first time that day. Yes, she might wish her life to be a little fuller, but the world no longer seemed such an empty desolate place.

Lill slept a dreamless sleep and awoke on Monday morning determined to take charge of her life. Again. The weekend had been bloody awful. She was not up for a repeat every seven days for the rest of her life. She supposed if she lived in St. John's she could go to some sort of therapist and get herself sorted out, but such amenities were not available in scrawny Port Grace. She'd simply have to shrink herself.

She started with diet and exercise, and ate fairly well all week. In spite of the predictable late spring snowfall she went for long walks every day, and she banished negative thoughts from her mind. She even got a new hairstyle, taking a good inch off her twenty-year-old page-boy and adding a discreet mix of ever-so-slightly blond highlights. Katie Hillier, who'd been cutting her hair for years, told her it brought out the flecky gold bits in her eyes. Lill hadn't known she had any and was pleased to discover something new, and positive, at her age.

Everything was swimming along beautifully until Friday morning, when she woke up so aroused she actually blushed, all alone in her bedroom. The tingling feeling between her legs had been dormant for so long that she barely recognised it at first, and when she did she leapt out of bed and hopped in the shower before she could do anything about it. Not that she would, or could. As she lathered herself under the steaming hot water, she blushed to think back on the times she had tried to do something about it. The magazines had made it sound so easy, so normal, healthy even, but she had never been able to figure out exactly what she was supposed to do, or what she was supposed to do it with. The mere thought of going to the drugstore in Port Grace and asking for a vibrator had Lill crossing her legs and cringing with embarrassment. The idea was ludicrous. Self-fulfilment! Hah! The only thing she'd been filled with was frustration, combined with a niggle of self-disgust for which she'd felt inexplicably grateful.

As a teenager, Lill had tried not to think too much about sex. Yes, she'd giggled with her girlfriends, but mainly because if she didn't, they would have noticed. It had shocked her how easily some of them talked about it—what a boy had done the night before, how far they'd let him go, how long they were going to make him wait, and how hard it was, for them too. Lill had never talked like that, and doubted she ever would. Nor did she find it difficult to resist the boyfriends she had in high school. Like Bobby Power. Every time they went out he tried to get his hand inside her bra, but she always pushed him away, even though they'd been dating for months. The same went for Sean Foley. And Billy Brennan. She couldn't imagine ever letting one of them touch her, especially in private places. The very thought made her feel dirty, which made her stop thinking the thought. When Lill did daydream, her hero was more likely to be a movie star or a famous singer—always older, always wiser. He was strong, quiet, and masculine, definitely not the pimply-faced boy next door.

Nevertheless, she usually agreed loudly with whatever the other girls said even though she often wasn't sure what they were talking about. As she'd heard her mother tell Noreen more than once, "it wouldn't do to be different." Noreen usually nodded but said nothing, which made Lill pretty sure it was good advice. Noreen always had something to say, especially to their mother. Unfortunately, neither was very talkative when it came to sex. Lill's questions remained unanswered.

Years later, her husband had been just as reticent.

"Steve? I was wondering about something," she ventured one night as they were getting ready for bed. She'd broached the subject before, a number of times, but he always managed to avoid the discussion.

"Sure, what is it?" he asked, unbuttoning his shirt.

It was a Saturday. They hadn't made love for several weeks. Lill suspected they would that night.

"Well, it's kind of personal," she said.

He continued to undress, silently.

"It's…it's about us, and, well, you know…"

He frowned, then shrugged. "No, I don't know."

"Well, do you think…I mean, could we slow down a little?" What she meant was, could he slow down a little.

"Slow down? Slow down what?"

"When we…you know, when we go to bed?"

"You want to stay up?"

"No, I mean, when we're in bed."

"Lill, what are you talking about?" His voice had grown wary, suspicious.

"I'm talking about sex," she whispered, glancing around the room as if she half-suspected someone else might be there.

"Good Christ, Lill, not this again!"

"What? I just want to talk about it." Her voice had risen slightly.

His finger rushed to his lips. "Shhh! The children!"

"They're asleep, Steve."

"They won't be for long if you keep this up. What's the matter with you?"

"The matter? Nothing's the matter. I just want to talk." She softened her tone. "Look, we've been married a long time. This happens to couples."

He grunted. "What happens? Nothing's happened to us."

"No, what I meant to say is that things get a little stale, it's not as exciting."

"Things are fine with me." He reached into the closet for a hanger.

"Okay…but what about me?" she asked, speaking to his back.

He hung up the shirt but did not turn around. "Lill, you're fine. We're fine."

"Yeah, but it could be better." She took a deep breath. "Women these days are experiencing lots of things, it's not just about intercourse."

He spun around. "Did you learn this in at the university?"

"Steve, I've only taken one course—"

"Then where?" he jumped in, his cheeks flaming. "Magazines? What's this about?"

"It's about us. I just want to make our sex life—"

"Lill! For God's sake, the boys are right next door."

"I'm just saying we should—"

"Oh for Christ's sake, that's it." His hand sliced the air. "I'm not talking about this anymore. I'm going to bed."

"But we haven't talked about it at all. We never do. You always run away. Can't we—"

"Fine, I'll sleep in the living room."

"Steve!"

He shook his head and stormed out of the room.

Lill stared at the empty doorway, then slammed the door shut. Why couldn't he just listen? What was so wrong with talking about it, especially with your own husband? Sex. Such a simple little word. Why did it scare people so?

As aggravated as she was with Steve, however, she was even more frustrated with herself. She should have approached him differently, coaxed him gently into the topic so that he was better prepared. But how? How do you tell your husband that he's no good in bed? After all, that was essentially what she was saying, and to Steve of all people, a man who went crimson whenever she dared to raise the subject.

The next day, when David asked his father why he'd slept on the couch, Steve muttered, "Ask your mother!" his voice burning with resentment. As a flush of embarrassment swept through her entire body, Lill decided that was it. She would try no more. She gave up and accepted her fate—quick and quiet intercourse with her husband, in the darkness of their bedroom. No thinking necessary.

Until that morning. Waking up to thoughts of sex had her up and about extra early, full of energy, ready and rearing to start the day. She even arrived at school twenty minutes early. Despite a lingering embarrassment, she felt a vague sense of excitement, a peculiar energy that made her body feel infinitely more alive. It was hard to keep the smile off her face. Her neck felt flushed and rosy as well. She wondered if she was mistaking it all for a hot flash.

She was grinning madly to herself when Rod Corcoran walked into her classroom. After their brief conversation at her birthday party, she'd noticed that he'd begun to treat her differently. Whereas before he'd done the "hi's" and "how are you's," now he talked to her as if they were long-time colleagues, friends even. He seemed to seek her out, always sitting next to her in meetings or at lunch if there was a chair available. Enjoying the attention, she began to look forward to seeing him each day, a bright handsome spot in her otherwise mundane existence.

"So, listen," he started right in, sitting on the edge of her desk. "I went and did something, and now I'm wondering if I should have talked to you first."

"Oh? And what would that be now?" she asked, looking up from her lesson plan. He seemed to be squinting, as if he was trying to figure something out. "Rod?"

"Sorry. It's just…did you do something to your hair? It looks really nice."

"Oh…thanks," she said dismissively, even though he was the first person who'd noticed.

"Anyway," he continued, "I think I've gone and made more work for you, but I didn't mean to." He gave her a guilty smile, charming nonetheless.

"Just what have you done, Mr. Corcoran sir?"

"I'm afraid I opened my big mug to our beloved principal, told him how much help you were when I needed a hand with Jenny, and now he wants you to help me with the guidance job on a regular basis."

As he talked, she found herself looking at his mouth and thinking that it wasn't big, it was perfect. Soft lips that smiled a lot, clean white teeth. She imagined that he had nice breath. She imagined getting close enough to find out.

"Lill?"

Her eyes shot back up to his, and the red raced from her neck to her cheeks. "Sorry, I was just thinking about something else."

"Do you mind?"

"Mind?"

"Helping me out?"

"Oh! No, that's fine. Sure. Let me know when something comes up, okay?" She just wanted to end the conversation and get to work. Away from that mesmerising mouth of his.

"Well, now you mention it, something has come up."

She couldn't believe the image that jumped into her head. Springing from her chair, she hurried over to her side cupboard and pretended to rummage around for supplies. "Sure, what is it?" she called over her shoulder.

"Jim wants the guidance manual updated. It hasn't been done since the nuns were running the place, and it's in desperate need of an overhaul."

"I imagine it would be," she agreed wholeheartedly. "When do you want to start?"

"Anytime. It'll probably take a while. Might even be good for a laugh or two, come to think of it."

Lill chuckled, her head still partially hidden. "Sure. How about Monday lunch hour?" she asked, chancing a peek in his direction. Still pretty darn cute.

"Staff meeting, remember?" He hesitated, then inclined his head. "You know, I've got my usual weekend ahead of me with nothing to do. I could start tomorrow afternoon if you're free?"

Lill's weekend social agenda was as bare as her cupboards. "Free? Well, I'll see if I can tear myself away from the laundry. How about two o'clock?"

"Great. Where do you want to meet? We could do it at my house but I'm still sorting the place out since Mom and Suzie left."

"Well, I don't want to spend my Saturday here. Five days a week is enough." She sat back at her desk. "Why don't you come over to the house? The boys will be in and out, but I'm sure we'll get some peace and quiet to work in."

"Sounds good to me. I'll bring along the old manual and we can go from there?"

"Makes sense. I'll see you then."

"Great. Thanks again, Lill."

As she watched him walk to the door, she recalled the heroes she'd dreamed of as a teenager. Rod's body seemed strong and solid, the dark slacks not too tight, but snug enough. Nice bum, she thought. His green shirt was of a new soft fabric, and the material seemed to caress his wide shoulders as he moved. Little wisps of hair curled around his shirt collar where it hugged the back of his neck. He would have a hairy chest, broad with dark tendrils swirling all about, surrounding his nipples, thinning out as they made their way down to his belly button, then—

"Lill?"

Jesus! He'd stopped and turned around. She realised that her eyes had been closed. "What?" she asked, grateful that she hadn't still been sizing up his bum.

"Catching up on your sleep? You said two o'clock, right?"

"Right," she croaked out, barely able to look at him.

"Okay, see you then."

He was gone, thank God. Lill sucked back a long deep breath. Coffee, that's what she needed. Really strong, very black coffee. And lots of it.

Saturday started out much as Friday had done, but this time Lill did not rush into the shower. She lay still in the warmth of her bed, trying to catch the wisps of a dream that hovered and teased in her semiconscious brain. A man, dark-haired and tall, almost familiar. He beckoned to her; she moved towards him. Hands touching, warm and close, safe. A naked chest, dark soft curls at her fingertips. Moments of breathlessness. And then, it was gone. She was awake.

The morning was filled with errands and house cleaning and grocery shopping. Unable to decide what to put out for a two o'clock meeting, Lill had finally settled for store-bought brownies. Everybody loved chocolate, she figured. She'd also splurged on some good steaks for herself and the boys, and fresh asparagus, the first of the season. God, she loved springtime.

Up in her room, she looked down at her faded old jeans, dirty and bagged at the knees. They had to be changed no matter who was coming, she told herself. She pulled on her other pair, and immediately regretted not buying some new ones last time she'd been in town. Rummaging through her closet, she tried on her track suit, then her khakis, and finally a denim skirt. But she'd never felt comfortable in skirts and dresses; today was no different. She reached around to take it off, but with the first tug of the zipper, she met a wall of cloth. She pulled again. Nothing. She pulled harder, nothing still. Damn it all, she thought, feeling the heat of frustration flush her neck and face. Then, just as she started to wrestle with the waistband to try to move the back of the skirt to the front in hopes of gaining better leverage, the doorbell chimed. The zipper stopped right on her hip. Head and shoulders twisted sideways, she tried to see what she was doing but her left breast made that impossible. No further ahead, but now with the skirt on half backwards, she yanked blindly at the tiny piece of metal attached to the zipper, but it refused to budge, no matter how hard her fumbling fingers pulled. By now she was sweating. Looking straight ahead she took a deep breath, determined to calm down. That was when she caught her reflection in the mirror. Her dark brown hair was all over the place, some strands sticking out, others stuck to her damp forehead. The skin on her face and neck looked as if she had an all-over case of roseola. What the hell was she going to do, she wondered, as once again she frantically tugged on the scrawny clasp that had her locked into its little denim prison. The damn skirt had always been too tight and now she was trapped in it, with her stomach bulging out and her cheeks near to bursting.

The bell chimed again. Max and David had gone to play ball, so it was up to her to answer the door. Wrenching the skirt back into its rightful position, she grabbed a sweater from her closet, pulling it over her head as she ran down the stairs. Without a hint of make-up, her hair a mess and her skirt partially hitched, she opened the door.

Rod smiled back at her. His face had that just-shaved look, smooth and clean, and he was dressed smartly in black jeans and a deep red polo shirt.

"Hey Rod, come on in. I was just changing."

"My God, you've got legs. I've never seen them before."

She pulled on the back of the sweater to make sure it covered the errant zipper. "Yeah, I don't wear skirts very often."

"Well, you should. Looks good."

Lill blushed, flattered beyond reason. After all, what was he supposed to say—good God, cover up them ugly gams? "Thanks," she mumbled. "Come on in and we can get set up."

As they sat at the kitchen table, he reached into his leather satchel. There was a rustle of paper, and his hand came out to place a brown bag on the table. "This is for you, a thanks for helping me and all. Hope you like it."

"You didn't have to do that," she admonished happily. Reaching in, she was pleased to find a very good bottle of Australian wine. "Ooh, Shiraz, one of my favourites. Are you a wine drinker?"

"I kind of got into it in Toronto. Hung around with that kind of crowd for a while."

"That kind of crowd?" she laughed.

"Yeah, you know, Mr. and Mrs. Ono File, Candy Cabernet and Randy Chardonnay," he explained with exaggerated snobbishness. "Home-made hooch will never pass these lips."

"You wouldn't blame them if you ever tried my brother-in-law's concoctions. Sort of burns going down, you know?"

"Good reason to stick to beer."

"Not a bad idea. I'll have to try that next time I'm over at Ted and Marlene's."

They were just getting started on the manual when the front door opened and heavy footsteps charged towards them. Max and David appeared in the doorway.

"Mom, can we . . . Oh hi Mr. Corcoran," said Max, his face opening up into a huge smile. "I forgot you were coming over." He pulled a chair out from the table and sat down.

"Hi fellows," Rod answered. "What are you up to?"

"Well, that's the thing," said David, with an impatient glance at Max. "Sean and Mick are going to Grenville to see their grandmother and then they're staying to see that Jet Li movie after. Their folks are going out to supper and picking them up later on, and his father said if we wanted to come, we could, and that we might as well stay the night because it'll be so late by the time we get home. But we got to be at their house by three o'clock if we're going."

"What about supper?" asked Lill. "I bought some great steaks, prime rib." Hardly a good ruse to get Max to stay home. The boy would live on peanut butter sandwiches if she let him.

"Mr. Corcoran can have mine," Max offered. "I'll get chicken and chips at Chase's Take Out."

Rod glanced at Lill. "A steak dinner? Sounds good…but no, no, that's okay. Save them for tomorrow for you and the boys."

Lill laughed. "If you're up for it, then so am I. At least I'll have someone to share the wine with."

"If you're really sure, Lill. I'd hate to put you on the spot." Looking straight at her, he added, "But I'd love to stay."

"Okay, then. These two will have more fun at a movie than home with their old mother anyway."

"So, can we go?" asked Max.

"Sure," she answered. "Sounds like fun. Don't forget your toothbrush."

Minutes later, they were out the door and on their way.

"Okay then," she said, "looks like we'll have lots of peace and quiet. We should be able to make a dent in this thing after all."

They settled in to work on the manual. The latest edition had last been updated about twenty years before, back when the school system was still solidly in the hands of the Catholic Church. Every stitch of advice was cloaked in religious overtones, providing them both with more than a few laughs at the expense of the good nuns from days gone by.

Rod had just come back with the coffee pot when she pointed to the bottom of a page. As he filled her cup, he leaned over to look.

"'Children should be encouraged to visit the confessional more often during the teen years,'" she read, "'especially boys. Their minds are often filled with impure thoughts and extra prayers will help to keep them chaste.' Well! What's a mother of two boys supposed to think of that, huh?" she chuckled, turning to look at him.

He was looking straight at her, but he blinked and glanced away immediately when their eyes met.

"Yeah," he coughed, "sounds about right to me." He took the pot back to the counter.

About a third of the way through the manual, she heard a rumbling across the table.

"Was that you?" she asked, laughing.

"Good God!" he exclaimed, his hand rubbing his belly lightly. "I think it was. Excuse me."

She looked up at the clock. "Well, it's no surprise. It's almost seven o'clock and we haven't had a decent bite except for a few brownies. You must be starved to death."

"Well, I could use a break. How about you?"

"Definitely. Why don't I start supper? Glass of wine?"

He stood and stretched, eyes closed, arms arched backwards. His shirt spread tight across his chest, and little hairs trickled out at the V. Her thoughts from the day before rushed into her consciousness, and she smacked herself mentally. "Get a grip, Lilly girl. He's Janie Corcoran's son, for God's sake."

"I'd love one," he answered, picking up the bottle he'd brought over. "Why don't I open this?"

"Grand idea." There was no harm in a glass of wine, she insisted to herself.

In the kitchen she got out the corkscrew and the asparagus and potatoes. Pouring two glasses, he held one out to her. "Cheers, Lill."

"Cheers," she answered, clinking his glass. As she raised hers to her lips, she was aware of his eyes looking at her over the rim of his. She reached for a potato. "How should we cook these, boiled, baked?"

"Why don't we do it all on the barbecue? Start the potatoes now, then add the asparagus, and then the steaks."

"Where did you learn to cook?" she asked, surprised.

"Not from Mom, I can tell you," he laughed. "It was always the same old chicken and fish with her. She used to kick me out of the kitchen."

"And now you got the whole place to yourself."

"For the most part. They'll be coming back some weekends."

"And then Ida'll take over the kitchen again, eh?"

"Fine with me. I don't really cook so much as I barbecue, anyway. Less to clean up and the food gets some flavour without too much work."

"Barbecuing is cooking," she defended him.

"Yeah, but winter can be pretty lean," he shuddered. "Canned ravioli looks some frigging good when the snow is drifting, I tell you."

Laughing, Lill went to start the barbecue. When she got back, he was about to cut the ends off the asparagus.

"Here, let me show you a trick Mom taught me." Taking a spear, she snapped the bottom off. "It breaks at the point where the toughness ends and the tender begins. Try it."

He did exactly what she'd done, but still seemed surprised when only the bottom fifth came off in his hand. "Hey. Look at that!"

As Rod topped up their glasses, Lill realised she was enjoying having a man in her kitchen. When she was little, she'd liked to help her father cook what he called lobscouse, which was always interesting because the recipe changed from week to week. Steve had never liked to cook, and had given the kitchen and everything in it over to her. Being there with Rod was completely new, two adults sharing wine, preparing a meal they would eat together.

"So, what do you do for entertainment, Lill?"

"Hah! Not a whole heck of a lot. A good friend of mine from University has a cottage just outside St. John's, and sometimes I go in and meet up with her for a visit. There's not too much to do in Port Grace. And when you're a teacher, you really got to watch yourself as well."

"Yeah. Wasn't really like that in Toronto, or not that I noticed."

"What do you do with yourself all the time?" Sipping her wine, she realised the glass was nearly empty again.

"I'm finishing up my thesis, but other than that I watch a lot of hockey or baseball or football. Or golf," he added. "I started running to try and get some exercise, but I'm not very good at it."

"Me neither. I keep waiting for those endorphins they talk about to kick in, but they never do. You ever get those?"

"No. Then again, running's not my idea of an endorphin rush," he said with a raised eyebrow.

She was surprised to hear herself giggle, the glow of the wine warm in her empty stomach. She glanced up to find him staring at her, and she looked quickly away. "It's warm in here, isn't it? Or maybe it's the wine. It's really good."

She reached for the bottle to read the label, more to take her mind off endorphins than for any real interest in the winery. The late spring day was coming to a close outside the small kitchen window. Only the overhead light from the stove lit the room. Setting the wine on the counter, she went to move past him to turn on the ceiling light. His hand reached out and he touched her arm. She turned to look at him, sure that it had been just an accident. He was staring intensely at her, standing so close she could hear him breathing.

"I was just going to get the light," she murmured.

"Okay," he said, his hand still on her arm. "Lill…" he whispered, his body leaning in towards her.

She felt hypnotised as his mouth inched closer to her face, spellbound by the simple possibility of a kiss. Her eyes closed just at the moment his lips touched hers, and she felt their soft full brush on her mouth, lightly at first and then pressing harder, his breath fragrant with wine. For a moment she remembered what it was to be sixteen, on a first date, waiting for the kiss that would end the night.

This was different. At sixteen she was a virgin and determined to stay that way. A kiss was all she ever got or gave. Lill was forty years of age now. For the first time in her life she was on a first date, or something like it, as an adult. When he put his wine down and brought his arms around her, she realised she could do whatever she wanted.

Just this once, she told herself. God forgive her, please, but she could not for the life of her imagine saying no. Who knew when she'd feel this way again, or get another chance?

His mouth moved from hers, down to her throat, and she heard a moan escape her lips. She couldn't help herself. Strong firm hands caressed her back, then moved up front to touch a breast. Her knees went weak and he pulled her closer still. There was no sound in the house except their panting breaths, his as heavy as her own. "Oh, God, Lill," he sighed into her ear.

Her hands followed the curve of his back, then moved down his tight buttocks just as he pressed himself against her. It had been so long since she'd been anywhere near an erection that the hardness startled her at first, but then she had to touch it. Grinding against him, she brought her hand up to his belly and slipped it between them, then slowly moved it down the front of his jeans. It felt so big, so sure in its purpose, especially with his hands pulling at her skirt. He tugged at the zipper.

"It's broken," she groaned. "The zipper, it's stuck."

Nudging her towards the wall, he pulled up her skirt at the same moment she got his fly button undone; his pants unzipped easily. Warm hands slipped inside her underwear and slid them down. She kicked them off. Lifting her up, he held her against the wall and she wrapped her legs around his waist. Penetrating full and deep, his penis glided inside her, his body pushing into her against the wall, their breath hard and fast. Blood rushed through her, building and raging as his penis probed and plunged, her own body sucking him back every time. Soon, they were both gasping, their bodies moving faster and faster, his hips bucking into her, her legs squeezing after every stroke, over and over, until she felt the most incredible relief, as wave after wave of erotic release rolled through her. Holding him tight, the most astounding surges shook her body, her nerves alive with a pure pleasure she had never known before.

They were silent then, each leaning in to the other, slowly catching up to their breath. She noticed the material from his jeans digging into her leg, her sweater bunched up around her neck. Next would come the moment after, the disentangling of bodies, the wiping down of private parts. Just as she was starting to feel embarrassed, he whispered in her ear, "Sure beats running, doesn't it?"

Laughing shyly, she nodded. "Yeah. Guess I forgot."

"Forgot? This is not the first time since…?" He leaned his head back to look at her in the near darkness.

"Ummm, afraid so."

He hugged her tighter. Grabbing a cloth from the counter, he slipped it between them and eased out of her. After they'd quietly cleaned themselves up, he found their wine glasses and brought them over. "You're beautiful, Lill."

She blushed. He moved close again and kissed her on the lips. "Do I still get dinner?" he asked, straightening her sweater.

"Oh my God, the barbecue's still going."

"Hasn't actually been on all that long," he said wryly. "Sorry."

Lill had never been comfortable talking about sex, and her early attempts to discuss it with Steve had made her even more gun-shy. Sex was something you did and sometimes even enjoyed, but then you let it go. She said nothing.

"I didn't mean to go so fast," he told her in an apologetic tone. "It's been a while for me too. Guess I got carried away."

"That's okay," she mumbled shyly.

"Maybe next time we'll slow it down." He touched her cheek. "Will there be a next time, Lill?"

Her breathing had sped up with his innocent graze of her skin. He leaned in and kissed her, slowly, gently, his tongue lightly pressing hers. Her body responded instantly.

"Can I turn off the barbecue?" he asked, his voice hoarse.

Not trusting her own, she nodded.

When he came back in, she was standing at the foot of the stairs. She'd already told her brain to shut up. One time could be justified by uncontrollable passion, or something of that nature. But having a second go was a conscious act, a purposeful decision to have carnal pleasure. So she smothered her misgivings, her guilt. This night would be hers, lived fully and completely, for one time. She led the way up to her bedroom.

His hands skimmed up her sides, sliding the sweater over her head and turning her around. With a firm tug, he released the zipper and let the skirt fall to the floor. The bra was next, his warm palms cupping her breasts from behind, kneading the mounds and tweaking her stiff nipples. She leaned back against him and let her fingers slither down the sides of his jeans. He moved away and with several quick motions, his clothes were gone. They stood naked together. She traced her fingers through the wiry black hair of his chest. He shivered, smiling.

Their second time was different. Rod was a big man compared to Lill, but he had a gentle manner that seemed made for love, his hands warm and tender, touching her in erogenous places she'd never known existed, the sides of her thighs, the soft skin in the crease of her elbow. They enjoyed each other leisurely, two bodies intertwining, lusting one second, delicately caressing the next. Sex in the kitchen had lasted barely five minutes, but in the comfort of her bedroom they built slowly on what they'd started. Having already tasted satisfaction, they took their time and savoured it.

In all of her years with Steve, Lill had never spent a night like it. As shy as she had been about sex, he'd been even worse. Foreplay was not a word in their personal dictionary, and certainly not one that Steve was willing to explore.

So if sex with Rod was a mistake, if what they had done together was wrong, if the extraordinary pleasure she'd felt with this man was a sin, well then, to hell with it, she'd just have to take the consequences.

When they were done, they lay on their backs on the bed, their fingers laced. Lill couldn't remember the last time she'd felt so relaxed. Sated was the word, she decided, completely and utterly filled to the brim with sex. She closed her eyes.

"Lill?" he whispered against her ear. "It's eleven thirty."

She awoke instantly. "Oh my God!" Her mind immediately shot to David and Max, then she remembered that they were at Sean's. "It's that late?"

"Would you rather I didn't stay the night?"

In the dusky light, her eyes traced the outline of his face. "Oh…" That nudge of embarrassment was back to haunt her. "I think it'd be best if you didn't, right?"

"You sure?" He spoke softly in the darkness, his voice almost a whisper.

"Yeah, the boys…you know, right? And the neighbours."

"I know."

He pulled her close for a long moment, then swung out of bed. She started to get up.

"No, stay put. You look so peaceful. I'll just lock up from the inside on my way out." He leaned in and kissed her lightly on the mouth. "I'll call you tomorrow, okay?"

"Okay." Yes, it could all wait until tomorrow, she decided. The worry, the guilt, everything.

"Good night, Lill. Have a good sleep."

"Night, Rod. You too." She almost said "thank you," but in the end, she just smiled softly to herself and closed her eyes again.

5

When I was ten I was afraid to fall asleep at night. I was terrified that I might wake up blind.

Mom and I weren't getting along so well at the time. I felt like she was always picking on me, but she said I was too contrary to live with and that I should stop whinging and whining all the time. When she wasn't looking, I used to make the most awful faces at her. She must have known what I was doing, though. One day, just after she'd yelled at me for tripping over the stool and spilling the milk, and then using her good tea towel to wipe it up, I made one of my disgusting faces, screwing up my mouth and twisting my lips and making my eyes go so cross-eyed that the room tilted in all directions. Before the fridge and stove had a chance to right themselves in my head, I felt the thump as her fist hit the arborite table. My face righted itself in an instant.

"Lillian!" she railed. "So help me God, you keeps making them faces, He's going to take away that nice one He gave you and keep the ugly one on it. That's what happens, you know."

My mother was known to rant a little when she was angry, so I probably would have ignored the remark if it hadn't been for my father. He was sitting in the stuffed chair by the stove and had seen the whole thing.

"You better listen to her, honey," he said. "Your mother knows what she's talking about there."

That made me stop and think. Dad was not the type to use scare tactics or make idle threats. Soon after, when I went into the living room to get out of Mom's way, I found Noreen doing her homework in front of the television. A badly disfigured woman was speaking on the screen; her ravaged face looked almost as if someone had taken it apart and rearranged it. Remembering what Mom and Dad had said, I asked Noreen about it.

She nodded as if that was the easiest question in the world. "Sure everyone knows that," she said, glancing at the TV. "What do you think happened to that one there?"

My father never lied to me. Neither did Noreen.

I stopped making faces after that.

Then the whole episode with Alma Fuller happened. She was a blind, retarded girl, a couple of years older than me. I had always assumed she was born that way until the day I heard Mom and Mrs. Murray talking over the fence about Alma's mother. I was lying in the high grass right next to them, dreaming I could fly as I counted crows and gulls and anything else that passed within my range of vision. They must have forgotten I was there, as usual. "That poor Sara," Mom was saying, "she don't know what to be doing with her anymore. And she got no one to help her." Mrs. Murray scoffed at Mom. "Poor Sara, my arse. A woman like that only gets what's coming to her, Marg. She got no one to help her 'cause she couldn't keep her hands to herself. Make no wonder poor Martin took off and left the pair of them. Men don't stand for that sort of thing." I had stopped daydreaming and was watching them under lowered lids. "I knows you're right, girl," Mom said, shaking her head, "but that young Alma is something else altogether, my dear, the poor retarded thing. Blind as a bat, too. Imagine losing your sight, having it and then not having it at all. And sure she's always at herself, rubbing and rooting and everything." "Hah!" Mrs. Murray grunted, "and look where it got her, can't see the hand in front of her face." She lowered her voice in that whispery way that, more often than not, meant something dirty was coming. "You know what they says, Marg, about fooling with yourself like that. Leads to blindness, it does, pure and simple. Well, she's living proof, ain't she though?" Mom started to say something, but Mrs. Murray just waved her hand and went on back into her own house.

I knew I'd overheard something I wasn't supposed to, but I didn't think any more of it. Not until Sunday. Not until I was sitting directly across the aisle from Alma Fuller in church. We were both on the ends of our pews, with the empty main aisle in between. Mom and Mrs. Murray's words came back to me, and I kept glancing over at Alma. It wasn't long before she started, rubbing her breasts, poking at her crotch, leaning back and stretching and rubbing harder. I watched, fascinated, as what had begun as a slow, seemingly absentminded touching, progressed quickly to a frantic grabbing and groping, until finally her mother twisted around and slapped her loud and hard on the hands and arms. Mom had turned at the same time and saw what was happening across from us. And caught me watching. She grabbed my wrist, jerked my arm and pushed my head forward. Dad started to say something but Mom gave him the loudest "shhh" I'd ever heard her make in church. I leaned my burning face on the pew in front of me and prayed to God that I wouldn't start to cry.

That's when I made the connection. That's when my world started tumbling down and around inside my head. The woman on the TV flashed before me, the woman who kept making faces until God taught her a lesson, her mangled mottled head proof positive of the power He had over us all. And then there was Alma's face, so godawful stupid-looking, and dead blind. "Oh holy Jesus, help me," I cried inside. "I'm so sorry, God, I promise I'll never do it again." Because, just the night before I had done it. Marlene was pretending to be sick so she could sleep with Mom and Dad. I had the bed to myself. Under the heavy covers, I let my hands go down there, stroking and teasing. It felt so nice, and it made me feel warm all over. I fondled it for a while and then I must have gone to sleep. Sometime later I woke up. I had that special tingly sensation I got sometimes, in the middle of the night usually, when I was so filled with sleep that I could never be sure if I was awake or dreaming. It was a hard feeling to describe, like I needed to pee, yet different in some way I couldn't figure out. Without thinking, my hand kept squeezing, over and over, until I gave up and went to the bathroom. I sat on the toilet in the dark for a minute or so, but nothing came out. When I went back to bed the feeling was gone and I fell back to sleep.

Sitting there in the church, I felt physically ill. I thought I might throw up right in the middle of Mass. Across the aisle, Alma slumped in her pew. Blind. "Oh my God, please don't make me go blind. Please, please, please Dear Jesus?" What would Mom and Dad say? They would figure it out. I knew they would. They would know. And everyone else would guess. And maybe I'd get as bad as Alma. Maybe I'd do it in front of everybody. Right in church, right during Sunday Mass. Yes, I'd end up just like Alma, too blind and too stupid to know better.

From then on when I went to bed I kept my hands under my cheeks or behind my head, or straight down and out, not touching my body. Whenever one of those old urges or thoughts came into my head, I'd slam it shut in my mind, killing it with prayers to God to make me be a better person. Nevertheless, some nights I'd wake up and there I'd be, squeezing it, my body pushing back into my hands, and I'd let myself do it a couple of more times, pretending not to be awake yet. Then I'd make myself stop. And the next morning if I woke before I opened my eyes I'd lie there in terror. Would this be it? Would this be the day that I only saw black, or white, or whatever colour it was that blind people saw? What did God have in store for me when I forced my eyes to open?

After a while, if I woke up in the black of night with my hands there against my will, I learned to rip them away and go straight to the bathroom. For some reason, that always killed the tingly feelings. Then I could go to sleep unafraid of the morning. I remember hoping that Jesus saw how hard I was trying. Surely to God that had to count for something. Surely to God, if He was all-knowing and all-seeing, He'd understand that I needed His help, not His punishment. And I think He must have, because one night it occurred to me that I was no longer awakened by those middle-of-the-night incidents.

I thanked God then, and said a prayer to my guardian angel, to protect me and keep me safe throughout the still, silent night.

Lill awoke slowly on Sunday morning, gradually allowing the world to seep into her consciousness. Her limbs felt suffused with a sense of calm, a peculiar lightness of being that pervaded her entire body. The night before replayed itself in her mind, and she could feel a wickedly guilty grin spreading across her face, as if she'd gotten away with the most delightful caper. Except for one thing; she had a really sore crotch. Not exactly appropriate for the widowed mother of two boys, who also happened to be a good Catholic schoolteacher in a small community in Newfoundland. But God, what a night! Lill was still amazed at what she'd done. Had it simply been that little whisper of mortality that comes with turning forty? Or was her true identity actually an oversexed woman who'd had the bad luck to spend the first half of her life in an undersexed world? Or maybe she was just horny, but *normal* horny. Maybe this is how most women felt on a regular basis.

Lying alone in bed, her initial self-analysis took only a few minutes. Then the guilts crept in.

Her first thought was "so much for safe sex." After all her lecturing about the importance of condoms, she'd used no protection whatsoever. It hadn't occurred to her as she'd preached at the boys that she'd be the one who needed it. With work and family commitments, there was little time or energy left over to think about having sex. But really, now that she had after so long without, she couldn't be unlucky enough to catch some disease, could she? No, surely not, she insisted to herself.

Next, she counted back on the calendar. Thankfully, her period was due any day, so she'd know soon enough if she'd been more stupid than sexy. In truth, she wasn't too worried. It was pretty late in her cycle to have gotten pregnant. Still, she knew she'd be waiting.

Moving on down her conscience, she blushed to think that she'd actually let a man she'd never even dated have sex with her. But then, right away she backed up. She hadn't "let him have sex with her" damn it; she'd chosen to have sex with him. "Making love" was hardly the right term, no matter how it had felt the night before. You made love with someone you loved. She knew Rod well enough to like him, but love wasn't an accurate sentiment for how either of them felt. Still, she'd had sex with a man she really didn't know very well, twice, and much sooner than the requisite number of dates socially recognised as appropriate before getting naked together.

She'd often heard her sister talk about loose women, Janie Corcoran being one of them. Lill had never contributed much to these self-righteous rants and did her best not to get cornered into one of Marlene's tirades. In the back of her mind, however, she suspected a little part of her envied the freedom those women seemed to have. Even so, Lill had never imagined herself as one of them. Until today. And with Janie Corcoran's first-born son.

A sudden thought hit her like a sledgehammer. What if the boys had come home? Holy Mother of Jesus, she cringed to think what a scene that would have been. Max's innocent face, David's knowing one, both shocked and dismayed to find their mother naked and—No! Enough! The whole idea was so repulsive, she thrust it from her mind.

Just as she was getting out of bed, the phone rang. She rushed downstairs, reaching it just as the machine clicked in and Rod's voice came on the line, deep, warm, intensely male. Simply hearing his familiar baritone made her feel more alive, keenly aware of her own breathing, of the rise of her chest with each intake of air, of that air slipping past her lips, lips that were still tender from the night before. Unsure of what to say, she just stood there, listening, until he hung up. She called him back a minute later.

"Hello," he answered with an expectant lilt.

"Hi, Rod." Her throat caught slightly as she said his name, and she felt a blush rise up her cheeks.

"Lill." His voice was strong and husky, and she felt that little rubbery feeling all over again. "How are you this morning?"

"Fine. Sorry I didn't get your call, I was still upstairs." She held back from saying she'd been in bed, the last place he'd seen her, naked beneath the sheets.

"That's okay. Listen, I'm going into St. John's today, bringing in a load of stuff to Mom. Don't suppose you can come along, eh?"

"Oh, thanks, but I can't."

He hesitated. "Okay. Well—"

"I'd like to," she blurted, "but the boys have been gone since yesterday and I got to get everything ready for work and school and I got to get a salad to take to

Marlene's tonight, we're going there for dinner, and thanks but—"

He laughed. "It's okay, Lill. Just thought I'd ask."

"Thanks."

"Well, see you tomorrow."

"Yeah."

There was a moment of silence that she was dying to fill. She just didn't know how to say what was on her mind.

"Okay, then," he said.

"Rod, wait. About last night."

"Yeah?"

"Maybe, you know, we shouldn't say anything—"

"At school?"

"Yeah."

"Sure, makes sense."

"Thanks."

"You got to stop thanking me, Lill. I'll get the wrong idea or something here."

"Oh, sorry."

"Now that's even worse. Can we go back to thanks?"

She actually heard herself giggle. "Okay."

"Last night was great, Lill," he said in that husky voice. "You're not sorry or anything, are you?"

That feeling again. Breathless. Warm shivers down her neck. Her hand caressed her stomach. "No," she mumbled. "I'm kind of surprised, but I'm not sorry."

"Good … I'm glad, Lill." His quiet breath reached her over the phone lines. Neither spoke for several seconds. "Well," he said finally, "I better get on the road if I want to get back at a decent hour. So … I'll see you tomorrow, right?"

"Right. And Rod?"

"What?"

"Thanks."

He laughed, deep and throaty, rich and warm. "No, no. Thank you. Bye."

It was barely nine-thirty, and she knew David and Max would be gone at least another couple of hours. More than likely they'd show up after eleven o'clock Mass, which she decided then and there she would miss. She'd let the boys assume she'd gone to the nine o'clock, and if they or anybody else were nosy enough to ask, she'd claim a morning headache.

In fact, her head had never felt better. Putting on a pot of coffee, she defrosted a couple of muffins and cut up some cheese and fruit. She'd wait for a shower. For one thing, she was starving, having missed dinner the night before. Plus, she was in no hurry to wash the night from her body. Maybe she wouldn't shower at all that day. Hugging her fat fleece robe close to her chest, she waltzed her way to the bathroom.

To her surprise, her period had started already, probably triggered by all the activity of the night before. And even though she hadn't been worried, it was a relief to see the bright red blood.

It was a good omen, she thought. She hadn't been a bad girl, she'd done the right thing hopping into bed with such a nice man. Life really was funny sometimes. Just the week before she'd been filled with despair. Yet today she was dancing on air, happy with the world, even happy to be on her period. She decided she'd have a long hot shower after breakfast.

~

Arriving home from Lill's, Rod had tiptoed through the house, still unused to the fact that Ida and Suzie and her dog no longer lived there. Besides, he wasn't thinking clearly. His mind and his body were still in shock from the unfamiliar pleasure he'd just experienced. Never had he felt so at one with a woman, so in sync, all his senses tuned to another person. It was a connection he was more than ready for. Lying next to Lill as she'd slept, he'd been filled with a profound sense of peace. He felt as if he'd come home. Lill was a real woman, a whole woman. A balanced woman who just might help to equalise the other women in his life, past and present. It almost felt as if Lill Dunn was the woman he'd been waiting for all these years, or the last three anyway. The thought shook him to his core; still he smiled.

From the first day he'd seen her in the staff room, he knew she was different. Totally unlike Janie or Ida or Suzie. Or Pamela, especially Pamela. There had been a quality about Lill, her warm and ready smile, her quick sense of humour. She seemed to belong to the space she inhabited, and that made him feel he belonged there too. It wasn't any one of those things in particular, but all of them and more playing together, that made Lill Dunn stand out in his mind. Her compact curves didn't hurt either, not even the small softness around her middle. It was a body lived in, he could tell. So unlike his ex-wife, her perfect physique a testament to a sterile life.

"Lill, you remember Rod Corcoran," Jim White, their principal, had said to the woman stirring her coffee at the counter. "He just got back home from Toronto."

She turned around and gave him that wonderful smile, then extended her hand. "Hi Rod. Welcome back to Port Grace. How long you been away?"

"About fifteen years, though it sure doesn't seem that long," he answered, his hand reaching out for hers. Smooth skin glided into his, her handshake firm but feminine. "But it's good to be back."

She raised her eyebrows the smallest bit. Rod was a man familiar with sideways glances, with smiles that bordered on sneers. He was used to the fact that the people of Port Grace would always eye the Corcorans a little differently. He'd learned to ignore it. But the little lift of Lill's brow made him laugh.

"We'll see how you're feeling when the snow sets in," she said, chuckling. "Seriously though, good to have you. It'll be nice not to be the new teacher anymore."

"Oh?"

"Yeah, this is just my second year on the job. Late bloomer," she laughed again, glancing at her watch. "Good God, I got a million things to do. See you later."

He watched her go, eyes fast on her back. Even after she rounded the corner and disappeared from sight, he still saw the brown hair bouncing away as she bustled from the room, still pictured the face that laughed so easily. The images stayed with him all day.

He couldn't help but notice her after that, to look for her even. Eventually he realised that just seeing her at work brightened his day, and gave him something to look forward to on Monday mornings. Unfortunately, she gave no indication that she felt the same about him. She was always friendly, but she was like that with everyone. It wasn't until her birthday party that he felt she'd noticed him at all. And to his amazement, within weeks they were having the best sex of his life.

It had been no surprise that he was the first since her husband had died. He'd asked a few casual questions, just enough to imply a general interest in a colleague. It seemed that with work and family commitments, Lill Dunn was a busy woman, or at the very least, too busy for anyone in Port Grace.

As for himself, Rod hadn't had sex in over three years. It was a self-imposed abstinence, one he hoped would clear his head and clean his mind. Having grown up surrounded by his widowed mother and Suzie the mute virgin, and occasionally Janie, who couldn't seem to decide if she was an adulterous slut or a frigid man-hater, he knew he had a jaded view of sex. He'd never been given "the talk", nor had there been anyone from whom he could pick up cues about normal sexual behaviour. At home, the subject was taboo, dirty. They didn't discuss it, joke about it, or read about it. Combined with the rumours and mystery surrounding his own conception, he could understand why his attitude towards sex was at best inhibited, at worst, downright unhealthy.

Not that he'd always felt that way. In fact, when he first discovered the joys of sex in university, he became consumed to the point of addiction and went to bed with any girl who'd have him. Surprisingly, there were many. He would undoubtedly have caught a disease or two if not for his insistence on wearing a condom—there would be no mutant little Rods if he could help it. On the few occasions when the girl took offence, he went without. No condom, no sex with Rod Corcoran. Never knowing for certain if his biological parents shared the same gene pool made him more than cautious about pregnancy; it made him downright paranoid. He vowed never to bring a child into the world unless he knew it was safe.

Finally, when he was thinking of marrying Pamela, Ida relented, just a little, giving him only enough information to relieve his fears. But that's all she would tell him, not another thing, no details, nothing. He settled for that.

By the time he met Pamela, Rod had grown weary of one-night stands, weary of seduction, perhaps even weary of sex itself. Which was fine with her. It was even fine with Rod for a while. He was just happy to be starting his own life, away from Port Grace, with a woman who was normal, completely different from Janie and Ida and Suzie. Sex was not so important.

But gradually, he found himself increasingly frustrated.

"Come on, Pamela," he urged her one night as they were lying in bed. The room was completely dark, the heavy drapes blocking any hope of light that might have filtered through their small bedroom window. "It's been weeks."

"No it hasn't."

"It has. In fact, it's been twenty-two days."

"You're counting?" She was lying on her side, turned to the wall.

"Well, there's nothing better to do."

"Look, I work hard all day. I don't want to come home to this."

"To what?"

"This."

"This? You mean me?"

The bed shifted as she flipped onto her back. "No, I mean this arguing."

"Oh, so it's not the sex, it's the arguing?"

"Right."

"Well, if we had more sex," he suggested, making his tone teasing and light, "we wouldn't be arguing." He tried to tickle her. She pushed his hand away.

"You can't force me to have sex."

"Christ, Pamela, I don't want to force you. I want you to want to have sex."

"But you're always on about it. You're obsessed, you never let up."

"That's because we hardly ever have it. And anyway, I'm not obsessed. When was the last time I even tried?" His voice sounded so pathetic in the pitch black room, he was glad they couldn't see each other.

"I don't know. It doesn't matter. Besides, at night I'm too tired."

"Then let's do it earlier."

"There's no time earlier."

"We could make time. It's important. Sex is important."

"Is that why you're always thinking about it, always trying to get me to do it?"

"Isn't that supposed to be a good thing in a marriage, to want to have sex with your wife?"

"Yes, but not all the time."

"It's hardly all the time."

"It is. Even when we kiss, I can feel it. As soon as we start, you're thinking about sex."

"But we need to have sex sometimes. It's been weeks."

The argument would go on in circles, following a similar pattern time and again. Occasionally, they did make love, Pamela flat on her back, Rod grunting above her. It never took long. Yet it seemed Pamela could find the time for everything else that mattered to her, nights out with her girlfriends, working out at the gym every morning, fighting about sex. And it was sex, inadvertently, that ended the marriage.

After his divorce, Rod discovered that women were still easy to come by. Unfortunately, he was not as diligent as he'd been in his earlier promiscuity. Before he knew it, he found himself at the doctor's office, embarrassed, humiliated and scared. Was Pamela right, he wondered as he waited for the results, was he obsessed with sex? After all, look where sex had gotten him this time. A phone call from a woman he barely remembered, yet one he'd done the most intimate things with, a call that made the fear rise up in his throat. Then the days of not knowing, berating himself for being so stupid, so careless. In the end, he was lucky. It was nothing that couldn't be cured with a dose of antibiotic. Thank God.

What it did cure him of as well, however, was sex. After a childhood spent in repression and ignorance, chased by a decade of consuming everything put on his plate, and followed with two years married to a woman who ultimately struck at his very manhood, he'd had enough. He needed time to think, about himself and his future, about what he was looking for in life, about sex and love and intimacy. He couldn't do that with different women traipsing in and out of his bed. The answer, he finally decided, was to give up sex altogether.

At first, it was easy. Avoiding parties and bars, he opted instead for golf and hockey. Even the locker room talk of his buddies didn't bother him, and he pretended to be as ribald as the next guy. After a couple of months, however, he found himself increasingly tempted by women, that is, his body was. His mind was another matter. And for once when it came to sex, he was determined to let his mind have the deciding vote. So he joined a gym, spending most nights in the pool or on the squash courts.

And that was where he met Theo Sidorski, a sixty-year-old irreverent psychiatrist who quickly became one of the most important people in Rod's life. Within a month of their first match, Rod was seeing him twice a week at his office and had spent his last couple of years in Toronto on Theo's couch. And in the end, just as Rod thought he was done, that he and Theo had figured most of it out and he was as close to normal as he could ever hope to be, Sidorski sent him back to Port Grace.

"Go face your fears," he told him.

"Good Christ, Theo, what for?" Rod asked. "Things are good now. What do I want to go back there for?"

"To visit your mother, or your sister, or whoever she is."

"Funny guy. Get serious, Theo."

"I mean it. Go. Hold your head up in that town, show them who you are."

"Jesus, that's like the last place on earth I want to be."

"Maybe so, but it's the first place you'll find answers. I've got no more for you. It's time for me to retire, time for you to go home."

"I don't want to do that. I don't need to do that."

Theo had patted him affectionately on the head. "You need to leave the nest, little Roddy," he teased, then added more seriously, "you need to finish growing up."

He'd come a long way under Sidorski's care. Theo had helped him come to terms with his very existence, to accept who he was and where he'd come from, even the parts he didn't know. As bizarre as his last piece of advice seemed at first, the longer Rod thought about it, the more sense it made. When Ida told him about the opening at the school, he applied for and got the job.

Then he met Lill. He knew instinctively that he'd entered a new phase in his life, and that all the work he'd done might just pay off. Three years of abstinence did provide a certain clarity.

Still, it had been a long eight months since the day he'd first seen her in the staff room. Crawling into his childhood bed, he breathed a satisfied sigh. Lill's face swam behind his closed lids. He couldn't imagine going another three years, not with Lill Dunn around.

6

When I was eight I saw my father naked. I knew it was an accident, but he was still naked.

After he was forced to quit fishing because of his bad back, he eventually got a job at the funeral home. By that time, Mom was working at Hynes' store, just to tide us over, but neither one of them got paid much so she stayed there. Every night, or morning, depending on his shift, Dad came home and went straight to the bathroom. We girls had learned not to be in there when it was time for him to get off work. Even though he was usually a kind, easy-going sort of man, he had no sense of humour about that at all. The first thing he wanted was a bath, "a good long soak to get the dead skin of the place off me". That bathroom was his for a good twenty minutes every day, and we learned to stay far and away from it. Except for Mom. Occasionally, she'd tell us she was just going to go in and wash his hair for him, so to leave them alone. The twenty minutes usually stretched to thirty or more then. One time I heard them laughing in there, and I remarked to Noreen that Dad must really like Mom washing his hair. She looked at me strangely, then stuck her fingers in her mouth like she was trying to throw up. Anyway, by the time he came out of the bathroom he was always his old self again.

The day I saw him naked he had come home early from work, but I didn't know that. Thinking it was one of my sisters in the bathroom, I opened the door and walked right in. He was soaking wet, standing with his back to me. I had never seen my father without his clothes on, so I never had a chance to get a good look at the back that he was always complaining about. "It's gone out on me again," he'd moan every so often, limping through the room. In my child's mind, I would see his back up and leaving the rest of his body and heading out the door. Or he would talk about his slipped discs, and I'd picture these round hard things sliding like crazy all over the place inside of him. So when I saw him standing there with nothing on, my first thought was to check for the scars on his back that I knew would have to be there, maybe even something that looked like a disc. But he was so used to having that small portion of time completely private from his daughters that he obviously assumed it was my mother who had come in.

"I'd about given up on you, Margie girl. Come here and give it a squeeze, eh?" When he turned around, he had a big grin on his face and there was something in his fist, pointed right at me.

It seemed as if my stomach flipped over inside my body, and I had trouble thinking clearly. What was in his hand and why did he say for her to squeeze it? Deep down I think I knew, but I wouldn't admit it. I didn't want to know that my mother let him do that awful thing Noreen had said about sticking it in her, and I hated to think my father would want to, would even smile about it, especially after how sad he was when Mom had lost the baby two years earlier. I felt sick. I was afraid I might even throw up. For some reason I kept seeing his white bum before he turned around, and it frightened me more than anything. In my mind I saw somebody else's face, not my father's, a face I didn't know. I opened my mouth, but nothing came out. Then both his hands shot forward to cover his front and he yelled at me. "Lillian! Get out. Go on, get out of here right now!"

I spun around and ran from the room, down the hall, and out the door. I kept running until I hit the beach and I stayed there for hours, watching the waves beat up against the rocky shore. It felt as if they were crashing right into me, spitting salt water in my face before pulling away and coming back and doing it all over again. My heart felt sore and bruised, like it had been beaten with a ham-

mer. Dad never yelled at me. He didn't yell much at anyone, but never at me. Mom did quite often, so I was used to her doing it. She had to, she said, it was the only way she got heard most of the time. But my father rarely yelled. Especially not at me.

That night after supper, he sat me on his knee in the front room where he liked to read the paper and look out the window at everyone going by. The new radio Mom had given him for Christmas was on, and a man was talking about a place called Vietnam. I was finding it difficult to look at my father, partly because I was still hurt but also because of what I'd seen. The image of a white bum still had me a little shaky. I'd spent most of the day trying not to picture it in my head, but it kept popping in there when I didn't expect it, whenever I let my guard down.

"Lilly? Look at me, Lillian, please," he said.

I looked at him then. I had to when he asked like that. Taking a deep breath, I stared straight at him. The only thing I saw was his kind familiar face, smiling gently at me. I was so relieved I started to cry.

He hugged me close. "I'm sorry about today, Lilly. It wasn't your fault and I shouldn't have yelled at you. I was just right shocked to see you," he blushed, "and for you to see me."

"I'm sorry too, Daddy." I so much wanted to tell him about the other bum I kept seeing in my head, and how it frightened me, but I didn't want to spoil things. "I promise I'll knock from now on."

"That's a deal, my darling."

I snuggled into him then, thankful that we'd found our way back to being happy. "Daddy?"

"What is it, love?"

"Why do you always have a bath after work?"

His eyebrows arched upwards. "Well, I'll tell you, girl. The place is right smelly down there in that basement. We has to use lots of chemicals and stuff, and I don't want to be stinking of them all night long after I'm gone from there."

"If it's so bad, why don't you work somewhere else?"

He sighed, long and deep. "I wish I could, honey. But it's the only job around here and I'm right lucky to have it, I tell you. Better not complain, somebody might hear me and put me out of my misery." He tilted his head then and pursed his lips. "On the other hand, maybe I'll do that myself soon, God willing. Sure would be nice to be gone from there."

He was quiet then, as if he was thinking really hard, and I remembered a conversation I'd overheard between him and Mom. It was after Suzie's father died and Dad was the one who had to get the body ready. There wasn't a big party like there was when old Jim Evans passed away, or Mr. Pomeroy. The Corcorans just had tea and cakes at their house, and we all went and gave our condolences and came on home out of it. Mom and Dad went up right away to change out of their good clothes, and when I walked past their door I heard them talking about Suzie. I tiptoed to the side and breathed very quietly.

"Ida's some worried about her, Hank," I heard my mother say. "The girl's not said one thing since the night he died. Not a word!"

My father grunted. He must have been leaning into the closet because I didn't hear what he said, only the clatter of hangers.

"Do you think there's something to it then?" she asked.

"All I knows, Marg, is that there was marks on it, and from the looks of them, they must have happened right before he died. At least that's what I figure from reading the books down there about all that stuff."

"What did Lester say when you showed him?"

"I didn't."

"What? Good God, Hank, he's your boss. He owns the place and knows how these things happens."

"That's what I was afraid of. When he came in I pulled the sheet over his middle and pretended like I was just finishing up. If them were what I thinks they were, then what might he make of it? Who would he tell? Ida's a good woman, Marg, and she and them girls have suffered enough with that bastard."

"True. Oh, that poor young Janie. She was awful quiet back at the house, wasn't she?"

"She was that. Except when she caught me having a smoke out by the road. You were still in saying your good-byes to Ida. She asked me how I liked it down at the funeral parlour, and she looked at me right strange. I had the awful feeling she was trying me out, to see if I saw anything."

"What did you say to her?"

"I said it was a job I'd rather not have to do, but that I did it and no one else. Then I told her if she needed anything, to come see us, and not to worry about her father. He was gone to his just rewards, I told her, and she muttered a thank you and left."

"So you're going to let it go then?"

His voice was like heavy snow, cold but full and deep, a voice I didn't know as his. "There's not a whole lot gets done to men like him, Marg. They gets away with blue murder half the time, or worse to their daughters. If something happened that night, it should be let be. The man had it coming to him."

"Maybe you're right, Hank. I honestly don't know what to make of it anymore. Still, makes you wonder why young Suzie's not talking no more, don't it?"

Dad made a sound like a shudder. I could hear them moving towards the door, so I snuck back into my room and pretended to be reading on my bed.

As they went down the hall, I heard him tell her. "I'm getting out of there as soon as I can, Marg. I can't seem to wash the place off me anymore, and I don't feel the same man since I been there."

"Okay, Hank. Can't say as I blames you."

Eventually, he did too, just up and quit. Claiming his back was as good as new, he joined up with his old crew and returned to fishing. Although he hardly ever complained about the pain, I got to where I could see it in his eyes when it was really bad. Mom could tell too, and we both tried very hard to make him as comfortable as we could. Hot water bottles, or sometimes ice, pillows and footstools, and good stiff belts of whiskey or rum. He claimed it was for medicinal purposes.

My mother often had one with him, which made little sense to me at the time. There was nothing wrong with her back.

Not since she was eighteen had Lill been nervous about running into a guy from the night before. After her first date with Steve Dunn twenty-two years earlier, she'd seen him at church the next morning. They'd exchanged glances across the aisle, barely making eye contact before looking away. Then after mass, stuck behind a group of slow-moving parishioners determined to wish Father Fyne a good morning, she'd spied him through the crack in the church door. His hands were shoved deep into the pockets of his grey dress pants, his eyes peeled to the doorway. At twenty-six, he'd been quite shy. And even though she normally wasn't, she felt shy around him, a man, so much older than she, so much more mature than the boys she usually went out with.

Right from the beginning, she'd felt there was something different about Steve. He wasn't like the fellows back in high school, looking for a cheap hook-up at the end of the night and whatever came with it, hoping for at least a quick feel. Not that they got much from her. She knew what people said about girls who did that, and she wanted nothing to do with it.

But Steve wasn't like that. To start with, he didn't even try for more than a kiss. He had his own apartment and a car, and he worked full time at the water works, a good steady job with a real future. On top of that, he'd actually phoned her up and asked her out on a formal date, just like she'd read about in books. Dinner and a movie – people actually did that. They'd gone for fish and chips and then to see *Grease* with John Travolta and Olivia Newton John. He'd seemed more interested in listening to what she had to say than talking about himself, which was quite a change from the juvenile bluster of most of the boys, always going on about hockey and ball and cars. And when she tried to be funny, he was ready with a quiet smile and a light laugh.

She'd been inordinately flattered that this attractive young man found her so appealing, and she married him less than two years later. They made a handsome couple, even she could see that. Steve, six feet tall with dark thick hair and deep brown eyes, his teeth so beautifully white and straight, towering over her. Yet she always seemed to be in charge—little Lilly Penney, deferred to by such a big strong man. She'd felt so grown up, knowing that he looked to her to lead the way.

It was a new role for Lill. As the middle child, she'd learned to be less demanding, less noticed than the other two. Noreen was the responsible one, taking care of the household when her mother got a job after their father's back got so bad he couldn't fish anymore. And Marlene was the baby, always and forever. Even after she'd outgrown it in years, Marlene's supposedly weak disposition and her ability to call upon minor illnesses at will kept her in the coddling chair. Lill bounced between them all trying not to cause too much work for Noreen or her mother, distracting her frustrated father with games of crib and forty-fives to keep him from going batty after his surgery. That part was easy. Her father entertained her as much as she did him, showing her how to whittle a piece of wood, telling her stories about growing up or when he used to go out fishing, concocting strange new dishes in the kitchen. She loved it best when her mother wasn't there because he wasn't as careful about what he said. He even swore sometimes, especially when Lill beat him at crib. Other than that, she tried to stay out of trouble and help when she was asked to. Nothing further was expected.

Steve needed much more than that, however.

"What kind of car do you think I should get?" he asked her one Saturday night as they walked home from church. They had been dating for almost a year.

"I don't know much about cars, but I like Toyotas," she said. "Are you buying a brand new one?"

"Do you think I should?"

"Yeah, sure! Our family's never had a new car before. Dad always buys a second-hand one."

"A new car sounds nice. So, you think we should get a Toyota?"

Lill noticed immediately how he'd phrased the question. She felt a little speechless at the implication.

"Lill?"

"Yeah?"

"This could be a car for us, you know what I mean?"

"I think so."

"Well, do you want to?"

She was terrified that she was getting it all wrong, that he didn't mean what she thought he meant. "Well, yeah…maybe…do what exactly?"

He was still walking, not looking at her. She stopped and waited until he turned around.

"You know," he said, kicking at the loose rocks on the side of the road. When she didn't answer, he coughed and looked up at the sky. "Maybe we could see the priest?"

This was not the way she'd imagined a man might ask for her hand. In her dreams, she'd been whisked off her feet over a candlelight dinner, or serenaded on a horse-drawn carriage under a full moon, or been surprised with a beautiful diamond on Christmas Eve. For just a moment she felt as if she might cry. She blinked hard several times, then squeezed her eyes shut. When she opened them, Steve was walking back to her. Then he knelt down right in the middle of the street. He looked so shy and so sweet, his face filled with hope as he stared up at her, that her heart melted. After all, she told herself, it wasn't his fault that she had such grand expectations. And he did go down on one knee.

"Yeah, I guess we could," she finally answered, feeling just a little shy herself.

"Really? You mean it? We're going to get married?"

For an instant, she wasn't sure if he looked frightened or happy, but she was just so relieved that he'd finally said the words that she wrapped her arms around his head and said, "Yes, Steve, I'll marry you."

He jumped to his feet and lifted her up to the sky, holding her so tight that she forgot all about his clumsy proposal.

The next weekend, Steve signed the papers for a brand new Toyota, cherry red, Lill's favourite colour.

The wedding went off exactly as she'd always imagined. When Steve insisted that whatever she wanted was fine with him, she was pleased that he had so much faith in her. They hired a good local band that didn't cost too much, and there was a hot roast beef dinner instead of the normal cold plate. Her sister Noreen even agreed to be maid of honour. Most of the faces were the same as in her dreams, too. Steve's parents were dead and his older brother lived in Toronto, so his only family in attendance were an aunt and uncle from Stephenville. He did invite several people from work, but they were friends of the Penneys anyway. Other than that, the guest list was Lill's.

And after the wedding, she decided when it was time to own a home, and that they should build a brand new one, a two-storey with three bedrooms. It was a decision she came to regret. Buying an older house in Port Grace would have been half the price, but Steve never made mention of that until several years later, after she'd quit her job as a secretary at the school to stay home with David. Then the bills started stacking up.

She planned their vacations, determined when it was time to trade in the car, arranged their social life, and made most other decisions, big and small. Steve was happy to let her do it. But she grew tired of being the boss, of having no one but herself to turn to, or to share the blame with when things went wrong.

Once she was at home full time, she decided to register for a University extension course, and she asked Steve to take over some of the minor responsibilities. It was not a role he took to. Before Lill could clue into the problem, the phone was disconnected for lack of payment, the electricity was almost cut off, and the car broke down for want of basic maintenance. When she confronted him, he raised his hands in despair; he always had been the strong silent type. Eventually she gave up and did it all herself.

Until they had their second child, Maxwell Paul Dunn. It was a difficult pregnancy and delivery, and by the time it was over, she and the baby were both exhausted. She asked Steve to name him.

"No, you should choose," he insisted. "After all, it's your baby."

"Our baby, you mean."

"Yes, of course," he conceded, "but you're the one who had him."

"So maybe you could at least pick a name?"

"But what if I pick the wrong one?" He actually looked scared.

This went on for three days, until it was time to leave the hospital. Still, he deferred it to her. As she sat on her bed filling out the forms so that she could go home, an old Beatles tune ran through her head. Looking up at Steve, she stared at him so long and hard she felt as if her eyes were paralysed on his face. What she was really seeing, however, was a boy named Maxwell with a shiny silver hammer in his hand, and he was banging him on the head, over and over and over. In a fit of rage, or postpartum hormones, she scratched the letters onto the page.

She probably would have changed it, but everyone was so relieved the child finally had a name and they made such a fuss over what a great choice it was that she let it be. It was another decision she learned to live with, alone. She never told a soul where the name came from, ever.

Rod Corcoran did not strike Lill as the sort of person who was easily led anywhere, which suited her just fine. She'd done her share of leading. On the other hand, she was too old and set in her years to start following anyone either.

Monday morning, she woke before the alarm. She'd slept like a baby, carefree, dreamless, at least as far as she could remember. Luxuriating in the blind warmth of her own body heat, she let her thoughts drift back to Saturday night, to the man who'd lain there with her, how he'd felt against her skin, how she imagined she could still catch the scent of him on her sheets, on her bed, the bed that she'd lain in with Steve for eighteen years. It crossed her mind that she felt no guilt about that part of it.

Suddenly the phone was ringing. She heard David's booming voice shouting at Max to get it, followed by the slam of the bathroom door. Max yelled something back, then she heard big feet thumping down the stairs. Finally Max called out to her, once, then a second time, as his voice came closer and closer to her bedroom door.

She sprang guiltily from the bed. As she pulled on her housecoat, she hauled the quilt back up over the sheets before running out to grab the phone.

"Hello," she said crossly into the receiver.

"You forgot your salad bowl," Marlene's voice shouted over the receiver.

Lill moved the phone an inch away from her ear. "Yeah, okay, I'll get—"

"When you were here for dinner, you forgot it."

"Right. Like I said, I'll get it—"

"So do you want me to drop it off?"

"Yeah, sure."

"I'm going into the school again. I swear I'm the only mother in there half the time. Why nobody else cares about their children's education is beyond me. Last week..."

Lill held the receiver away from herself and waited for the noise on the other end to stop.

"Lill?" Marlene's voice yelled out to her.

Lill put the phone back to her ear. "Yeah, I'm here, Marlene."

"So do you want me to drop it off on my way? It's no problem. Like I said, I'm going into the school again anyway. The kids really love it when I'm there and—"

"Fine, whatever! Yes, I mean, please, just leave it on the front step if I'm not here."

"Boy, you sound cranky. What's—"

"I'm standing here soaking wet, Marlene!" she lied. "I'll talk to you later."

Lill dressed carefully. At first she put on a red blouse, then thought better of the colour. She switched to white and then to beige, neutral, unobtrusive. Several new skirts hung in her closet, bought almost two years before when she thought skirts and dresses might be more appropriate for a teacher to wear to school. They'd languished on their hangers ever since. She removed the green one and pulled it on. Feeling slightly underdressed, she went down to make breakfast.

Max whistled when Lill walked into the kitchen. "A skirt! What's the big occasion?"

"Can't a person wear a skirt on a warm spring day, for God's sake?" she snapped at him.

"Well, it is different, Mom," David poked his head out of the fridge to pick up for his younger brother.

When one of them so quickly jumped to the other's defence, she knew she was in trouble. "Sorry. You're right. Maybe I'll change it."

"No, really Mom, it looks good," said Max.

Now she was in a pickle. If she didn't change it, it would be obvious to Rod that she'd worn it on purpose, an instant reminder of lust in the kitchen. If she did change it, Max would think he'd insulted her, and the last thing she wanted to do was start his week on a sour note.

She smiled at him. "Okay. Thanks, hon." She poured them both a glass of juice and popped some bread into the toaster. "Who wants toast?"

"Sure," said Max. "Any bakeapple jam left?"

"In the fridge somewhere. It's the last jar."

As he rummaged for the jam, Lill glanced down at her legs. They seemed so out there, conspicuous. They really didn't look right, sticking out from under that dark green skirt. Somehow she had to cover them up before she left the house. Frustrated with such a ridiculous problem facing her so early in the morning, she slammed down the lever on the toaster, then felt her hand slipping sideways, hitting the full glass of juice and knocking it over. The orange liquid splattered across the counter before racing down the front of her brand new skirt. "Shit!" she yelled in an extra loud voice.

Both boys stopped to stare at her. Their mother didn't often swear in front of them.

"Aw, Mom, and you looked so nice, too," said Max.

"And now what a mess! Oh Lord, and it's almost time to go. David honey, will you wipe this up while I go change?"

"Sure," he answered, reaching for a cloth.

Upstairs in her bedroom, she cringed to think she might have spilt the juice on purpose, then thought better of it. Who would ever know, or care, for God's sake? Putting it deliberately from her mind, she hauled on a pair of black pants and a burgundy sweater, not very spring-like, and not very special. With a quick comb of her hair, she ran down the stairs and grabbed her toast. "Hurry on, you two, we're late."

It was a nerve-wracking morning. Every time someone walked by her door, she was afraid to look up in case Rod poked his head in. She prayed he wouldn't. She didn't expect him to, really. But she was over-agitated nonetheless. Several times she noticed bewildered glances among her students. Had she said or done something inappropriate? Or could they just sense what had happened two days before? By the tone of her skin, or her voice. Could they tell, these young almost adults, some of whom had probably done a similar deed on the Saturday night, that she'd been witless with want? And with their very own Mr. Corcoran?

Finally it was noon. Just as she was hurrying to leave her classroom, Jenny Hayden came to the door.

"Hi, Mrs. Dunn. Got a second?"

Lill looked at her earnest face and smiled. "I'm just heading to the staff meeting but that can wait a minute. How's it going?"

"Pretty good, actually." She bowed her head shyly. "I just wanted you to know I got a scholarship, so I'll be heading off to UBC next year. I couldn't have done it but for you."

"Oh, Jenny," Lill reached out and took her hand. "You deserve every bit of it, you know that, don't you?"

"Thanks, Mrs. Dunn." Her voice was barely audible.

"I'm just glad I could help, Jenny. Everything going okay?"

She shrugged, finally looking like the innocent teenager she was supposed to be. "Yeah, it's okay. Not great all the time, but better."

"You're not sorry, are you?"

"God, no!" She shook her head adamantly.

"Good. And you're still determined to move clear across the country?"

"Definitely. The farther away, the better."

"We'll miss you around here."

"Thanks, Mrs. Dunn. But I got to get out of here. He'll be back, and I don't know what I'd do if I ever saw him again. I tried to get Mom to move too, to take the boys and make a break for it, but she won't go. Said this is her home and he's her husband and God would want her to do her duty by him when he comes home." Jenny's worried face looked at her. "I think she's gone a little nuts, and I'm scared a bit for the boys."

Lill smiled sympathetically at her. There was nothing left to say to a girl whose stepfather, the only father she'd ever known, had destroyed every iota of her love and trust. "Lloyd and Sammy are growing boys, Jenny. Soon they'll be able to fend for themselves, and your mother too if they have to."

"Oh, God, I hope that's true. Maybe I can write to you, or email you or something? Just to keep in contact with someone, find out how everyone is doing."

"I'd like that. When are you leaving?"

"Right after exams. Auntie Jean and Uncle Bob are already watching out for summer jobs for me in Vancouver."

"Come see me before you go, okay? I'll give you my e-mail address."

"Okay. Thanks again, Mrs. Dunn, for everything. I'll never forget all your help."

"You're welcome, Jenny. And congratulations on that scholarship."

"Thanks. Bye."

Lill watched her leave, the long ponytail swinging behind her. She'd had many doubts about what she'd done for Jenny Hayden, the clandestine arrangements made through her friend Gwen Mercer in St. John's, the sworn secrecy, the lies to cover other lies. It had been more than enough to lose her job and her reputation if anyone found out. But one look at Jenny today compared to the girl who'd been sick with despair a month earlier, and Lill knew she'd do it all again if she had to.

Arriving last for the meeting, the only spot left was at the far end next to Rod.

"Sorry," he said, removing his coat from the empty chair. "Have a seat."

A large bundle of thick handouts was just coming his way and he took the top one. As Lill sat down, he passed her the stack, his hand flat under the bottom. His fingers slid over hers as she took them. She could feel his eyes on her face. For the life of her, she could not look back. Instead, she focused her total attention on the pile of papers he was holding, as if the very pressure of her staring was the only thing that kept them from sliding to the ground.

Throughout the meeting, she was conscious of his every move. When he spoke, or picked up his pen, or shifted in his chair, she noticed. It wasn't that she'd fallen madly in love with him or anything remotely like that. She just couldn't seem to wipe Saturday night from her consciousness. It kept creeping into her mind, little vignettes of what they'd said and done. Especially what they'd done.

"Well, if that's it, we're done." The authoritative voice of the principal broke through her reverie. Jim White was the type who came straight to the point, which kept staff meetings short and intense. Lill realised she had no idea what this one had been about. "Thanks, everyone," he continued. "Have a good lunch. Oh, I forgot. There's one more thing. Lill's going to be helping Rod out with the guidance duties from now on so there'll be two of them at it."

Rod looked directly at her then. His eyes were crinkled in the corners, and his mouth, with those even white teeth and those soft lips, smiled at her. His naked body flashed in her mind.

"I know it's extra work, Lill," Jim was saying, "but I really appreciate it. If the two of you could come together on this, it would help a lot."

There was the tiniest nudge of a foot under the table.

"Sure Jim, glad to help," she managed to mumble.

"I'll see about getting you both some extra prep time to work on the manual. Maybe we can go over a few ideas I have after the meeting."

"Okay, sure." All she wanted was for the meeting to end so that she could blush in peace.

"Anything else?" asked Jim to the room. "Great. That's it then."

Jim walked between Lill and Rod as they headed outside to talk in the warm May sunshine. Students milled around in small and large groups, eating, talking, and occasionally, if they were a couple, kissing and touching each other surreptitiously behind the teachers' backs.

"So," said Jim, "what I was thinking for the manual was to bring it up to millennium standards."

"That's a job and a half," laughed Rod. "You wouldn't believe what's in there."

"Oh wouldn't I? I was brought up with that, you know, back in the old days."

"Nobody's that old, Jim."

"Except the church. So your job is going to be reconciling the needs of these kids," he waved his hand to include the whole schoolyard and everyone in it, "with the limits placed by the Board."

After giving them some advice and a few ideas, he left them to it and went inside. But just as he did, Bonnie Regan, a first-year teacher, pranced up and tucked her arm into Rod's. From St. John's, Bonnie was loud in her resentment at having to leave the city for job experience.

"So, did you have a good weekend, Rod?" she cooed at him.

"Oh, hi Bonnie," he said, leaning away from her.

"Hey, I went to that new café I was talking about. It was awesome. Too bad you were too busy to come."

"Yeah, it's been kind of hectic."

"Well, you have to eat, you know," Bonny chided him.

"Yeah, usually." He poked Lill in the side with his free arm.

"What about this Saturday, then? You can come into town and we'll try that other new restaurant I told you about?" So far she had not acknowledged Lill's presence, and Lill was beginning to feel uncomfortably invisible.

"This weekend? Ah, let me see…No wait, I can't, I'm busy all weekend with Little League."

They stopped to watch a group of boys playing ball. Freeing himself from her clutch on his arm, Rod bent to brush a twig from his shoe. When he stood back up his arms were folded tightly across his chest.

"Don't you need to be a dad to coach Little League?" asked Bonnie petulantly.

"It's with my sister's kids."

Lill glanced quickly at him, but he didn't look at her.

"Oh. Fine. Some other time then," said Bonnie, tossing her long hair. "So, Lill, you're helping with the manual?"

"Hello, Bonnie. Yeah, it really needs an update."

"Well, I offered to do it a couple of times, but nobody took me up on it. Jim thinks I'm too young, but God, I'm twenty-three."

The ball rolled right up to Bonnie's feet. Picking it up, she held it out to Marty Cunningham, a second-year grade twelve student who was chasing it. She could have tossed it to him, but instead she waited until he came right up to her. "Here you go, Marty, here's your ball."

"Th…thanks, Miss Regan." His face glowed a brilliant red, and he stammered something else that was completely unintelligible, all the while looking in the vicinity of her chin or her neck, but not her eyes. Then he ran off to his buddies, stumbling all the way.

"Oh well," Bonnie giggled, "maybe Jim's right. Rod's already got the young perspective anyway, you can be the old and wise one."

Lill was looking right at her as she said it, but Bonnie didn't seem to grasp the fact that she'd insulted her. How old did she look in this girl's eyes, Lill wondered? Probably as young as the "girl" seemed in hers—five years older than David.

Feeling like Mrs. Robinson herself, Lill pretended to watch the ball go back and forth a couple of times. "I think I'll be heading in," she said as politely as she could. "I've got some prep to do before class." Without glancing at either of them, she walked away. Followed by the dwindling chatter of Bonnie's voice, she imagined Rod's eyes on her back, and she hurried to get out of range.

After a morning on edge, she spent an afternoon on self-recrimination. How could she have been so stupid, falling into bed with him, allowing a man she wasn't even dating to do those things to her naked body? Twice! A man whose mother she'd played with as a child! And the boys! Oh good God, what if they found out? What if their friends did, and told them? And teased them, about their own mother, the town slut! How would she ever look them in the eye again, or try to give them motherly advice? She felt so old suddenly, old and frumpy and fat and ugly, far beyond the forty years she'd had the gall to celebrate.

At four o'clock she was packing up to leave for the day when he slipped quietly into her room.

"Get your prep done in time?" he asked, fingering the tin cup of pens on her desk.

"Yup." She wasn't in the mood for banter. Since Saturday she'd deliberately shirked the issue of age, but young Bonnie Regan had gone and smacked her in the face with it. And the fact that the little bitch hadn't even meant to do it made it worse. In Bonnie's mind, Lill was too old to take exception to the word.

"Want to grab a coffee before you go?"

"No." She piled her books on top of her binder.

Rod stopped fiddling with the pens. "Okay. Are you going to talk to me, Lill? Tell me what's wrong?"

"Nothing. There's nothing wrong." The books slid off onto the floor.

"Here, let me help—"

Lill stooped to pick them up, pushing her hand out to stop him. "I can do it."

"It's Bonnie, isn't it?" he asked, a hard edge to his voice.

Lill didn't answer.

"It's what she said at the end, right?"

She thumped the books on the desk and grabbed her purse. "No big deal. She obviously thinks she's more suited to you than some old wisewoman."

"Jesus, Lill!" His voice rose slightly. "I don't give a damn what she thinks."

"It won't be just her thinking it. For God's sake Rod, I used to play with your mother. I even remember when you were born."

His hand reached over and pressed hers. She looked directly at him for the first time, the hint of afternoon bristle shadowing his cheek, the thick brows almost touching over dark green eyes. A strong face, the face of a man she could grow used to.

"Lill?"

"What, Rod?" she sighed, looking away again.

"This is silly. You know that."

"No, I don't know that. This is a small town, a silly town too when it comes to stuff like this."

He took his hand away. "Remember how old Bonnie said she was?" His voice was tight, on the edge of anger.

"I don't know. Twelve? Thirteen?"

He didn't laugh. "Twenty-three. I'm thirty-two. That's nine years difference. How many years between you and me, Lill?"

The math was easy; the calculations were far more complex. "Rod, I got to live here every day. With the neighbours and the other teachers and the students and their parents. But that's not the worst. My sons have to live here too. With their friends—our students, no less—

who'll be looking at us different and making snide remarks, 'Old Lill Dunn and young Mr. Corcoran.' Oh God!"

"But Lill—"

"It's not fair to them, Rod," she continued. "Think about it."

"Well, it's not fair to us either." His eyes blazed out at her from his earnest face.

And it was such a nice face, she admitted to herself as she grabbed an armload of books. "Look Rod, we're big and ugly enough to take care of ourselves. But the fact is, it's my job to take care of the boys. Max, anyway."

He moved to stand directly in front of her, his warm hand holding her arm. "You're sure this is what you want, Lill?"

"I'm sure this is how it has to be," she answered, staring as hard as she could at him.

"Ah, Lill. That's not the same thing."

"It is to me, Rod," she said, and walked away.

7

When I was seven, Suzie Corcoran got a baby brother. Her family didn't appear to be too excited about it, but the rest of the town sure did.

The tongues at Hickey's store were wagging like wildfire. All the old biddies were so eager to talk about the new Corcoran baby they didn't even seem to care who overheard them.

"That poor Ida," old Mary Rowe lamented, "now what's she going to do with such a wee one in the house?"

"Yes, imagine having a baby around at her age!" Jean Hickey agreed, adding up a grocery bill.

Roberta Ryan shook her head at them all. "Well, but isn't that just like a Corcoran for you, having a youngster out of wedlock? Not worth talking about it, it's not."

They all nodded and sighed, then went right on talking.

I wasn't sure what wedlock was, but it didn't sound good. One thing I did know was that the baby was part orphan because Suzie's father had died the year before, and that there was something shameful about it. I couldn't figure out what was so wrong with this, so I asked my mother. But all she said was, "Leave it be, Lillian, and don't be talking about them. Let the poor child alone." Her tone of voice and the way she shook her head made me feel so guilty, although I had no idea what I could have done to the "poor child", or even if the "poor child" was Suzie or the baby. I wished I'd asked my father instead; he usually gave me a straight answer.

I felt bad for Suzie's little brother, who would never know his father, and for Suzie as well. Most of the time she didn't seem overly sad, but her face would get very solemn and serious whenever some adult tried to console her. They would pat her head and call her "poor little thing", then give her a dime or twenty-five cents. When that happened, we would go to Hickey's and buy a bag of mixed up candy. We liked it best when Randy Hickey was serving because he always gave more than he was supposed to. Then we'd head for the beach and throw rocks in the water and eat until the bag was empty. We never went to Hynes' store because my mother worked there.

At first I used to hate it when someone stopped to pity Suzie because she would instantly get sad and teary-eyed. Didn't they see the long face she got the minute they started talking? But soon we began to hang around places where she might find some sympathy, like the store or the church grounds. Twenty-five cents bought a lot of candy.

When I first heard that the Corcorans were getting a baby, I remembered how big my mother's stomach had grown the year before. This didn't happen with Ida Corcoran. Ida was always kind of fat, but she didn't get any bigger, and her belly stayed about the same size as always. At the time I wondered if that had something to do with the baby's father being dead. When I asked Suzie, she sort of nodded but I wasn't sure what she meant. She couldn't talk anymore, and I was certain that had something to do with her father's death because I heard Mom and Dad whispering in worried voices. They never seemed very sad about Mr. Corcoran being dead though.

I would have asked Janie but she wasn't very friendly anymore. She'd always been nice to me, I think because she knew I picked up for Suzie at school and in the playground. But she'd gotten quite mean, like I heard teenagers sometimes did. All she did was sit around and watch television, soap operas and game shows, whatever was on, though she didn't seem to enjoy them very much. One day Suzie and I were watching with her when, out of nowhere, she started yelling at the people on screen. "Goddamn stupid woman! Tell the bastard to fuck off." Then she looked right at me and said, "Men only wants to hurt you, Lilly, to stick it in and hurt you.

Don't you be letting them at it." She stormed out then, like she was mad at me or Suzie.

Ida wasn't getting fatter, but Janie certainly was. I rarely saw her eating, but she must have been because she had grown so big, even her face, which used to be pretty but had gone pale and puffy. She was cranky too, always cross at everybody, especially her mother. I really didn't like going to their house anymore. Someone was always sad or mad, and nobody ever seemed to have fun. In bed at night, I'd wonder if that's what happens when your father goes and dies and leaves you all to take care of yourself. Then I'd feel ashamed for avoiding them all.

When school was over that year, the whole Corcoran family went away, even their grandmother. Ida told Mom they were going to Marystown for the summer, where all the aunts and uncles and cousins lived. It sounded very exciting, going away on vacation. Our family never went anywhere, but no one else did either. I thought Suzie and Janie were so lucky, and couldn't understand why they weren't happier about it, until I remembered their poor dead father.

They came back to Port Grace at the end of August with the new baby, but without their Nana, who had died in her sleep on a hot night in July. They arrived home just in time for Suzie to start school. We were in the same grade together; she was the oldest and I was the youngest. Mom had told me that Suzie was born too early so she wasn't really as old as her birthdays. That sounded about right to me; I had been bigger and smarter than Suzie since grade one.

Janie didn't bother going to school at all that year. She turned sixteen at the beginning of September, and told Noreen she was moving to St. John's to get a job, which she promptly did one week after her birthday. She just up and left Port Grace and moved to the city, all by herself. I couldn't wait to grow up.

Suzie rarely went to school from then on either, except when the truancy officer got after them. There was no point in it, Ida told

Mom, "she don't talk and I'm not so sure she hears much either, what's she going to do in the school all day long for God's sake?" I remember Mom shaking her head and giving Suzie's mother that smile, the one that Mom used to get when she was trying not to cry.

I kind of stopped hanging out with Suzie during that year. She never wanted to do anything except stay in the house all day. The only time I'd see her was when Janie came out from town. The two of them would walk a lot then, usually down to the beach. I followed them once, but I couldn't find them when I got there.

When I was seventeen, I heard some of the old biddies at Hynes' store gossiping that Janie was getting married, that she had to get married. "Again", they'd added, their eyebrows dancing at each other. Marlene said to me that she didn't know Jane Corcoran had been married before. By that time I'd heard all the rumours about Suzie's brother, little Roddy Corcoran. And even though I didn't have much to do with Suzie anymore, I still felt an odd loyalty, to her, but also to Janie. I sensed a connection between us, although I could not have said exactly what that connection was. So I had no desire to repeat the local gossip, especially the stuff about Suzie's father, or Roddy's mother or father. And especially not to Marlene, who was as annoying at fifteen as she had been at five.

"She wasn't," I said, and left it at that.

Jane tramped out of the doctor's office, slamming the door behind her. The gall of him, telling her not to be asking for another one. She was on her own this time, he'd said, he wanted nothing to do with it. Who said she even wanted one, she'd almost screamed at him, who said she wouldn't keep this one, huh? But goddamn it all, now what was she going to do?

Jack was waiting for her in his truck, patient as always. Flinging herself into the passenger side, she wriggled her butt on the seat trying to adjust her jeans. They'd been riding her all day and she wasn't used to that anymore. After she'd moved to St. John's eight years before, the fat had just started falling off her bones. Not that she'd tried to lose it. She just didn't eat much. As she liked to say at the bar where she worked, "Why spoil a good drunk with food?"

"Everything okay?" Jack asked, leaning his long thin frame forward onto the carpeted steering wheel.

She could feel his eyes straining to see past the side of her head. After a minute, she turned. His shaggy-bearded face looked so pitiful trying to find out what was wrong when she wouldn't even let him see her face. "Yeah, sure." She lit a cigarette.

Still he didn't start the engine. "I'm serious, Janie."

He was the only one besides her family who called her Janie anymore. She sucked back another drag, adding a layer of tobacco smoke to the stink of motor oil rising from Jack's clothes and hair and everything around him. His skin seemed permanently stained from working on motors and mufflers and whatever else went wrong in a car. But he was a decent man, better than anyone she'd ever gone with before. She'd given up trying to figure out why he was so good to her. After she'd told him she wasn't interested, he'd kept coming around the bar, ordering coke after coke, leaving big tips in her cup. Even the nights he watched her leaving with other men, he still kept coming back. Finally, she went out with him, more to break the spell he seemed to be under than for any real interest. His devotion spooked her.

Then, over time, she started to like him. He was hard not to like, really. The problem was, she didn't respect him. He gave her what she wanted, when she wanted it, and when she didn't want something, he went out of his way to find something she'd like. He loved to cook for her, always her favourite things, and was happy to bring her out to Port Grace whenever he could.

But for Jane, by far the most important thing about him was that he was real nice to Suzie. Always brought her chocolate bars, Oh Henrys, her favourite, and spent lots of time just sitting and watching TV with her, sometimes even when Jane dolled herself up and went to a local dance or party. Nobody else had ever bothered to pay any attention to what Suzie wanted. That made Jane try harder to respect him.

"Did the doctor say there was something wrong?" he insisted.

She should never have let him drive her to her appointment, should never have told him she was even going. He'd not leave her alone now. She lit another cigarette off her first one. What the hell, she decided. "Nothing's wrong. I'm pregnant, is all."

"We're going to have a baby?" he whooped.

"No." She blew out a mouthful of smoke and turned to glare at him, deliberately narrowing her eyes. "That's not what I said. I said, I'm pregnant. 'Don't know nothing about having no baby'," she smirked, brushing some loose ash off her tight T-shirt.

"But it's mine? Right?"

She didn't blame him for asking, not the way she used to carry on, and the way she still talked like she did. Sensible question, that. He went up a notch. "Like I said,

I'm pregnant. Me. No one else. It's nobody else's concern."

"Aw, come on, Janie. I knows it's mine. I knows you don't do that no more."

"Oh you do, do you?"

"Sure I do. A man knows them things, you know. We're not all stupid all the time," he said, his cracked front tooth grinning out at her.

"What makes you so sure?"

He looked at her guiltily. "A man knows when a woman likes it and when she don't. And when she's tired of pretending she do. That's you, Janie. But I don't mind, see. I don't mind at all. You don't have to be like that with me."

She didn't know if she should laugh or cry. How did this big stupid lumbering man see that? How did he know that she saw sex as something done to her, as a thing to get done, to be got through? Did she dare to believe him, to think that maybe he was different from almost every other man she'd ever met? How could she? Yet if only she could. She was tired, so utterly tired of it all. He was right on that.

"Let me take care of you, Janie. We'll have that baby and give her a good home, bring her up right."

Her? Better a "her" than a "him", that was for sure. Too many "hims" in the world for Jane's liking.

She glanced at Jack, the prospective father. His smile shone back at her, full of hope and optimism. Christ, he was just too gullible. It was time he knew who he was dealing with. "It won't be the first baby, Jack."

"Oh?" he squinted at her. "What's that about then?"

"Well, there's Rod. I had him, not Mom." There. It was the first time she'd ever actually said it out loud. It was easier than she thought.

"Oh. Nobody ever said nothing to me."

"Hah! Hang around out in Port Grace long enough and lots of them will say, they'll all be glad enough to let you know about the Corcorans."

"I don't care about any of them," he insisted. Then he added, "Is the father out there?"

"No, most of them thinks the father is dead." She swallowed. She'd never told anyone, never dared to talk about it. "Most of them thinks my father did it to me. But they don't know nothing."

"Why didn't you ever tell them the difference?"

Tossing her head back, she took a long deep suck on the cigarette. "None of their fucking business. Hah! More fun watching them squirm, just thinking how bad he was, that goddamn prick."

They sat there in silence. She'd already said more than she'd intended.

He started the truck. "Let's go tell Suzie we're getting married. Bit of happy news will do her good."

The thought made Jane smile. Suzie might like a wedding, and Ida would be relieved; she was always going on about what a good man Jack was. Jane had to admit her mother was right about that. She just wished he had a little more backbone.

She should tell him the rest, the other almost-babies. He had a right to know. But she suspected he didn't really want to be told, and she wasn't all that sure she wanted to tell him. She looked over at him. He smiled back at her hopefully.

"Aw, fuck it," she said. "Why not!"

~

Jane had two sons in two years, big boisterous boys that soon made her forget the things she never wanted to remember. She was too busy buying diapers. And changing diapers. And washing diapers. Too busy tripping over toy trucks and model trains and baseball bats. Overrun with training wheels and hockey skates, birthday parties and sore knees and hurt feelings. Every minute of every day, there were two little people who turned to her before anyone else, who were up one side and down the other of everything in sight, never stopping to slow down or catch their breath or let her catch hers. She felt God had given her a lease on life.

God had given her Jack too. Good old Jack Pitts. When she looked at their children, she was never sorry for saying yes. Even in bed, when he rolled over to her, she didn't regret it. After all, he seldom broke down and asked for it, knowing her like he did. And again, when she thought of the boys, she knew it was worth it.

They lived a simple life, the sort that people lived who didn't have to constantly hide the darkness inside them. They worked and paid their bills, cooked their meals and ate their suppers, went out for darts or to a dance or for fish and chips. It was all part and parcel of being a family, raising children and keeping them safe.

As often as they could, they went out to Port Grace. Ida was getting older and Suzie, even quieter, each day moving farther away from the rest of the human race. It was a silence that Jane often found hard to accept, one she sometimes felt the irresistible need to break.

"You want to put chocolate chips in?" Jane asked one day as she and Suzie mixed up a batch of double chocolate brownies.

Out of the corner of her eye, Jane saw Suzie nod.

Jane ignored it, pretending to peer into the upper cupboard. "Huh?" she asked again. "Chocolate chips?"

Again, Suzie nodded as her fat arm stirred the batter with a wooden spoon.

Jane kept her eyes averted. "Suzie, do you want chocolate chips or not?" she asked, raising her voice just a little.

There was a noise then, something between a cry and a grunt.

"Fine with me," said Jane as if she hadn't heard. "No chips."

The noise was louder this time, more of a screech. Then suddenly Suzie flung down the spoon, sending chocolate batter splattering all across the wall and onto Jane.

The thwack of the spoon on the counter startled Jane and she lost her patience. "Oh for Christ's sake," she yelled, spinning around and grabbing Suzie by the arms. "Just tell me. Tell me anything. Tell me to fuck off, for all I care. Just open that big mouth of yours and say something."

Suzie's round plump face paled instantly. Her big body started to shake, followed by a dull guttural hum that escalated by the second, her mouth slobbering with spit. Her desperate eyes locked onto Jane, and Jane realised that her sister didn't need to talk for Jane to understand what she wanted to say, that Jane was her sanctuary, that only Jane could possibly understand why she couldn't talk, and that if Jane didn't understand then how could anyone else ever hope to.

Jane wrapped her arms around Suzie's wide shoulders and pulled her close. "I'm so sorry, my little Suzie. I didn't mean it, honest, I'm sorry." She held her sister tight until the humming stopped, but even then, Jane still heard it, as clear as the day it had started years before.

Jane hated when that happened, when the memories would not retreat and the noises inside her head threatened to overpower her. She feared she would go crazy, that she was, in fact, already crazy. There was only one place to go then. She'd head to the beach, picking her way among the rocks and driftwood, through the bushes and dense dark overhang of firs, until she reached the light again. She would stare into the limitless ocean, as vast and endless as the sky above. It was the place she craved to be, especially on a windy day, when the sound of the water and the surf and the waves would pound into her brain and knock out all those other thoughts, the ones she'd stuffed far away, the ones that had been nudged by talking to Suzie.

Occasionally when she was out around the bay she saw Lill and Noreen, sometimes their sister, a pouty little thing who didn't seem to belong with the other two. "How old are your boys now?" they would ask. "And how are Suzie and Ida?" They were always friendly, interested in her life in St. John's, asking after Jack and wishing them well. Then, when Lill got married, they were all invited to the wedding. And even though Jane had grown apart from the Penney sisters since their berry picking days, she was not surprised. The two families had always seemed bonded somehow, what with Marg Penney sending a big basket of goodies each Christmas, always with a note to

Ida, "her oldest friend". Old Matt invariably scoffed when the basket showed up on their doorstep, but Ida had accepted it gratefully, and always sent a batch of shortbread in return.

Suzie didn't go to the wedding, of course. She stayed home with Jane's two little ones and Roddy, who at twelve was more responsible than Suzie would ever be. Janie had to admit that her mother had done a good job with the boy, better than with her own children, that was for sure.

Leaving the others at home, Jane and Jack and Ida dressed up and joined the celebration. When Lill walked down the aisle, so beautiful beside her handsome young man, Jane felt a hidden sense of relief, of accomplishment even, for a job well done. She was proud to know that she'd had a silent hand in helping Lill become such a strong and confident young woman, or at least in preventing the opposite. It didn't matter that no one would ever know the truth of it. Truth rarely mattered to Jane anymore.

When Jane got pregnant again that next year, she was not happy about it. "Christ almighty, Jack!" she stormed, slamming a frying pan onto the stove. "I told you to get something done. Now look what went and happened."

Jack, however, was thrilled, and tried to wrap his arms around her. "Don't be fretting, Janie love. This one'll be a girl, just you watch."

She shoved him away. "What the hell does that matter? It's another baby, and I said two was enough. I'm dog-tired all the time, b'y. Now what'll I do?"

Jack's worried face looked at her. "Like I said before, why don't you quit the bar? That place is killing you, it is."

"And like I said to you, we needs the money. The bills don't pay themselves, you know." She didn't add that she needed the bar. There were days when she only felt sane when she walked through its doors. Immersed in the blare of the jukebox, the din of shouts and laughter, the fog of cigarettes and beer fumes, she could breathe. He wouldn't understand that, and she knew she couldn't explain it.

"Come on, Janie. I'll work more hours. I can get—"

"Stop it, Jack," she ordered. There was no point talking, the damage was done. This time. "What you can get is a doctor and get that thing fixed right now."

His skinny face paled, and his panicked eyes stared out at her. "But Janie, honey, there's no rush now to do… you know, to get…" He stopped, his mouth twisted as if the words were rotten.

"Good Christ," she said, disgusted. "Look, I got to have them, but you got to stop them." She scraped at the frozen hamburger meat in the pan where it had stuck to the bottom.

"What?" he asked, his face bewildered. "Stop what?"

"Jesus! Babies, b'y! Having youngsters is what I'm talking about. I don't want any more. Christ, I don't want this one, but it's too late for that, isn't it?"

"Aw, Janie," he said, his face lighting up, "don't you want a little girl?"

She didn't. Two boys were plenty for her. Still, there was nothing to be done now, at least nothing that Jack would ever consider. "Look, I'll make you a deal. I'll put up with this if you get yourself fixed. Okay?"

"Sure," he agreed, his face aglow. "Don't you worry. I'll handle that later."

Having no choice in the matter, she settled in to have the baby, dragging herself from the house to the bar and back again, lugging kids to and from playschool and the babysitters and everywhere in between. It was a long, heavy drawn-out pregnancy. Her stomach ballooned right away, as if it knew exactly what to do. And it did, of course. It had climbed this mountain three times before, and had threatened to several other times as well. It was probably glad to get another chance to show her what it could do.

Day after day, she put up with it, until finally, in her last trimester, she gave in. As she lost sight of her toes, she began to see her daughter in her head. And her daughter looked like Suzie, the little sister Jane remembered before it happened, before Suzie's world fell silent. With the hormonal insight of pregnancy and motherhood, Jane saw it all then. God was watching her. This was her chance to do it right, to take that baby and reverse the tide. He was giving her a little girl to bring up, to raise right, safe in Jane's house. Safe with Jack.

In her eighth month she had to stop working at the bar. "You're always banging the customers in the head with your gut," her boss laughed. "Not good for business, that."

She knew Norm was right, at least about the size of her belly. She felt as big as a side of a barn and about as graceful. Besides, she could use the time. There was always so much to do and no time to do it. She hadn't even been out to see Suzie in over a month. So on her first day off, a cold wet grey sort of day, she buckled the boys into the back seat and, shivering from the dampness, squeezed herself behind the wheel. With Jack working extra hours, they would have to head out to Port Grace on their own. Jane was looking forward to the break, having Ida to cook and Suzie and Roddy to play with the kids. A rest before the next one arrived.

About halfway there it happened. Out of nowhere. An animal, huge, threatening, careened towards them. Matted hair, dirty and thick with the sludge of winter. Before Jane knew what was what, it had hit the car, smashed the windshield, and bounced off again. The wheels had a will of their own. They kept moving, turning, nonstop, this way, then that, and back again, for ages, forever in mere seconds, and even though her hands were frantically trying to steer them clear and stay on the road, to not lose complete control, to keep a grip on whatever piece of pavement she could, the car kept spinning and turning, until finally it pitched down a small embankment where it was stopped abruptly by the trunk of a tree. She felt her body and head pitch forward violently, then slam back against the seat.

Odd how her father's face had whipped through her consciousness.

For a split second Jane sat frozen, stunned beyond place and time. Then the sounds of crying from the back brought her into reality again. But as she tried to turn around to check on the boys, a blast of pain ripped through her body. The last thing she heard was the distant murmur of voices and someone banging on the door.

It was two days before she opened her eyes, at least as far as she knew. Jack's face was there, above her, the furrows in his forehead even deeper than she remembered. When she tried to say his name, nothing more than a groan came out.

"Janie? Honey? It's me, Jack."

She wondered why he would say that. Of course it was him.

"You're going to be okay, Janie. Yes. Yes, you are."

There were tears in his big brown eyes, tears that threatened to scare the life right out of her. If she was fine, why was he crying? Her head pleaded with her to shut down, but she couldn't, not yet. "The b…?" she tried.

"It's okay, Janie. Everything's going to be okay."

"The boys?" she wanted to scream at him. "The boys? My boys?" But she couldn't make her mouth work.

He must have read her mind. "Johnny and Henry are fine. Don't worry, honey. You must have had them buckled…"

She didn't hear the rest. She didn't need to.

When she came to the next time, she heard people talking, their voices reassuring to her semiconscious brain. If she could hear, she must be alive.

A young nurse hovered over her. She seemed to be taping something to Jane's head. "How are you feeling, Mrs. Pitts?" she asked in a firm yet kind voice.

Jane didn't quite know how she was feeling, but she figured if she was breathing that was something. "Okay," she managed to mumble. Her mouth felt thick, and she wondered if that was where the foetid smell was coming from.

"You've had quite the go of it, eh? I just got back from days off, so I been reading up on your chart. That's some gash you got on your head there. Lucky you weren't killed, eh?"

Jane tried to nod, but stopped immediately when her head ricocheted with pain.

The nurse moved down and started rummaging with the blankets and Jane's lower body. "Is it hurting much? We got you on a drip, but now you're awake we can figure things out a bit better, huh?"

"Mmmm," Jane said, not wanting to risk the pain again.

"The stitches down here are looking good too, and the incision's nice and clean. They did a neat job for an emergency section. Still, I suppose bikinis'll be a thing of the past, eh?"

Jane's heart skipped. C-section? What had happened? Good God, was she born already then? Where was she? Was she okay?

"Well, better that than what could've happened," the disembodied voice continued, the person attached to it prodding and poking at Jane's skin. "We could've lost the both of you, from what I hears. I know that's hard to take given she was about ready to come out, but at least you're here to take care of the rest of your family, right? And it's not like you ever knew her. Got to look on the bright side, eh? Right?"

There was a vague sensation of her bare skin being covered, then the nurse reappeared above her.

"So, you need a bump-up for the pain?" she asked, her concerned ignorant face peering down. "Might as well take advantage, eh? No sense suffering, is there?"

Jane nodded, ignoring the screeching in her head. Her eyes felt like melting ice. Frostbitten, the thaw moments away, the flood just below. She closed them against the light in the room, but the tears seeped through. As they washed down her face, an immense sadness overcame her, an all-abiding sorrow she feared would last a lifetime.

The minutes grew into hours, the hours into days. The sorrow did not abate.

Jack arranged for Ida to be there when she got home from the hospital. Jane didn't care one way or the other. Dressed in flannel pyjamas and Jack's heavy robe, she sat in her bedroom looking out the window onto the street, watching cars going by, people walking, sometimes stopping to talk to each other. Occasionally they waved. Her hand was too heavy to lift in reply.

She sensed the life bustling around her, in and out, eating, talking, moving, everybody always moving, children crying. When it got to be too much, she left her soft yellow room with it's flowery border and burrowed into the basement. It was dark there, and she would sleep. Most evenings that was where Jack found her. She hated to hear the heavy tread of his footsteps on the stairs because she knew he would make her leave the darkness and return to the living above her. She had no energy, no desire, for that. Her only wish was to be left alone in her blackened tomb. If only he would do that, then eventually she could cease to feel. Cease to be.

She did not think about what had happened at all. Every time it seemed she might have to, she would fall asleep. Her body was so very tired, just the thought of what it had endured was enough to exhaust her.

Ida and Jack tiptoed around, placing cups of tea in her hand, or bowls of soup. Sometimes she ate or drank what they gave her without realising what she was doing, or that she was hungry or thirsty. Half a sandwich would disappear, and she would feel the food in her mouth, her teeth chewing reflexively. They gave her pills too, several times a day. She'd learned to look forward to that, and not just for the pain. The pills helped her forget.

After a week, the medicine ran out. The doctor said there would be no more.

Jane felt as if she was waking from a prolonged slumber, only to find that the peace she'd found in her dreams had been just that, a dream. She was forced to face her world. Her mother and husband, their concerned faces peering at her, constantly asking was she okay, how did she feel, did she want to talk, could they get her anything. God, would they never stop? And then there were her children, those two innocent boys. Henry, the youngest, asking why didn't she play anymore, when was she going to take him to the park again, what were they having for supper? Once, she happened to glance at his older brother, Johnny, at five years old so like his father, his serious kind eyes, the frown lines even then beginning to show above them. Johnny had been staring at her, almost into her it felt like, and when she didn't answer, couldn't answer, he'd grabbed his brother's arm and dragged on it. "Quit pestering at her, Henry. She'll be at that stuff when she's better. Come on out now." Jane had tried to nod, tried to smile at him, but her face was stuck. Johnny looked as if he'd aged years in mere weeks.

That was when the true pain started, a pain that she could not dull, could not avoid. It was always there, constantly lurking behind every conscious moment. She'd have cried if she could but she was too numb for that. There were no tears that she could find to shed, just a dull aching emptiness in a sea of pain.

Finally, she asked Jack to send Ida home, and to take the boys with her, promising them all that she would get better sooner if she was on her own. In reality, she couldn't bear to spend another day surrounded by people all the time. She wanted only to be by herself and not have to pretend to care, or to be feeling anything at all. With the house to herself most of the day, she would have hours to be alone, and that aloneness was what she craved.

Until she got it. And then she feared she would lose her sanity in the silence. Her head rattled with all the bad things, the screeching of tires, the stench of the hospital, the pain of recovery. Everything except her daughter, the tiny precious infant girl that never got the chance to live. As soon as her mind would start to veer towards that dead baby, she could feel her body shift inside so that she had trouble even breathing. Trying desperately to zoom away from any thought of her, Jane would hit on the first noise she could find, rattling pots and pans, jumping into the shower, raising the TV to full blast. Anything but her.

But eventually all the racket in the world could not have stopped the thought that had to come. That it was all her fault. That, like all the others before this one, she had not wanted the child from the beginning and so would not be given her. That God had decided Jane was unfit to raise a daughter and had taken her away.

The idea that God had done this to punish her was more than Jane could bear. She took to her bed and stayed there. She might never have left it again if Ida had not rooted her from it.

It was a Sunday morning. Jane knew that because Jack had gone to Mass, giving her a single hour of solitude in two days. When she heard the door open, she closed her eyes and prayed for sleep, but it didn't come. She kept them tightly shut all the same.

"Time to get out of bed, Janie."

The sound of Ida's voice surprised her. She opened her eyes. "Mom? What are you doing here?"

"Jack called. Told me what you were up to."

Jane noticed the matter-of-factness of her mother's voice. It was no longer worried, or cajoling and pleading like it had been before she'd returned to Port Grace the week before. "What do you mean, 'up to'? I'm not up to nothing. Leave me alone."

Rummaging in the dresser, Ida laid out a sweatshirt and loose pants. From the top drawer she fished an over-sized pair of panties and a bra.

"Get on, Mom. Leave my stuff alone."

"No. Time to be up, Janie."

Her mother hadn't told her what to do in over ten years, ever since her father had died. They'd been more or less equals after that. In Jane's opinion, this was no time to start getting bossy. She rolled over, her back to Ida.

There was a loud sigh, followed by her mother's weight and presence beside her on the bed.

"Are you blaming yourself, then? Is that what this is?"

The bluntness of the comment threw Jane off guard, and she whirled around. Ida's face was bright with colour, in stark contrast to her drab brown housedress. "What the hell are you talking about?" Jane demanded.

"You're not the first this happened to, you know?"

"Right. Now leave off and go."

Ida shook her grey head, her faded eyes filling with tears. "I lost one of my own, Janie, before you were born. I was about six months along, could feel him kicking and everything."

Jane wanted to scream at her to shut up, that she didn't care, that this was different. She did not feel like sharing the pain. This was her grief, her sorrow, her fault. Ida could not be allowed to take it from her. "Hardly the same."

"No?" Ida asked.

"No. It's not the same at all. She was almost due, she was practically alive for Christ's sake."

"True," Ida conceded. "But the rest is the same, about feeling like it's your own fault."

"What the hell would you know about it?"

"Plenty, Janie. More than I ever wanted to."

"But you were only six months. And it wasn't your fault, was it?"

Ida's hands covered her face, her fingers digging into the soft wrinkled skin. "I'm going to tell you a secret, one I never told nobody before. The thing is, I used to think it was all my fault. It's only since I got old that I don't think it was. I hope you don't have to wait that long."

Jane eyed her suspiciously. "What do you mean?"

"It happened two years before I had you. On one of them nights, you remember, when he'd go nuts. Well, this one night when he was drunk he came after me, pushed me on the floor and then knocked me down the stairs. The next day I started to bleed and that was that. I always thought it was my own fault, if I hadn't made him mad at me, or I'd cooked him something different, or a bunch of other things. But it wouldn't have mattered. He would have beat me anyway."

"You knew what he was like and you stayed with him? Even when you had no children? For the love of God, why?"

Ida tutted, and blew out a breath of air. "For the love of God? That's what you said, right? And that's what it was, that's why I stayed. May God forgive me."

Jane stared at her mother. She could hardly believe it. She'd always thought that the evil inside her father must have grown over time, that the pressure of a wife and children and no money had gotten to be too much for him.

But here was Ida admitting that he'd been like that forever, and she knew, and she stayed with him anyway. All because of the goddamn church.

Suddenly Jane felt sick, sick of them, sick of herself, of her mother and especially her father, who she'd almost managed not to think about in years. It was everybody's fault, and it was nobody's. If Norm had not told her to quit working, if she had not gotten into the car that day, if she'd been driving just a little faster, or slower, if Ida had not stayed with Matt Corcoran, if Matt Corcoran had never lived, then maybe, just maybe, they all wouldn't be in the sad mess they were in. But most of all, if Jane had truly wanted the child in her womb, then she might have deserved to give it life.

Well, fuck it, she decided. She was stuck with the facts of her life, the mortgage payments and the heating bills, the laundry and the cooking, the husband and two growing boys who needed someone to take care of them, even if it was her. It was time to put that dead child away, the baby girl she'd never gotten to know. Somehow, she'd have to cope with the empty space inside her soul, or find some way to put up with it, and with her mother, who should never have been.

"Go back home, Mom," she said, leaving no room in her voice for discussion. "Go take care of Suzie and Rod. I'll be fine."

With that, Jane rose from her bed. Two days later she was back at work. And it was there, amid the constant haze of smoke and booze, that she found a form of solitude, in the music and the noise, in the banter of her customers, but most of all, in the taste of liquor.

8

When I was six, we almost got a baby brother. When we didn't, we were the saddest family in all of Port Grace.

My mother especially. There was a stuffed chair by the stove and she'd sit there for ages, her hair often greasy and uncombed, big sweaters over her housecoat even on the warmest days. I had never seen her so quiet. Mom was always a busy person, looking after my grandmother, cooking and cleaning, hanging clothes on the line or taking them off, gossiping with Mrs. Murray, cleaning out a cupboard or filling one up. It was endless. She rarely sat. But that spring and summer she did almost nothing. I knew that she was sad because of the lost baby; so was I. But I felt scared as well. Mom didn't seem to care about anything or anyone, not even Marlene, who spent most of that summer even more confused than me. Although my father did what he could, he wasn't much better than Mom most of the time, although he pretended everything was normal whenever she was around. But I knew better. I would watch him sitting in his chair by the window in the evening, reading his paper. Some nights he hardly turned a page, just sat and looked at the same spot for ages. There were days I thought we'd never laugh again.

I first suspected something was going on around St. Paddy's Day. We were having Irish stew for supper, and Dad got up to get a beer from the fridge. When he asked Mom if she wanted one, she said she'd just have a sip or two of his and then, rubbing her stomach, said she had to watch it. Still she went on to eat two bowls of stew. I had noticed as well that she was getting fat, always eating crackers and moaning about what a size she was, then she'd laugh and go and eat something else. And nobody seemed to mind. They all—Mom, Dad, Noreen, even my cranky old grandmother—acted like it was no big deal. All they could talk about was the new baby we were supposed to be getting. And they went on and on about how it would be a boy, surely to God this one had to be a boy, they all said. "We'll call him David," they finally agreed, even though we weren't supposed to be getting him for months yet. Nobody ever talked about a girl's name.

One day I asked Dad why they didn't just order a stupid boy if they wanted one so bad. He laughed and hugged me and said it didn't work that way, that you couldn't put in an order. Besides, he didn't really care one way or the other what it was as long as it was healthy. Boy or girl, it was all the same to him. I immediately felt better about the new baby, and began to daydream about having a brother.

Something he'd said stayed with me though, and one day I asked Noreen what he meant by it "not working that way." "The baby's inside Mom," she told me. "It starts out small and grows until it comes out of her bum after nine months." I thought that was the strangest thing I'd ever heard, but then she told me how it got there. Her eyes grew large and round, and her mouth stretched wide open across her teeth when she said the word. "Sex." Her voice was low and secretive. Then she told me under her breath how a man's thing, "his cock" she whispered bluntly through clenched teeth, got really big and he put it inside his wife and that was how a baby was made. She shivered when she said it, and sounded so disgusted that I acted disgusted too. In truth, I was more scared than anything, scared of what she'd said, even scared of the words themselves, "sex" and "cock". My brain reeled with questions—how big was it anyway, and how big could it get, and where did it go, in the belly button? But I was afraid to ask. After all, look where my curiosity had taken me already. I wasn't sure I wanted any more answers. Besides, with everybody always laughing and talking so excitedly about the new baby, it was easy to push my concerns aside.

Then one day all the laughing and excitement stopped. I was in the living room. Dad was working and Noreen was out playing hockey, as usual. The warm smells of garlic and onions and tomatoes reached me from the kitchen where Mom was cooking up a pot of spaghetti, a family favourite. Marlene was home too, but she was in bed with "a spring fever". I was playing with my doll cut-outs, dressing them up in the new clothes I'd cut from the summer catalogue, when I heard the clatter of dishes, followed by a horrible moan. It was an awful sound, like someone was twisting a knife right in her. I jumped up from the coffee table and ran out to the kitchen. Mom was leaning against the fridge, hanging onto the door handle. Her other fist was clutching a big metal spoon. It was sticking up in the air and the red tomato sauce that coated it had trickled down the long handle onto her arm. Tiny dots of sauce spotted her apron. I noticed there was a puddle of sauce on the floor between Mom's legs, and her calves underneath her plaid shift were streaked with it too. Confused, I looked up at her. Her face was pale as a sheet. The knuckles of the hand holding the spoon were whiter still. When I looked down again, the puddle had grown and her shoes were splotched. It was then I realised that it wasn't the same colour as the sauce at all. It was too red. The red of roses, or meat at the butcher's. Or Dad's finger when he'd cut it the week before. It was blood red.

"Lill," she mumbled, groaning loudly and sinking to the floor, "go get Mrs. Murray...somebody, anybody." I stood there stock still, not able to move my feet. Then she whispered "please" in such a tiny voice that it sent me flying from the house and over the fence to the Murray's house. Once I'd told them what happened, they said I should stay there while they took care of Mom, that everything would be fine but I needed to stay out of the way. When I got home later she wasn't there. I wished I hadn't listened to them then.

It felt like she was gone forever, but it was only a week. The days passed by so slowly, the house quiet and still except for Marlene.

Even she was more subdued than usual. We were all just waiting for Mom to come home. When she did, the days went no faster.

I heard Dad say over the phone that it had been a boy after all. But that was it, there couldn't ever be any more. They had to take it all out, "the works" he said, and used some big word I'd never heard before, "his" something or other. That's when I knew it was "his" fault, the baby's, perhaps even Dad's, for putting it in her in the first place. But then I heard him still talking on the phone, and there were tears in his voice, and in his eyes when he hung up. Was he so sad because it was his fault, I wondered? Without a word, he sat down and squeezed me so hard I could barely breathe. But I didn't say anything or try to get away. It felt so good to be hugged.

It occurred to me that my sisters and I must have been made the same way as the brother who died. I wondered how God decided if a baby would be a girl or a boy, and whether it would live or die. I wondered, secretly, if it was just up to God. How did He pick and choose between us all, who would be born and who would not, who would lead happy lives, and who would wallow in misery? How much of this was left to chance, to luck, to our own devices? Who was to blame for my brother's death?

Feeling my father's loving safe arms around me, I decided that it couldn't have been his fault, not my wonderful caring father. I also decided that I was never going to let a man put it in me. Not if it caused all that blood, and so much sadness.

It was Friday, just after three o'clock. Lill was sipping tea at her desk, hard at work, trying to put thoughts of Rod and what they'd done together from her mind. But the same questions kept hammering at her, just as they had all week long. How could she have let it happen? What on earth had made her lose control like that and fall into bed with a relative stranger? After so many years of managing to not have sex with anyone outside of marriage, and even then certainly not so fraught with desire as to be out of control, what had come over her in that insane moment? Where had her principles gone? Twice!

Jim White's voice boomed at her over the intercom, for a moment making her forget what she was trying not to remember. A welcome reprieve. It was short-lived.

He wanted her and Rod to come to the office to discuss ways to speed up the guidance manual.

Rod arrived just after she did. "So, what's the big hurry, Jim?" he asked when they'd all sat down.

Lill could feel him glance in her direction. Except for a quick hello when he came through the door, she hadn't looked at him. It was hard. She kept catching little sideways snippets of him, and she had to force herself to concentrate on Jim's face instead.

"Because I'll be gone in a couple of weeks." He'd been promoted to head up the curriculum department with the board, he told them, and he didn't want to leave the manual unfinished. "I promised to finish the stupid thing two years ago, but I kept putting it off. So, can you get it done for me?"

Jim had given her a break when he hired her fresh out of university two years before, and she felt she owed him. Still, she hesitated. "There's a lot left to do, Jim. I don't know—"

"You'd be doing me a big favour."

She felt Rod look her way, then he planted his hand on the desk. "Listen Jim, don't worry about it. I'm just hanging around that old house with nothing to do. Lill's got a family to take care of. I'll get on it by myself this weekend."

Jim shook his head. "Well, that's nice of you but it needs a woman's point of view. If Lill can't do it, we'll have to ask Bonnie." He nodded sympathetically as Rod groaned. "And quite frankly, she's a little immature for the job. I want two people who are young enough to still be in touch, but old enough to have a little experience and common sense."

Smiling his particular principal smile at her, he tapped the tips of his fingers together in a pretence of praying. Before she knew it, she'd caved in and she and Rod were out in the hallway.

"So, when do you want to start back at it?" he asked.

"Right away, I suppose."

"The weekend's pretty flexible for me."

"Thought you had Little League? And a sister with little kids?"

"Oh, that. Sorry, but I'm all out of excuses with Bonnie."

"Why not the plain truth?"

"There's not much left to the school year. No sense hurting her feelings now. Anyway, what are we going to do, Lill?"

It took her a second to figure out what he was talking about.

"Why don't you come over first thing in the morning. The boys like to laze around on Saturdays, so they'll probably sleep till noon." But they will be there, she thought, in the house, large as life.

He looked at her for a long moment. "I'll try not to wake them. Nine o'clock too early?"

Dragging her eyes from his mouth, she answered tightly, "No, that's fine. I'll see you then." She hurried back to her classroom, her own lips pressed together, as if that could block out the recurring image of his mouth coming towards hers.

The next morning she got up at eight, showered and put on a pair of old jeans and a baggy sweater. Purposely avoiding make-up or perfume, she clipped her damp hair close to her head and answered the door. Rod was looking equally casual in track pants and sweatshirt. After seating him at one end of her seldom-used dining room table, she went to get the coffee.

"I've got some bran muffins too, in case you're hungry." It was hard to get more unromantic that bran.

"Sure, let me help," he offered, standing back up.

"No," she blurted. "Stay there. I'm already up. I'll get them."

When he was seated firmly in his chair at the table, his laptop opened in front of him, she went back into the kitchen. Every time she went in there she saw them together, their bodies pressed against the wall, clothes hanging off them. Just yesterday the image had hit her so hard she'd had to lean against the fridge for support. She did not want him having the same reminder.

She took a seat at the opposite end of the table, far enough away that he would have had to lie across its length to reach her. He gave her an odd look when she sat there, but then returned to what he'd been reading on the monitor, his eyes creasing in concentration. Still, she could have sworn there was the tiniest grin at the corner of his mouth. While they worked away for the next couple of hours, she made sure his cup was never empty, that he never had to go to the kitchen to get a refill.

Despite her obsession with keeping his coffee topped up, they managed to get a fair bit of work done, and have a few laughs as well.

"Listen to this!" Rod chuckled late in the morning. "'While it is no longer necessary for a girl to put a sheet of paper between them if she sits on a boy's lap, the act of sitting on laps should be greatly discouraged.' My God, they didn't really tell them to do that, did they?" he asked, finishing the last bite of his second large muffin.

"Hard to believe, but they did." She got up to get the coffee. "Noreen's grade nine teacher, Sister Bonita I think was her name, told her to do just that," she called over her shoulder.

"What good would a sheet of paper do?" he asked, just behind her.

She spun around. They were standing approximately where it had all begun. "I can do this," she stammered. "You go on back—"

"You trying to keep me out of the kitchen, Lill?"

Aromas of coffee and aftershave teased her nose. She turned away. "What? No, don't be silly."

"Could have fooled me." He looked at the guilty wall. "I don't need to be in this room to remember."

"Rod—"

He touched her cheek. "I miss you, Lill."

A delicate little shiver shot up the back of her scalp, as if someone had tickled her brain with a tiny feather. She shook her head at him. "How can you? We barely got started."

"I know. But doesn't that tell you something?"

"Oh Rod, don't—"

"Just tell me the truth. You miss me too, don't you?"

She looked away, her eyes intent on the freshly brewed pot of coffee, the steam still wisping from the top of the machine. He was right. It made no sense but she did. She missed his sense of humour, his easy familiarity, his touch, all that after only one night together.

"I think we deserve a chance, Lill."

"Why? Why me?"

"Why not you? You know, you don't strike me as insecure, but you sure are funny about this."

"It's just that there are lots of single women in Port Grace. Young women, with nice tight little bodies, not old widows like me."

"Believe me, the last thing I want is another woman striving for perfection. And quite frankly, since I've been back I haven't met anyone who could hold a candle to you. You might not realize this, Lill, but I've wanted to get to know you better ever since I started at the school."

"Really?"

"I'm not surprised you didn't notice. I could never seem to get your attention. You were always busy with students, or rushing off somewhere. It wasn't until your birthday party that I thought you knew I was alive."

Her heart was pulsing. She could feel the heat in her face. "I don't know, Rod, it's still—"

Moving within a hair of her, he gently raised her face and kissed her on the mouth. She felt as if her body was floating, and only his lips kept her grounded. Leaning back, he looked into her eyes. His fingers came up and brushed some stray hairs back off her face. They were both silent. Then he kissed her again, letting his lips linger on hers.

"Mom?"

Lill shoved Rod away and instinctively wiped her mouth. David towered in the doorway in T-shirt and boxers, but instead of looking shocked, he had an embarrassed grin on his lean handsome face.

"Sorry. Uh…hi Mr. Corcoran."

"Hi David. Yeah, well, we were just—"

"I just wanted some juice," David cut in, his brown eyes widening.

Rod jumped away from the counter. "Sorry, I'm in the way here."

"No, you're not in the way, Mr. Corcoran. It's fine."

Lill glanced at Rod. After all his talk, she was surprised to discover that he was the nervous one.

Max trudged in, his eyes thick with sleep, his dark hair a pile of kinks on top of his head. "Hi Mr. Corcoran. Morning Mom. Where's the juice?"

It was abnormally quiet in the crowded kitchen.

"What? What's going on?" asked Max, looking dazed.

"Nothing," muttered Lill at the same moment as David. He grinned at her. "You guys want a bran muffin?" she asked.

"Yuck," Max grimaced. "Bran muffins are for old people, Mom."

Both boys took their juice into the living room and turned on the television. The overzealous voices of sportscasters filled the background.

She grinned at Rod. "How many muffins did you have?"

"Two."

"You're older than you look."

"That's what I keep trying to tell you." He nodded towards the living room. "Sorry about that Lill. I never heard a thing. Hard to believe they could be so quiet."

"Yeah, really! Normally there's not a quiet bone in their bodies."

"What should we do?"

"I'll talk to them later."

"David seemed pretty cool about it, didn't he?"

She laughed at him. "Cooler than you. 'We were just' what? What were you going to say?"

"Oh God, I don't know," he grinned, red faced. "Okay, so maybe you were a little bit right. This is awkward. But that's all you were right about."

"I don't know, Rod. Let me think on it. And let me feel them out about it."

"Okay, whatever you need to do." One finger reached out to touch her chin. "Maybe I should go for now. I'll take the manual home and input some of the changes. Jim had Betty scan it into the computer yesterday. After I print it off, we can have a read through, see how it's sounding. Okay?"

"Sure. Why don't you bring it over after lunch tomorrow?"

"Okay." He looked down, then almost shyly, back up at her. "Guess I'll just go."

Smiling, she nodded. There'd be no kiss goodbye.

Once he was gone, she joined the boys at the TV. They'd switched over to a rerun of Ripley's and Max stared mesmerised, fascinated as live snakes squirmed around a scantily clad woman's body. David seemed less absorbed.

"Any homework this weekend?" she asked.

"A bit." He rubbed his bristly chin.

"Anything else going on?"

"There's a party at Kev Bartlett's tonight. I'll be out pretty late."

"Who's driving?"

"Sharon, so don't worry. She never drinks."

"Just make sure you come home with her and not someone else, okay?"

They both knew his days of being told what to do were numbered. He'd be off to University in a few months, living with strangers. She wouldn't be there to remind him anymore, to keep him safe. Still, they kept up the charade.

"Grilled cheese for lunch?"

"Yeah," Max piped up.

She made the sandwiches and poured milk for them all. As they munched away at the kitchen table, Max entertained them with imitations of some of his teachers, her colleagues. She shouldn't have laughed but she did; he was pretty good at it. He had his father's chocolate brown eyes, even darker than his brother's, and they twinkled back at her.

"You got an imitation of Mr. Corcoran?" David asked, glancing at her.

"Nah, he's too normal. Nothing weird enough about him."

Lill coughed. "Do you guys like Rod, I mean, Mr. Corcoran?"

"Yeah, he's great," said Max. "Everybody likes Mr. Corcoran."

David made a show of clearing his throat. "And do you like Mr. Corcoran, Mother? Or should I say, 'Rod'?" he asked in mock seriousness.

"Well, I—"

"Or, more importantly," he interrupted, obviously enjoying himself, "does Mr. Corcoran, a.k.a. 'Rod', like Mother?"

"David!" she warned.

Max was looking at them strangely. "What's going on, Dave?"

Lill jumped in before he had a chance to answer. "Pay no mind to that brother of yours, Max. The truth is, Mr. Corcoran and I, well we… he asked me out on a date. I told him I needed to talk to you two first."

"You mean like out to dinner or something?" Max's brow creased over very serious eyes.

"Yeah, like that."

"And you want our permission?" he asked, looking confused again.

"Sort of. Not really, I suppose, but kind of." Good God, what *did* she mean?

"Wow." At fifteen, Max was inordinately shy with girls and hadn't started dating yet.

"So, should we let her, Max?" David teased, leaning nonchalantly back in his chair. "She's a little out of practice with men. Maybe she should take some lessons first."

"Ha ha, very funny," Lill said.

"That's what you always make us do with something new," David reminded her coyly.

"I was married to your father for eighteen years, you know. I'm hardly new at this."

"Being married is not like dating, Mom," David informed her. He gathered their dirty plates together and dumped them noisily into the sink. "Things have changed in the last few decades."

"You should listen to him, Mom, he knows what he's talking about," Max added, glancing respectfully towards his older brother.

"All right, enough out of you two." Lill joined her hands together and leaned forward on her elbows. "Listen. Really, how would you feel if I went out with Mr. Corcoran?"

"First off, you got to stop calling him 'Mister'."

"David! You know what I mean. Be serious for a minute, please."

Her sons looked at each other and laughed. They made it seem so easy.

"I think it'd be great," said Max.

Sitting back down, David turned serious. He looked so much like his father at that moment, it took Lill's breath away. "Sometimes I feel sad when I go out on a Friday night," he said, "leaving you here alone with nothing but the television and a glass of wine."

Max nodded in agreement.

She hadn't thought they'd noticed, and was sorry they had. An image of a lonely old drunk flashed through her mind. "What about him being younger than me?" she asked, shoving the previous thought aside.

"He's younger?" Max looked puzzled again. All in all, it was turning out to be a very baffling morning for the poor boy, thought Lill. "You look about the same to me," he added.

"What's the age difference?" asked David.

"Seven years. Well, eight until his birthday," she added guiltily.

"It's usually men who are older than the girls, aren't they?" Max asked.

"Yeah, but that's kind of sexist," said her enlightened oldest. "If men can do it, why not women?"

Lill smiled, surprised. She'd often worried if she sounded like a broken record on equal rights, and not just for women. As a mother of two boys, she'd sometimes felt they were more discriminated against than females, by teachers, and storekeepers, and many others who didn't understand the teenage male species. She was as committed to their equality as she was to her own. And when it came to girls, she'd been just as watchful and worried about who David dated and hung out with as any father of a teenage girl would be. She didn't want some pushy or insecure young girl getting either of her sons into sex before they were ready, or at least before they made their own conscious decision. But as much as she'd harped on about all of it over the years, she was never really sure if they were listening. It was nice to see a little payback for all her preaching.

"That's true," Max readily agreed.

"What about the neighbours though? And your friends?" Lill persisted. "What would they think about your old mother going out with one of their teachers?"

"First off, you're not that old. And second, who cares?" David answered with the carefree innocence of one who'd never been ridiculed. "What do they know about anything?"

Max nodded but said nothing.

"You might feel different if you heard them making remarks about me sometime, though. I don't want to put you in that position." She spoke to David, but she was watching for Max's reaction. He was by nature the less confident of the two, and she'd often wondered if not having a father during his early teens had exacerbated that. He looked to his brother for the answer.

"Mom, if you want to go out with Mr. Corcoran, whatever Mick or Charlie might have to say about it really doesn't matter," David assured her. "What matters is that you're happy and not so alone."

"I'm not alone!" she insisted, spreading her arms wide. "I've got you two."

"Yeah, for another couple of months. Then it's just you and Max, and he'll be gone in a couple of years. What are you going to do then?"

"It's not your job to be worrying about me. It's the other way around, remember? And if me having a date is going to cause either one of you trouble, then I don't want it and that's that. It's just not that important." She leaned back and folded her arms across her chest.

"Well, all I can tell you is that it's fine by me. How about you, Max?"

Lill didn't want it to be like this, with Max on the spot. "You know," she interrupted before he could answer, "I'd rather you both thought about it a little bit first. Then when you're ready, tell me what you think? Okay? Please?"

David rolled his eyes and said sure; Max copied him to the last raised eyebrow.

Jumping up, she went to start the laundry, grateful for the mindless tasks before her. She needed time to think, about her children and her sisters, about her colleagues and neighbours. About why she was putting up road-blocks. Both boys seemed fine with the idea of her dating. And really, she asked herself, what if they weren't? Didn't she deserve a private life? Was she just using the boys as an excuse not to go out with Rod, as a reason to stay in her safe little life, night after night after lonely night?

She didn't think so. But then again, maybe?

Later that afternoon she was sorting the clothes, dreaming about summer when there'd be enough time and sunshine to hang them on the line, when Max sauntered into the kitchen. In the last year he'd grown several inches and was finally taller than her.

"Need some help?" he offered.

"You sick or something?" she laughed. "Never mind. Dig in."

He picked up a shirt and began to fold it. "So, you want to go out with Mr. Corcoran, eh?"

She flicked her hand as if waving it off. "Maybe."

"He's a pretty nice guy, Mom. You could do a lot worse, you know."

"Again, maybe. I'm doing okay without him or anyone else right now, so it's not as if I'm dying for a date."

"You must get kind of lonely sometimes though. Me and David are gone a lot. And he's right, you'll be all alone in a couple of years."

Yes, she did get lonely. Damn lonely. It was only now that Rod was in the picture that she realised how incredibly lonely she actually was. But that was her problem, not her sons'. "I'm a big girl, Max. Maybe I'll get a new hobby or something. And it's not like you'll be gone forever, you'll be home on weekends and stuff."

"But that's not the same as meeting somebody," he insisted, pretending to fold a pair of gym shorts while he studiously avoided looking at her. "I never thought about you that way before, you know, dating and stuff, so I was kind of surprised today. But wouldn't it be nice?"

He was so earnest, his young serious face bursting with concern. He deserved for her to be just as straightforward. "Oh, Max, it would only be nice if there was no way you would ever be hurt by it. I'd never want it to come between us or give you any grief."

"It wouldn't, Mom." His gaze was so intense, it was like he was asking for the moon. "Honest to God, it never would."

She put down the shirt she'd been holding and studied him for just a second. "Max? Are you trying to talk me into it?"

He blushed. "Ah…no. It's just that it'd be kind of cool, you know?"

"How so?"

"Well, Mr. Corcoran would be around here a lot then, wouldn't he?"

"I suppose."

"That'd be cool."

"You like him, don't you?"

"Yeah, he's not like the other teachers. I think he really likes kids, and he's always been real nice to me."

"Really?" This was the first she'd heard of it, but that was hardly surprising. Max was not the most forthcoming with casual chit chat.

"Uh huh. Showed me a couple of great wrestling moves in gym when he subbed for Mr. Smith. I love it when he subs for him. Old Smitty's useless on the mats. Everywhere else too. You know, he subs for him a lot lately. Is Smitty sick or something?"

"He hasn't been feeling very good lately. Poor old Ned's getting up there."

"Up there! He's ancient, and round as a barrel, not like Mr. Corcoran. Now, he's in shape."

Lill smiled at the compliment, as pleased as if he'd said something flattering about her. "You're building up some good muscle yourself there, bud. I've been noticing you're really filling out."

Max beamed. He was always trying to keep up to David. "Mr. Corcoran says I've got the makings of a great wrestler. He said I'm probably the best in my weight category."

"Really? That's great."

"It's awesome." He thought for a moment. "If he was over here more, he could help me train."

"I should go out with him so you can learn how to wrestle?"

"No, I didn't mean it like that. But if you did, then he could, right?"

"I suppose so, Max. I'll take that into consideration."

"Anyway, whatever you do is fine by me, Mom. Just so you know."

"Thanks, kiddo, I'll keep you posted." She gave him a conspiratorial little grin. "In the meantime, don't say anything about it, okay?"

"You mean like to Aunt Marlene?" he laughed.

"I swear you can read my mind." She opened her arms and he wrapped his around her.

The doorbell chimed into the CBC news. Lill switched off the radio. It was the same one she'd listened to for years sitting on her father's knee after supper, and it took pride of place on the oak shelf above the fridge. She heard David answer the door on his way out, and a series of rushed hellos and goodbyes before the door shut once again.

She poked her head around the kitchen archway. "Go ahead and set up over there on the couch. I'll be right in."

By the time she'd gathered the tea and cups and cookies, Rod had spread papers over the coffee table and was seated on the couch. He was holding his laptop, but it remained unopened. He seemed lost in thought.

"Everything okay?" she asked, pushing some of the papers aside to make room for the tea. He immediately leaned forward to help her.

"Yeah. Sure. Max home?"

"No, he's babysitting at Marlene's again, poor kid. He wanted to cancel when he heard you were coming over, but I wouldn't let him."

"Oh, good. I mean… we can talk if it's just us, right?" He glanced around, as if someone might appear out of the woodwork any second.

Remembering his embarrassment of the day before, she smiled. "I suppose so."

"So, what did you say to the boys?"

"That you asked me out on a date," she answered, noticing his curly hair still damp from the shower. "And I wanted to talk to them first, to see how they felt about it."

"And?"

She felt shy suddenly. He was pretty up-front, and she wasn't used to that. "They both said it was fine. David seemed happy that I might get out of the house on a Saturday night, and Max was even more pleased that it was with you."

He leaned towards her. "So? How do you feel about it now?"

Lill sighed. "This dating business is complex, you know that? On the one hand, I'm relieved they're so easy-going about it all. On the other, I worry." She paused. "David's not the problem, and maybe Max isn't either. It's just I always think of him as vulnerable. Steve died when he was so young, I'm never sure he gets enough of a male take on things. If you come into the picture, it scares me for Max."

"Wait now. If he likes me, that should be a good thing."

"True." She frowned at him. How could she explain that that was the problem? That she was afraid Max might get too attached, and then when, or if, they broke up, he might pay the highest price. She wasn't going to begin to think about how she'd feel. "Okay, here it is. I'm just going to say it because so far we've been pretty honest and I'd just as soon keep it that way. Yes, I'd like to see where we can go, but I'm realistic. I'm not assuming we're going to last, or that we're not. You can't start a relationship with either of those predetermined. But the fact is, I worry that if we don't last, then Max could end up being the most hurt of us all. Do you see where I'm coming from?"

"I think I do, Lill, girl." Looking hard at her, he rubbed his chin. "How honest we getting here, anyway?"

She swallowed, staring back at him. "Look, I know men are not supposed to talk about feelings and emotions and all that, at least Steve never did, but I'm getting the feeling you're different. Anything to that?"

He sighed self-consciously. "I sure as hell hope so." He stopped, his eyes fixed on hers. "The thing is, Lill, the last two years in Toronto I was going to a shrink."

"A shrink?" she blurted before she could stop to think.

"Yeah. I met him playing squash, and ended up seeing him twice a week in his office."

"Oh." She hesitated briefly. "Was he any good?"

"He was. He had a wall full of degrees and diplomas, and a big fancy office downtown Toronto, but it was even more than that. Theo Sidorski really knew his stuff."

It occurred to Lill that going to a psychiatrist could explain a lot about Rod. Such as the fact that he had always struck her as being more evolved than most men she knew, and could talk about things, feelings, without having to be cajoled into it. Perhaps too easily though? She glanced sideways at him, and wondered if he had decided to tell her about the psychiatrist before they went any further, to see what her reaction might be. He sat quietly, patiently waiting for her to speak. She'd have been chomping at the bit if the tables were reversed, anxious to justify herself, impatient to find out what he thought. Then again, maybe that was it. Maybe he wasn't normal. After all, he'd had to go to a shrink. Maybe he wasn't quite fixed yet. Maybe he was nuts, certifiable. Maybe that was why he'd been attracted to her in the first place, and was so determined to go out with her. She glanced at him again, then immediately looked away. Good Christ, what had she gotten herself into?

He stood up abruptly. "Look, I'm sorry, Lill. Guess we weren't ready for this much truth." He sighed again, and she caught the edge to his voice. "Wasn't such a big frigging deal in Toronto to go to a shrink. Still is here, though, I suppose."

He was good and angry now, she could tell. His face had whitened, and his nostrils flared slightly. But mainly she knew by the timbre of his voice, so rough and deep and full of frustration. And rightly so, she realised.

"Good Christ, Rod, I'm the one who should be sorry. I didn't mean to clam up like that, it's just I was so surprised. The ridiculous truth is I've never known anyone who's ever gone to a psychiatrist."

"And now you do." He remained standing, but she thought she detected a slight softening in his voice.

"Yeah well, maybe you're the lucky one. There's plenty here that could use a good shrink. In fact, a couple of weeks ago I was wishing for one myself."

"You?" he asked, eyebrows raised.

"Yeah, me," she answered defensively. "You're not the only one with problems, you know." Well, wasn't this just ducky. They were fighting over who was crazier. Lill had a sudden fear that she might win.

He burst out laughing. "Sorry. Didn't mean to corner the market."

She could feel the red rushing to her face. "Good God, never mind…"

"Lill," he cut in, sitting back down and grabbing her hand. "I am sorry. Honest. Sorry for dumping this in your lap. Sorry for upsetting you just now. But I'm not sorry about the shrink. I'll never be sorry for that. In fact, I'm not sure where I would have ended up without Theo."

His fingers were gently stroking her hand, and his skin felt warm and safe against her own. She wanted to kiss him, on the hand, on the mouth, anywhere, to touch her lips to his warm male skin. "He really helped, eh?" she asked instead.

"Helped? If it wasn't for Theo, I wouldn't be sitting here today. He helped me put my life together, and then he sent me back here." He paused for just a moment. "Home. To Port Grace."

The way he looked at her, his face so serious and sincere, she almost felt as if he'd added, "To you".

"So!" she smiled, but could think of nothing to add.

"It's okay, Lill. Go ahead, what are you thinking?"

What she was thinking was that he seemed so calm, so certain, so sure of himself. So different from Steve. "I was wondering why you went to a psychiatrist?"

He blinked at her. "You really have to ask that, knowing my history?"

"Yeah, your history. Is there anything else there I should know?"

"I'm guessing there's lots you already do."

"Well, I did grow up here," she said apologetically.

"Right. So you know Janie's my actual mother, and all the other rumours?"

"I've heard the gossip. I'm not sure how much any of it matters."

"It used to matter to me, one time. Still does, I suppose. But what can you say to rumours about yourself when you don't even have a clue what's true?" For just a moment, he looked more like a lost child than the self-assured man she'd come to know.

"Janie never told you?" she asked quietly, wishing for his sake that she didn't already have the answer.

"No, neither did Ida, at least not who else it could be."

"That's tough, not ever knowing."

He kept his eyes on the floor as he spoke, and she had the impression that it was tougher than he was letting on. "Yeah, especially when someone does know and they won't tell you. Makes you think the worst no matter what they say."

"I suppose it would." She took a deep breath. "What about your marriage?"

"Yeah, that. It wasn't pretty Lill, at least not after the first year or so."

"They usually aren't when they break up, are they?"

"Nope. This got uglier than most, though." He rubbed his forehead. "To make a long story short, we were together for two years and then Pamela got pregnant. Unexpectedly."

Lill had heard nothing about his having children. "What happened?"

"She aborted it. No discussion, nothing. Just went and had it done, like I had nothing to do with it." He shook his head and sighed. "The thing is, I never even wanted to have kids, never thought I should, actually, but that really hit me, when she did that."

His arms were crossed, his lips pressed tight together. He looked so hurt, and so angry. Reaching out, she squeezed his right arm where it was folded tightly over his left. Immediately, she felt the tension decrease. "I'm so sorry, Rod. What a rotten thing to do."

"Yeah, well, she wasn't sorry. It wouldn't have worked anyway, the marriage, but that killed it for sure."

He seemed edgy, as if he had more to tell, but was unsure of how to say it. She waited for a minute or two, then asked finally, "Is that why you brought Jenny to me?"

He looked puzzled, as if his mind was stuck somewhere else. She wondered if he was remembering his ex-wife, and what that memory entailed.

"Jenny?" he asked. "Oh, right, Jenny Hayden." He nodded, but then shook his head. "I don't believe in abortion, Lill. I think it's wrong in the eyes of God and the eyes of man. Especially the man, the father."

"Even in Jenny's case? Surely to God you can see that's not the same." Her voice had risen and she didn't try to lower it. If he couldn't see the difference between Pamela and Jenny, she needed to know.

"No, it's not the same. That's why I asked you for help. Jenny was different."

"I'm glad we agree on that," she said guardedly, "but I think that's all we agree on."

"How so?" He sat up straighter, more rigid.

She could tell by the line of his mouth that this was personal to him. Considering his past, she could hardly blame him.

"I'm not talking about what happened in your marriage, Rod. That sounds just as different as Jenny's case, but in almost the complete opposite way. You were married and having a life together. What I'm talking about is most of the time when a woman has an abortion. She's got to have a right to it, I don't care what the church says. It's her body and her life. I know it's the same old line, but that's because it hasn't changed in a million years." She noticed that her own back was stiff and upright, and made an effort to drop her shoulders.

He seemed to have the same inclination. "It certainly is a thorny issue," he said, his mouth softening as he smiled at her. "Did we just have our first fight?"

"Nah," she said, relieved. "Disagreement? Discussion, maybe?"

He brushed a stray hair from her forehead, then let his fingers trace her jaw line. "Hope they're all this calm. So, are we okay, about the psychiatrist and all?"

Her hand came up to meet his, and she smiled into his warm green eyes. "My father always said don't be too quick to judge. He was usually right."

"Sounds like a smart man. So, anything else you want to know? I'm in the mood for true confessions."

"It's some ridiculous, isn't it?" she asked with a light laugh. "And it's not fair. Just because this is complicated, it doesn't mean we can't leave a little mystery to it. Not many people starting out on a first date have to jump through this many hoops."

"I think we've had our first date, Lill," he said with a sexy grin, reaching out to tickle her arm.

Laughing, she pushed his hand away. "And that's another thing. I've got two impressionable boys in the house. I can't be caught doing what I tell them not to do."

"Can't be caught?" he asked, his eyes twinkling. "I like the way that sounds. It's a lot better than 'I can't do what I tell them not to do.' Which one did you mean?"

She blushed, fully aware which one she meant. The truth was, she couldn't get it out of her head. "I'm serious, Rod."

"I know, I know. And I agree. We'll be really careful, I promise," he vowed, even as he moved towards her.

Just then the door burst open and Max practically fell into the room. He looked as if he'd run all the way from Marlene's. "Oh, hi Mr. Corcoran." He managed to almost sound surprised.

"Hey, Max," Rod exclaimed, springing back. "Working on a Sunday, eh?"

"Yeah," he muttered with an accusatory glance at Lill. "But not by choice, that's for sure."

"Same here. Unfortunately, this manual's not going to write itself."

"That it won't," said Lill. "I suppose we better get to it." In fact, she was looking forward to it. Enough with the heavy conversations for a while.

"Will it bother you guys if I work on the computer?" asked Max, looking uncertainly from one to the other.

"Not at all. Go ahead," Lill smiled at him.

They settled down to work. Occasionally they interrupted each other with a question or made a comment or generalisation. It was a comfortable arrangement, one that seemed to suit all three of them. When David came home it was only natural to invite Rod for supper. He helped prepare the food and set the table, and they shared a relaxed Sunday evening dinner together of roast chicken, potatoes, and peas and carrots.

Lill felt a sense of satisfaction, then a niggling anxiety.

Too easy too fast made her nervous.

New as they were, and as controversial as they might be to a few narrow-minded people, they were in no hurry to venture out in public. Max and David seemed to understand this, and said nothing beyond the house.

Although weekdays were busy with work and family and all the minute details that went with both, she and Rod, and Max usually, spent large chunks of the weekends together—cooking nice dinners, watching videos, playing cards. It was a chaste time of getting to know each other, a time to try on their personalities to see if they were a good fit. All in all, Lill thought they were much like the salt and pepper on the kitchen table.

The chaste part was not by their design. Max had suddenly lost interest in most of his normal pursuits, and spent the weekend evenings with them. Lill did not think for a second that he was doing it out of some need to keep them chaperoned. He truly appeared to like their company, and for her part she found it hard to resist his obvious pleasure. He acted very mature around them, talking to Rod about wrestling and sports, offering youthful suggestions about the guidance manual, and generally acting as if the three of them were a set. There were no sibling shenanigans like when he and David were together. This was Max the person, not the brother. It was a joy to spend so much time with him. For the most part.

Eight o'clock one Saturday morning, the phone rang. Lill was surprised to hear Rod's voice on the other end.

"What's up with you so early in the morning?" she asked, pouring her first coffee of the day.

"I left my sunglasses there last night. They're on the shelf in the closet."

"I'll put them away for you."

"I need them now, Lill."

"Oh…sure. You coming over?" She rummaged in the cupboard for the bag of sugar. Much like the toilet paper roll, the boys never refilled the sugar dish either.

"I was kind of thinking you could bring them to me."

"Yeah, okay. I got a bunch of stuff to do, the groceries and all that." Finding an empty bag at the back of the shelf, she mentally added sugar to the list. "I'll drop them off later on. Anything you'd like for dinner?"

"I was thinking more of breakfast actually. Something we haven't had in a while, a special breakfast," he said, his voice softening.

She put down her coffee cup. Her midsection had suddenly gotten a deliciously giddy feeling. "Give me fifteen minutes."

The boys were still sleeping and probably would for a couple more hours. As quietly as possible, she showered and dressed, wrote them a vague note about running errands, then made her escape. She arrived at his door in exactly eighteen minutes.

The second the latch sounded behind her they were on each other. Tumbling towards the bedroom, their lips and teeth sucking and biting along the way, Lill felt like she was in an erotic fairytale as their clothes marked the path from porch to bed. Her body just took over. Again. And she let it. Gladly. Even as it did, it registered how unreal it all seemed. She, who had learned to lay there, under Steve, resigned to a quick finish but yearning for more, had become an animal with Rod. She writhed against him as she held him tight, her mouth starved for his lips, her tongue teasing his nipples, her breasts straining against his chest. One minute she was on top, the next she was on the bottom, her legs wrapped around his waist. She could not believe the urges that ripped through her. Yes, she'd glimpsed them before, but had been rejected once too often early on in her marriage. After a while, the urges had gone away. At least when she was awake.

And she was fully awake, as awake and alive as she'd ever been. But except for an occasional mutter or moan, she said nothing and neither did he. As they dove into each other, Lill couldn't stop her hands from trailing all along his skin, relishing the feel of his muscular arms and broad shoulders. It was as though her fingers had their own urgency, a hunger to touch and pinch and grasp, to savour the feel of his tight bum, his curly hair and furry chest. At times they were almost fighting for position, each trying to caress some neglected nook or erogenous dimple. Then he was inside her. It seemed to happen automatically, without any placement or planning, as if it knew where to go, and when to go there. She felt her body swell as the heat inside her rose up, filling her with pure lust, pure pleasure. And like the first time with Rod, she knew waves of fulfilment she'd never imagined with her husband of eighteen years.

Nestled into the curve of Rod's body spooning hers, Lill glanced at the clock. Their after-sex snuggle had lasted several minutes, yet it was barely a quarter of an hour since she'd knocked at the door.

Rod pulled her closer and wrapped his legs around her. "Just the appetizer, right?"

It was irresistible not to do it again. Slowly. And tender, oh so very tender.

By eleven she was home with the groceries, bags and bags of the most indiscriminate shopping she'd ever done. Articles had flown into the cart, filling it up in record time, proof that she'd been an industrious little mother and not out shagging the school's new vice-principal. Her face was flushed, presumably from running up and down the aisles.

She was still unpacking when David wandered into the kitchen. Looking like he'd just rolled out of bed, he was dressed in his rowing gear and his hair was uncombed. "You're on the go some early," he grumbled, opening a fresh bag of cheese bagels.

"Early bird gets the worm," she chirped happily.

Rubbing his eyes, he looked at her strangely. "A little chipper this morning, aren't we?"

"I thought I'd get a head start on supper, maybe marinate something."

"Sure, whatever." He picked up a small tuna-sized tin. "We get a cat?"

Lill stopped and looked at the can he held out to her. A grey tabby stared back, his pink tongue halfway around his lips. "Ah…no… but there's a stray sometimes, comes around. Always looks hungry."

"Oh, okay. I'll be home about six, all right? The boys are off to St. John's for a concert, but I've got too much studying to do to be up all night with them."

"Glad to see you're taking your finals so seriously, David." Lill had always had to nag him about schoolwork, and she'd long feared that his grades would be too low to get him into the program he wanted at university.

"Like I always said, mother dear, MUN is not going to be looking back to my grade six marks to decide if I get in or not."

"Well, you may be right. Still, if you'd studied more, maybe you'd be able to go to that concert tonight." It was a new twist on a familiar sermon.

"Let me see." He pretended to think, rubbing his bristly chin in deep consideration. "Twelve years of studying stuff I'll never need, or one night out with the guys. Hmmm. Perhaps you're right, Mother!"

She snapped the tea towel at his legs. "Get out of here, you brazen brat."

To her surprise, he kissed her on the forehead and smiled down at her. She was thankful he'd taken time to brush his teeth. "You seem happier lately, Mom. Things are going okay, huh?"

The question jolted her, and she realised what an unexpected position she was in. Her first-born was turning the tables, making sure that all was well in his mother's life. Stranger still, it did not seem unnatural. In fact, it felt great. "Things are good, David. I don't know how long it'll all last, but right now I'm just having fun."

"I notice our little Maxy is too."

Lill thought for a moment, wondering how far she could trust their new roles. They had always been able to talk easily to each other, a bond that had grown stronger since Steve's death. David was fast becoming an adult, already was one really, and it dawned on her that he would make some girl pretty darn happy someday. The thought saddened and cheered her all at once.

"Mom?" he interrupted her reverie.

"Oh, sorry Davie. Yeah, listen, can I talk to you about something, and will you promise to keep it just between us?"

"Sure, Mom. No problem." Grabbing an apple from the counter, he chomped back a quarter of it in one bite.

"It's about Max. He's always with me and Rod, which is great, don't get me wrong. I love having him around, and he seems to love being with us. The problem is, what if it doesn't work out? What if Rod and I don't keep seeing each other? What will that do to Max?"

Frowning, David shook his tousled head at her. "Max is tougher than he looks, Mom. You really do treat him like some over-sensitive little nerd sometimes."

"I do not!" she snapped, then stopped short. Okay, so maybe she did, but Max was her baby, and part orphan, for heaven's sake. "And even if I do, it's because he needs it. He's not wired like you, there's more of your father in him. Sometimes I'm afraid he'll get run over by everybody else on the way out the door."

David patted her back like a tolerant uncle. "I know you worry about him, but I see him at school. He can take care of himself. He's different there and around his friends, you know."

"You mean he fakes it around here?

"No, not like that. I mean when he needs to, he does just fine for himself. He doesn't have to so much when you're around, so he doesn't. And I don't mean that in a bad way, it's just that when he's home he can let you take care of him, and away from here he's got to act more grown up. You know what I mean?"

Lill groaned. Why was every conversation so complicated lately? "I suppose. It was hard enough keeping track before, now I'm afraid I'm making matters worse by adding another person to the worry list."

"Jesus, Mom!" He rolled his eyes at her. "For the love of God, just go and enjoy it. You've been taking care of us all these years, it's time to relax."

"Maybe. I just hope it doesn't come back to bite me on the arse."

David laughed. "Well, at least it's loosening you up a little. That's got to be good for you."

Yes, she thought, it certainly felt good. To hell with it, she might as well give in and enjoy the ride.

Rod rolled over and stretched luxuriously. After seeing Lill off, he'd gone back to his room to get dressed, but the bed had beckoned. Just for a minute, he told himself, or maybe five. He'd dozed off, wrapped in the sheets that held Lill's fragrance. He could still smell her warm honey scent on his body, feel her soft skin beneath his fingers, hear her laughter as he tickled her toes.

It had been quite a month. Never before had he been so satisfied with his life. He had a job he loved, he was near his family again, and for the first time in his life, he felt at peace with Port Grace. But most of all, there was Lill. Lill completed the picture. Rod felt such joy in hearing her voice on the phone, such pleasure in sharing a simple cup of coffee, such excitement at the touch of her hand. Being with Lill was different and better than anything he'd ever experienced.

Rod's only fear was that somehow he would screw it up. During his sessions with Theo Sidorski he'd learned much about himself, such as the fact that he didn't truly know how to be happy. He didn't trust that he deserved happiness, that he had just as much right to it as the next guy. On the bright side, he also learned to quit being so hard on himself, and to accept that some things were beyond his control; when things went wrong, it was not necessarily his fault.

During his marriage to Pamela, he'd blamed himself for most of their problems. Maybe he didn't pay enough attention to her, or maybe he paid too much and she was smothering; if only he could be more assertive, or less; perhaps if he made more money, was more educated, came from a better family. These doubts had plagued him even before they were married, but he'd pushed them aside in his relief at having found such a seemingly normal person. Pamela was from a regular family—a mother and father and a sister and brother. He didn't know them well, and found them uncomfortable to be around, but he assumed that was his fault. They were all educated and cultured, with season's tickets to the theatre and opera. They drank wine and martinis, not rum and beer. To Rod, Pamela's life had followed an idyllic track, from ballet classes to cheerleader to homecoming queen. Her model existence was reflected in her apartment—meticulous, the crystal figurines and other collectibles always arranged just so, the towels perfectly placed along the racks. Even their infrequent sex life had a pattern, at least at first, but he didn't mind. He always knew when and how it would happen, no guessing, no games. Above all else, Pamela was about order, precision, a time and a place for all things. Rod longed for such a life.

It didn't take them long to realize their mistake, although neither rushed to admit it. Rod would have liked to be able to look back and say he'd worked at it, that he'd made a decent effort to save his marriage, but the only thing he'd done consistently was deny the problem. Even when Pamela had tried to broach the subject, which wasn't often or with much conviction, he'd managed to avoid any worthwhile discussion. He only knew that if his marriage did not succeed, it would prove that the people of Port Grace had been right about him and his family all along. After all, he'd married the perfect woman. If it failed, the fault could only lie with him.

And then Pamela had the abortion. He would never have known if he hadn't lost his credit card. Fearing it had been thrown out in one of Pamela's cleaning binges, he was searching through a bag of garbage she'd tied up ready for the trash when he came across a pregnancy test kit. It had been a particularly bad week in which they'd had little nice to say to each other. Seeing the box, he began to wonder if a pregnancy was at the root of the problem. They didn't have sex that often, but it only took the once. Could it be possible? He decided then and there that if it was, if Pamela was pregnant, then it was time to work on his marriage. He would do whatever she wanted, be whatever she asked, say whatever she needed to hear.

With a renewed sense of hope, he went to find her.

She was standing at their twelfth floor window, staring off into the muddle of buildings that made up their landscape.

"Pamela? Are you pregnant?" he asked, the discarded box in his hands.

Her face seemed to freeze, and her hands curled up into fists.

"Honey, did you hear me?" he asked as gently as he could, trying to quell the fear and excitement in his voice.

"Yes, I heard you, and no, I'm not."

He could hardly believe his disappointment. The shadow of parenthood had hung for mere minutes, yet it seemed as though something precious had been snatched from his hands. "Oh. Sorry."

"Sorry? Why on earth would you be sorry? And why," she demanded, grabbing the box from his hand, "were you hunting through my garbage?"

"I wasn't," he tried to explain. "I was looking for—"

"Looking for what? Snooping around, checking up on me, watching me all the time."

Rod had no idea what she was talking about at first. Then he remembered the odd phone calls, how on several occasions she had abruptly replaced the receiver the minute he entered the room, and twice the week before she'd locked herself in the bedroom and told him to leave her alone when he'd asked if she was okay. And that was after she'd taken a sick day but didn't answer the phone when he called her from school. He'd tried to reach her all morning to see how she was, and, increasingly worried, had finally come home during his lunch hour. She wasn't there. Later that evening when he asked her about it, she said she'd slept till noon and then had gone for a walk. At the time he'd let it go even though it had sounded suspicious.

Standing there looking at her, the obvious explanation hit him—Pamela was having an affair. The thought initially struck him as odd because she'd never really enjoyed sex. His biggest surprise, however, was his own reaction. He didn't care. In fact, he felt somewhat relieved. Better her than him.

"I'm not watching you," he said innocently. "Why? Is there something you're trying to hide?"

"No."

"Then why do you think I'm watching you?" He found himself treating it as a game, like cat and mouse.

"Coming home from school to check up on me! How dare you? And now going through the garbage, for pity's sake."

He flipped out his credit card. "Found what I was looking for. And then some," he added.

"Well, goody for you."

He decided to take a chance. "Came across a strange phone number too. Not my handwriting, yours most likely."

She gave him a sideways glance, then looked swiftly away. "Big deal, a phone number."

"Wonder whose number that is, who I'd get if I rang it up."

"Shut up, Rod, and mind your own business."

"I think this is my business."

"No, it's my goddamn business. It's got fuck all to do with you." Pamela's normally pale face was flushed with defiance. She rarely swore.

"Bullshit! Of course it has to do with me." He was feeling far less calm as the conversation progressed.

"Maybe, but it's still my decision." She stared directly at him, purposely holding his gaze.

He held hers as well. "Who is he, Pamela?"

The defiance melted somewhat. "Who is who?"

"You know damn well who. Christ!"

She started to laugh then, an unpleasant mocking chuckle that rang hollow throughout the room. "You think I'm having an affair! Jesus, you really are stupid."

It was Rod's turn to be confused. "What? Then what was all that?"

She turned a patronising smirk on him. "I'm not having anything. I already had it."

"Pamela, what the fuck are you talking about?"

Her face hardened; for an instant she reminded him of Janie. "I had an abortion, that's what I had. God, an affair! Like I'd want more sex. What a laugh!"

He was stunned. "An abortion?"

She wasn't laughing. "Yes, an abortion. I wasn't bringing a baby into this marriage. No way."

"But you didn't even talk to me about it? How could you just go and—?"

"It's my body, Rod. I get to make the decisions about what happens to it."

"But it—"

"Look, the bottom line is—"

"Fuck the bottom line! You had no right—"

"I had every right." A satisfied smirk ran across her face. "Besides, it's done now and there's not a damn thing you can do about it."

In a fit of impotent rage, he grabbed her arms. Furious fingers dug into flesh, the bones beneath hard and thin. He closed his eyes and squeezed because that was all he could think to do. Unless he took his hands from her arms, and then he didn't know what might happen, what he might hit, or break, what his hands might do if they weren't squeezing her arms.

Only her whimpers brought him back. He opened his eyes and looked into the terrified face of his wife.

Pamela. Even after three years away from her, three years in which he'd analysed his life from top to bottom, her memory still made him cringe. Perhaps it always would. Perhaps there were not enough hours in a lifetime to do the job justice. He could live with that.

Now that Lill Dunn was in his life, he thought he could live with just about anything.

9

When I was six, I still slept with my older sister, at least for the first part of the year. I always felt safe with Noreen lying beside me.

One day I saw Noreen and my mother whispering together after they came out of the bathroom. I had seen them act secretive like this before but they would never tell me what they were talking about. And I really did want to know because I had noticed that it always made Noreen grumpy, and I hated when she was cross like that. So that day, after they were gone, I went into the bathroom and looked around. I was just about to give up and leave when I noticed something lumpy in the garbage can. I shut the door and listened to make sure no one was coming, then I snuck it out and unfolded it. It was a long soft pad that had gone harder in the middle, and it had reddish brown stuff soaked into it. I was dying to know what it was, but since I was pretty sure I wasn't supposed to see it, I couldn't ask.

About a month later I was in the bathroom again after Noreen had used it. In the garbage I saw another clumpy thing with toilet paper wrapped around it. Wishing there was some way I could lock the door, I took the thing out of the trash and opened it up. My breath caught. There was blood on it, and I realized then that it was probably blood the time before too. Did this happen to Noreen all the time, I wondered, feeling suddenly frightened. Maybe she had been bleeding ever since the last time I'd seen the pad and I just hadn't noticed, and no one had told me something was wrong. But here was proof that my big sister, who I loved more than anyone in the world, except maybe my father, had some horrible disease. But again, remembering all the whispering and secrecy between her and my mother, I knew I couldn't ask about it. I slumped onto the toilet seat, imagining Noreen getting skinnier and paler as she died a slow and painful death. I was so upset that I didn't hear the footsteps coming closer. There was a tap on the door and then Noreen walked in, leaving me no chance to put the pad back in the garbage. I was caught red-handed.

"Lilly, don't touch that!"

As soon as I looked up at her, my lips started to tremble. I couldn't believe I'd gone and made it worse. Noreen was probably dying and now she was mad at me too. I burst out crying.

"Oh Lilly, it's not that bad," she said, kneeling next to me.

"It is so that bad," I sobbed. "Look at all the blood."

"Oh, that. That's nothing." Her voice sounded so disgusted I knew it wasn't nothing.

"Why are you bleeding Norrie? Are you dying?"

"Lilly!" she laughed. "No girl, I'm not dying. This'll happen to you too in a few years."

I shrank back against the cold toilet. "Are we all going to get it?"

"Just the girls, Lilly. Dad's the only one that won't, the lucky dog."

"But all the blood? What's wrong with you?"

"It's called a period. Girls get them when they get older." She rolled her eyes then and blew out an angry breath. "It's supposed to make them into women, and every month they bleed. Every single month for years and years and years, so help me God. Anyway, it's normal. Don't worry about it."

I did worry though. Periods came after sentences, at the end of them. Was this Noreen's sentence, and was it up? I watched her like a hawk, waiting for signs of feebleness, anything that might tell me she needed me to take care of her. But it turned out she was right. She didn't get sick, and she certainly didn't die. She did start to grow little bumps on her chest though. I overheard my mother say-

ing they would buy her a bra on Dad's next payday, and Noreen swearing and yelling that there was no frigging way she was ever going to wear it.

One night I came to from a deep sleep. My hand was touching something soft and warm. Opening my eyes a tiny bit, I realised my sister was putting my hand over her little lumps, first one and then the other. She closed her eyes and let my palm rest on her chest. Her breathing was very hard, and her eyelids fluttered. I shut my eyes, but not too tight, like I'd seen hers when she was sleeping. I tried not to move. Soon, she moved my hand back onto the sheet. Then she rolled over and went to sleep.

What she had done really worried me. Part of me felt it must have been wrong, but I was afraid to ask Mom or Dad. I suspected it had something to do with what Mom called the S-word, which was not something we talked about. The only reason I even knew about it at all was because I'd heard Mom and Mrs. Murray talking about some dirty old man who nobody could catch but who had the town half frightened to death. Mrs. Murray said he was sex-crazy, and Mom was so mad at that she actually swore at Mrs. Murray. "Sex don't have a goddamn thing to do with it, girl," she declared. "Whoever he is he's just plain crazy, and dirty and sick too, to be after little girls, especially poor retards like that Alma Fuller. That's not sex, my dear, that's not." I decided then that sex was something dirty or sick or crazy, and that it scared people. So I never told anyone what Noreen did because I was pretty sure they'd be mad at her, and probably at me too. I was too embarrassed to ask Noreen herself. Still, the same part of me who thought it was wrong wished she'd do it again because I'd forgotten what it felt like. The rest of me felt a little sick about the whole episode.

I don't know if Noreen did do it again. I often tried to stay awake until she came to bed, just in case. Usually I drifted off, too tired to wait for her. So maybe she did, and maybe she didn't.

My grandmother died later that year. She was old and crabby, and although everybody cried and spoke nice about her at the funeral, I didn't think anyone would really miss her. I was wrong. Her dying opened up a whole new bedroom in our house. Noreen, being the oldest, moved into it. So in the end I missed my grandmother more than anybody else because she took Noreen away from me.

When my older sister moved out of our room, the younger one moved in. My father gave me a speech about being good to little Marlene, and how it would be up to me to help take care of her now. As much as I missed Noreen, I took my new responsibilities very seriously.

Marlene was furious about the move. For four years she'd slept in a cot at the foot of my parents' bed, close enough to reach out and touch them. Being sent to sleep with me was like a slap in the face. Every night she kicked and screamed, and every night my mother got more frustrated with me for not doing something about it. But I had no idea how to shut her up. I begged her to stop, I tried to bribe her with candy, I told her that God was watching and was not very pleased. When that didn't work, I told her Santa Claus was even less happy with her behaviour. She actually seemed to stop and think about that one, but she must have decided that Christmas presents were hardly worth being stuck in my bed. And still my mother blamed me, night after night.

Finally, one evening when Marlene started kicking at me under the blankets and calling out for Mom, I lost control. Jumping up in the bed, I took hold of her wrists and glared at her. "Listen here, you little witch. Stop it right now. If you don't shut up I swear on the bible I'll hurt you really bad."

She seemed quite scared at first. Then she narrowed her eyes and her lips scrunched together in a spiteful bunch. I could see her nostrils flaring at me as I sat on top of her. "I'm telling on you," she hissed.

I knew if I let her win this one, she would always win. I'd had it with her, with her crying and screaming and snivelling, and I wasn't going to take it anymore.

She opened her mouth and took a long deep breath, gathering all her energy to yell as loud as she possibly could. Then her lips came together to sound the beginning of "MOM". With the very first noise that started at the back of her throat, a noise that I knew from experience would build into a roar that should have been impossible for any normal four-year-old, I pounced on her and smothered her small mouth with my hand. Clamping down as hard as I could, I looked her dead on. "Are you going to shut up?" I spat down at her. "Are you? Huh?"

Her eyes grew wide and frightened. I felt kind of scared myself, but that just made me crazier. "Answer me, you little monster. Are you going to shut up from now on or what?"

She stared and stared. I pressed harder, suddenly worried that if she didn't shut up I probably would have to go ahead and kill her. Finally her head bobbed under my fingers. Before I took my hand away, I added. "And you better not go telling either. Right?" I asked as fierce as I could.

She nodded again. Letting go completely, I rolled over in the bed and breathed a huge silent sigh of relief. Then I pretended to be asleep. After a while I felt her moving, as if she was getting out of bed.

"Lie down, Marlene," I ordered in as dark and as grown-up a voice as I could find inside me. "Close your eyes and shut up."

She scurried back under the covers. Eventually, she must have fallen asleep.

It didn't take long before she wasn't frightened of me anymore. But by that time, too many nights had passed for her to tell Mom what I had done. Gradually we got used to sleeping in the same bed, although we never did snuggle and whisper in the night the way Noreen and I used to. I missed that.

Some years later, I began that process I'd first heard about through Noreen. My period came, and I wrapped the used pads in toilet paper, always making sure to hide them deep beneath whatever else was in the garbage. I noticed my breasts too, growing from tiny buds below soft nipples into small mounds on my chest. As I lay in bed one night with my younger sister snoring lightly next to me, I remembered the time I'd found my hand on my other sister's breast. I wondered how Noreen had felt, and I began to wonder what it would feel like to have someone touch me there. I looked at Marlene, her mouth open just a bit, smudged from the cookies I'd seen her steal from the pantry before bed. Her face and arms and hands were soft in sleep, completely relaxed, not at all like the bossy cranky sister who stomped through my life day after day.

She grunted and turned to the wall, her dark hair a mess of tangles about her head. I rolled over and went to sleep.

"You knew darn well what time we were going out, Ted." Marlene's voice was sharp, brimming with barely suppressed anger.

Standing in the porch, Lill glanced at Max, who frowned back at her as if asking what they should do. She shrugged. "Just go on in," she whispered.

"Why the hell didn't you call me earlier?" Marlene hissed. "I'm sitting here ready to go."

It was a Thursday evening, and Lill was dropping Max off at her sister's to baby-sit. He didn't really want to, but he hated to say no, and not just because Marlene was his aunt. She paid really well. According to Max, with her kids she had to.

Marlene's eyes narrowed slightly as they lit on Max and Lill coming into the room. A tight smile jumped onto her face. "Never mind, it's okay honey, we'll go as soon as you get here. Just toot the horn and I'll be out."

"Trouble?" asked Lill. She barely stopped herself from adding "in paradise".

"Trouble? Don't be silly, Lillian. Poor man works so hard, I hate for him to be stuck there when we've planned a night out together." She was sitting at the kitchen table, her dyed blond hair stiff as a board, her perfectly made up face scowling at Lill.

"Isn't he supposed to be the boss?" Lill asked.

"Yes," Marlene explained as if to someone not quite bright, "which is exactly why he has to work such long hours. He has lots of business dealings going on, and the hardware store doesn't run itself, you know."

"Ohhh…anyway, here's Max. And now that you're delayed, I guess we can have a little visit." In truth, she was hardly in the mood, considering that even when her sister was in good spirits, Lill didn't particularly enjoy her company.

"Just as well, I've been meaning to talk to you about Dad anyway. That nosy head-nurse from the Home called to tell me they had to change his medication, something about the last stuff making him sick or something. God, that bunch drives me nuts. What's the good of telling me, for Christ's sake? Just change the frigging pills."

"Well, I'm glad they keep us informed, though they usually just tell us on Sundays. Wonder why they didn't this time?"

"They didn't this time, Lillian," Marlene preached at her, "because no one was there on Sunday, as you well know."

"What? How would I know? It was your turn."

"It was not!" Marlene grabbed the calendar from her desk and flipped it back a couple of pages. Her index finger stabbing from Sunday square to Sunday square, she recited whose turn it had been for the previous ten weeks. "Me, you, Noreen, me, you, Noreen, me, you, Noreen, me." Her finger hovered over the square. Starting over, she did it again, with the same results. "Now how on earth did that happen? I was sure it was your turn."

"Oh, you know how it is, we all get busy. Mistakes happen, Marlene."

Marlene looked at her as if to say, "not to me, sister", but Lill let it go. She didn't really care whose turn it was, or who had made the mistake. What bothered her was that no one had been to see her father in almost two weeks, which meant that no one who truly cared about him had patted his arm, or smoothed the thin strands of hair over his head, or kissed his cheek. No loving hand had touched him in eleven long lonely days.

"So, anyway," Lill sighed, deliberately changing the subject. "How you been? Anything new?"

"No, nothing much. Ted's thinking of opening a..." She stopped abruptly, her eyes lighting on Lill. "Never mind that, enough about me and Ted. I haven't talked to you in ages. Yes, I think it's time we do some catching up."

Catching Max's eye, Lill shrugged. Grinning, he mumbled something about going outside with the kids and quickly left, passing Noreen on her way in.

"Hey, look who's here. How's it going Lill?" she asked, wrestling her motorcycle helmet from her head.

Marlene rolled her eyes, barely hiding her annoyance. "Oh...hello Noreen. Ah, what the heck. You two want a cup of tea? Or how about a glass of wine?" Lill was about to decline when Marlene added, "I'll open one of them good bottles Ted's suppliers gave him last Christmas. "

When she'd left to get it, Noreen whispered at Lill, "Wow, a store-bought."

Lill smiled back, happy not to have to drink Ted's awful excuse for home-made wine, and pleased that Marlene was making an effort to be nice.

Handing her a full glass, Marlene asked primly, "How's work, Lill?"

It was one of those topics, and there were several, that Lill tended to avoid around her younger sister. Inevitably, Marlene would turn the conversation around so that Lill felt pitied for having had to go to work, which was not the way Lill saw it at all. Certainly she'd been nervous about starting university as a wife and mother, but that was at least partially because Steve wasn't very supportive. By the end of her first course in basic psychology, however, she loved it. It was never a hardship after, except when she had to be away from the boys. But thanks to her mother and Noreen, they'd managed, even the brief periods when she'd had to go full time. Every day she learned something new; often it was about herself. At times she felt as if her eyes were being dragged open, the better to see the bigger world that existed beyond Port Grace. There was so much more to know and do, and especially, so much more to think.

"Fine," she answered cheerily. "Jim's moving up so we're getting a new principal, someone from Mount Pearl apparently. Anyway, we'll find out next week."

"I heard you got a new vice too."

"A vice?" Lill asked, her stomach becoming increasingly unsettled. What was the little witch up to now, she wondered?

"Principal," Marlene explained in her own uniquely annoying way. "You got a new vice-principal, didn't you?"

"Oh. Yeah, Rod Corcoran's taking over from Janice Shaw. You knew she was going over to your kids' school as principal, right?" Lill asked, hoping hopelessly to change the subject.

"Uh huh," Marlene muttered with a flick of her hand. "This new vice-principal, he's pretty young for the job, isn't he?"

The wine was beginning to sour on Lill's tongue. When would she learn that her sister always had an underlying motive? "He's thirty-two, Marlene."

"But you're much older than that. They should've given you the job, what with two big boys to feed."

"For God's sake, Marlene, it's not about age. He's got two degrees and he's almost finished his Master's." How on earth did she get stuck in this position, defending Rod?

"Makes sense," agreed Noreen. "You've only got a couple of years behind you."

"Back to Rod," said Marlene, a peculiar emphasis on his name. "You seem to know a lot about him."

"I work with him."

Marlene gave a mirthless little chuckle. "From what I hear, that's not all you're doing with him."

"What are you talking about now?" asked Noreen, giving Marlene an exasperated look.

"I'm talking about Lill robbing the cradle," she sneered. "With Janie Corcoran's son."

Just the way she said it made Lill feel dirty, like an old pervert. Through the crystal-clear window she saw Max playing with Jordan and Jessica, and was grateful he wasn't in the room. It likely would not have stopped Marlene.

"Lill?" Noreen asked, her eyes glinting.

"Yeah, Lill. Tell us all about him," Marlene taunted.

Lill cleared her throat. "Yes, I've been seeing Rod Corcoran socially as well as professionally." Socially might have been a bit of an exaggeration; she and Rod mostly stayed home. They were perfectly content with each other's company, sharing a glass of wine, listening to music. Sometimes they even danced in the privacy of Lill's living room, the lights down low. They enjoyed long leisurely dinners if they were home alone, usually something that they cooked together, sipping wine, sneaking kisses around the stove. Rod was becoming quite handy in the kitchen, and had taken to showing up at her door on Friday evenings with an armload of groceries and several new recipes, some of which were more successful than others. Just the weekend before they had made Indian food, but it was so spicy they both had tears in their eyes and beads of sweat on their foreheads by the time they'd finished eating. By far his favourite meal, and hers, was Saturday breakfast. Except for the one time when Suzie and Ida came out for the weekend, Rod always cooked for her on Saturday mornings, omelettes or pancakes or scrambled eggs, around ten o'clock, before she went shopping, after they'd made love. It was a meal she looked forward to all week long, one that made her go weak just thinking about it. Lill had been amazed to discover how sensual a woman she was. How had those urges, those desires of the flesh, been subdued for so long, only to come charging to the surface when she and Rod were together? It struck her that if Steve had not been killed, she might never have known that part of herself, might never have felt that flutter of excitement at the touch of a man, or her own weak-kneed reaction to an innocent tendril of chest hair. Her sad lonely life might have been forever deprived of the joy and wonder and pure longing that Rod aroused within her.

"Get out of town!" Her sister's exclamation jolted Lill from her reverie, and she wiped the smile from her face. "How come you never said anything?" asked Noreen.

"Well, I've hardly laid eyes on you since it started."

"Oh, never mind. What's he like?"

"He's nice," Lill answered, wishing she was having this conversation with Noreen somewhere else.

"Nice?" bellowed Marlene. "My God, Lill, is that all you got to say? He's a good ten years younger than you. And for God's sake, look at the family he's out of. And don't pretend you don't know what I mean. His father, or lack of one!"

Lill was about to tell her where to go when Noreen let out a big round laugh. "Is he really, Lill? Ten years?" She emptied the rest of the wine into their glasses. "Wait now. Janie would've been about—"

"He'll be thirty-three his birthday," Lill interrupted, trying to keep her voice level and calm, "and I just turned forty."

Marlene opened her mouth, but Noreen jumped back in. "All right, Lilly! When did all this happen?"

"Oh, some weeks ago. We've been working on a project together, updating the old guidance manual. And it just kind of started from there."

"Noreen! Don't tell me you approve of this. Someone in your position can surely see how inappropriate it is." Marlene's voice rang with indignation.

"Oh go blow it out your arse, Marlene!" Noreen snapped, eyes blazing. "For your information, I might not be married, but that doesn't mean I've been a model citizen all these years. Even an old librarian like myself likes to let loose once in a while, you know. So get the hell over yourself."

"How dare you!"

"I dare because I damn well can. So, there's eight years between them. If it was the other way around, no one would say a word. They're consenting adults, for Christ's sake—he's a handsome consenting adult too—so what's the harm?"

"But the boys! What about Max and David?"

"Actually, I cleared this with them beforehand," said Lill. Well, almost, she thought to herself.

"You actually discussed this with them?" Marlene had moved from shock to anger. "For the love of God, why drag your children into this dirty sort of thing? Getting involved with them Corcorans! Crazy Suzie and foolish old Ida. Really Lillian, you should have more sense."

Noreen smirked. "Marlene, what the hell are you talking about? What 'dirty sort of thing'?"

"S-E-X is what I'm talking about," she hissed. "There are two innocent boys in that house. Who knows what kind of behaviour goes on there? I think Lill—"

"I think you should mind your own goddamn business!" Lill spat at her, not even trying to keep her voice down. The gall of the woman! "I'd never behave like that around Max and David, so you keep your filthy mouth shut."

"Well, if you're not going out with him for that, then why are you picking up men young enough to be your own son?"

Lill glanced over at Noreen, whose mouth was hanging open. They both burst out laughing.

"Christ almighty, Marlene, would you listen to yourself. First of all, she'd have to be pregnant at seven for that, and second, give Lill some credit. If and when she chooses to do something with Rod Corcoran, I have no doubt she'll use good judgement. As for the boys, one of them will be living on his own next year, probably doing exactly what you're accusing his mother of doing. If he hasn't already."

"Oh, Jesus!" Lill moaned. Normally, no one in her family ever talked about sex. She didn't want to be the one to change that, at least not today. "Can we not go there? I'm not in the mood to discuss my sex life and my son's in the same breath."

Marlene shuddered. "I really thought you'd have better sense, Noreen."

"Hah! I'm more jealous than anything. Go for it, Lill, have a ball."

A car horn blew in the driveway and Marlene rushed to get her coat. "I've got to go. My husband and I are going out to dinner. Be careful, Lillian. I wouldn't want you to get a bad name." Grabbing her purse and patting her hair in her pocket mirror, she scurried out the door.

After Max and the kids were settled inside, Lill walked out to the driveway with her sister.

"She's some stick in the mud, isn't she?" laughed Noreen.

"Yeah. Unfortunately, she just said what lots of the old biddies will be thinking, or saying behind my back."

"Let them, Lill. If you really like him, just go for it. No sense saving it."

Deliberately looking right at her, Lill gave her a guilty grin.

"You little devil!" Noreen squealed. "Give me details or I'm telling Marlene on you."

Lill giggled; sometimes lately she felt like a silly schoolgirl. "Suffice it to say, it may have been a couple of years, but it was worth the wait."

Noreen turned serious suddenly. "I'm happy for you, Lilly. You deserve this, so don't mind what anyone else says. You can waste a lot of time doing that," she added wistfully.

"Think you'll ever find someone yourself, Noreen?" she asked. It was a question she'd often wondered about. It made her sad that her favourite sister was always alone.

Noreen seemed to hesitate, as if about to say something, then shook her salt and peppered head. "Not in this town, Lilly my dear. Not in this frigging bloody town." She gave Lill a quick tight hug, then got on her bike and drove away.

When Lill got home, David was sitting at the kitchen table. He nodded significantly at the open envelope in front of him.

"Guess what that is?" he said with a smug grin on his face.

"Oh, David, is it from MUN?" She sat on the edge of the chair next to him.

"Sure is."

"And?"

"And I'm in!"

"Oh honey, that's wonderful news."

His face became serious. "Of course, I still haven't heard about a student loan."

Lill frowned. "I know. But listen, no matter what, we'll manage."

"How, Mom? University's going to be pretty expensive."

"You let me worry about that." If push came to shove, she could re-mortgage the house, but she wasn't about to tell David that.

"Well, thanks, but…" He hesitated.

"But what? What's up?"

"I got a chance to make some money."

"Oh? At what?"

"Laying pipe."

"What do you mean, laying pipe? And where?"

"Well, that's the thing, it's out west. Mick's uncle works out of McMurray, and they're looking for men for this pipeline they're working on."

"Fort McMurray? But that's so far!"

"I know, but the money's great. And there's lots of overtime, so I could make a really decent buck in two months."

"Yeah, but you'll spend most of it getting there and back."

"Well, not really. They're willing to pay our way out if we stay for the whole summer."

"The whole summer?" It struck her then, finally, that he really was going away. Whether he went in a couple of weeks to Fort McMurray, or in a couple of months to St. John's, David would soon no longer live under her roof. All of a sudden, her eyes filled with tears. She blinked rapidly, trying to stop them from escaping down her cheeks.

"Aw, Mom, don't cry." He reached over and squeezed her hand. "Please?"

"I'm sorry, Davie, I don't know what's the matter with me."

"Is it because of McMurray? I know it's far but—"

"No honey, it's not that. Or it is, but…I don't know…I'm just going to miss you so much, no matter when you go."

"I'll miss you, too, Mom. Really, I will," he insisted.

She smiled at him. "It's okay, Davie, honest." She took a breath and swiped at her eyes. "About this pipeline job. Do you really want to do this, spend your last free summer out in the bush, so far away?"

"I really think I should, Mom. First, there's the money aspect. It'll make a good dent in tuition. And then there's the job experience. If I'm going to go into geology, working a pipeline will look pretty darn good on my resume. And think about it, it'd be so different, heading out west, I can go to Calgary and Banff and all those places. I haven't really travelled very much, you know," he reminded her.

"Yeah, I know. There's that money thing again, eh?" She laughed, then turned a serious eye on him. "Sounds like your mind is made up."

"As long as it's okay with you?"

She let herself really look at him then, his rich brown eyes, his lightly bristled upper lip, the small rise on his nose. He was a grown man, ready to go out on his own and face the world. Even if she wasn't ready for him to go. She had purposely avoided thinking about the fall. There'd be plenty of time for that in the summer, she'd figured, plenty of time to prepare herself to say goodbye to her older son. And now she would have to do it two months early.

She rose from her chair. "Come here and give me a hug, would you, b'y." As hard as she tried, she couldn't stop the crack in her voice.

David stood and smiled softly at her. "Thanks, Mom," he said. Then, reaching out, he drew her in and folded his arms around her.

With Rod turning thirty-three and David heading out west at the end of the school year, Lill decided to make them all a lobster dinner the last Saturday in June so they could celebrate together. It was such a beautiful night they decided to set the table out on the deck. Noreen, who was spending a rare weekend at home, came over as well. Having her there with them on such a special night made Lill extra happy, though she didn't make a big deal of it. Max built a fire in the pit late in the afternoon to get the perfect coals, and in the evening David put a canner of salted water on to boil. Once it had, they tossed in a bunch of peppercorns and bay leaves, then some baby potatoes and fresh corn. Thirty minutes later, the lobsters followed. Lill filled a small dish with melted butter and lit the candle underneath to keep it hot. A hamburger for Max and a crunchy green salad from Noreen completed the spread, except for the chocolate cake that Lill had ordered specially from the bakery.

The umbrella over the patio table was festooned with all colours of balloons and ribbons, and the table was laden with bread and wine and all the food fresh from the fire. As they took their chairs, the last of the sun was still peeking through the tops of the trees, providing a soft glow to a picture-perfect meal.

"To the chefs," Rod said, raising his glass.

"Hear hear, cheers." They all joined in regardless of who had cooked.

David lifted his glass of beer. "To Mr. Corcoran. Happy birthday, Rod."

Lill smiled contentedly. David and Max had finally gotten used to calling Rod "Rod" at home and "Mr. Corcoran" at school. Still, it must have seemed a little odd for David, sitting across from his vice-principal drinking alcohol on a Saturday night. Over the past year, Lill had taken to offering David an occasional glass of wine or beer when she was having one herself. Yet even though she knew he drank with his friends, this was the first time he'd accepted her offer.

They all toasted again, to David's trip out west, then dug into the feast that awaited them.

"This is the best lobster I've ever eaten," Noreen vowed after the first bite, dipping a second chunk of tender tail meat and popping it into her mouth.

Rod grinned, his lips shiny with butter. "I feel like I've died and gone to heaven. This is so good, all cooked up with the spices and everything together. Some scoff, Lill girl," he said, his eyes twinkling at her over the rim of his glass.

"Yeah, good stuff, Mom. You should try a taste, Max." David had recently added shellfish to his list of favourite foods.

"No way," Max cringed. "I saw them go in the pot, I'm not touching them. Did you see their eyes? Bulging out of their heads, they were." He took another bite of his burger.

"Max, enough already!" Lill scolded. "We're trying to eat here."

"Oh well, more for us if Maxy doesn't like it," Noreen piped up, sliding another dripping morsel into her mouth.

It was a long leisurely meal. Tunes from Great Big Sea played in the background, loud enough to hear but low enough not to interfere. They all talked about nothing and everything, and they laughed as much as they talked. At one point, Lill had just returned from getting more rolls from the kitchen. Something particularly funny must have been said because everyone else was laughing. She was about to ask what it was but stopped herself. She didn't care. It was just such a pleasure to watch the most special people in her life enjoy each other's company that she chose to simply wallow in the moment. Noreen sputtering wine into her napkin as she tried to cover her mouth, David smiling coyly into his plate, so obviously the one who'd started it all, Max pointing at his aunt, his open giggling mouth full of food, and Rod, blushing slightly but grinning, the willing brunt of David's humour yet again. Her heart felt full, as bountiful as her table. She only wished her father could have been there.

After dinner the boys cleaned up, something they'd agreed to do before Rod arrived. "He can't clean up on his birthday," Lill had told them. "And if I get up to do the dishes, then he will too. You know what he's like. Why don't you make this his birthday present?" David had rolled his eyes at her and nodded, then Max had followed suit. After looking at the mess in the kitchen when she'd gone inside searching for some warm clothes, she was glad she'd made the arrangement.

The air cooled swiftly once the sun disappeared, and they quickly snuggled into the thick sweaters Lill brought out. Despite the chill, it was still a glorious evening. The sky was clear, with silvery stars hanging gaily from the ebony night, the moon large and luminous, as if God Himself was smiling down on them. They sipped their wine, murmuring contentedly over the meal and the beauty of the night. A Van Morrison CD moved into position on the stereo.

After a while, David stuck his head out the patio door. "Me and Max are heading out for ice-cream. You guys want to come?"

They groaned in unison. "I wouldn't know where to put it. I'm stuffed to the gills," Lill answered.

"Okay, see you in a bit."

"Bye."

"It's amazing what they can put away, isn't it? Did you see how many potatoes David had, and with all that butter on them?" asked Noreen. "If I did that, I'd be looking like the blimp."

"Me too," Lill agreed. "And you, Mr. Corcoran sir. I noticed you helped yourself to the butter as well."

He grinned saucily back at her. "It's my birthday. And I'm going to eat and drink whatever I feel like, thank you very much. Which reminds me, a nice brandy would really help the digestion. Ladies?"

Lill and Noreen looked at each other. They'd already shared two bottles of wine between the three of them.

"Oh, what the hell!" said Noreen. "I can walk home. What do you say, Lill? Should we tie one on?"

"Sure she will. Three brandies coming up."

Jumping up, Rod kissed the top of Lill's head, his warm fingers caressing the nape of her neck, sending little goosebumps down her spine. She sighed, content.

The unopened bottle of brandy had been in the cupboard since Christmas, a gift from a secret Santa at the staff party. As Rod poured them each a drink, the strong sweet scent drifted upwards in the still night air. Raising their glasses to each other, they savoured the first sip.

"Well, this has been some nice, Lilly girl," said Noreen. "Thanks for including me."

"It has been, hasn't it?" Lill smiled at her. "We don't get much of a chance to do this, what with you gone almost every weekend."

"Got to strike while the iron's hot, you know."

"Ooh, funny girl," Lill laughed. "You got to take me with you some time. I'd love to learn how to golf."

"That's a great idea," said Rod. "I played a bit in Toronto. Maybe we can get a foursome?"

Lill glanced expectantly at Noreen, who smiled but said nothing. "What is it, Noreen? Don't you want to play with us?"

She took a long time to answer. "Well, yeah, I do," she said finally. "But the thing is, it's not just the golf I go away for."

"Well, how about that!" Lill grinned, more than a little relieved. Her sister had always been so close-mouthed when it came to sex, Lill had sometimes wondered if she had any interest at all. "Is there a special someone in town?"

"Maybe," Noreen answered, unusually coy.

"Come on, Noreen, fess up. Who is he? I promise not to tell a soul."

Noreen took a sip of brandy and a deep breath, staring into the amber liquid as it swirled back towards the bottom. "Her name is Sandra," she answered finally.

Lill almost dropped her glass. "Sandra?"

Noreen nodded, glancing nervously at her, then Rod.

Laying his drink on the table, Rod cleared his throat. "I'm not much of a gossip, Noreen, but if you don't want me to hear, I can leave."

"Too late for that," she answered.

"Yeah, I suppose it is."

Lill took a slow sip of her brandy, trying to bring her mouth back to life. She knew she had to say something, but her tongue felt thick, numb with shock.

"Lill?" Noreen was staring at her, all the pleasure of the meal wiped from her face.

Lill tried to smile. "Sorry. Just give me a minute here. I'm a little bit stunned."

"I know. And I'm sorry. I always wanted to tell you, but I just never could."

The sight of Noreen, her usually confident face riddled with insecurity, made Lill swallow her own misgivings, at least for the moment. "That's okay, girl. I just got to get used to it, is all. Anyway, Sandra, eh? So, what's she like?"

Noreen looked gratefully to her. "She's pretty special."

"How long have you… has it…?" God, she couldn't even say it.

Noreen laughed nervously. "I think I knew in high school. No, I know I did, but I never admitted it. Can you imagine telling that to Mom and Dad?"

"Lord, no!" Lill cried. "Mom's probably rolling over in her grave this very minute." She paused. "How long with this Sandra, though?"

"Well…about three years now. She's the golf pro at the club."

"Three years! Oh my God, that long?" The simple lonely fact that something so important had been happening to Noreen without Lill knowing the first thing about it made her incredibly sad. Where had she been while Noreen was discovering this new life? Had she been so wrapped up in herself, in the sudden reality and instant fear of being left all alone to cope with raising two sons, that Noreen, who'd spent decades on her own, had been abandoned yet again?

"Yeah, it's been a while."

"Is she the first… you know, did you ever…?"

To Lill's amazement, Noreen blushed. "Yeah. And no." She took a sip of brandy. "I'm after spending a lot of years pretending, Lill, wishing I wasn't different. Avoiding the questions people always asked, wishing I could just feel the way everybody else seemed to feel. Wanting to talk to you about it, then not even being able to help you when you needed it, terrified you'd find out my dirty little secret." She stopped, glanced at Rod, then guiltily at Lill. "Sorry. Me and my big mouth."

Lill blushed. It was the first time either of them had even vaguely referred to what had happened all those years ago. She and Steve had been married about a year, and everything seemed to be fine. And it was, almost. Except at night, when the lights went out in their bedroom. Which they did immediately. Steve did not like to lie in bed and read, or talk, or cuddle. They went to bed to go to sleep. Except for Saturday nights, after Steve had had a few drinks at the bar. The lights still went out, but they didn't turn from each other right away. Not for five minutes anyway, ten at the most. After which Steve would roll off and over and sleep like he was in a coma. Lill usually stayed awake much longer, with the lights out.

Eventually this bothered her to the point that she tried to talk to her mother, who hurriedly interrupted before Lill could even tell her about it, and told her to count her blessings and thank the good Lord that she had a husband with a job and a car and who never raised a hand to her. Still determined, she went to her sister who, although she wasn't married, was five years older and had always been a font of information. To Lill's amazement, however, Noreen practically bit her head off. "Jesus Christ, Lillian, what's the matter with you? That's private stuff between you and Steve. My God, don't you know any better than to be talking like that about your husband behind his back. Good Christ, girl, grow up, would you!" Lill had been so humiliated she could barely look Noreen in the eye for months afterward. The only person left to talk to was her father, and she actually contemplated it. But in the end, she just couldn't bring herself to raise the subject. Then she got pregnant with David and the Saturday nights dwindled to once or twice a month. By that time, she'd learned to pretend not to care, and by the time Max came along, she actually didn't. Instead she counted her blessings; her boys, her parents, her home. And especially Noreen, who took to being an aunt like Lill took to being a mother. In their pure pleasure with David and Max, she and her sister put aside the memory of what had happened and became as close as they'd always been, able to talk to each other about practically anything, almost.

"It's okay," Lill whispered, shocked that Noreen had brought it up, yet not upset with her at all. She could feel Rod's eyes on her, but she didn't look his way. Maybe she would tell him later. "Anyway, you were saying?"

"Oh...yeah. Look, all I wanted was to be normal, but I knew I wasn't. So in the end I just decided not to do anything about it. At least, not till I met Sandra. And then I stopped pretending, when I'm with her anyway." She leaned forward, her elbows on the table. "I know this is a lot, Lill, but are you okay with it?"

Lill felt a sudden strange urge to laugh. She'd been so worried about her own situation, and look at her sister! A lesbian! She smiled and shook her head. "Well, I won't pretend it's what I'd want for you, Noreen. It's a hard road you're on, even these days. But if it's what you want, then I'm here for you, you know that."

"Thanks, Lilly. I knew I could count on you. Are you shocked?"

"Well, to be honest, I suppose I shouldn't be, not totally anyway. I remember when you and Mark Whelan broke up, how relieved you seemed, like the weight of the world was off your shoulders. Almost too relieved for a normal break up. And I've never known you to date since."

"Poor Mark, such a good guy. He knew it, you know. He wanted to get married anyway, said we'd work on it together. I almost did too, I wanted so much to have that normal kind of life. Like you were having. Then the night I decided to say yes, that I'd marry him, I got so sick you wouldn't believe." Noreen shook her head and shivered. "My God, I've never puked so much in all my life. So I put it off, but a couple of days later when I went to tell him, I could feel the nausea building up in my throat. I knew then I couldn't, that it wouldn't be fair to either one of us. And that's when I faced it."

"That's a tough one in a town like this, isn't it?" asked Rod.

"Certainly is. Which is why I go away so much. In fact, I've been thinking of moving into St. John's later this fall. Sandra wants us to move in together, maybe buy a house or something."

"Oh." Lill was instantly saddened by the prospect. For such a listless town, Port Grace kept insisting on changing every time she turned around, and it seemed it wasn't about to stop. First it was her mother, the gradual decline and then the sudden heart attack. Her father's stroke followed shortly after; for all intents and purposes, he was as good as gone. Steve's death had been the ultimate blow, his quiet life lost from the house, from her bed, from her sons' lives. Now with David going away and Noreen thinking of moving, she was faced with losing two more, although thank God, not permanently. "I'll miss you some lot if you go, girl, but I can't say I blame you. Are you going to let us meet her before she steals you away from us?"

Noreen, looking happy again, grinned at her. "How serious are you about wanting to try your hand at golf, maybe get a foursome?"

"That'd be great," Rod jumped in. "Wouldn't it, Lill?"

"Well, yeah…but I don't have a clue about golf. How am I supposed to play with all of you?"

"Don't worry about it," Rod said, reaching over to squeeze her hand. "I'll give you a few tips, and everyone plays at their own level anyway."

"So it's set," Noreen announced. "You figure out a date and I'll talk to Sandra."

There was an edge of excitement in her voice, a keenness that hadn't been there in a long while. Lill wondered if people thought the same thing about her lately, now that Rod had come into her life. She certainly felt more alive, just like Noreen looked at that moment. Could it be love, she wondered, or was it just plain old lust? What on earth had happened to the Penney girls anyway, Marg and Hank's dutiful daughters? Noreen in love with a woman, and she with a younger man. In lust, anyway. The neighbours would have a field day when they got wind of it all. Suddenly, she laughed. What about Marlene? Lill could just imagine what the youngest Penney daughter would have to say.

Making her expression as severe as she could, she peered sternly at Noreen. "I'll golf with you on one condition." She paused a second. "I get to be there when you break the news to Marlene."

Noreen's face broke into a wide grin. "It's a deal, Lilly," she laughed. "I think we better bring Rod too, make sure we get out in one piece."

10

When I was nine, I found myself with no friends for a little while. Time goes pretty slowly when you're nine and there's no one to play with.

Out of boredom, I started cooking. My father was happy to show me the little he knew, pancakes, scrambled eggs, the ever-changing lobscouse. But Mom wasn't used to sharing her kitchen with another person all the time, and was constantly badgering me to clean up after myself.

One afternoon I was trying my hand at Pavlova. Egg shells littered the counter and sink, and the floor was slippery with the sugar crystals that had spilt when I shook out the nearly empty bag. Without thinking, I lifted the beaters out of the bowl, but my mind was a million miles away and I forgot to turn off the electric mixer first. Splotches of meringue flew in all directions, plunking little fluffy clouds of white all over the place. It must have pushed Mom over the edge.

"Good God, Lillian," she yelled. "I'm some sick of stepping around you all the frigging time. Now for Christ's sake, just clean this up and get out from underfoot of me."

I knew I'd made a big mess, but I was lonely and hurt and angry with her for shouting at me. So I struck back. "Underfoot! What a stupid word!" I said brazenly. "How can I be underfoot? And why is it foot? Why not feet? Feet makes more sense than foot. Stupid word."

When I finally shut up, I saw my mother's red puffy face glaring at me. Grabbing an empty pail off the counter, she threw it right at me and said not to step foot in the house until I had a bucketful of berries. As saucy as I'd been a minute before, I already regretted it, but I knew the best thing to do was to get out of her way. Still, I had no intention of going berry picking up in the marsh. There was no one to go with and I never went by myself anymore. Ever. Instead, I headed for the beach.

I was even lonelier there. It was one of those cold windy days when the water is covered in frothy white tips. They reminded me of the meringue I'd been whipping because I had nothing better to do, and that made me think of the friends I didn't have anymore. Suzie Corcoran still didn't talk, and we'd sort of stopped playing together. To make matters worse, my best friend Gina's family had finally gone and moved to Marystown like they'd long been saying they would. Gina and Suzie and I had always been a threesome, and although there were other girls my age around, I had never hung out with them. All of a sudden I was left on my own.

I spent the rest of that afternoon collecting driftwood and throwing rocks into the ocean. I was feeling pretty sorry for myself, and wished only that Gina could have been there to comb the beach and scale the rocks with me. I missed Gina terribly, but I knew I didn't really miss Suzie. A part of me had always secretly thought she actually was a little bit stupid, although I never would have said it out loud. Deep down I was afraid that if I hung around with her, especially now that she didn't talk, people might start to think that I was stupid too. I would have liked to see Janie though. It had always been fun to watch her and listen to her stories when I was over at Suzie's. But Janie wasn't even there anymore. She lived in St. John's by then. I thought she was the luckiest girl to come out of Port Grace.

I remembered the empty bucket in my hand and went in search of berries, but the pickings near the beach were pretty meagre. At suppertime, I ventured back home, a single layer of blueberries lining the bottom of my bucket. Mom never said a word about the shortfall. She just hugged me about the shoulders and kissed the top of my head, then told me to go clean up for supper.

Bored with books and television, and no longer welcome in my mother's kitchen, I jumped at the chance to make a new friend. Charlize Brown had just moved into our town and when she started school, the teacher asked me to show her around. I liked her right away. She reminded me of Gina because she talked so much, and because of the way she carried on, like there was always something interesting happening even when there wasn't. She seemed far more mature than Gina though, mainly because of the things she talked about, like men, and men and women together. Some of the stuff she said sounded pretty strange. "Do you know they can rub it and make it bigger?" she asked me once. "And they can make it spurt, too." I didn't know what that meant, and I didn't ask. I just nodded as if it was old news, and hoped she would shut up soon. "They can make women spurt, too," she added, "when they put their things inside them." She would go on and on about all the things they did to each other, all of which left me feeling excited and guilty at the same time. I was not sure my mother would have approved of the things Charlize knew about, or claimed to, at least. Sometimes I wasn't even sure I wanted to listen to her myself, but I didn't know how to stop her. Later, when I decided that I really did not want to hear what she had to say, I would sing in my head when she'd start in. I knew I should have told her to stop, but I really did want a best friend.

If I hadn't been so "underfoot", I doubt if Mom would have been quite so happy about my friendship with Charlize. First of all, Charlize didn't have a father. Well, she had one, but he wasn't with them. Apparently he lived in the States somewhere, and she hardly ever saw him. I heard the old gossip bags at Hynes' store whispering that he'd divorced them and gone off, their old-women voices tutting and sighing, saying that it was no wonder the mother and daughter were like they were, coming from that kind of a home. I had never known anyone who was divorced, but it was the one and only thing I knew about Charlize's father because as much as she loved to talk, Charlize never wanted to talk about him. Or about her mother either, who she always seemed nervous around. I didn't blame her for that. Mrs. Brown made me uncomfortable too, though I could never quite put my finger on why.

The second strike against Charlize was that she was Protestant. After she started in our school, whenever we had religion Sister Philomena would stare down her long beaky nose at Charlize and tell her to stand up and go to the library. Sister would wait for the door to be completely shut before she started teaching, as if Charlize should not be allowed to hear one word of the religion lesson being taught that day. Charlize always left the classroom very slowly, with just a hint of a smirk on her face, and we all watched her in total silence, especially the boys. I thought she was almost as lucky as Janie Corcoran on those days.

When Mrs. Murray heard that the family wasn't Catholic, she said she was hardly surprised, that surely the two, being divorced and Protestant, went hand in hand. The only other Protestants I knew at the time were the Macleans, and they had always seemed happily married. Mrs. Murray didn't always make much sense to me back then.

Charlize and I did everything together. We played house up in the woods, making up husbands who had important jobs and went to work in suits and ties. We'd kiss the trees when they were coming and going, much like we'd seen on TV. Except that Charlize would kiss for the longest time, and she used to run her hands all up and down the tree trunk. She claimed she was going to be an actress so she needed to practice. Nevertheless, I was always embarrassed watching her, and wished she would stop.

Charlize had gotten a baking set for her birthday, and we loved to bake the tiny cakes that came with it. When they were all gone, we saved up enough money to buy a regular sized cake mix to refill the empty little boxes, then baked them again. After eating the cakes, we would spend hours looking through catalogues, dreaming about the clothes and the models who wore them. I'd try to skip over the men's pages, but Charlize always made me stop there. She'd stare really hard at some of them, especially the underwear ones. I'd go to the bathroom, or to the kitchen to get something to drink when she did that, anything to act like I didn't know what she was doing. When we got sick of doing "girly" things, we'd comb the cliffs at the beach or take turns racing her bike down Cemetery Road. She always won. I was far too afraid to go as fast as her, but it gave me a thrill to see her long blonde hair flying behind her as she whipped past me at the middle point of the hill.

Mom made no secret of the fact that she did not think highly of Charlize's mother. Nevertheless, she was always nice to Charlize. In fact, she acted too nice sometimes, as if she was trying to make up for something, and it made me uncomfortable because I couldn't understand why. Then one Saturday morning I heard her talking to Mrs. Murray over the fence. As usual, they seemed to forget I existed and proceeded to talk about my best friend like I wasn't alive. "I don't know how you can let her run around with the likes of that one," Mrs. Murray said. Mom shook her head. "Oh she's harmless enough, poor child. I feels bad for her not having a good home, and people thinking mean things about her. I mean, it's not her fault what her mother does." Mrs. Murray gave a snide little chuckle. "Sure enough, it's not, Marg. But have you watched the way the child struts around, just like her mother, sticking her front out and swinging her hips. She got no one else to look up to but a heathen who has all kinds of men in and out of that place. What can you expect?" Mom saw me then and sent me into the house with the first basket of laundry. I was glad to leave.

On my way to bed that night I heard Mom relaying what Mrs. Murray had said to Dad, and asking him what he thought they should do about me and Charlize. I stopped dead in my tracks.

Surely to God they shouldn't do anything. As uncomfortable as Charlize made me at times, she was the only friend I had. I knew she talked too much about what men and women did to each other, but I never for a minute thought she did any of those things herself, at least not with boys. And just because she was Protestant didn't mean she was bad, I thought, no matter what her mother did or what Mrs. Murray said about it. Besides, I reassured myself, Dad was always fair. There was no way he would stop me from playing with Charlize. But just as I started to relax, his words hit me like a red brick. "Marg," he said, "I knows just what you mean. The girl makes me some uncomfortable. Just today herself and Lilly were going through the Eaton's book the way they do, and one time when I looked over at them she was staring at me some odd, and I saw they were on the page with all the brassieres and drawers and stuff. I had to leave the room, I did." I remembered that moment, how she had acted so strangely and wouldn't let me turn the page even though I knew Dad could see what we were looking at. After he'd left the room, I had gotten really mad at her and she'd gone home in a huff, swinging her hair behind her.

The next day her mother called. It was right after Mass and we were just about ready to sit down to dinner. I was in the living room with Dad when he answered the phone. He was very polite, his normally big happy voice all quiet and correct, a sure sign something was amiss. He made no comment until everybody was finished eating and only he and I remained in the kitchen. "That was Charlize's mother on the phone before. She wasn't very happy. Seems she thinks you're a bad influence on her daughter." The way he said it struck me as very odd; he seemed mad, but not at me. Still, I felt a cold shiver in my stomach, and my eyes had started to sting. "Mrs. Brown said you were always going on about girls and boys and stuff," Dad continued, "and wanting to look at dirty pictures, and you were all the time swearing, and—" Suddenly I was bawling, broken-hearted with guilt. Dad put his arm around me and let me cry it out. "Lilly," he said after a minute or so, "sometimes you can get into trouble just by being around a person. Do you know what I mean?" His voice was soft, which surprised me because I knew he should be angry with me. I nodded between the last of my sobs. Deep down, however, I was starting to get pretty mad myself. All I'd wanted was a best friend. That's all. Everybody else had one, but not me. Gina went and moved to Marystown, and Suzie wouldn't talk to me or anyone else anymore, and now Charlize was telling stories about me and they weren't true, or not really true anyway. What was the point of trying to have a best friend, I wondered, if they did stuff like that? I realized that Dad was still talking although I hadn't heard all of it, something about not trusting people, and I figured he was referring to me. I made myself stop crying then, and wiped my face as hard as I could. "I'm sorry Dad," I said. "I won't be hanging around with her anymore. Don't worry." When I looked at him he gave me a sad sweet smile, which made me feel even worse. I decided then and there that I would prove to him that I wasn't bad, and I would start by not speaking to Charlize ever again. I was through with best friends.

In the end none of it seemed to matter.

Two days later Charlize's father was waiting for her after school. He was just standing there outside the classroom door. None of us children knew who he was, but when he picked Charlize up and hugged her, I figured it out.

I never saw Charlize again. According to the gossip, her mother had taken her from her father down in California, and he'd been looking for her ever since. For two years he'd been searching, selling his house and car and borrowing money from anyone and everyone. Finally he tracked them to Newfoundland and found his long-lost daughter and took her back. It sounded so dramatic. The police arrested her mother and Charlize moved back to California with her father. It caused quite a stir in Port Grace, but it wasn't really a scandal. They were all from away, so it wasn't as if they had a rep-

utation to live up to, or extended family that would be affected. It happened and they left within a couple of days and it was over. People still talked about it, but with no one left to represent the guilty, there didn't seem much point.

Even though I was still mad at Charlize, I was glad she got her father back. Fathers were just as important as mothers, in my mind. Or more, even. I tried to imagine what my life would have been like if Dad had not been in it, but it was too sad and empty to keep on thinking about. And then I realized I wasn't even angry with Charlize anymore, just relieved that she was safe.

I wished I could have told her that. Perhaps we could have been long-distance friends, confiding our deepest secrets in letters for years to come. I never even got the chance to say goodbye.

"How about the end of the month?" Lill suggested. It was a Saturday morning, and she and Rod had just finished a leisurely breakfast. "Every year Max spends that weekend at Sean's cabin, and David'll be away at university."

"Yeah, sure, it can wait till then."

"Do you mind?"

Rod grinned at her. "No, it's fine. It'll give us more time to plan our wicked weekend."

Lill felt her face redden, but she smiled anyway. She liked how he called it that, or maybe she just liked the light in Rod's eyes when he said the word, wicked. They'd been trying to schedule their golf excursion with Noreen and Sandra, but with David gone all summer, Lill hadn't wanted to leave Max. The truth of it was, she'd missed David even more than she'd expected to, perhaps because she didn't have work to keep her so busy. And Max, although he probably wouldn't have admitted it, missed him too. Watching the goofy television shows they both liked to make fun of wasn't nearly as entertaining without his brother around.

Then, when David came home at the end of August, Lill had wanted to spend time with him before he left again. He only had a week before he was off to university. Golf, and everything else, could wait.

Lill was grateful to have plans of her own for that weekend. With the prospect of both boys being away, she was afraid she'd feel disproportionately lonely in her quiet house, even with Rod's company. As it turned out, Rod was equally relieved by the time the weekend was upon them. Ida and Suzie had come out the Friday before and decided to stay over for the week; he was feeling a little crowded.

It was the perfect time to go, no responsibilities, nothing to keep them at home. As she said proudly to Rod, "a great opportunity to hit the links, tee off, putt around." She wished hitting the ball could be as easy as learning the lingo. The only puzzle in her new vocabulary was what to call Noreen's golf pro. Friend, girlfriend, lover? What would people call Rod, she wondered, then immediately decided that "lover" was not the answer. Plain old "Sandra" would have to do.

As the weekend drew closer, Lill grew more excited. And like Noreen, it wasn't just for the golf. She'd arranged to borrow her friend Gwen's cabin just outside St. John's. Even though Gwen had offered it to her many times, Lill had only ever taken her up on it once, when she and the boys had gone there for a weekend after Steve died. David and Max had been pretty bored, but she'd loved every minute of it, its quiet serenity a balm to her saddened heart. With its huge fireplace and big picture windows overlooking the water, it was the perfect place for her and Rod to spend their first weekend together. And since it was barely outside the city limits, it would be easy to go back and forth for golf or dinner.

In truth, except for their golf game and maybe a lunch with David, they planned to stay put. Their private times together were usually somewhat hurried due to the fear that someone, David or Max, Ida or Suzie, would walk in on them. To be able to laze in bed, to talk and snuggle and revel in each other for hours at a time, was a delicious luxury that they both looked forward to. For weeks beforehand, they talked about what they needed to bring, labouring over the menu, steaks or seafood, maybe both, the salads, the wine, the coffee and croissants. It was almost as much fun planning their getaway as they expected to have when they got there.

Finally, it was the Thursday before the long awaited weekend. They'd both worked late and were walking out of school together. The sun was beginning its descent in a rare cloudless sky.

"I just got to get Max organized when I get home because they're leaving right after school tomorrow," Lill said. "Then I'll concentrate on our stuff."

"Great. What time do you want to take off?" he asked as they reached her car.

"Six o'clock? That'll get us there by seven-thirty or so, time to settle in and have a bite to eat."

Rod gave her a sultry once-over. "Settle in, eh? Wonder how long that'll take?"

She was about to answer with a wisecrack of her own when his expression changed from teasing to serious. He was looking behind her. She turned around.

The man walking toward them would have been tall except that his shoulders were hunched inward, as if grown weary from constant weight. What was left of his hair was a dull grey, and it stood about his head in curly bits that looked as if they'd been recently tamed to stick closer to his skull. His face was clean-shaven but his clothes were old and had obviously seen better days. Lill guessed him to be about sixty, or maybe less. Something about him seemed younger, yet his face had the cracks and creases of a man who'd spent much of his time outside.

The closer he got, the more familiar he became, as if she knew him from somewhere else. Then she realized she'd seen him the day before at the post office, just a side view, but in the same clothes. He did not belong to Port Grace. A stranger passing by, she'd wondered at the time, then thought no more of it.

Reaching them, he stopped, his eyes never once touching on Lill. "Are you Rod Corcoran?" His quiet voice had a nervous edge.

Rod tensed beside her and she put her hand on his arm. Still the man didn't seem to notice her.

"Yes," Rod said. "Can I help you?"

Finally the stranger looked at Lill. "I'm sorry Miss. Could I speak with him alone, please?"

Rod took Lill's hand. "You go and get Max ready. I'll call you later."

"You sure?"

"Yeah," he squeezed her fingers. "Go on." Uncharacteristically, he leaned over and kissed her lightly on the lips; demonstrations of affection were generally confined to their homes. When she glanced at the stranger, he was looking at Rod.

Lill got into her car, backed out and drove from the parking lot—slowly, watching them in the rear view mirror. Nothing much happened at first. They simply stood there, presumably talking to each other. She turned onto the street and glanced through her side window. Now the man had his hands out, but she couldn't tell if they were extended to give or receive. Rod took a step backwards. As she moved towards the main road, Rod retreated several more steps away from the man. Then she lost sight of them.

By the time she got home a small nut of fear had lodged in her gut, but she had no time to analyze what it was or why it was there. She and Max were too busy running around trying to get everything he thought he needed for the weekend, which meant two trips to the store to replace items that refused to be found in the house. It was almost nine when they threw a frozen pizza in the oven for supper.

"Here's my cell phone," she said, passing it to Max. "You got all the numbers where you can reach me, right?"

"Yes, Mom," he groaned. "Quit worrying. We're only going fifty miles."

"I know, but I won't be here, so I'll be lots more than fifty miles away."

They talked briefly about where she and Rod were going and the prospect of her first golf game. He didn't ask for more details, nor did she volunteer any. He had contact numbers for Noreen's cellphone, Sandra's apartment, the golf course and the cabin. They both avoided the topic of who was staying where, and with whom. At ten o'clock, he kissed her goodnight and went to bed.

Although she kept busy packing for her own getaway, as the minutes crawled by the uneasy feeling in her stomach turned into a hard ball of worry. In their five months together, she and Rod had developed a level of trust that went beyond friendship. They did not play mind games, and there were no power struggles, real or imagined. Perhaps because of the inherent complications in their relationship, honesty came naturally. If one of them was going to be late, or if something came up, each immediately let the other know. They did this spontaneously out of a sense of respect, and something else that she hadn't put her finger on just yet. It was too soon to mess with the 'L' word.

Just before midnight, he knocked on her door.

"Rod! Come on in." She took his arm and led him into the kitchen.

Weary-eyed and pale, he slumped into a chair at the table. She didn't need to ask if something was wrong. "I'll make some tea." He nodded.

As she got the teapot and cups, she glanced over at him. His eyes were closed, but his face was creased almost as if in pain. While the water boiled, she made a small stack of sandwiches. When she placed the food in front of him, he touched it gingerly at first, but after a couple of bites, he wolfed back the entire plate.

Draining his mug, he looked up at her leaning against the counter. "You're so good for me, Lill."

She smiled, happy with the complement and feeling much the same way about him. Still, there was something about the way he said it, a sort of yearning in his voice that made her nervous.

"I mean it, Lill. Before I came back to Port Grace, I thought I'd never trust a woman again." He smiled wistfully at her. "But then you happened."

His hand came up. When she moved closer to take it, he pulled her in and buried his face in her belly. She wrapped her arms around his head, and he held on as if his very life depended on it. "Thank you, Lill," he whispered, his hot breath permeating through her housecoat and into her skin.

She held him for a minute, and then gently eased back. "What is it, Rod? What's wrong?"

"Oh Lill. If only I knew."

"What do you mean?"

He hung his head for a moment, and when he looked up at her, the sadness in his eyes struck her full force. "That man? He was my father."

PART III

11

The stranger extended his hand. Without knowing why, Rod backed off. He watched the man's face, the haunting, oddly familiar eyes.

The man's left hand joined his right, reaching out, palms up as if beseeching. "Please?" he said. "I have to talk to you."

Rod wanted to shake his head no, but seemed to have lost the will. He waited.

The stranger looked to the ground, then back up at Rod before exhaling a long deep breath. "I'm Dan Walsh. I think I'm your father."

Rod heard himself gasp, felt his legs moving backwards, retreating from this inconceivable apparition claiming to be his flesh and tainted blood.

"Please? I just want to talk to you, Rod."

Something in his voice made Rod stop. Perhaps the way he pronounced the name, so full on his tongue. Rod studied the person in front of him, the wavy curls that resisted control, that indefinable something about the shape of his face. He tried to imagine the man shaving, tried to picture him as he would look in the mirror, carefully drawing the razor down his cheek, staring intently through the glass, studying his face, peering into his soul. A ritual reserved for a man's most private moments, to see beyond his outer self. Would they each see a little of the other in their bathroom mirrors?

Then and there, he knew that this stranger held the answer. It was a question he'd given up asking, a search that no one but him deemed important. Refusing to even acknowledge that somewhere a truth existed, his entire family had toed the line, the uncrossable border between fact and fiction, fiction and denial. When Janie and Ida said "Let it go, Rod," the steel in their voices told him it was useless. Suzie said nothing. She never had in all his thirty-three years, only hummed the same monotonous white noise over and over. Every so often he would get her alone and ask about his father, but her reaction was always the same. The drone would grow until it transformed itself into a buzzing mantra, so loud that he couldn't hear himself speak, and always Ida or Janie would rush into the room and stare at him accusingly as they led her away. He learned to leave it alone. He learned to fear the answer. He might find out that he really was his mother's father's son. His own mother's brother.

So when a stranger stood in front of him and claimed to be his father, Rod's first reaction was hardened denial, mixed with the same sense of alarm he got from Ida and Janie and Suzie. He pushed it aside when Dan Walsh began to speak.

"I didn't know you even existed, Rod, until two days ago. I swear to God I never knew."

The faded eyes seared into Rod's, and he knew this man was telling the truth as he knew it.

"How did you find out then?" Rod asked, his voice so hoarse he barely heard himself.

"I saw your mother, I saw Janie. First time in thirty-three years."

Nobody ever called her that. His mother. Rod waited.

"Do we have to talk here? Is there somewhere we can go?"

Rod led him across the road and down a path through the woods. The short walk to the beach gave Rod a chance to think, a few minutes to take back the breath that had been sucked out of him at the word "father".

They walked to a weathered makeshift bench by the breakwater and sat down. There was no one around.

"Where do you want me to start, Rod?"

"Good God, I don't know. No, wait a minute. Where did you see Janie?"

"At a bar in town." His tone was apologetic.

Knowing Janie's behaviour when she was drinking, Rod wondered now if his mother had unwittingly tried to seduce his long-lost father. "Well, that makes sense."

"She a drinker?"

"Yeah. Sort of."

Dan Walsh nodded his head as if that didn't surprise him, as if he'd expected it.

"So, what did she tell you? About me?" asked Rod.

"Nothing at first. It was late and dark and she didn't recognise me. Guess I've changed a lot in thirty-some years. But I knew who she was right off. Janie Corcoran," he said, gazing off into the autumn sky. "Janie Corcoran from Port Grace, not a girl I was likely to forget. A man doesn't forget his first love."

His words took Rod by surprise. "You were in love?"

The grey head jerked. "Yeah, well, it was a long time ago, I guess. Anyway, I stopped into a bar on Duckworth to use the phone and saw her. She was in pretty bad shape by the time I showed up, could hardly stand up at the bar. I had to convince her who I was. So I sat her at a table and went to get some coffee. I'm not a drinking man, and

I could see she had more than enough in her for one night." He took a breath and sighed. "When I come back to the table there's another man there and I asks him to leave, and he says who the hell am I and tells me he's been buying her drinks all night and I should get lost. So I said I was sorry, that I was an old friend of Janie's. That's when she looked up. 'Hah!' she said. 'Some old friend. The boy's father, he is.' Then she puts back another drink, I don't know where she got it from. That other man, I suppose. Well, I was right confused, thought she had me mixed up with something else. It was too long ago for there to be a 'boy'. But she looks at me suddenly, and her eyes, they're just that bit clearer, and she says, 'By the Jesus, he's the spitting image of you back then.' I was getting nervous by this time, and I says to her, 'Who?' and she shouts at me, 'Rod, for Christ's sake! Don't you know your own boy's name?' By now the other fellow is getting pretty pissed off at me, but then another man comes in, stone cold sober, and says he's her husband, and it looks like there's going to be a bit of trouble at first. But he throws twenty bucks on the bar for the other fellow and then hustles her out of there looking like he's done it a thousand times. I was in a daze or something, 'cause by the time I tried to catch up to them, they were gone. He must've had his car right outside the door, I swear. They just seemed to disappear into thin air."

Sitting on the battered old bench listening to Dan Walsh, Rod gradually felt his heart slow to a normal rhythm. It wasn't that he'd grown accustomed to sitting next to someone who claimed to be his father. It was more the man himself, his cadence of speech, the sense of tranquillity surrounding him. Dan Walsh seemed inordinately at peace with himself, especially for a man who'd just discovered he had a grown son. Still, Rod felt instinctively that Dan would have earned his peace, that his serenity had not been easily attained.

Rod pictured the scene in the bar. Janie, drunk as a skunk, some old guy just as looped trying to pick her up, and poor Jack coming to the rescue again. He'd seen it happen on more than one occasion. The woman didn't know how lucky she was.

"So, what did you do then?"

"Well, the bunch at the bar were no help. Wouldn't tell me a thing about them or where they lived, just that I should get lost and leave Jane and Jack alone. And I didn't know her married name, and there was nothing in the phone book under her maiden one. There was nothing left to do but come here," he said, his voice lowering as if trying to keep it under control, "and see if I could find you."

Finding it hard to sit still, Rod sprang up from the bench. He walked towards the ocean and scooped up a full handful of rocks, then pitched them one at a time into the water. Soon only one remained—flat, smooth, perfect for skimming.

Footsteps crunched behind him. They both watched as the stone danced on the surface, five, six, seven times before it disappeared.

Dan Walsh broke the silence. "Can you tell me about yourself then, Rod?"

"Yeah, I suppose so. Let's see. I'm a teacher."

"I heard as much. Found that out at the post office. I was one too, you know," he added shyly.

"Yeah? Where did you teach?"

"Right here in Port Grace. I wasn't from here though, I was in from St. John's. I taught at the old school, but I see they tore it down. Nice new building you're in compared to that one."

"It's not so new anymore. But I guess that was a long time ago, eh?"

"Thirty-four years. Seems like an eternity."

Thirty-four years, thought Rod—just enough time to have a thirty-three year old son. His body shivered with the knowledge, with the nearness of the man he'd spent a lifetime wanting to meet. And although he'd known him barely ten minutes, he felt he knew him well. What was even more amazing, he trusted him.

Rod had so many questions he didn't know where to start. Finally, he blurted out, "What about you and Janie?"

Dan's head sunk down onto his chest. "I was a teacher. She was in Grade eleven, or she was supposed to be, anyway. I never met anyone like her before."

Rod turned to look at him. "How old were you?"

"Nineteen. It was my first teaching job. When they offered it to me, I grabbed it even though I didn't look much older than some of the bigger fellows, especially ones that had failed a year or two. I was young for my years, and I didn't know I was four years older than her, or that she even went to the school." He stopped. "I'm sorry, Rod. I'm not trying to make excuses. I know darn well how wrong it was."

Rod was thinking about himself and Lill, their eight-year age difference, twice as much as between Janie and Dan. Those years mattered more the younger you were, and they mattered most if you were teacher and student. That was wrong whatever math you used. For the life of him, Rod could not fathom having that kind of relationship with one of his students.

Still, it was only four years. And two teenagers.

"How did it start?" He did not feel at odds asking such a personal question from someone he'd just met. After thirty-three years of not knowing, he felt he had a right to, and Dan Walsh seemed to think the same thing. If only Janie had had a similar conscience.

"It was all pretty innocent. I didn't know anybody so I'd go walking on the beach after supper, feeling kind of lonely being away from home. I seen her there the first night when I went, but she was walking the other way. The second night she was there too and coming towards me. I recall her looking right at me, and she nodded her head. And then the third time, she sat down on the rocks as I got closer to her, and when I got there she looked up at me and smiled. We got to talking and before I knew it I was sitting next to her. She seemed so worldly, which I know was kind of odd. I was from the city and she from the bay, so you'd expect us to be the other way around. But my parents were right religious and I didn't know much about girls and life and all of that. She did though. At first I wondered if she was older than me. I remember when I asked her if she was married. She stared at me real strange for a long time, then said no. I was so relieved."

"How come she wasn't in school?"

"Turns out her father wouldn't let her go, and in the end she didn't want to anyway. He was some bad man, he was. You were lucky you never knew him."

There was a new tone, a bitterness in Dan Walsh's voice that made Rod uneasy. The closer they got to the heart of the story, the more Rod began to question whether he had the right or the desire to know all the details. "Are you still teaching?" he asked.

The grey head slumped forward again. "No, not since then."

"Why?"

Dan stared off into the distance. "There's some things a teacher shouldn't do, things a person shouldn't do. I broke the rules, Rod. Thing is, when you break one rule, there's usually a couple more that follow, whether you want to or not. A teacher's got to be above all that."

There was resignation in his voice, an acceptance that he'd dealt his own hand and had to live with it. Rod wondered what other rules had been broken.

"Did someone find out about you and her? Is that why you quit?"

"I stopped teaching because I didn't deserve to do the job anymore." He looked at Rod and asked in all seriousness, "Don't you think it's a privilege to help shape young minds, and if you betray that privilege you should lose it?"

Rod had never put it into quite those words, but it occurred to him, with some surprise, that he agreed. Although he'd become more pragmatic, more cynical with age, as long as he could remember he'd planned to be a teacher. It was more than a job to him—it was a calling, a vocation. He'd kept that to himself, however, and simply went about his business of teaching children and loving his job. People felt so free to complain about his profession, to paint all teachers the same watered-down colour of the few who didn't measure up. It was unfair, but he understood it. He'd met a few of the bad ones in his time. Like Pamela. He wouldn't have wished her on Suzie's dog.

Looking at Dan Walsh and listening to the conviction in his voice, he sensed that it was the same for him. An involuntary smile broke out on his face; within hours of meeting the father he'd wondered about for most of his life, they'd found a connection on such a profound level. Maybe he wasn't a cynic after all, thought Rod. Good God, was he a closet idealist at heart?

"What are you smiling about?"

"Nothing," he answered, embarrassed, feeling like a naïve schoolboy looking for links to his long-lost daddy. "So what have you been doing all these years?"

"I ended up out west. The oil patch was just starting to heat up in Alberta and they needed lots of strong men for the rigs. Well, that's all I wanted to do, work hard and make an honest living, try to forget about…other things."

Rod felt inexplicably sad for him. "Did you ever get married?"

"Nah, never was good with the women. Except your mother, she was the only one." There it was again, that same note of nostalgia Rod had noticed before when Dan talked about Janie. It was gone when he continued. "No, no wife, no family. That's the way things were supposed to be."

"And now you find out you've got a son," Rod said, staring intently at his hands, anywhere but at the man who claimed to be his father. "How about that?"

Dan Walsh blew out a short burst of air. "It struck me dumb. I never suspected a thing. After I left Port Grace I never heard from her again. That was just something we agreed to do, though I didn't really have any say in it. I did send her my address the first couple of times I moved, just in case she ever needed me. But she never did get hold of me, and I suppose I understand why." He rubbed his chin, and Rod could hear the brush of whiskers. "I wish I'd known though, it would have been nice to know there was someone out there that kind of belonged to me, not to be alone in the world."

"No brothers or sisters? Parents?"

"I got some cousins and stuff, but I was an only kid. My folks were older when they got married and I think I was kind of a surprise to them. Dad died almost forty years ago, Mom went about six years later."

Rod thought for a minute. "Right around the time I was born."

"Yeah, it would have been. She never understood why I quit teaching, why I left Newfoundland and went so far away. I couldn't tell her the real reason, couldn't ever admit it to her. And then the next summer she got sick and died, just like that. There was nothing to bring me back after that."

"Why'd you come back now?"

Dan Walsh shook his head. "That I don't know. Just felt the call to come."

Two crows flew by, followed quickly by two more, their ebony wings spanning and soaring up to the sky. The sun had set behind them. The sky was closing in.

Dan stood and stretched. Rod suggested a walk, and he led the way, casually, as if he had no destination in mind. As they approached the house, Dan slowed his pace and stared up at it, as if in fear.

It stood about a hundred yards from the road. There were no pretty flowers or trees lining the way. In the middle of the yard, someone had placed two old tires. The leftover stalks of summer plants protruded from them, dead now that they'd had a few nights of frost. One of the dark brown shutters over the windows had come loose and flapped against the clapboard. A muted light shone from an upstairs window. The kitchen was at the back, unseen from the front entrance. Rod started around the side of the house.

"I've only ever been inside once, and I don't really want to go in there now." Dan stood still on the road, hands deep in his pockets.

"Why not? It's just Mom and Suzie."

"Janie's in there?"

"No." Rod stopped. "Mom is Ida."

"Oh." Dan turned and looked behind him down the road. Turning back, he caught up with Rod and followed him into the back yard.

It was somewhat nicer there than in the front. Suzie liked to try to grow things, and every year attempted a new plant or shrub, nurturing it from spring until fall. Only the hardiest survived.

Rod opened the storm door and went inside, motioning for Dan to do the same. As the door shut behind him Dan stopped, rooted in the shadows of the dark porch, looking into the deserted kitchen. The last moments of dusk filtered through the window above the sink. An unpleasant hint of cabbage lingered in the air.

"Mom?" Rod called. "You home? Suzie?" He turned on the lights. Supper dishes drained on a rack, and the old rectangular wooden table had been cleared except for the perennial salt and pepper shakers in the centre. The clock on the electric stove said eight-fifty-seven. "Guess they're out."

There wasn't a sound except the drone of the fridge and the tick of the cuckoo clock on the wall, a gift from Rod when he'd travelled to Europe after graduating from university. Ida had always wanted one, and he'd carried it carefully from country to country until he got it safely home.

He wondered briefly where they were before remembering that it was bingo night at the hall. Ida didn't like to play on Thursday nights though, only Saturdays. On Thursdays she sometimes helped out for an hour or so at the concession selling cokes and chips and bars, and then she came home early. Suzie must have gone for a walk with the dog. She never went anywhere without him, but at least since she'd gotten him, she didn't mind being left alone for a bit.

"Come in," Rod said. "You can't just stand there. Mom'll be coming through the door any minute and she'll have a heart attack if she sees you there."

He was only half joking. Ida had been having trouble with her heart the last few years, just like her late husband. The nitro tablets were always close by, usually in one of her pockets. Rod knew she lived in fear of going the same way old Matt did, apparently just seconds away from the magic little pill that might have saved his life.

Dan stepped into the kitchen and looked around, his head revolving in a slow motion arc. He jumped as the clock struck, then cuckooed nine times. Just as he sat on the edge of the stool by the woodbox, Ida limped through the back door.

"Hey, Mom," Rod called from his seat at the kitchen table. "How were all the gamblers tonight?"

"Hah! Stupid bingo. Giving it up, I am." She kicked off her old running shoes, carefully sliding the orthotics back in.

"Yeah, right. You say that every time you go."

"Means it this time. Never saw so many stupid people, smoking their brains out, sucking back the cokes and chips, spending money like crazy trying to win twenty dollars." She slipped her bunioned feet into the fur-lined slippers that Rod had given her for Christmas, then hobbled into the kitchen. "Old Bet Linehan won the fifty-fifty, then spent it all on…" She stopped when she saw the man by the stove. Her round face pinched into itself while she tried to see who it was.

"We got a visitor, Mom."

"Yes. Hello. I just needs my spectacles," she said politely, fumbling with the string around her neck where a pair of glasses hung suspended onto her deceptively large chest. It was only half as big as it appeared. One breast had been removed years before.

"Do you know who this is, Mom?"

She glanced at him. "No. Should I?"

"Maybe not. It's been a long time," Rod answered.

Dan stood up. A puzzled frown came over her face, then the slightest hint of recognition.

"Ida," he said. "How are you after all these years?"

As he walked towards her, the light from the ceiling illuminated his face. Suddenly, every trace of pigmentation drained from Ida's skin, and her hand rose up to rest on the missing breast. "Sacred Heart of Jesus have mercy on us," she gasped. "Is that really you, Dan Walsh?"

"Yes, it is. Hope I didn't frighten you, Ida."

"Lord no, well yes, yes you did now I tells the truth." Suddenly, she looked madly about. "Good Christ, where's our Suzie at? She never saw you, did she? Did she?" she repeated frantically when Dan didn't answer immediately.

"No, she's not here," he told her, his hand reaching out to comfort her.

"Blessed be the Lord."

"It's okay, Ida."

As they talked, Rod watched and listened, acutely aware of the man who stood in his mother's kitchen, the lean frame, the unruly hair, the lines around his eyes and mouth. Why did he feel such an affinity for this stranger? Why was he so drawn to him, to the point that he wanted Ida to be nice to him, wanted them all to be careful not to break whatever it was they might have a chance to build in this spotless old kitchen?

Ida turned to him. "So what have you two been talking about, then?"

The question was directed at Rod, but he noticed that she glanced quickly at Dan. He suspected that more was being asked than the words allowed.

"I know I'm his father, Ida," Dan said.

"Oh! You do, do you! And how's that now?" she asked tensely.

"Well, I ran into Janie in St. John's. I thought she would have phoned you by now."

"Was she drunk?"

"Yeah, pretty much."

"Probably thinks she was getting the hag again, if she remembers at all. She gets them D.T.'s sometimes."

Rod had not known that. Then again, there was so much he didn't know about Janie, like how she'd managed to attract Dan Walsh, or for that matter, Jack Pitts.

"She wasn't in the best of shape," Dan admitted.

"Does that a lot, our Janie. Ever since..." She stopped speaking abruptly and busied herself at the sink. "So what is it you're after then, Dan Walsh?"

"Mom!"

"It's okay there, Rod," Dan instantly reassured him. "I got a son, Ida, a son I knew nothing about. I know I promised never to come back, but he was never in the deal. It's been thirty-four years. Surely to God I've done my time."

Ida was looking out the window, craning her short neck to eye both directions. "Maybe so, but I'm not sure it's a good idea—"

"Why the hell not?" Rod asked, increasingly aware that this would not go smoothly.

"Ida, I just—"

"Now listen to me, Dan, you got to understand—"

"Understand what, Mom?"

The three of them were all talking at once, Dan placating Rod while Ida kept trying to get them to leave. The back door flew open and Suzie trudged into the porch, her dog Belle charging past her on the way to his water dish. At the sight of Dan he came up short and bared his teeth. Growling, he broke into a full-fledged bark, his black-rimmed mouth foaming at the sides. Ida reached out to calm him.

Dan knelt down and held out his palm. "It's okay, boy," he whispered. "It's all right now."

Belle barked again, with slightly less intensity. Opening the basement door, Ida took the dog by the collar and shooed him down the steps. "Get on down there, boy. Go on now," she said and shut the door.

As Dan stood up, Suzie walked in. Her face took on the look of a startled kitten, divinely innocent yet instinctively fearful. She stared at Dan as if she couldn't quite comprehend his presence.

"Thanks, Ida," he said. "Some dog you got there. Good security."

At the sound of his voice, Suzie's body went rigid and her pale lips stretched across her wasted mouth. For over thirty years, she'd used it to do little more than eat and hum. Occasionally she moaned, if she cut her finger or bumped her knee. Sometimes she made noises that could have been mistaken for laughter, but it never lasted long enough to call it that for sure. When she worked in her garden, there often came a sound that was almost musical, a lyrical lilt that came close to pleasing the ear. The same happened when she kneaded bread dough.

But as Dan's mouth closed on his last word, she started to keen, a shrill buzzing noise unlike any Rod had ever heard from her, or from anyone else. He stood transfixed as it grew and the others moved towards her. When Dan's hand touched her arm, it seemed to catapult her over some edge of sanity and she crumpled to the floor, moaning and gasping, her brown hair a tangled mass in front of her.

"Suzie, please," Dan begged, immediately falling to his knees in front of her. "Please, I'm so sorry. Oh God, I shouldn't have come back here. Don't do this, little Suzie. Please stop."

And she did. She stopped. Looking up, her hair fell back off her forehead. Rod gasped at the madwoman before him. Eyes blazing in her red-blotched face, her lips seemed to pry themselves apart. A foamy spittle coated her teeth. All at once a new sound, like one might expect from a crazed lunatic, whipped past her lips. Yet for all its feral intensity, the single word was unmistakable as she spit it into Dan Walsh's face. "Killer!"

The word hit the air, and stayed there. For an instant, nothing moved.

Rod's eyes flew to Dan, who rebounded from Suzie as if he'd been shot. His elbow struck the floor and he scurried backwards until he hit the wall. It seemed to Rod as if he was actually pushing against it, trying to move further away. He was gulping the air into his lungs, his eyes whipping frantically back and forth from Ida to Suzie.

"What did she say?" Rod asked once he'd recovered from the initial shock of hearing Suzie talk.

No one answered.

"Mom? Dan? What's going on here?" Rod felt a sense of panic that it was all going to be lost again before he'd had the chance to get it firmly in his grasp.

Ida hauled Suzie up off the floor. "Nothing! There's not a darn thing going on here. Come on, girl, let's get you up to bed."

Keening frantically, Suzie tried to push her away, but Ida had a firm hold and dragged her out of the room, shoving Rod's arm aside as he tried to stop them. Seconds later, he heard the rattle of a pill bottle from the bathroom, then the water running in the sink. There were some human sounds that seemed to be in protest. They were short-lived. Heavy footsteps down the hall, then quiet.

Dan remained huddled against the wall, knees to his chest, eyes shut tight. Looking down at him, Rod tried to keep his voice calm. "Listen, you got to tell me what's going on here. Please, for the love of God, talk to me."

There were tears in Dan's eyes when they opened. His lips parted; for a second, he seemed about to answer. Then, jumping to his feet, his fingers dug into the bones in Rod's shoulder. "Ida's right, I should've stayed gone from here. This was an awful big mistake, Rod. I got to go."

"Go?" Rod yelled. "You can't just go. No goddamn way. They never told me a thing all my life. So now you've got to."

The floor creaked unevenly above them with the weight of Ida's limping steps.

"You don't understand, Rod—"

"No? I understood what Suzie said, what she called you. The only word I ever heard from her."

"What?" Dan asked, looking incredulous. "What do you mean?"

Rod could feel his brain spinning as it tried to make the connections. How long had Dan been gone? When had Suzie stopped talking? Why were Suzie and Ida so horrified that Dan was back? Yet why had Dan seemed so calm until he'd seen Suzie? Nothing was adding up.

"Suzie doesn't talk," Rod told him. "She hasn't for years, since before I was born. The only thing I ever heard from her before now was humming, never a word."

He'd been watching Dan's face carefully while he spoke, and the confusion he saw there mirrored his own.

Ida came in. "You heard nothing, Rod," she warned. "Nothing. Dan, it's time you left."

Dan shook his head as if to clear it, then nodded sadly. "Yes it is. Good bye, Ida. And I'm some sorry."

She waved her hand at him. "Not your fault. Never was."

"What's not his fault?" Rod yelled at Ida. What he wanted to do was grab them both and hang on, to take them and tie them up or something, before it all got away. Good God in heaven, how was he going to stop what he knew in his heart was coming?

"Rod!"

When he was young, Ida's tone of voice could freeze him in his tracks. But he was no longer a child, and though it startled him momentarily, he kept on. "I heard Suzie, Mom. What the hell was she talking about? And what are the two of you trying to hide, what 'never was his fault'?"

Ida looked hard at him and shook her head, then turned to Dan. "Goodbye Dan Walsh. May God be with you."

"And you Ida. Take care of them for me." He walked up to Rod. There was an overwhelming sense of sadness about him, in his searching eyes and his solemn, lined face. "Let it be, son. Thank God I got to meet you." He placed his hand on Rod's shoulder, then reached out and pulled him close. Before Rod could react, his father had turned and rushed from the house.

Almost spellbound, Rod watched him go, then spun back to Ida. "No … Jesus no, he can't. I got to go get him."

This time, however, Ida's voice did stop him. It shuddered from her twisted mouth, wracked and broken, sending the most ungodly chills throughout him. "Please, Roddy. For the love of God, please leave this be." Steadying herself against the table, she practically fell into a chair.

He had never in his life heard her beg. Nor did she ever ask much from him, this woman who had given him a life his own mother had been incapable of providing.

"Mom?"

"If you ever wanted to do anything for me, Rod, now's the time. Let that man go, for his sake and ours."

"Will you tell me what happened?" The minutes were ticking away, each one moving Dan Walsh further from him. "Well? Will you?"

"Oh Roddy. I'm sorry, my boy. Only Janie can do that."

"Goddamn that Janie, it's back to her again, is it?" He wanted to scream, just scream and scream until they carted him away. But he knew no one was listening.

"Yes, it always comes back to our Janie. Not that she ever wanted it to."

If Rod had any hope of catching up to Dan Walsh, he should have already bounded out the door after him. But Ida's pleading voice hovered in the air.

"Fine. He can go for now, but I know who he is and I'll find him. This time that goddamn Janie's going to answer some questions. I'll just have to sober her up first." His eyes fell on Ida slumped in the chair, her lined old face and hard round body. "You okay, Mom?"

She shrugged. "Oh…I suppose."

"What about Suzie?"

"That's the real question, ain't it?" she said, her eyes drifting upwards to the silence of the floor above. "What about our poor little Suzie?"

All of a sudden, the tears started. Rod had never seen her cry with such force, and could hardly believe she was capable of the raw emotion that shuddered through her solid shoulders.

"Aw, Mom, I'm sorry. Here girl, let me get you a cup of tea or something."

She didn't seem to have heard him as her body slid to the floor. The sight took the breath right out of him, strong dependable Ida falling apart before his eyes.

"Mom! Good Christ, what's going on?" He knelt beside her and lifted her face. "Is it really that bad?"

She stopped crying for just a moment to look at him. "Oh Roddy, if you only knew. God help us, I wish I never did." Then the sobbing started again, inconsolable, a lifetime of tears, a watershed of sadness.

He held her for a long time, silently. When the tears subsided, he helped her up, then led her up the stairs to the bathroom. "Where's the stuff you gave Suzie?"

She showed him the pills hidden behind the toilet paper, and he took one out and placed it in her hands. "Your turn for a bit of peace, I think, Mom. Get a good night's sleep. Maybe it won't seem so bad tomorrow."

She took it and washed it down. "Not enough pills anywhere for that."

Returning to the empty kitchen, Rod turned off the light and sank into a chair. As the darkness washed over him, he wished that it could creep into his mind and shut it down for just a little while. He was too confused and agitated to think clearly, yet his head hurt from trying to sort through the images that bombarded him, his mother crying on the floor, Suzie, eyes wild and scared, keening like a crazy woman. But most of all, he saw the gentle face of Dan Walsh. His father.

Finally, he peeked in on Suzie and Ida. When he was certain they were sleeping soundly, he went through the house, turning off lights and checking the furnace and stove to make sure everything was set for the night.

Leaving the dog in charge, he locked the doors and headed straight for Lill's.

Rod's dark head pressed against her stomach, Lill nestled him close, all the while trying to make sense of what he'd told her. It was hard to believe the mystery that had plagued him all his life was finally solved, at least partly. Unfortunately, what he'd learned had raised more questions than it had answered.

She knelt in front of him. "Are you okay then, Rod?"

He smiled sadly back at her, his green eyes filled with heartache. "I suppose. Confused, but okay."

"Yeah, I guess you are. God, what a night, eh? So what are you going to do?"

He rubbed his forehead and blew out a breath. "I don't know. Mom's been so good to me, all my life. And she's not even my mother. How can I push it if she's so broken up about it?"

"Ida's an awfully good woman."

"But oh Christ, he's my father. I never knew him for thirty-three years, my whole life. For half of that I thought nothing but the worst. I sure as hell never dreamed he'd be anybody decent."

Pulling up a chair, Lill took his hand and sat quietly.

"You know how I discovered all the rumours about who my father was?" he asked her. "And that my sister was my mother?"

She felt the hurt in his voice, and she knew it would not be an easy answer. "How?" she finally asked.

"I was fourteen, in grade nine. Can you believe I still didn't know, at fourteen frigging years old? Jesus, how stupid! Anyway, Missy Collins was in grade nine too. I thought she liked me. In fact, I was pretty sure she did because Anne Smith told me so, said that Missy had broken up with her boyfriend because she really liked me and wanted to go out with me. Well, I'd never been out with a girl before. I was frightened to death of them, to tell the truth. But this looked like a sure thing, so I thought maybe I should give it a shot."

He laughed, but there was no humour in it. "I should have known something was up. Missy Collins was one of the most popular girls in the school, and Anne Smith was trying to set us up. Anne Smith never gave me the time of day before that, always seemed to look down on me, in fact. Especially back then. I was short and pimply and she was this long tall skinny thing with braces, of all things. Anyway, there she was being right nice to me and I was falling for it. So she told me Missy wanted to meet behind the gym right after school, but not to be a second late or she'd leave. And like a goddamn fool, I went."

He drained his mug of tea. Lill refilled it.

"Missy was there all right, waiting down at the end of the building, alone, or so I thought. 'You wanted to ask me something?' she said right off. Well, I had to do it then. She'd practically asked me to ask her out. So I did. 'Can I take you to the dance tomorrow night?' I said. It hardly came out, I was sweating so bad. All over the place, even my head, and I could barely see for the sweat in my eyes. And I had to use the bathroom so bad because I didn't go after school since I was in such a rush to get there. 'What did you say, Roddy?' she asked. 'I didn't hear you. Could you repeat it?' I remember how odd it seemed, that she was talking so loud and pronouncing each word just so. But I figured the sweat and the need to go were just screwing up my brain. So I said it louder, almost shouted it. Next thing I know there's five or six of them, big guys, and one of them goes over to Missy and kisses her right in front of everybody. Then they're all around me, and the one that kissed Missy is talking at me, something about leaving alone his girl, who did I think I was, a frigging retard, and something about a granddaddy for a daddy, and a slut sister for a mother, and they were shoving and pushing and I remember I fell down, and I remember thinking why was the ground so wet, and then I felt some of them kicking at me, and Missy yelling at them to stop, that this was no fun anymore and she was leaving if they didn't let up, and how I felt so grateful to her, and then they were all gone."

Lill's heart was pounding. "Oh God, Rod. The little bastards."

He continued as if he hadn't heard her. "I picked myself up off the ground and made it into the bathroom. I remember my head was kind of spinning, the words all running around together—granddaddydaddy and sister-slutmother. There was no one in there, thank God. I was pretty dirty from the ground and had a few scrapes and cuts, but they hadn't really hit me as hard as they could have. So I brushed off some of the dirt and ran home through the woods."

He looked over at her, and she could see the anger and the despair that he had felt all those years ago. "I went into the bathroom, Lill. The bathroom. I wiped myself up as best I could and I left. That's all I did in that room."

She understood then. A fourteen-year-old boy, about to ask a pretty girl out on a date, a girl he knew would say yes, and instead he'd found out the most shocking detail of his own life, and gotten beaten up as well. Then he'd peed all over himself, right in front of everyone, on the ground, helpless.

Kneeling before him again, she kissed his eyes, his cheeks, his lips, tasting the salt from both their tears. "I'm so sorry, Rod. Oh my love, I'm so sorry."

Her heart felt as if it was crying, she was so sad for this man she held in her arms, for the scared sad boy he once was, and for the fear for her own shy child, her innocent young Max. If she had a silver hammer, she'd give it to him tomorrow, and tell him to bring it down on the first person who ever tried to hurt him like Rod had been hurt.

She looked into Rod's eyes for a long moment. Then they kissed, a deep hungry kiss that wanted to last forever. They buried their faces into each other and held on for a good long time. Finally she noticed how still he'd become, how quiet.

"There's more, isn't there?" she asked.

His red-rimmed eyes tried to smile. "That's the first time I ever talked about it. Or cried about it either."

She kissed his eyes again. "What did you do then?"

"All I knew was that I had to get home. Mostly to see Janie. I needed to see her to know, to see how much I hated her, and how much she hated me."

The words shocked Lill. Although she knew they didn't have a normal relationship, she would never have thought that Rod and Janie hated each other. "Hate? What do you mean by that?"

"It was just something I knew, something I'd always felt inside us. Me and her. I always wondered what would happen if it ever came out in the two of us. That night I found out. When I confronted her, she started to beat the life out of me, and I let her. If it wasn't for Mom, she might've kept at it forever. I didn't even care anymore while she was doing it, although later I felt like punching her back. That was the first time I ever came close to hitting someone."

"Holy Jesus, Rod, who can blame you? What a horrible way to find out, and then have her beating on you as well."

He looked down at the floor, and his head dropped into his hands. As he rubbed hard at his face, the scratch of his beard was the only sound between them. "Oh Lill. There's something I need to tell you. It's not the only time I felt like that. Years later that same urge hit me. After I found out what Pamela had done." He looked up at her then, right in the eye. "But this time I did something about it."

Lill held her breath. "You hit her?"

"Not exactly, but just as bad. God, I wanted to. There was nothing on earth I wanted to do more. But I didn't, I just held her arms in my fists, held them there as tight as I could so I couldn't let go and smack the face right off her. Squeezed them so tight I left my fingerprints in her skin. I was afraid if I let go I'd pound her to a pulp. Finally she started crying and I sort of woke up and opened my hands." His voice was tight and tense, as if determined to say it once and for all. His eyes never left Lill's the whole time.

She stared back at him, unsure quite how she felt about what he'd said. For all intents and purposes, he'd assaulted his wife. She knew she should be alarmed and angry that a man had used such force on a woman. But she wasn't. That was the real shocker. "What did she do?" she asked.

"Pamela? Hah! Pamela did what she always did, found a way to make me pay. The marriage was over that night, and I never saw her again until we were in court. When we got in front of the judge, she hauled out these pictures, big blown up copies they were, the most awful colours of bruises. I couldn't believe I did them, that I was that kind of animal. I was ready to agree to anything then. She could have whatever she wanted, alimony, the bank accounts, furniture. I didn't care. Thank God my lawyer had more sense than me, and got me to tell the judge about her having the abortion. Jesus, we must have looked like the most awful people, at least that's how I think the judge saw it. He told us we were the saddest excuse for human beings he'd ever met, and it was too bad we weren't together anymore because it looked like we were made for each other. Then he told us to get out of his courtroom and stay away from each other forever."

A long painful sigh swept past his lips. It was as if the telling had finally emptied him. "I can only say I'm sorry, Lill. I've never hurt another soul in my life, honest to God. Do you think I'm a monster?"

She squeezed the hand she still held. "God no, Rod, you're not a monster. You're one of the sweetest men I know. And the truth is, nobody knows how they'll react in a situation like that." She hesitated. "Can I ask you a very personal question?"

"Anything," he answered immediately. "Whatever you want to know."

"Well, I was wondering, weren't you worried about you and Pamela having a baby, you know, considering all the rumours." She didn't think she needed to spell it out for him.

He nodded, then shook his head. "That's just it, you see. By then I finally believed that I wasn't some mutant, some incestuous by-product from the sticks. I spent years making sure there was no chance, always used a safe, never took the risk. But then I decided to get married. And even though I didn't plan on having kids, I thought I could use the whole marriage thing to get the truth from Mom. And I got it, or a bit of it anyway. One night when I was home for a visit I deliberately made her a couple of big stiff drinks. I felt a bit rotten being so underhanded, but I figured this way she'd have a good excuse if I managed to get anything out of her. After I set the third one in front of her, I brought the subject round to having youngsters and being a parent and all that stuff. I told her that I was thinking about getting married but that I couldn't because I didn't know if I should ever have children, that

I was afraid what they'd turn out like if I was the result of incest."

"What did she say?"

"Nothing at first. Then she got up and poured her drink down the sink and said she was going to bed. I remember being so frustrated. She still wouldn't tell me! I was going to go to my grave never knowing the truth. At the doorway she stopped. 'If I tells you this one thing, will you promise for the rest of your life to leave it be?' she asked me. I said yes, of course. 'I means it, Roddy,' she said. 'I'm going back on my word to Janie here, and she got her own reasons for wanting this left alone whether I agrees with her or not. Do you swear to never ask about it again?' I swore to God I'd never say another word. 'Okay,' she said. 'Listen up good. Your father was from away. It was not your grandfather. And that's the truth.'"

"So you finally knew?"

"I did, sort of. She wouldn't tell me any more, so I had to trust her. But I kept my promise. I never mentioned it again, until tonight."

"God, yeah, tonight. What are you going to do?"

"Jesus, Lill, I don't know. I wish Theo wasn't retired, maybe I'd phone him and get some advice." He shrugged helplessly. "Does the promise to Mom still hold now that Dan Walsh has shown up?"

"That's up to you, isn't it?"

"Yeah, I suppose it is." He sighed slowly, then stood up. "Look, it's late. I better head home."

As they walked towards the door, they passed the stairs, and Lill inclined her head towards it. "You're welcome to stay. You can sleep in David's room, you know."

"Ah, Lill, I wish I could. I wish to God I could just curl up next to you and go to sleep for a week. But I can't. Suzie and Mom are over there all alone. I got to be there when they wake up."

"I guess we'll forget about the golf game?"

"Yeah, not really in the mood for golf right now. But hang onto the cabin, you never know what might happen tomorrow. Let's see how things shape up in the morning, okay?"

"Okay."

He looked at her, a long deep searching look. "I want to be with you Lill, and not just for a weekend."

"Oh Rod—"

He touched his finger to her lips. "No, don't say anything. I just wanted you to know that, okay?" He smiled at her then, a beautiful sad full smile that flowed deep into her soul.

A door opened above them and Max started down the stairs. "Hey, what's going on?"

She dragged her eyes away from Rod's. "Nothing, hon," she answered. "We're just saying goodnight."

"Yeah, I better be going," Rod agreed. "See you, Max, and have a good weekend." He took Lill's hand. "Goodnight, my Lill. I'll see you tomorrow, right?" he asked, a lonely smile curving his lips.

With Max standing in the stairwell, she reached up and kissed Rod softly on the mouth. "Tomorrow," she said. "It can all wait until tomorrow."

"I can't do it, Lill. I have to go after him, or at least find out more from Janie."

Seven hours after he'd left, Rod was once again sitting at Lill's kitchen table. Max had just left for school; she would have to follow in a matter of minutes.

"I've got everything covered for today," he added. "Jim is going to cover my classes, so I'm heading right into town after this."

"Can't blame you I suppose. How's your mother? And how's Suzie?"

"Poor frigging Suzie. Jesus, what a night! She got me up around four in the morning, petrified. Had cold sweats, trembling and shaking. Mom was right in the bed next to her but she didn't wake up, thank God. I was really getting worried about her last night—she needed a good rest. I wasn't sure what to do with Suzie at first, but I knew where the pills were, and I got her to take one of them. She's still knocked out over there now."

"And Ida?"

"That Mom, tough as nails she is. Woke up this morning just like her old self."

Lill smiled. "Sounds like Ida. Does she know what you're planning to do?"

"No, not really. All I said was I had some things to do in St. John's, and that I thought she should stay out here with Suzie. She's not stunned though, she can probably guess what I'm up to."

Lill looked at her watch. Her first class started in ten minutes. "I have to go. Sorry, Rod."

"I know, that's okay. Just one thing. I was wondering, seeing as you had the cabin all arranged for the weekend, do you think you could come in this evening? Max is away till Sunday, right?"

"He is." She hesitated. "I could come, but should I? I mean, there's a lot of family stuff you need to figure out. I don't want to be in the way."

"Ah Lill, you could never be in the way. I don't know what's going to happen, but I do know I'd love to be able to come home to you when it's all said and done." He smiled at her for a moment. "As for family, I don't want to scare you off, but you come more to mind than anyone else lately."

A day ago, such an admission might have surprised her. But after what Rod had gone through since then, she knew the rules had changed, even the few they had between them. Still, if they were going to be honest, she had something to say as well.

"Does Janie know about us, Rod?"

"Janie? I don't know, maybe. Why?"

"Because I used to go berry picking with her before you were even born. What's she going to think about me and you together?"

"I don't much care, to tell the truth. Look, myself and Janie don't have much to do with each other anymore. Never did, really. I thought you knew that."

"I do. But she is your mother."

"That's where you're wrong, Lill. Ida's my mother. And you know darn well she thinks you're the best thing that ever happened to me."

It was true. Ida had told her exactly that a month earlier. "Lill," she'd said, "I never seen our Rod so happy. He's been like a new man since the two of you started going around with one another." That had been the final straw. With the boys and Ida on side, she'd quit trying to find excuses why they shouldn't be together.

His hand reached over and caressed hers. "So, will you come to town?"

He seemed so lost and lonely, his grave eyes searching her face, the pressure of his fingers stroking her skin. There was so little she could do to help him.

"Well…I suppose I could drive in after work. It's all arranged and everything, might as well take advantage of it."

"Thanks, Lill." His unshaven face looked instantly relieved.

They arranged to meet at the Irving's on the edge of town, but she gave him directions to the lake just in case. "Max has got my cell phone, so you won't be able to get hold of me. So if either one of us is not there, the other one should just go on to the cabin. Gwen said the key is under the chair cushion on the front step. Okay?"

He nodded, then kissed her long and hard, his unshaven face leaving a hot glow on her own long after he'd gone.

Lill managed to muddle through most of the school day, then arranged for another teacher to take her last class so she could get an early start to St. John's. There was an unscheduled stop she'd decided to make along the way.

The Home hadn't changed. Still bland and brown, it sat back off the highway, unobtrusive unless you knew what it was. She wished she didn't.

He was in bed when she arrived, a late afternoon nap they told her. She wondered if they'd put him there earlier and forgot about him. Then she wondered if the people who worked there had similar thoughts about her and her sisters, that they'd stuck Hank Penney in a home and forgotten him.

"I have a family," she felt like yelling sometimes, even though the staff were always polite and friendly. "I have two sons and no husband. I'm even trying to have a life," she wanted to add.

She wanted to tell them, and him. Especially him.

She stood by the side of his bed. The rail was up so he wouldn't roll over and onto the floor. That had happened once before. Hopefully, only once. He didn't normally move much, but he must have had a dream or something, they said. Anyway, he'd fallen off the bed, his foot catching onto the end bit of rail on the way down. She still remembered how she'd found him, his body contorted between the bed and the floor, his eyes open, and, she could swear, frightened beyond measure. She had cried off and on for days after, filled with sadness that there was no one there to catch him, no one there who loved him and could stop him from falling onto the hard cold linoleum. It was after that when she started secretly praying for God to take him, to end his misery, and hers.

He opened his eyes and looked at her. She could have sworn they were the same smart eyes that had smiled at her every day growing up.

"Hi, Dad. It's me, Lill." In her mindless hope that he was "with it", she'd raised her voice. "Sorry, you're not deaf, are you?"

Was there a glint in his eye? She took his hand in hers.

"I'm just going into town and thought I'd drop in. How are you? Can you squeeze my hand?"

She waited. Was that a slight pressure, or was it simply her squeezing him?

"I was planning to play golf with Noreen and Rod. Do you remember Rod Corcoran, Dad?"

A squint maybe, then just vacant eyes staring at her.

She lowered her voice. "I've been seeing him, dating him, you know. He's Janie Corcoran's son. You remember Matt Corcoran, don't you? He died years ago."

This time she was sure of it. His brow went tight, and he seemed to be trying to remember or say something. But as usual, nothing came out.

What the hell, she thought. "Rod's a good man, Dad, a really good man. Not like his grandfather at all. I've heard all that stuff about old Matt, and all the other rumours too. But don't worry, he's long gone now, thank God."

The veil of fog she was used to had descended fully by then. She wondered if he always woke up just a little more lucid, a tad more sane, just a bit of the Hank Penney she'd known and loved with all her being, and who'd loved her just as fiercely.

Oh God, she prayed silently, I hope not.

He closed his eyes again. She watched him for several minutes, his chest rising and falling peacefully, his face serene, untroubled.

"Bye Dad, I'll be back on Sunday. God Bless."

Placing a kiss on his warm dry forehead, she tucked the blankets around his neck. She walked out, past the nurse's station where she nodded pleasantly, on past the lounge area where the more mobile residents hung out. She waved happily as several caught her eye. At the main door, she calmly pressed in the code, one number at a time. She got it right the first time and was buzzed out.

Yes, damn it, she would see him on Sunday, never mind it was Marlene's turn to visit. Wouldn't she be surprised? And undoubtedly, not too pleased that Lill was messing with the system. Lill didn't care. She was coming to see her father on Sunday on the way home from town, and she'd come any time she could from here on in. It was time she started following her own instincts, quit worrying what anybody else thought. Someday she might even bring Rod with her, when the business with his own father had been settled. To hell with Marlene.

12

Rod went straight to Janie's house. When no one answered the bell, he knocked hard on the door. Still nothing. After another ring, he banged the door a couple of times, then was about to leave when he saw the curtain shift the tiniest bit. Janie didn't own a cat.

"Janie?" he yelled instinctively at the window. "Goddamn it, Janie, open up."

The silence felt forced, artificial. He knew she was in there.

"I'm not going away. Open this damn door before I get out half the neighbourhood to watch." It wouldn't take much. The multicoloured houses were all connected in a long row up and down the street.

He waited. Nothing.

"I know all about it, Janie," he shouted, leaning against the wood, his nose almost touching it. "Now open the goddamn door." His clenched fist banged harder than before.

It opened then. She stood there, hair tousled and matted, her face a mess. There was a bruise on one eye, and the scar on her forehead seemed more vivid than usual.

"Jesus, what happened to you?" he asked, barging past her into the small cramped living room.

"A little scuffle in the bar. Should see the other bitch."

His mother. No matter how much he denied it, she was his mother. She'd never been a delicate creature, but the passage of time had steadily eroded whatever grace he imagined she might have once possessed. As a young boy, even though she rarely paid him much attention, he'd looked forward to seeing her. She and the kids brought a noisy energy to the house, a welcome reprieve from the stillness of Ida and Suzie. But as he grew older, he came to like Janie less and less. It wasn't hard. Always crabbing at him and Ida, constantly complaining about the boys, spewing cigarette smoke wherever she went. Janie made little effort to be nice to people, except for Suzie, and to a lesser degree, her two young sons. Then came the accident. From then on, Janie seemed to be in a steady downhill spiral. It was as if she'd lost more than a baby when that moose hit her car and she'd slammed into the tree. A cloud of gloom came over her, its shadow casting far and wide to everyone else around.

And then that fateful day he heard the rumour, that dark irretrievable moment when he discovered the ugly piece of truth that she didn't deny. They were both different people after that, and he tried to avoid her, staying as far away as possible when she was there. Not that she'd cared. In fact, again except for Suzie, she didn't appear to care much about anything. She would visit at odd times, with or without Jack and the kids, showing up unexpectedly in the middle of the day. Or night. Sometimes sober, more often drunk. Always angry. It got worse over time, the drinking, the anger, the hostility, towards him, towards Ida. Sometimes it seemed to Rod that she was rotting from the inside out, decaying right there in front of everybody, and he'd wonder how, or why, a person could change so much. Nevertheless, watching her decline made it easier somehow to ignore his parentage, to resist the occasional impulse to find out more about it.

Until now.

"We need to talk, Janie," he said.

"'We need to talk, Janie,'" she mimicked him. "What the Christ is so bloody important that you had to wake me up to talk about?"

She looked at him then, right at him. Her face seemed to freeze, yet it was almost as if she wasn't really seeing him. She shook her head and blew out a breath of stale air. "Anyway, whatever. Suzie okay? Mom?"

"Yeah, they're okay." He watched her rummage through the litter on the coffee table until she came up with her cigarettes. "I met Dan Walsh," he said flatly.

Her hand started to shake so badly the cigarette had trouble finding a spot to lodge in her mouth. She tried to strike a match, but the top broke off and the flame barely flickered. Taking the box, Rod lit one and held it out to her.

"I said I met my father. He's come back, he's here in Newfoundland." He didn't bother to add that he was probably gone again. Just as she'd done for years, he also could hold his information close to home.

She whirled on him then. "What the fuck are you talking about? Your father is dead."

"It's too late, Janie. You had my whole frigging life to make up a story, it's no good starting now."

"Oh, mother of Jesus, I can't take this now," she moaned, heading for the kitchen.

He followed her in and waited as she popped the cap on a beer and raised it to her lips. Half the contents slid down the inside of the bottle and into her mouth before she slammed it on the counter. "So, I didn't dream it. He really is here."

"He said he saw you in a bar, and you told him about me."

She laughed, though not with any humour. "I thought I dreamt the whole goddamn thing. Fuck! After all these years," she said, her eyes glassy.

"Yeah. After all these years." He looked her straight on. "I need to know about it now, Janie. And you've got to tell me."

She snarled at him. "I got to tell you fuck all, mister. Don't be telling me what I got to do."

He could hardly believe she was still at it, still determined to have her own way. His head rocked with fury. "Well, here's the way I fucking see it. I'm going to find out, you see. One way or another. I know who he is now, and I can ask him. Or I can push Mom, or Suzie, or everybody in Port Grace." He gave her a moment to absorb it, and himself a chance to catch a calmer breath. "The point is, Janie, how much shit do you want stirred up? Because once I start asking questions, I'm not stopping until I get all the answers."

Her bloodshot eyes narrowed. "You little pisser. Do you have any idea what you're doing? Don't you give a shit about Mom and Suzie?"

"You've held that over my head for as long as I can remember. I never knew why, and I still don't. But quite frankly, I don't think Mom's afraid of anything, and Suzie's too nuts to know." He held up his hand as she started to protest. "It's the goddamn truth, Janie. You're the one who's most afraid. Why? Please, would you just tell me why you're so petrified of the truth?"

She slumped into the tattered armchair by the stove. Letting her head fall back, she closed her eyes for a moment. "Because I hate the truth. You got to understand, Rod. I don't know if I can go through it all again. I don't know if I can stand that."

He hunched down in front of her. "Janie, you know I'd never hurt you, don't you, or Mom or Suzie? The last thing I ever want is to hurt either one of you."

She nodded dismissively, as if that were only a small part of it. "It's not so easy, Rod, there's more to it than meets the eye. You might be sorry you found out."

"You let me be the judge of that. Now tell me, damn it, tell me what you're so afraid of."

She sighed. "I'll need a stiff drink for this one, Rod."

"Not this time, Janie. A stiff cup of coffee is more the ticket for this."

She eyed him disgustedly. "Ah, fuck it, just as well. But you better make it a big pot. It's an awful long story."

Janie turned fifteen years of age on Labour Day. A Monday. A holiday. A last chance to rest up. A time to put things in order for the hard year ahead.

When her father came to her bedroom that night to give her his special birthday gift, she was ready for him.

The room was almost dark, but not quite, especially if a person had been lying there waiting, eyes growing accustomed to the dwindling day, pupils expanding with each minute, enlarging to allow more light, increasing their width and depth the more a person thought of what might happen in a darkened bedroom with no one to see, no one to witness, no one to believe. No one.

She knew this would be the night he did it. She'd seen it in his eyes after dinner, watching her clear the dirty dishes from the table. Those eyes, varicosed, dripping with lust and stained with blood from the drink and the wanton cruelty that bred inside of him, they followed her. She knew the look. She'd known it since her own first blood, when she was eleven.

Not much had changed since then, at least not for the better. At fifteen, Janie Corcoran no longer thought herself a child. She hadn't in years. She decided that tonight would be different, a birthday present to herself. She had the knife. She was ready.

It was nine o'clock. Sitting on her bed, she heard the footsteps lumbering down the basement stairs. Reaching beneath the pillow, she touched the wooden handle, letting her fingers creep up to feel the razor sharpness of the blade. She'd honed it right after she'd washed it, then snuck it under her blouse so that she could get it down to her room, trying to slide nonchalantly past him where he sat in his rocker drinking beer. She didn't look at him, but she knew he was still staring at her. His eyes had followed her all evening, until his wife went to his mother's house to tuck the old lady in for the night, and he'd sent his nine-year-old daughter off to sleep in her lonely bedroom, warning her not to come out, that her mother would not be there to spoil her, no one but him to smack her and send her back to bed.

On the nights when he came to Janie's room, he always knocked at the door before coming in. She wished he wouldn't do that. The soft tap always sent her blood hammering and racing all over her body, so fast and wild that she forgot to, or could not, breathe. She wished he would just come in and do it, but that wasn't his way. After knocking, he would enter quietly and sit on the edge of her bed, bringing her with him if she'd been standing. She'd learned it was better to just be there so that she could get it over with faster. Once they were seated he would begin to talk to her.

"How was your day?"

"Fine," she'd whisper.

"What did you do?"

"Nothing."

"You must have done something." Taking hold of her hand, he would squeeze her arm. "Tell me what you did." She would hear the rustle of clothing and know he'd opened his pants. "Tell me!"

Sometimes she remembered something that had happened that day, and other times her memory blocked and she made stuff up. It didn't seem to matter to him as long as she talked. One time she tried not to, but he left bruises on her arm, and more on her leg. Big pinched bruises.

"I went to the store."

"Uh-huh." His hand would move hers over to his knee, then he would inch it higher up. Slowly. "Did Suzie go with you?"

"Yes, Suzie went with me." She'd try to pull back, but his fingers would clamp on her wrist like a steel vice.

"Who else went with you?" His voice would get raspy, like he was having trouble talking. He would slide her hand higher still.

"Noreen and Lill."

As soon as she said it, he would slide her hand the last little bit onto his penis and squeeze her fingers around it. She'd learned that this was his favourite answer, one that would get her to the end quicker than any other.

"Tell me about Lill and Noreen." He would start to move her hand up and down.

"Lill is Noreen's sister. Lill has brown hair and blue eyes." Janie did not actually know the colour of Lill's eyes, nor did she care. Sometimes she said her hair was black, and others brown. Nothing mattered to him as long as she kept talking and saying their names and he kept moving her hand. So she did, and he did. Until it was all over both their hands. Then he would leave.

As the years passed they moved beyond the pretend innocence of sitting on the bed. Slowly, month by month, year by year, the degree of body contact increased. At thirteen he moved into her mouth, at fourteen her vagina, where his visits were timed by what she put in the bathroom garbage can—she'd seen him check. By her fifteenth birthday, there was only one place left to go. As innocent as she still was, she had never considered this possibility until he put his finger there the last time. Then she knew what he had in mind.

And she knew it was time to stop him.

The footsteps came towards her closed door. She waited for the knock. But it did not come. Instead, he shoved open the door and stood there with a belligerent smirk on his face. He walked towards her, never taking his eyes from hers.

"Where is it?"

Janie's fingers instinctively inched towards her pillow. "What?" she mumbled.

"I know what you're at. Give it here."

Janie couldn't speak. She tried to swallow but her throat felt paralyzed with fear. It had risen up from her stomach, and was filling her whole body, her head and her mouth and her brain.

He stood in front of her, his zipper near eye level. She had imagined him undoing it and taking the thing out, and that was when she was going to get the knife and cut it off. Then, as he writhed on the floor, she was going to stick the knife in his gut, his heart, his head, his brain. She'd fantasized about it for weeks, and now that it wasn't going to happen, the intensity of her disappointment killed her fear and she lunged for the knife under the thin pillow and made a wild stab for anywhere she could. She just wanted it in him, somewhere, anywhere.

He caught her hand, squeezing at first, then twisting the wrist until the knife fell onto the bed and lay there, dry and bloodless. He picked it up.

Janie only wanted to die, and decided if he didn't kill her right there, she would do the job herself when he was finished what he came to do. She'd had the thought many times before, but now there was just no other choice, and she felt a sense of peace. Her body relaxed into itself, grateful that the end was near.

She heard his voice. It seemed to be far away at first, and she couldn't make out what he was saying. Then the words became clearer. "…been watching her. More than ready, I'd say."

"What?" Janie whispered.

"I said if it's not you, it'll be your sister," he snapped at her, as if annoyed about being brought out of his day-dream. "Goddamn stupid girls. Now get them pants off of you and turn around." Throwing the knife onto her battered old dresser, he undid his button and fly.

"No, don't. Please." Janie started to cry. Always before, fear had kept the tears bottled up until he'd left, but this time they poured out of her, her body shuddering and shaking as she gasped for air between the sobs.

"Shut it up, goddamn you," he hissed.

She tried to stop, sucking back her breath and holding it in, but it didn't matter. As soon as she let it go, the tears wracked her again.

"I said shut the fuck up!" he screamed, and his big wide dirty filthy hand swooped in to whack her full force across the side of her head. That stopped her. That shut her up.

"I won't be warning you again. Now it's you or your sister, don't matter to me. She's looking pretty good right now."

Janie didn't answer. Her voice was still buried in the stunned reverberations in her head.

He took the knife off the dresser. "Right. Her it is then. As far as this goes," he warned, holding up the knife, "if you ever thinks on doing anything, remember it'll be her that gets it in the end."

Zipping himself up, he turned to go upstairs to where her younger sister lay in her bed. Janie stood up, her tears dead behind her eyes. "Leave her alone."

He glanced at the knife, then at her. "Well now, that's up to you, ain't it?"

Janie looked past him to the concrete walls of the basement. Some day she would make her escape, somehow she would get herself and Suzie out of there. Her father could rot in hell then, and her mother could rot in the church.

His rough ugly hands went to the front of his pants.

"Just leave her alone," Janie said. She turned around.

Rod felt sick to his stomach. He had a wild urge to rush outside, to suck back great lungfuls of clean fresh air, to let the oxygen wipe his brain free of the images that Janie had so clearly laid out for him. When she'd said Lill's name, his mind had frozen for an instant. Janie had kept on going, though, and he'd raced to catch up. He hadn't wanted to miss a word.

The story wasn't over. He knew that. He knew Janie had more to say, and that this time she would indeed tell him. He doubted he could stop her.

Janie stood up. Hands on her hips, eyes closed, she stretched backwards. Rod felt a moment of fear that she'd lean back too far and fall, without realising or caring how far bent she was. She had always produced that kind of dread in him, that she could or would hurt herself simply through not caring. That it wouldn't matter to her either way.

"Jesus, Janie," he said to the back of her head when she straightened up. "It's hard to believe someone could be so evil. I'm some sorry, girl."

"Sorry, are you?" she said, her voice coated in sarcasm.

She turned around then and looked at him. Just stared at him for a long quiet moment, her eyes moving slightly, as if studying his features. He couldn't remember her doing that before, ever giving him more than a fleeting glance. He'd always felt that most of the time she couldn't rip her eyes off him fast enough.

She filled their coffee cups, then topped hers up with a shot of whiskey. Gesturing towards the bottle, she raised her eyebrows at him. He shook his head.

"Did you ever tell Mom about it?" he asked.

She let out a disgusted snicker. "Yeah. Once. She wouldn't believe me."

"Wasn't there someone you could go to? The priest, a teacher?"

Janie took a big gulp of the liquor-laced coffee. "Don't be so fucking stupid."

"Come off it, Janie. They're not all bad."

"Hah!" she snorted. "And Mount Cashel never happened. Roddy, my boy, you don't know shit. That stuff was going on all over the place. As for him, before he got at me, he used to take it out on her. I don't know exactly what he did, only that she put up with it and tried to hide it. And the priest! He told Mom to be a better wife. As for the teachers, they were scared shitless of the church, and the school was run by the nuns who were run by the priest. Nice fat circle, it was." She paused to light a cigarette. "Besides, if your own mother don't believe you, why would any of them?"

"Christ! When did she find out you were telling the truth?"

Janie's hand came up. "Hold your horses. You waited this long, don't rush me now."

Getting up, she went to the phone and punched in some numbers. "Norm," she said shortly, "it's me, Jane. Listen, I'm not coming in this afternoon…no, no, I'm fine…a family emergency…no the kids are fine, just someone out in Port Grace. Listen, I got to go, I'll see you tomorrow."

"What time you supposed to go to work?" Rod asked when she sat back down.

"About an hour. They'll get someone else, won't be busy till later anyways."

"When does Jack get home?"

"He won't be home till tonight. Don't worry, we got time." She sipped her coffee, her black eye peering at him over the rim. "I'm just not sure you're going to want to hear the next part."

"Well, it's not really something anybody wants to hear, is it? This kind of awful stuff happening to a person."

She inclined her head slightly. "Yes, it is rather distasteful, isn't it?" she said grandly, then gave him a coy look. "The next bit's a little different, though. Might hit closer to home. It's about someone you know."

"So was the last bit. I think you're someone I know, Janie."

"Just thought I'd warn you."

"Okay. Consider me warned." And in fact he was. Who did he know better than Janie? Himself?

"You sure you want me to go on?"

He hesitated. Good God, was this where she told him another truth, that he really was Matt Corcoran's son? But that was impossible. Wasn't it? "Yeah," he said, despite the beginnings of unrest in his gut. "I'm ready."

"Well, baby, so am I," she said, her eyes glinting.

It was Friday, four days later.

She watched her father watching Lilly, who was giggling and laughing with Suzie, chattering on about all the fun they would have at Gina's that night, and how sad they'd be if Gina really did go and move to Marystown. Knowing him like only she did, Janie could guess what was going through his mind. For four years now, the easiest way for her to get him finished was to talk about the Penney girls. Noreen had been his favourite for a time, but he'd quickly had his fill of her. After that, Lilly seemed to be the one that finished him the quickest. And God knew, she needed it to be over with fast, now more than ever, now that he'd done that awful thing to her on Monday.

Janie looked at the two brown-haired innocents in front of her, Suzie's serious round face, Lilly's happy pink one. It was hard to believe that so much purity could inspire such evil, that the mere thought of this child could satisfy the vilest beast of man. Although she felt guilty for using Lilly like she did on those awful nights, she justified it with the belief that it probably saved Suzie from a reality far worse.

"Her mother makes the best fudge," Lilly exclaimed.

"I know. Mom's always trying to cook it as good as Aunt Donna but sometimes we end up eating it with a spoon. Mom's is still good though," Suzie answered loyally.

"You want to see my new pyjamas?" asked Lilly.

"Sure. When did you get them?"

"Last week, but I never wore them yet. I was saving them for Gina's." Lilly held up a pair of pink pyjamas with tiny red flowers all over them.

Janie saw her father's eyes, heavy-lidded with drink, staring at the small pink pj's. She couldn't wait until next week when he would be leaving for his new job.

"Oh!" Suzie cried out in envy. "They're babydolls! I asked for babydolls for my birthday but I didn't get none." Her face was crestfallen.

Lilly shoved them back in her bag. "That's okay, Suzie. They're not that nice anyway. The bottom part where the elastic is kind of digs into your skin."

"Oh," Suzie mumbled, seeming unconvinced.

"You can wear them if you want," Lilly offered tentatively.

Suzie's face brightened.

"Now Suzie," Janie cut in, "you can't be wearing her brand-new pyjamas." She noticed Lilly's grateful glance.

"But I found a pair the other day you might like that I grew out of a few years ago."

Her sister's little face became more hopeful. "Where are they?"

"Why don't you two come on down to my room and you can try them on?"

Janie led the way down the basement stairs and into her bedroom, followed by Suzie and then Lilly, who ran in and bounced on the bed.

"I wish I had a room like yours, Janie," Lilly told her earnestly. "You got so many neat things, and it's so private, away from all the noise and everything."

Janie tried to smile. "Yeah, it's private all right."

Lilly got up and went over to touch the knickknacks on the shelf, and Janie told her where they had all come from—the trophy for fastest berry picker and the ribbons for best pie at the fair, the stories behind the stuffed elephant and the little basket of used stubs and receipts. Even though she'd heard it all before, Suzie sat attentively, looking proudly from her sister to her friend and back again.

After she was done, Janie rummaged about in her dresser and brought out the pyjamas. "Here you go, Suzie. Try these on."

"Oh, I like them better than mine," Lilly declared, fingering the baby animals on the faded cotton. "Look at the little kittens and puppies. I like animals better than flowers," she told Suzie with a touch of envy in her voice.

"Why don't you try yours on too, Lilly," Suzie suggested.

"Yeah. Maybe we can run over to Gina's with them already on. It's not that far."

They grinned at each other as if they were about to pull off a great trick.

"Wait here. I'll run up and get them for you," Janie offered.

She ran up to the living room where Lilly's bag had been left on the couch. It wasn't there. She looked under and around the cushions, but it was nowhere to be seen. Finally she went into the kitchen and yelled down the basement stairs. "Lilly, is your bag down there already?"

"No," came the immediate answer. "I think it's on the chesterfield."

"I couldn't find it there. Look around and make sure you didn't bring it down."

She waited, leaning against the door.

"Nope, not here," the two young voices shouted from below a minute later.

Muttering to herself, Janie went back into the living room. There it was, on the couch, right where she'd thought it should be. Right where it hadn't been a minute before. The elasticised bottoms were sticking out of the top of the bag, as if they had been stuffed in quickly.

She picked the bag up and started to leave the room. Still puzzled, she stopped at the archway and glanced back. Her father's head was moving past the corner of the far hallway. He then proceeded up the stairs, his belt hanging open from the front loops. As she watched his retreat, she was struck with a dull throbbing in her gut. She dropped the bag back on the couch.

"Hey, you two, come on up," she called down, her heart thumping so bad it hurt even more than her stomach. "It's too cold to change first. You'll have to put them on over there."

"Awww," came the little voices. "Please, Janie?"

"No," she said firmly, almost breathless with the pain. "Now hurry up. You're going to be late."

When they got upstairs she bustled them out of the house as fast as she could, relieved that for one night at least, she would not have to worry about her sister, or Lilly. She walked to the road with them, grateful that the ache in her chest seemed to be subsiding. "Sleep well, you two, and have fun."

"Bye Janie. See you tomorrow," they yelled in unison.

The four little legs skipped down the street. Turning, Janie started to walk back to the house, but a movement in the upper window caught her eye. Her father stood looking out, watching the two children running and jumping their way to Gina's house. Then he stared down at Janie.

Turning again, she went the other way. Five minutes later, she was on the beach and a familiar stranger was walking towards her.

Janie had long sought solace at the ocean, sometimes by herself, and sometimes, if her father was drinking beer in his chair at home, she dragged Suzie with her. On the evening she first spoke to Dan Walsh, she was on her own. Suzie was safe at Gina's.

"Hello," she said as the quiet young man came closer. She'd seen him earlier in the week but hadn't said anything to him.

He looked up from where his eyes had been searching the ground. He seemed surprised. "Hello," he answered back. "Beautiful day, huh?"

"Indeed it is."

He smiled at her then, and she liked the way his thin face curved when he did that. Unlike hers, which was always round and plump. In fact, Janie knew she was more than just plump. At five foot one inches, she carried one hundred and seventy pounds of soft pudgy flesh, the doughy dimples in her short stout arms like the nooks and crannies of a fairytale house. Her mother had been pestering her about her ballooning body for years, but Janie had learned not to hear her anymore. Until yesterday, when Ida compared her to her sister, and talked about what a lovely figure of a girl that Suzie was getting to be. Janie's father had looked from one to the other of his daughters and nodded, but Suzie had just seemed confused about the attention. Oblivious to its implications. Much like Ida. Janie had wanted to stuff her fist into her mother's blind face, to poke the balls out of those nervous eyes that refused to see what was under her very nose. Grabbing Suzie's arm, she'd rushed from the room and down to their grandmother's house. Nana could barely move anymore, but she was always good for cookies and milk, and an unwitting safe haven from her only son.

"You're not from here, are you?" she asked the young man smiling shyly at her.

"No. From St. John's."

"What are you doing out this way?"

"I'm the new teacher starting at the school."

"Ohhh." Careful, Janie, she told herself. "Where you staying?"

"I have a room with the Whelans for now."

"The principal's house. Oh well, you won't get fat living there," she laughed.

"What do you mean?" he asked, his eyes sparkling, cheeks red.

"Have you eaten anything there yet?"

"Yes. Mrs. Whelan has cooked some fine meals," he said stiffly.

"Oh, she has, has she?" Janie grinned up at him.

After a moment he grinned back. "Well, I'm not starving."

"What's your name, anyhow?" she asked, scooching over to make room on her boulder.

He sat on the edge. "Dan. Dan Walsh."

"Well hi, Dan Walsh. I'm..." she hesitated just a second. "Janet. Do you like combing the beach then?"

"Yeah, I do. We don't live near to one like you do here. Some peaceful, isn't it?"

She looked off into the horizon and the endless water. "My favourite place to be, rain or shine."

"What do you do, Janet?"

"Me? Oh, you know, different stuff. My grandmother needs a lot of help, she's old and sick, so I got to take care of her most of the time."

Just that morning her mother had told Janie that she might have to move in with the old woman. It was getting to be too much for Ida going over every night, and it wasn't enough anyway.

"That's too bad, about your grandmother. It must get lonely for you."

"Probably not as bad as for you being away from your family."

"It's okay," he said. She heard the lie in his voice.

"I bet they miss you. You have any brothers and sisters?"

"Just my mother and me. Kind of quiet."

"That's good. It's pretty quiet at Nana's house, too. I wish Suzie and me could just live there."

In fact, she'd told her mother she would only go if Suzie came too. She didn't want to think what would happen to her little sister if she wasn't there, if Suzie was the only one for their father to stare at and watch endlessly. Ida had told her not to be stupid, Suzie was going nowhere.

Fine for now, Janie had thought. She'd see about it later, after he got back. God, she wished he'd just go ahead and die out there, fall overboard and never ever be found. Thank God he was going away for a while. Out of work for most of the year, he'd finally found employment on a trawler and would be gone indefinitely, maybe even a couple of months. At last they'd get a break from him.

"Do you come down here a lot, Janet?" he asked.

She liked the sound of her new name on his tongue. "Every day," she exaggerated. "Sometimes I go in at the back where it's quieter. The youngsters comes down here lots of times and makes a racket. Nicer back there though."

"Oh. Sounds nice."

"Maybe I'll show you next time." She stood up. "I got to go now."

"Okay." He stood too. "I'll be here tomorrow," he added, blushing.

"Yeah, sure. See you then, maybe," Janie called over her shoulder as she bounced away. Tomorrow. Something to look forward to.

The next day was Saturday, two days until her father was gone. Janie was staring out the upstairs window, the same one he'd stood in the night before. Just then she saw him coming up the road. Even from a distance he looked slimy, his dark hair wild about his head, his clothes dirty and tattered. A curl of smoke rose from the cigarette lodged between his lips. Suzie and Lilly trailed behind him on their way back from the sleepover at Gina's house.

Janie wondered why he was leading them. It wasn't like Matt Corcoran to worry how or when his children made it home. Not unless he wanted something from them. She shot downstairs and met them on the road.

"You'd best be off home now, Lilly," she said immediately. "Do you want me to walk with you?"

The child had looked strangely at her. "No…I know where it is."

"Sure I knows that. Just thought you might be tired after a late night up with Gina and Suzie."

"We were still sleeping but Dad came and got us," Suzie explained. "Said we got chores to do."

Janie looked at him. "What chores would that be now?"

"Never you mind there, Jane Corcoran. My business when my youngsters should stop in to their own house after a night out."

"What you want I should do, Dad?" asked Suzie, looking confused.

"Nothing! Christ, always saucing, never stops. The both of yous, in the house." He thrust a small bag at Lill. "Here, take this and get on home."

Lill pulled it close to her chest, her eyes wide and scared. "Thanks for carrying my stuff, Mr. Corcoran. Bye Suzie, bye Janie."

Janie looked at the bag that had just passed from her father to Lill. She noticed that Suzie carried her own; he obviously hadn't offered. She turned to her father. "Bill Barnes called from down at the hall. Said the bunch from unemployment wanted to know why weren't you there getting your stuff for Monday."

"Jesus bastards! Some impatient, that lot. They can bloody well wait, they can."

Janie had visions of her father being passed over for the trawler job, just as he had for so many others when he'd deliberately defied authority before he'd even begun his first day's work. She saw the weeks ahead, him sitting in his chair, knocking back the brews, complaining bitterly about the ungrateful sods at the unemployment office. Her hopes of seeing the back of him in two days began to fade.

"I think he said something about all the hired hands going to the bar after to celebrate," she lied. It wasn't much of one, really. More likely than not, that was where they'd end up.

His face scrunched with the effort of thinking through the pros and cons of gaining employment. The threat of having to work soon lost to the weight of a night of heavy drinking with his friends. "Ah, fuck it anyway. Tell your mother I'll be back later." He left in the direction he'd come, but faster this time.

Janie washed the dishes right away after supper, then went straight to her room. Peering into the mirror, she studied her face. It had been some time since she'd bothered, but she had overheard a couple of old biddies outside the church the Sunday before. They must have thought she was deaf, or stupid. "Such a pretty face on that young Janie Corcoran," they'd bleated more or less to each other, "shame she's so fat, eh?" Janie certainly had to agree with them; she was awful fat.

Her father hadn't come home since the morning. Apparently they'd spent a good part of the afternoon listening to government types spout off about their new duties and the workings of the trawler and what was expected of them. Thirsty work. She doubted he'd be home before midnight.

She went upstairs and found her sweater, the pocket bulging with the piece of cake she'd neatly wrapped and put there earlier. It was cooler this evening, but still nice enough for a walk on the beach. Seeing Suzie in the back yard, she went out the front and ran off down the street.

As she rounded the corner and approached the wharf she saw him, his head rising above the edge of the grass, his body gradually ascending the closer she got, as the foreground receded and the beach grew larger. She stopped running. Trying to catch her breath, she strolled onwards, towards the beach.

She came up behind him. "Hi."

He spun around, his face beaming at her, even more handsome and wholesome than she remembered. She realized he'd taken hold of her hand. They stood there, just breathing and smiling, for what seemed like ages. When she took her hand away to reach into her pocket, he looked worried until she took it out and placed the wrapped piece of cake in his palm.

"I thought you might need something else to eat," she said, laughing lightly.

"Thank you."

Janie turned and led the way across the beach. Dan walked beside her, silent. She was quiet too, her mouth filled only with the joy of him.

They could hear approaching voices and the squeals of young children.

"Come on," she urged. "I'll show you the back way."

Without a second thought, they hurried through the woods. Once sheltered by the trees, they slowed down, heavy limbs of evergreens fanning leisurely around them. Janie led the way into the dense growth, towards the light that shone at the far end. Soon they came to an opening, and Janie watched, satisfied, as he gaped open-mouthed at the vista before them. Endless water rippled and glinted in the low-lying sun, and red-tinted sky stretched forever and beyond, into infinity on three sides. There was no sign of the town or its people, their clapboard houses or rusted fishing boats. No roads or schools, no noise. It was the beginning of nowhere, a window into a world made solely of earth and air and ocean.

Janie walked out past the tree line to a small rocky beach, and there they sat for a good long while. They talked of life, not his or hers, but of the potential for living that existed beyond them, out into that limitless space that beckoned their souls. She had never shared her secret place with anyone, and had never expected to, except maybe someday with Suzie. She felt safe here, and had often thought of ending it all at the very spot on which she sat. She might have done it too, but again, except for Suzie. Still, it was a comfort for Janie to know that the option was always there. It gave her some peace in her other world, the world that ceased to exist when she was here, especially with him. They parted finally in the middle of the woods. He headed towards the beach, she to the road.

On her way home, her world smacked quickly back into focus. She was just about to pass by the Penney's house when a figure emerged from the shadows. The man kept slinking by, obviously not aware of her. Janie had been walking quietly, hoping not to be noticed, not to be asked questions about where she'd been at so late an hour, all by herself. She stopped, then moved into the shade. Lowering himself to a crouch, the man crept through the trees. A cat darted in front of him and he stumbled forward onto his hands and knees. His gruff tone just reached her as he swore, "Jesus goddamn cat," and continued on.

A knot of anger boiled in Janie's stomach when she heard the voice. That godforsaken bastard. What the fuck was he doing now? She had to stop him, somehow, someway. Because whatever he was up to, it could not be good. It never was.

She searched the ground until she found a rock, a good-sized one, nice and heavy yet small enough to throw with precision. Gripping it tight in her hand, she snuck around the other side after him. She knew the place well, having played with Noreen and Lill off and on for years, and was able to avoid the brambles and gouges near the trees. By the time she got there, he was peeking into a partially open window. Lill's window, she was almost certain. As she tried to think of what to do, he started to heave himself up off the ground, trying to get a toehold onto the ledge. After several attempts, his foot found a nook to hang onto. She could see the arms, one aiming for balance as the other disappeared inside. Janie was frantic with fear. For Lill and for herself and her family. For every time he'd ever knocked on her bedroom door. For the reputation the Corcorans had always had and could never get rid of, and rightfully so it would seem. She raised her arm. With every ounce of her strength she reared her hand back and pelted the rock through the glass. The last thing she saw was the back of his head smacking into the bottom of the windowsill. The clatter and crash of breaking glass followed her as she flew down the road.

When she got home, she told her mother that her grandmother was feeling extra poorly and had asked for her and Suzie to sleep over. They stayed there for two days, until Matt Corcoran boarded the trawler and shipped out.

Only then did Janie feel she could breathe again.

Janie hadn't known she would share her secret place with Dan Walsh. It had just happened, like lots of things did in her life. Except this was a good thing, she knew that right off. She could tell, too, from the look of delight on his face each time they went there that he loved her hideaway as much as she did, that he found it just as magical. He looked so peaceful staring out at the water, she wanted to hold her breath and capture his picture in her mind forever.

Janie had never been interested in boys, nor they her. Grown men, on the other hand, were a different breed, especially her father's friends. They always looked at her the same way that he did, and they weren't even related to her, she thought disgustedly. She wasn't sure why that was more disgusting, to be unrelated, it just was.

Except for the secret of her real identity, she and Dan talked to each other about everything, night after night. He confessed that while he was more than a little interested in girls, he'd always found himself tongue-tied when he was around them, whether it was at church, or school, or social functions. He had never asked a girl out on a date, and had begun to think that he never would. At times, this made him feel somewhat hopeless. His life seemed so small, he said, and he'd always dreamed of making it bigger when he grew up. In his mind, he'd seen himself meeting all kinds of folks, interesting people with interesting lives. He yearned to live fully, and saw a future with a large family, with important work in the school and church and community. To think that he might end up with less of a life than his parents depressed him greatly. He ached for more; he just didn't know how he would get it. He could not figure out how to meet all those people he knew in his daydreams, or even, God help him, one single solitary girl who might possibly like him.

Until now, he told her, until he met her, Janet. Janie blushed at the compliment.

They met every day at the same spot, regardless of the weather. Janie told Dan to follow the route she'd shown him, while she came through from the other side. Her father was overprotective, she told him, so it was best if no one knew about them just yet. While Dan did not have to make excuses for his absences, Janie created alibis as she needed them. Ida was usually too busy to worry about what her older daughter was up to after she'd done her chores, so the mention of seeing a friend or going for a walk usually sufficed. And Suzie seemed happy not to be dragged off to the beach like she so often was when their father was home. In fact, everyone was more relaxed now that he was gone.

With her father away, Janie's constant sense of desperation began to ease off. Nevertheless, as each evening approached, she could feel her pulse quicken whenever she thought of Dan. She had begun to bake on a daily basis, cookies, squares, cakes, so that each evening she had something fresh to bring to him, an offering. Her mother had complained at first that she'd only get fatter with all the sweets around, but Janie had lost weight. In fact, she barely had any appetite at all.

On the beginning of their third week together, Janie sat waiting for him. It was a Monday, and she hadn't seen him since the Thursday because he'd had to go home to help his mother and didn't return until late Sunday night. Before he left, they'd met in secret every single day for two weeks; the weekend had been almost unbearable without him.

There was a rustle within the trees and she looked towards it. There he stood, his gentle face smiling at her. As they moved closer, a rush of love flowed through her. She could have sworn she saw it shimmer on the air between them.

And although they'd only ever held hands up until then, it seemed as if both of them were filled with a need to have each other completely. They knew instinctively what to do, despite their lack of experience. It was nothing like Janie had ever dreamed, or felt, before.

They made love every night for a month. Then Matt Corcoran came home.

Thank God, was all Rod could think. Thank God, and thank Janie. Conflicting emotions ricocheted in his head—horror that Lill might have fallen into the hands of Matt Corcoran, relief that Dan Walsh was who he claimed to be, gratitude to Janie, for saving Lill, for loving his father. It was a disconcerting feeling after spending so much of his life resenting her.

But it was the little girl Lill that kept coming to the forefront of his mind. He could easily picture her, the happy cheerful youngster he imagined she must have been. The bright and lively hazel eyes, her joyfulness, so much a part of her adult self, radiating from her spirit so long ago, the naivete and innocence of a carefree child.

To think that his own grandfather would have killed those things in the woman he loved—yes, he knew it most definitely, the woman he loved—was unthinkable. If Janie had stayed longer on the beach, if she'd no longer cared what her father did or to whom, if old Matt had been as skilled at hiding himself as he was at concealing the truth, Lill would not be the Lill he knew today.

He looked at Janie, stone-still in her chair. Her face was sad, reflective. Was she remembering the young man, her mysterious lover, the boy she'd cherished?

"Janie?"

She turned to him, tears in her eyes. She was not a woman who cried.

He got up and filled her coffee cup, then held up the bottle of whiskey. "Top up?"

She nodded silently, the back of her trembling hand wiping at her eyes, then pushing the loose grey-black hairs from her ravaged face. "I haven't thought about him for a long time. It was always better not to, you know?"

"Yeah, I suppose so." So much had been said, there was nothing to add, at least nothing that would make any difference as far as he could see. "I'm sorry, Janie."

She lit another cigarette and sucked back a deep drag. "So," she sighed, exhaling a long trail of grey smoke, "what's this I hear about you and Lill?"

"I don't know. What have you heard?" He wasn't sure how to talk to her. He'd never really done it before.

"Rumour has it you're quite the pair, you two."

"Yeah, well, some rumours are truer than others, I guess."

She chuckled. "Guess so."

He wondered how she'd found out, and knew instinctively that it hadn't been from Ida. "When did you hear of it?"

"Ah, a few months ago. Getting myself a pack of smokes and a tub of ice-cream for Suzie over at Hynes', and they were all gabbing like crazy about it. They didn't know I was in the back."

"Oh? What did they say?"

Janie looked hard at him. "Nothing. Nothing important anyway. Bunch of goddamn biddies."

"Goddamn biddies who always got something to say. Come on, Janie. Tell me."

"Why? What does it matter what they said? Narrow-minded bastards."

"That's what I told Lill. She was worried what people would say and I told her it was none of their business, that it was between us. But now I want to know, so could you tell me please?" he asked, trying to curb his frustration.

"Fine," she snorted. "If that's what you want. Basically there was lots of little snickers and stuff, as you can imagine."

"Just tell me what they said, Janie."

She gave him a glance then that was almost pity. "Rod, you know what they're like. Don't mind them."

"Janie!"

"Oh Christ! Fine. They said she was awful old to be at that sort of thing, and what was she doing robbing the cradle when she just got her own boys out of it, and why would a young fellow like you want to be saddled with someone old as her. Okay? Happy now?"

He felt his face tighten. "Is that it?"

She looked at the floor. "No. There was one other thing. I wasn't the only one stuck in back by the freezer.

Her young Max was there too. He didn't know who I was but I knew him. Standing so still I thought he was frozen."

He almost wished he hadn't asked. It was the very thing that had been bothering Lill since day one, and now he understood why. And poor Max. He'd never said a word, no hint, nothing.

He went to the cupboard and came back with a glass. Drinking with Janie was not something he was inclined to do. She usually had too much, and when she did, more often than not she was a mean stupid drunk. Still, this was different.

"So?" she asked as soon as he'd poured himself a shot. "Tell me about you and her now."

"Yeah. I'm going out with Lill Dunn."

"Going out with? That all?"

He stared into the amber liquid, unsure how far to go. This was untested water, and he had too much at stake to jump right in. How much did he want her to know about Lill, and what would her reaction be? Uppermost in his mind, however, was Janie's own story, because he knew she still was not finished.

"Let's talk about that later, okay?"

"Sure," she smirked. "If you still want to."

"Why wouldn't I?" Again, she was making him nervous.

"The Corcoran men have always had a thing for the Penney girls, especially your Lill. You might want to think about that."

"Shut up, Janie."

"Oooh, testy, are we? Well, the fact is, she might want to rethink it if she ever finds out. Think about that!"

"You let me worry about me and Lill."

"Fine. So much for maternal instincts, eh?"

He thought she almost smiled, and he leaned forward slightly to check. If she was softening in her old age he wanted to know. But then she took another big swallow and started talking again. He had no intention of interrupting that.

It was a night that would mark them forever. A night that Janie foresaw as the start of a new life, but one that Ida saw early on was just the resumption of their old one. And as she told Janie afterwards, they were both more right than they could ever have imagined.

It had begun simply enough, Ida said, with a routine visit from the truancy officer.

"I done told you," she insisted to the irate official. "She got to take care of her grandmother down the road."

"I'm afraid the board is not satisfied with that anymore, Mrs. Corcoran. Jane is only fifteen and she needs to be in school."

"For God's sake, you knows I got no control over this. Why don't you just leave it all be like you did before?"

"Well, we need to make our report before the end of the month, so it's necessary—"

"Your report? So that's why you're bothering us, is it? Just so you can say you did?"

"Now Mrs. Corcoran. It's not like that at all. We needs—"

The back door flew open. There he stood, Matt Corcoran, home from the sea, his face a riot of overgrown hair, grease and dirt.

"Ida!" he yelled. "Who the fuck is this and what do he want?"

"You're home!" she stammered, her hand rushing to her throat at the language and the tone after almost two months of peace. "You should have told us—"

"Shut up, woman. Who are you?" he yelled at the officer.

The man barely started to stutter an answer before he was cut off.

"I don't care who you are. Get out."

"But I'm—"

"Get the fuck out of here. Now!" He took a step into the kitchen.

The quivering truancy officer had come by the front door and took a beeline for it, barely slowing to gather his vinyl briefcase from the table on his way out. Ida was relieved to see the back of him, until she turned around to see her husband shedding his filthy clothes in the middle of the kitchen.

"Run me a tub of water and get me a beer," he ordered. "Where's Janie?"

Ida had no idea where she was, nor did she care. All she knew was that Janie seemed different these days, happier, slimmer, full of energy. "She's over at your mother's," she lied. "She'll be back in a bit."

"Send her to me when she stops in," he said, then shut himself up in the bathroom with two bottles of beer and a glass of whiskey.

After picking up his dirty clothes and dragging his duffel bag to the basement, Ida opened the kitchen window all the way, a thing she rarely did. She had to get rid of the stink of him and the smell of rotting fish he'd brought with him. Then she left and went to their Nana's.

Suzie was there but Janie was nowhere in sight. Ida hadn't really expected her to be, but it made her wonder what Janie did with herself each evening. She sent Suzie on home with orders to finish her homework and get ready for bed. Settling her mother-in-law in with a cup of warm milk, she cleaned up the kitchen and tidied the living room before putting her own feet up for a few minutes of uninterrupted peace, the last she was likely to get for a while now that he was home.

Looking out the window at the trees half bent over from the raging wind, she thought his timing was about right considering the storm that had sprung up out of nowhere. She noticed two figures snuggled close together walking along the edge of the woods. Too exhausted to be nosy, she got up and did a final check of the house and her mother-in-law, then left to limp slowly home against the current.

Janie and Dan huddled into each other in the last minutes of fading daylight. His jacket was wrapped around her shoulder, as a gale force wind had come up off the ocean, blowing in unexpectedly. For the first time they'd left the beach together, having decided that she should tell her mother about them. It had taken some convincing on his part, but once he brought up the subject of marriage, she'd agreed, her head suddenly filled with visions of herself and Suzie free and safe from their father. Still, despite her impending liberation, they did not take the main road to her house, but followed along the line of trees past her grandmother's until they reached her own back yard.

"Wait here," she whispered. "I'll go on in and see if Mom's home from Nana's yet."

"Okay, Janet. I'll be here."

"Oh, and by the way," she hesitated, "the family calls me Janie, sort of a nickname. But I always liked Janet better. Just so you know. Back in a minute."

She crept across the mud and grass and up the steps to the back door. Quietly she pressed the latch and went inside, removing her dirty shoes in the porch. "Mom? You home?" she called in a low voice. She looked around the kitchen and living room, then listened at the foot of the stairs for any movement on the second floor. Not a sound save the roar of the storm. She went to the back door and signalled for Dan to come in.

"Are you sure?" he asked when he reached her.

"I think so. Mom should be home any minute, and this would be a good time to talk to her because Suzie must be asleep. Let's be quiet so we don't wake her, okay?"

Placing his shoes to the side, he stepped past her into the small clean kitchen. It was all neat and orderly just as she'd left it. Except the window was open. In fact it was wide open with the curtains deliberately tucked back, so that the freezing gusts whipped violently in and about the room. Janie wondered what had possessed her mother. She saw Dan shiver.

Taking off his jacket, she placed it on his shoulders. "Here, put this on and shut the windows. I'll run down and get a sweater." She kissed him lightly on the lips, loving the sense of intimacy it gave them. He smiled indulgently back at her. She tiptoed across the room and down the basement stairs.

Janie was nervous about talking to her mother about Dan, but she knew she had to do it. She also knew she should have told Dan her true age, but every time she'd tried, she just couldn't make the words come out. He was the only person in the world whose opinion mattered to her. Besides, she hadn't actually lied, she told herself, she'd just implied that they were the same age. He had seemed relieved and happy to let the subject go. It had never come up again.

There was another reason her mother had to know about Dan. Janie's period was late.

It was dark at the bottom of the stairs. She pulled on the frayed string attached to the ceiling bulb and looked towards her bedroom. That was when she first heard the noises. Grunting. Muffled groans. Whimpers that grew louder, almost familiar, as she crossed the concrete floor. Her stomach sick with fear, she turned the knob and opened the door into the unlit room. Fright bolted into rage. Suzie was on the bed in the same spot where Janie usually sat. She had on only a pair of pink and red flowery pyjama bottoms, instantly recognisable to Janie. Her hair was clutched in his big fist, and the thing was in her mouth, and he was gurgling something over and over as if in a spell, the echoing L's swelling then falling, killing the foul air, filling and spilling from his lips, from his smelly mouth, and then he was yelling, his belly pulling and rolling hypnotically with each plunge. Suzie's little face bulged; strangled gags erupted from her throat. A small hand grasped the iron bedpost, the tiny knuckles sharp and white. Her eyes were crossed and she didn't even seem to see Janie, her older sister who was supposed to protect her, to save her from this fate, the sister who'd been out doing it herself, doing it with one of them, doing that awful thing that men always did. Nor did Suzie appear to notice when Janie screamed like a banshee and jumped on his back. It was his turn to screech out then, and Janie was momentarily surprised that she'd caused such pain. Then she looked down and saw her sister's teeth on it, and he was still in her mouth, and then Dan came running into the room with Ida wild-eyed behind him, and her father fell out of her sister's face but he was having trouble breathing and his eyes had a panic in them, and Ida scrambled to reach into her apron pocket for his special pills that she always kept close by in case his heart decided to wonk out on him, and Janie saw her open the bottle and go to him where he'd fallen onto the floor, but her mother's fat hands were trembling so bad she couldn't get hold of a single pill as they tumbled from the upturned container.

Janie lunged at her mother. "Give me that." She reached in and took out one of the few remaining pills. "Stick out your tongue," she yelled at him, then tried to pry his lips apart.

She stopped. A low humming sound rose from the bed. Her father lay gasping on the floor, his pants open, his flesh raw and bare. She looked at Suzie, then stared at the little pill. Very slowly she closed her fist on it, then threw it across the room where it rebounded off the wall and landed somewhere on the floor in the semi-darkened bedroom. Ida dropped to her knees to find it or another of the ones that had fallen earlier.

"Don't touch that," Janie commanded.

Her mother's face shot up to peer at her. Janie gestured towards Suzie, whose reddened mouth seemed stained with blood but who said nothing, only hummed and stared blankly at her father on the floor.

"Janie, we can't—" Ida cried.

"Oh yes we can. We have to."

Dan had been standing as if spellbound, but abruptly sprang to life. "Good Jesus, he's hardly moving. Give him the pill! What are you waiting for?" he yelled.

Janie stared at her father. "I'm waiting for him to die."

"Jesus God Almighty, Janet, you have to help him," he pleaded. "Why are you doing this?"

"Because," she told him, calmly and deliberately, "what you saw in my sister's mouth has been in almost every part of me. For years now. Years, Mom!" she suddenly screamed. "Four years he's been at it. But you didn't believe me, and now he's at little Suzie, and we got to stop him."

Dan picked a pill up off the floor and started toward where Matt Corcoran lay dying in the middle of them all. "Janet, this could save his life."

"If you give him that pill," she vowed, "it'll be the end of mine."

"We can't just let him die. What kind of person are you?"

"Don't do it, Dan."

He moved forward.

Janie jumped on him. "Leave it!" she screamed, smacking at the hand that held her father's lifeline. "Who do you want to kill, him or me?" The humming grew louder.

Dan struggled to get by her, pushing her onto the bed. Suzie didn't react even when Janie fell against her, just kept up the monotonous drone.

"Suzie love, you okay?" Janie asked, touching her face. All at once, the sight of her battered little sister, the bruised mouth, the small naked shoulders, took all the fight out of her.

Fine, she thought, let him live, the bastard. She'd have Suzie out of there the next day, no matter how she did it. It was time to end it, for both of them, one way or the other.

She looked at the man, not much more than a boy, who might have saved her from all of it. "If you help him, Dan, you'll be killing me." Overwhelmed with sadness, she felt her body crumple to the bed as the tears burst from her eyes.

Dan had been crawling frantically around on the floor until, finally, his shaking hand came up with another pill. He scurried over to where Matt Corcoran lay and went to shove it into his mouth. Just as he did, Suzie bounded from the bed and onto his back, knocking the pill from his hand. She held on to him, squeezing his neck, her hands covering his face and eyes as she kicked and screamed at him to stop. But she was no match for a grown man, and soon Dan managed to push her aside where she landed on top of Janie. He found another pill and shoved it past the lifeless grey lips. Pulling the limp legs downwards, he spread him flat on the floor and reached in to feel around his neck. Then he put his ear to Matt's heart. Janie had the absurd fear that her father would reach up and grab Dan's head, but he didn't. He didn't move at all. He just lay there, eyes blank, unmoving.

"I think he's dead!" Dan's voice quivered, and he looked at Ida and then at Janie. "My God, what have we done?"

It was Suzie who answered him. "Killer!" she said, staring straight at him. The humming started again then, but it was more hysterical, and her eyes were wild and frantic.

Dan jumped to his feet. "We got to call the police. Come on, Janet, do something."

Janie stood up. So did her mother. Ida, who for four years had stood idly by, refusing to see what her daughter's life had become, what hell Janie had endured month after month, seemed to wake up all of a sudden.

"What's your name?" she asked.

"My name? It's Dan, Dan Walsh. I'm the new teacher at the school. Janet and I, we've been—"

"You don't have to explain," Ida waved her hand at him. "I'm sorry you got dragged into this, but it's too late now. He's dead, and that's the end of it. After we tidy up, I'll call the doctor. Now you better go."

"I can't go. Janct, tell her—"

"Mom …mc and Dan—"

"What? You and Dan what? Jesus Janie, look at this. What could you ever be now?"

"But Mrs…Mrs…?" Dan stood there looking bewildered.

Ida eyed him pityingly. "She didn't even tell you her last name, did she?"

"No. It didn't mattcr."

"Well, Dan Walsh, it's Corcoran. She's Janie Corcoran and I'm Ida. Would that ring a bell to you?"

Janie knew it would, of course. It had to. The name would have been bouncing around the school since he'd come. The girl who wasn't allowed to come to school. Whose father's name was uttered in whispers. As if saying it aloud would soil the speaker.

"Janet? You're Janie? Why did you lie?"

But Janet was gone, as dead as Matt Corcoran himself, and Janie didn't bother to answer. If he couldn't figure that out for himself, he wasn't as smart as she'd given him credit for. Besides, she was through explaining. This was it. Never again would she bother.

Ida took over. She turned to Dan. "Here's what's going to happen. You're going to leave here and never come back. I don't care where you go, but the further the better. You're to forget all about Janie, and all about this. Do you hear me? Because if you don't, it will land at your own two feet. You're a teacher from away, going around with a fifteen-year-old pupil whose father ends up dead in her bedroom where the two of you are. You can figure that out too, I'll bet. I mean you no harm, Dan Walsh, but I promise you, if you stay and play this out, it'll be the ruin of you and us, and I won't have that, not now. We're finally shed of him, and I'm not going to spend the rest of my years with my head down like I have the last fifteen."

"Janet?"

She could feel Dan's eyes boring in on her. Staring straight ahead into the black basement window, she deliberately kept her face impassive. It was easy, really. She doubted she would ever smile again. A day that had started out with such dreams, and almost ended with a real hope for the future, was now dead. What had happened in that bedroom could never be fixed, never be explained or excused, never be righted no matter how they tried.

Janie turned and looked at him one last time. "Goodbye, Dan Walsh," she said firmly. Her face tight and hard, she pointed to the door.

Oh Good God. Oh Holy Mother of Jesus. Rod had never really believed it could be worse than he imagined, but it was. They'd killed him, his mother, his grandmother, his father and his aunt. Between them all, they'd managed to end the life of another human being. Especially Janie. It had been her idea. Make no wonder she'd never wanted to tell him.

She sat impassively across from him, her face pale, body limp. He tried to imagine her at fifteen, the age of many of his students. The same age as Max. He thought of how Lill was so protective of her younger son, how she was always worried that someone would hurt him. More than anything else, Lill was Max's mother, and nothing was as important to her as him. Rod knew that, and he knew that Max knew it too, knew that his mother would go to the ends of the earth for him. Most mothers would.

Janie had never had that. No one had been there to save her from the horror that was her own father. Not until it was too late.

His mind veered back to Lill, and the image of his grandfather echoing her name while he bludgeoned his daughter's mouth. In that moment he understood why Janie had done it. He only wished he'd been there to help.

An early evening quiet had settled on the house, and the kitchen had lost most of its light. He rose from the table. Kneeling in front of his mother's chair, he took hold of her hand.

"I'm so sorry, Janie. I am so very, very sorry."

She looked at him then, her eyes sadder and fuller than he'd ever seen them. Her body jerked suddenly, then her mouth opened with a long mournful wail. For the first time in his life, he reached out and took her in his arms. As the spasms tore through her body, he felt the weight of all the years pour out from her. And for the first time that he could remember, she hugged him back.

13

Janie knew she didn't deserve it. She took it anyway. For thirty-three years she'd held back, giving nothing, taking nothing in return. Ever since Rod was just a boy, his face lighting up when she came into the room, so obviously happy to see her. It was not a feeling she'd reciprocated. All he did was remind her of what she'd had and what she'd lost, of what had been taken from her. She'd wanted nothing to do with him. If it hadn't been for Suzie she'd have never stepped foot over that threshold again.

Eventually, of course, he'd stopped caring too. When she came out to see her sister, her poor dumb mute sister, he would disappear for hours. She'd hear him come in at night, a teenager, and wonder what he'd been up to. But he never got in trouble. Never caused Ida much grief, except when Janie turned away from him. A silent grief, for all of them. That was the price she paid and he paid and her mother paid. After all, somebody had to pay. They always did.

And now he knew. He finally knew. She supposed she should have told him earlier, years before even. But she didn't, she couldn't. Then, when he'd shown up at her door that morning, something in him had changed. It had rippled through his anger-filled body, charged his deep familiar voice, blazed in his eyes. Dan Walsh's eyes, Dan's face.

Not like the faces that came to her night and day, the faces that sometimes persisted despite the booze. Matt

Corcoran's face. Eyes afire as he shouted some profanity at her or her mother, spit foaming on his hard thin lips. Unshaven and dirty, despicable with drink and hate, eyeing her sister. Leering at Janie as she passed him in the kitchen, his tongue just visible in his stinking mouth. Flushed and hot, gasping for breath while he took her. Why hadn't she done something then, she wondered, why hadn't she killed him on one of those times, when he was so vulnerable, when he would have been easy prey? Why hadn't she tried earlier? When she was eleven, or twelve, or thirteen, or fourteen?

She hated all those faces, but the one that truly terrified her was the one that came only in her deepest slumber, haunting her sleep, killing her dreams. It was the last one she'd seen, his eyes open, not seeing back. Her father's dead eyes had followed her every day since she'd done him in.

She had always feared if she looked too closely at Rod, she might see the devil who was her father. So she hadn't let herself look, really look, until today.

Dan Walsh had stared back at her, Dan Walsh's eyes at least, so filled with pain, rife with longing and sadness. And that was why she did it finally. That was why she told her son that at fifteen years of age, she'd killed her own father. Then she told him why.

She just wished she'd done it sooner. Life would have been so very, very different if she'd only done it sooner.

By the time Rod reached the lake, the day was fully gone. He parked at the back, then walked to the front of the cabin, the sound of music guiding him in the blackness.

Through the glass of the patio doors he saw her. She was kneeling at the fireplace, her dark hair framing her head, the small strong shoulders moving rhythmically as she fanned the flames.

How could he go in there and not tell her what he knew? It wasn't only that he hated secrets, and that he swore he'd never let them rule his life again. It was that this secret was actually about Lill. She had been part of his grandfather's evil, part of the sickness that drove him. His stomach shivered with guilt, the guilt of association, the guilt of blood relations. The sins of the grandfather.

How could he lie to her, after he'd been lied to all these years? She deserved better, even if it meant the end.

Lill stopped moving suddenly. She stood up and turned around.

They stared at each other for several moments. As she walked toward him, they continued to hold each other's eyes. She opened the door.

The truth caught in his throat. Just the sight of her there, the unspoiled wonder that was Lill, was enough to stop the words he knew he should say. Her warm hazel eyes were so full of hope, her mouth smiling nervously. No woman had ever looked at him with such intensity, with that quality he could only hope was love.

In that instant he decided. To hell with Matt Corcoran. He'd ruined enough lives. Rod would not let him ruin theirs, for his own selfish reasons, but also for Lill. If she would let him, he'd spend the rest of his life making up to her for what his grandfather almost did, and she'd never know.

He held out his hand.

~

Lill had not cried on the way into town. In fact, for the first time ever, she left the Nursing Home with something close to joy in her heart. The feeling was so unexpected she found herself actually smiling as she drove away, bright and happy images of her father filling her mind like a long-anticipated slide show. When she found her favourite memory, she allowed it to settle comfortably in her mind. In it, he was relaxing in his chair by the window like he had done almost every day of her childhood. Listening to the radio and reading his paper, his warm face looking up as a young girl interrupted his peace and quiet. He would always open his arms, the paper flapping about slightly until she'd found her spot on his lap, then he would catch the paper with his other hand and they'd read it together. He never turned her away, not once.

Then her mother was standing in the doorway, looking at the two of them, smiling. The child on the man's lap saw her out of the corner of her eye, saw the pleasure on her face, the love that enveloped them all, herself, her sisters, and especially her father. Marg Penney stood there for a long time, simply smiling. Then the child turned to the woman, and her mother said, "Time to set the table, Lilly." The smile had tucked itself away, but it was still there beneath the surface, behind the stern voice, still there in her warm motherly eyes.

Her mother was as much a part of the love she felt for her father as he was. Marg had allowed Hank to be the gentle one, the funny one, the father who couldn't say no, who loved his daughter endlessly. The love her parents had shared for fifty years came from both of them, and from them to their children. It was a love that Lill had known as a child, as their child. Unlike Marg and Hank however, she'd never had the good fortune to share it with her own husband.

So she remembered her mother too, and missed her. And she thought of the father she'd left behind in the Home. Even now he was still teaching her. Lill knew then that God had a purpose for keeping him alive, to help Lill understand the depths of love.

Marg moved from the doorway, and faded away. Lilly sat in his arms, never more loved, never more safe.

This man was her father. This was the man she would remember.

This was also the man she'd talked to that afternoon, however briefly. Telling him about Rod had released something inside her, as if some veil of secrecy, or illicitness, or whatever it was that she still could not name, had been lifted, so that whatever it was, it didn't matter anymore. She knew her father would have approved. Hank Penney had never been the type to worry needlessly about what others thought of him. He'd been a good man, and he lived a decent honourable life, so what was there to worry about? It was time for Lill to be more like him.

She pulled into the Irving station right on time, but after sipping a coffee at the counter for half an hour, she decided that Rod must have been held up and that she would go on ahead and wait for him at the cabin. As she was reaching for her money, a hand clapped her on the back.

"I thought that was you," Noreen said, plunking down next to her. "Got a head start, eh?"

"Hey Noreen," she smiled, filled with pleasure at seeing her sister. "Yeah, you too?"

"Uh-huh. Figured I'd sneak out early and try to get a few holes in before the sun goes down. Where's Rod?"

"Rod?" Lill thought quickly. "He had to go on ahead and do something for his mother. We're meeting later at the cabin." She didn't mention that they might not make the golf game. That could wait.

"Oh," said Noreen, ordering a bottle of water. As the waitress left, she turned to Lill. "You two getting serious?"

"Well…" Lill hesitated. Telling her father was one thing, telling her sister was another. Noreen could answer back.

Noreen held up her hand. "Ah, Christ, I'm sorry girl. Here I am not telling you a thing for years, and now I'm sticking my nose in your business. Don't mind me, okay?"

Lill grinned at her. "You know what, Norrie? I think we are. What do you say to that?"

Noreen looked surprised, but then she smiled. "I think that's grand. He's a good man from what I've seen. And he looks at you like there's no tomorrow."

Lill's grin widened. She couldn't stop it. "Yeah, Dad's okay with it too."

"What!"

"I popped in on the way by. Told him about golfing, and all about Rod. He had no objections."

Noreen grunted. "Funny he never mentioned it."

It was Lill's turn to be surprised.

Noreen nodded. "I dropped in too. I usually do when I come to town. Just don't tell that frigging Marlene on me."

"Ah, the heck with Marlene. I don't know why we put up with her."

Noreen smiled. "Because she needs us to, Lilly. That's all."

Lill thought about it for just a second. "Yeah, maybe she does."

The waitress returned with Noreen's drink and she stood up to go.

"So, I'll see you tomorrow, Lill. Have a great night and say hi to Rod." With a happy little laugh, she gave Lill a hug, then waltzed away. Lill watched through the window as her sister hopped on her bike and roared off.

Placing some money next to her cup, Lill left a few minutes later.

The day was setting as she pulled up, and she shivered in the coolness of the evening. Leaving her car, she walked down to the rocky shore. Straight ahead, the sun seemed mere inches above the water line, it's golden orange glow shimmering on the rippling surface. A bird trilled from a nearby tree, just as a tiny anonymous creature broke through the glassy skin of the lake. Breathing deeply, she stretched her arms luxuriously above her head, letting the tranquil air permeate her body. A single crow flew past, followed almost immediately by another. She waited. There were no more.

It took only an hour to get everything inside and their supper organized. When she was done, she turned off the kitchen light and found some soothing music on the radio. She wanted everything to be ready by the time he arrived. After his day with Janie, whatever had happened, he would need solace, and she wanted him to feel like he was coming home.

Because somewhere along the way, she'd decided that he was.

Lill had just gotten the fire going when she felt him there. Standing, she turned and looked through the glass leading to the terrace, then walked across the room to open the patio doors.

Rod stood on the step, still and silent. Behind him, a full moon shone down on the lake, its iridescent light illuminating the water from above and below. It fanned out to surround him, a surreal backdrop to his clear green eyes and solemn face.

Reaching out, Lill wrapped his warm strong hand in both of hers. She led him inside and shut the door.

THE END

Thanks and Acknowledgements

First and foremost, to my family - my husband Michael Jennings, and my sons Ian and Keith, for their unflinching support and belief in me, for putting up with me throughout it all, and for always having a sense of humour. Their constant presence and encouragement has kept me going.

To my writing group, Cecelia Frey, Cheryl Sikomas, and Dixie Baum, each of whom has critiqued this manuscript chapter by chapter, and again in its entirety. Their honest and constructive criticism was invaluable and always made me think.

To Kathi Gowsell, Lynette MacCulloch, and Karen Lowe, who provided early feedback when I was first trying to get the story together.

To Robert Finley, for his sound advice during our manuscript consultation at the University of Calgary.

To Donna Francis, Angela Pitcher and Creative Book Publishing; God love you all for giving me a shot.

To Maurice Fitzgerald for his wonderful and inspired cover design.

And finally to my editor, Carmelita McGrath, whose fresh eye and wise suggestions helped bring the manuscript to completion.

Thank you all.